Alan Dreams of Giants

Alan Dreams *of* Giants

A DREAMT UP FANTASY STORY

T.M. MAY

Published by the author.

Athens, Georgia

Library of Congress Cataloging-in-Publication Data
May, T. M., 1995—
Alan dreams of giants / T. M. May

p. 370 ; 23 cm.

Summary: Struggling with the recent death of his father, Alan Hendershot,
a grocery store cashier, escapes his dismal reality through lucid dreaming,
ultimately discovering his father's presence within a fantastical world,
leading him to reclaim his confidence and purpose by embracing the power
of storytelling.

ISBN: 979-8-218-49815-3 (pbk)

1. Fantasy fiction. 2. Dreams—Fiction. 3. Fathers and sons—Fiction. 4.
Grief—Fiction. I. Title.

Library of Congress Control Number: 2024917853

TO RAMONA
& HER GRANDPA

CONTENTS

I. Dreams as they used to be

June 9, 1971

If he made the oil touch the top dipstick eye on his first try, then Alan got to draw the circle for marbles. His dad held him up over the engine of the Thunderbird as though he were a puppet master, angling Alan's determined 5-year-old hands precisely for the pour. Alan tilted the oil jug gently, waiting for the shiny stream to flow.

He whispered Mississippi counts to himself as it poured. Alan smiled. He was good at this.

When he touched back down on the ground, there was no doubting his achievement. His dad pulled the dipstick from the engine with a great deal of theatricality, letting the oil glimmer in the sunlight. The tease of a furrowed brow and faux disappointment didn't fool Alan. He could feel the precise success in his bones.

***

Drawing the circle for a game of marbles wasn't a *significant* advantage. For Alan, there was something else to it. It meant he was the one creating the world in which they would play. Sure, it was nothing more than chalk on a driveway that would wash away next rain, but during the game, that's where he and his dad lived. And Alan had made it.

Smartly, he selected the gold chalk. That guaranteed that he would get dibs on his favorite cat's-eye marble, a silver sphere with gold streaks running through the middle like ink mixing in a well. The first time they played marbles, his dad had made the mistake of letting Alan in on a well-guarded secret: with the gold cat's-eye, it was impossible to miss twice in a row.

They gathered up the ducks and dropped them into the gold-chalked world, and with great hubris, Alan allowed his father to go first. A miss! Alan smirked as the black aggie rolled off from the circle, dejected.

Alan's turn next; he aimed for a pair of marbles half a foot from the outside edge. His cat's-eye bounced right over the pair on an uneven patch of concrete and veered toward the grass. A smile fast replaced the momentary disappointment, for he knew one miss guaranteed a hit to follow.

His dad got down on one knee and lined up the marble with his fingers, ghosting through the movement of the arc and release. He buttoned his lips and closed his left eye tighter, offered Alan a wink, and launched his aggie at a group of four marbles in the center of the circle. They were all disturbed, like breaking a game of pool, and one duck skittered hard outside the circle and came to a stop at Alan's feet.

A 1-0 lead was not unconquerable; Alan knew that for sure. But he also knew that he did not want to be losing *2-0*. He lined himself up again to aim for the same pair he missed the first round. After all, the gold cat's eye was on his side. With a held breath, he released his shooter, and with one bounce, it smashed into the marble on the left hard enough to send them both flying. There. 2-1.

The score progressed similarly as the sunlight became more golden, allowing the glimmer of the cat's eye to truly shine. Every time Alan's father drew close to a tie or a lead, the cat's eye hit an unmissable shot.

Alan nearly felt guilty, had he not poured the oil so exceptionally earlier. He had earned the choice of chalk and shooter. After all, his dad preferred for Alan to draw the circle for whatever odd reason. Maybe he just liked to lose.

II. Six puddings short

May 17, 1992

Today, the game of marbles was not more than a memory. This morning in particular, it had been a dream to be awoken from. And this afternoon, three minutes before his break from cashiering at Elmwood's on Elm (the finest grocer in southwest Ashtabula, Ohio), it existed as a wisp of a daydream that, for a moment, transported him elsewhere. He longed for his federally mandated fifteen-minute break to escape further, perhaps with a good book.

From the dark abyss (but a safe one) that was the undercarriage of his register, Alan fished for the register light switch as a slam of reverberating liquid and plastic sent a defeated chill down his bony spine. A red-headed woman with tightly curled hair and freckles had just smacked down a gallon of 1% milk on the belt, spraying condensation particulate like a mushroom cloud.

1% was a calling card in Alan's expert opinion. It's not that *every* customer who's procuring a fresh gallon of the half-skim, half-fatty homogenization is a pain in the ass. It's just that Alan cannot recall a single time where a patron was both purchasing milk and that individual was a particularly deplorable soul where the milk was not 1%. Approachable or kind 1% milk purchasers are often mistaken as nuns, volunteer firefighters, or public interest attorneys.

"Hi, miss. Did you find everything with a smile?" Alan pulled up the sides of his mouth into a faithless grin and pulled the milk over the scanner.

BEEP.

"Well, no. I can't even say that I found everything without a smile."

He dared to face her as he put the milk in a second bag. She was, in fact, *not* smiling, as she had reported. Her brows rose ever so slightly, begging for a retort.

"I'm so sorry to hear that. What was the problem?"

She slammed down a cardboard pallet of pudding onto the belt.

"This." She prodded the box with a well-manicured index finger in a spot absent of pudding. "I needed 48 puddings. Only 48. Nothing outrageous. Instead, what do I find?"

Alan took a moment, counting the puddings in threes.

"42?"

"Obviously." She spat and tried to shove the pallet over the scanner herself.

He laid the pallet on top of the bagging carousel and made his best attempt to avoid eye contact as he scanned the six-pack of strawberry pudding seven times. Beep. Beep. Beep. Bee-

"Do you have to do that with so much despair, young man? I do have places to be." She tapped her diamond-bedazzled wristwatch. "Some of us are seeing our children *all the way* through school."

Alan inhaled sharply as he scanned the last pudding. A slight smirk grew on the woman's face as she rifled through her pocketbook.

"Okay. Your total is $9.9-"

She held up a hand inches from his face. "Wait. I have coupons." Her fingers flew through the coupon portfolio like a well-oiled Rolodex before a thick stack manifested in an outstretched hand. One at a time, Alan redeemed them. Beep. Beep. Beep. *Bloop.*

Bloop? A quick inventory of the last two coupons scanned revealed the blunder immediately, and Alan sheepishly eyed the woman to gauge her potential eruption. The outlook wasn't great.

"I'm *terribly* sorry, miss. We don't double coupons." With a shaking hand, he pointed to a sign hanging on the front glass with big, bold red letters:

No smoking, no spitting, and <u>no</u> double coupons.

Her eyes widened. Her nostrils flared. She ripped the coupons out of his hand and grabbed the pallet off the carousel, slamming it into the cart, strawberry pudding splattering everywhere.

"Why you little..."

She huffed.

"You little, snot-nosed, societal-parasitic..." Her *P* sprayed saliva reeking of tuna and burnt coffee. "...LEECH!" She peeled the foil lid off one of the few intact pudding containers and squeezed it out on the conveyor belt. In a flash, she'd pushed her shopping cart into a display of alphabet soup and stomped out of the store.

Alan tapped the button on the belt to inch the pudding closer to him, little by little to ensure that the pudding didn't sneak its way to the underside of the belt. He felt as though someone were watching him and turned to see Mr. Vick, standing still like a melted candle of a man. He held a dirty cotton rag in one hand and a spray bottle of neon blue fluid in the other.

Vick was middle-aged, slightly overweight, with thinning black hair. He was unbearably overbearing and wore a nametag that read "Mr. Elmwood" even though his name was, in fact, Vick Vick. Alan always suspected that his mother changed his name to a redundancy once she'd gotten to know her child.

"Hendershoooot." His nasal voice shot out, "What did you do to rile up Mrs. Westbrook?"

Resistance was futile, but even more so an hour before a shift ends. "I don't — I don't know, I—"

"It doesn't matter. Your break started two minutes ago, so I'd clean that mess up quickly if you want to salvage any of it."

***

Alan took a seat at the singular table in the employee break room, a second-hand half of an old cafeteria table, with ketchup and dried egg serving as artifacts to the past. A mostly eaten container of noodles spun around in the microwave (for the second time today) as his mind drifted off to the fifty-cent paperback he held open with one hand. *Finally*, a bit of an escape.

At the moment, Alan was making his way through *The Wisest Wizard of Windenbergh*. It wasn't great fantasy, at least not compared to a lot of what he had read lately, but it was a hell of a lot better than being stuck out on the floor with Mrs. Westbrook. Ten minutes was 18 pages without chapter breaks, and even more if the spine was broke-in enough to eliminate the need for repositioning between pages. Five pages in, and the microwave buzzer had to blare a second and third time just to suck Alan back into the real world.

As he retrieved his noodles, he heard a banging on the glass behind him. Mr. Vick's office overlooked the break room with one large four by six-foot window, and he disrupted no less than half of Alan's breaks. He came storming out, staring down at a clipboard in his hand and angrily scratching marks with a cheap pen from the used car dealership down the street. He looked up and caught Alan's eyes at the microwave.

"Hendershot. Jesus Christ. Keep it down, will you? I'm busy." He held up the clipboard a little higher, as if it was proof of an ungodly workload.

"Yeah, sorry Mr. Vick. Won't happen again. Have you ever noticed that the buzzer is kind of qui—"

"Okay, you're boring me." He paused. "Is that a mustard stain on your Elmwood's shirt?" He asked as if there were a bloody knife sticking out of Alan's pocket.

It was true, however. As Alan presented his lanky self to his overlord, he looked down at the starchy, white polo and saw the mustard yellow about halfway down. It was there, no jury would deny it. But Alan hardly had the motivation to wash the single shirt every evening, particularly when an apron covered it on the floor. Nor was the mustard stain the most unappealing thing about him. His big toes had almost burst through either side of his once-white Reebok tennis shoes. His khaki cargo pants, as khaki was the color that Vick required, were the closest to his size that he could find at the thrift store, but they bunched up on his left thigh from too significant an adjustment with a belt. The bottoms rode an inch above the shoes. His face was less unsightly, though he hadn't had his shaggy blonde hair cut this calendar year, and he'd always felt that his Adam's apple was too big for such a narrow neck.

He looked back up at Mr. Vick, who was whispering to himself as he scratched three more harsh marks across the clipboard. "Yeah, sorry, mister. My washing machine…uh, I think it might be broken."

He snarled and spun around to return to his office. "Don't give me that shit, Hendershot. I know your generation doesn't have the self-respect to do laundry." His voice was almost inaudible now, as he turned the corner into the room. "When I was your age, I did the laundry for myself and my girlfriend. That's my wife now."

Alan thought about letting Mr. Vick know that *his* entire aura reeked of leeks and spoiled onions, so clean laundry should be the least of his concern, but it was much more convenient to imagine the putdown. Instead, he sat back down with his book, salvaging the last minutes he had with it while slurping down unevenly heated noodles. Soon he was riding side by side with Undor, on their way to the far-western kingdom of Ashenhill to let the wizard council know about the evil gnomes they had come across near the continent's edge—mischievous creatures indeed.

***

Alan's life, however fractured we may determine it to be, was in great repair compared to the driveway he'd just pulled into, with cracks so wide Moses would have been jealous of the ground's handiwork. According to his driver's license, he lived in the duplex it unfurled from, a 1952 ranch that truly required an act of God to save its curb appeal. Had you more time to read it, his license also recorded his brown eyes, weight of 160 pounds, height of six feet and two inches, and an absurd greed over his organs. He didn't have any reason not to be a donor, but when he was 16, his mother had recently read a short story about a man coming back to life an hour after an automobile accident had left him pronounced dead, and it would have given her "ungodly worry" if he had checked the box.

His license did not say what vehicle he drove, and he was thankful for that; if he was ever caught dead with his license but absent his car, perhaps everyone could just forget about it. A 1968 Volkswagen 411— it was the last "hot rod" that his grandmother had owned before the government forced her to give up her own license. Alan had always thought the paint color to be a hybrid between earwax and mucus, but it was difficult to decide which it favored more.

The duplex was less embarrassing on the inside. That was probably because Micah took care of 70% of the rent. Well, *Micah's parents* took care of 70%. Two years ago, Alan had moved in with him after Micah finished his biochem major (or, pre-dentistry, as Micah called it) and had wanted to "take a sabbatical before making it big." Alan had pushed to live somewhere even dumpier when he'd expected to split the bill, but Micah's parents said that this duplex was the dumpiest place they'd have their son living.

The lights were off and there were no other cars in the drive, as was usually the case on a Friday evening. Most weekend nights, Micah wouldn't get back until the wee hours of the morning, if he came back at all. Alan had no problem with it, as the alternative seemed to be Micah bringing people over to their duplex, and Alan had no interest in coming up with casual conversation to have at the ready when entering his own living room after a long day at work.

Instead, he was greeted by a cloud of frost billowing from the open freezer door as he stared into the cool abyss in search of dinner. Alan did cook. Or, at least, he *had* cooked in the past. But a few years ago, he had decided there was no longer a reason to do it, for *Chef Billy* of aisle 11 prepared frozen dinners of a caliber he was...well, completely *okay* with.

Tonight, the options were endless. Chef Billy's cheeky grin, wink, and finger gun were emblazoned upon the edge of four rectangular slabs of nutritional sustenance. He could choose from Salisbury Steak, Beef Bolognese, Fried Chicken, or St. Louis Ribs. He closed his eyes and shuffled the boxes around quickly, trying to forget which had been where, picked one, and opened them to the divinely mandated ribs. *Sure.* He popped the plastic a few times with a knife and kicked his shoes off towards the hall as the microwave hummed away.

Reading was tricky while eating ribs, so Alan had limited dinner entertainment options. There was a TV in the house, but Micah's parents had purchased it, and it sat in the corner of Micah's bedroom beneath a few Playboy magazines and a Nintendo. The two times they had a party in the house, Micah had pushed the setup out to the living room, but other than that, he was quite covetous.

The alternative was an 8-track player that sat on an old ottoman with a Peter, Paul and Mary tape inside. He bumped play with his middle finger to avoid getting St. Louis style barbecue sauce all over the button. As he turned, he saw a flashing orange light on their answering machine and mashed stop on the 8-track before hitting the playback button on the machine, while catching a free-falling drop of sauce on his sock.

"Your beep took a while, Alan..." It was his mom; she chuckled, "I guess those are mostly me...anyway, me and Nikki just wanted to sing you happy birthday."

Today? May 17th? Me? Another year older? Fantastic. Everyone says life starts at 26.

Alan heard his little sister cough into the phone and then the pair began singing Happy Birthday, quite out of sync with one another.

His mom spoke up again. "Okay, Nik, go to your room and finish your homework."

She took a deep breath. "I know it's hard, honey. We all miss him." Her voice broke a little. "Your dad...your dad was really something." A longer pause. "He wouldn't want you to be alone today, either. I really hope you think about coming to see us. It doesn't have to be today. But sometime soon, Al. Your sister was a little upset you weren't here today, so I told her we could throw a birthday party for dad. I know it's a few weeks away, but, ju—"

The tape in the answering machine screeched as the dial couldn't turn anymore. It was full. His mom was right, about the tape, that is. It racked up another two or three minutes about twice a week, and she was always the recording artist.

Alan sat still for a moment while his ribs grew cold, considering the fact that he had forgotten his own birthday. He was sad about it; he guessed. Alan would have liked to have been eating a birthday dinner with his family. He looked around the empty living room. It probably would have been at Pizza Inn. He would have liked for everyone to be with him tonight, and to not be a dining guest of *Chef Billy*, for everything to be normal. But that was just it—everything wasn't normal.

Alan's dad had passed away a little over two months ago. He had worked at a coal dock — to be honest, Alan knew little more than that. He remembered he operated some machinery, and that he had one or two people that worked under him, but nothing else. Something had fallen on him; they tried to save him, but he had passed on the way to the hospital. Alan, his sister, and his mom all got there after he died. Nobody said goodbye.

It was a lot easier being alone, Alan had decided. Nobody was there to ask him when he was thinking about going back to school, or getting some certificate, or how tired he was of being a cashier. It was easier being alone, because if he was alone, he didn't have to know what anyone else was doing. He didn't have to see his high school friends getting married, having kids, or even driving a car that wasn't a VW 411. Yeah, it would have been nice to blow out some candles, but it was a lot easier eating lukewarm ribs in an empty duplex.

III. The pirate captain who reads books

Have you ever gone grocery shopping on a Saturday? You probably have. People pick Saturday more than any other day of the week. Elmwood's was no exception to this, as the lumpy white tile and precarious, jumbled shelves played host to an absolute rampage of ornery, thrifty, stubborn individuals that all fed off the energy of one another. Miss Etta often said *it doesn't feel too heavenly here on Sundays, but Saturdays are the closest thing we have to hell.*

Miss Etta was a ray of sunshine among storm clouds, and Alan usually started the day sitting in one of the bakery booths, watching her put the finishing touches on cakes and pastries. Forgot breakfast? She had a day-old danish or an over-blueberried muffin with your name on it.

Today it was a raspberry danish, not even 12 hours old, but Vick always had the entire bakery inventory wiped clean before the Saturday rush. "They're our finest customers, and they deserve our best," he'd told Miss Etta. They both knew that this wasn't the case, as the proper reason was that Saturday shoppers had a whole lot of time on their plate to argue or complain. Thursday night you have to get home for family dinner, so you grab the first bunch of bananas you lay your hands on. But on Saturday, well on Saturday, Alan had once seen an older man sort all the bananas from green to yellow to brown and then count off one from either end to get the perfect bunch.

Today, Miss Etta was less available to talk than she normally was. As you might have already deduced, Alan isn't the most-practiced conversationalist, but Miss Etta seemed to be one of the few people that worked at Elmwood's that *got it*. Whatever *it* was, well, Alan would have a hard time saying, but at its fundamental level, it was an understanding. Even after working there for 34 years, she still had a small pursed smile on her face as she finished the lettering on a birthday cake.

"Why so busy today?" Alan asked, licking some raspberry jam from his finger.

"Hm." She dolloped a red balloon. "Well, I don't know. Lots of graduations. A few weddings. More than a couple of birthdays, too. People love to celebrate right now." She laughed and popped the plastic cover back on the cake she had just completed.

Alan grew squeamish as the first cars pulled into the parking lot.

"Now Alan," Miss Etta declared, watching his attention draw back, "can you tell me why you didn't think to tell *me* that yesterday was your birthday?" She laid down a bag of red icing and propped a hand on either hip in contempt.

"Oh, I don't know. No reason to bother other people with that sort of stuff."

She clicked her tongue. "Do not give me that. How long have I been telling you I was gonna make you a cake on your birthday?"

"A while."

"A while. So?"

"I don't know. That just seems like a big waste. I can't eat an entire cake all by myself." Alan was picking up some crumbs of danish he'd left behind on the napkin, avoiding eye contact.

Miss Etta remained quiet for a moment, smiled and shook her head before retorting, "A cake for you is not a waste. Besides, I just threw out four cakes and two pies yesterday. You think you're the one causing a waste?"

"Well, when you put it that way." Alan looked up at her and managed a half-smile.

"Good." She grinned. "Because I already started on it soon as I got here this morning. Come see me before you go home and I'll box it up."

Alan smiled and nodded before more slamming car doors pulled his attention back to the parking lot and a bushy-tailed Mr. Vick, who was marching ceremoniously towards the door to unlock it and unleash the horde.

"Well, that's my cue." He started toward his register before pausing and facing her. "Hey, how *did* you know yesterday was my birthday?"

"Honey, you know Mr. Vick owes me more than one or two favors."

As Alan migrated to his register and noticed a sticky spot of pudding leftover on the number pad, he took pleasure knowing that somewhere in the building, there were people that Vick owed favors to.

***

CUE MONTAGE

Mr. Rusden, a chubby, bald, bespectacled man wearing a starchy, white button-up and black trousers, came through Alan's line purchasing seventeen cucumbers, one case of mason jars, and two jugs of white vinegar. He yelled at Alan ceaselessly for 37 seconds after he asked if he was making pickles.

An unidentified black-haired woman, tall, and accompanied by two children between the ages of 9 and 13, had a shopping cart full of frozen dinners, toilet paper, cheese curls, and *cola*. She took ten minutes to write a check to pay for her order, because the younger of the two children snatched a pack of *mint* breath fresheners from the register display and got millimeters from disaster every time she took her eyes off them. She finally allowed it. Alan's hands were sticky for the rest of the day.

A younger woman, maybe a year or two into college, placed a basket on the conveyor belt without removing any of the items. Alan picked up the basket without noticing that the person next in line had already filled up the belt with their items, leaving him no room after the conveyor sped forward. She had also put seven different varieties of by-the-pound produce in a single produce bag. She asked to speak to his manager for touching her peppers with his hands when he took them out to weigh them. Mr. Vick made Alan re-bag each item into its own vessel and apologize profusely.

A woman that Alan knew to be Shirley Hillsdale, matriarch of Bo Hillsdale, the bully of Alan and every child attending Oak Grove Elementary from the years of 1972-1978, was buying only cigarettes. She came every Saturday to buy a carton of Virginia Slims. However, today she was more hungover than normal and spat her request at Alan. Nothing else happened, but it's hard to describe in words just how horrible her spit was. It smelled of cheap whiskey, ketchup, and, of course, Virginia Slims.

An older couple both queued at Alan's register in matching power scooters. Mr. Vick refused to pay for such "needless creature comforts," so they must have brought them from home. Each of their front baskets spilled over with an identical assortment of dry boxed and canned foods. There was an awful lot of green peas and macaroni and cheese. They were actually perfect customers until the man's toupee flew off as a gust of wind blew through the front doors. He then backed over the toupee, which got sucked up into the scooter wheels and soon began burning as the wheels continued to spin in place, which then stalled the scooter entirely. Alan had to push the man atop his scooter out to their car with the wheels *not* turning, while trying to stomach the stench of burnt toupee.

BACK TO SCENE

At around 2 p.m., the wait time for any register at Elmwood's will probably quadruple on average. Saturdays were even worse, and this one was no exception, as one cashier had called in sick. It was Nigel, the nephew of Mr. Vick. He hadn't gotten the job because of merit (which is difficult to do when you're being hired as a cashier), and he often became horribly ill right as it was time to come into work on a Saturday or Sunday.

Alan's line extended beyond the candy bars and the pickle-flavored chips on the end cap (Vick had mistakenly ordered 19 cases instead of 1 and was trying to remedy his mistake by promoting them at 15% off). Most of the customers at this point in the day had grown indefensibly irritable, probably because they were just now reconciling with the fact that they had waited until 2 p.m. to make the trip and were now dealing with the consequences.

Alan was tallying the groceries of one Mrs. Dudgeon. She had seven kids, and her two cart-fulls of food would probably last the household a little less than a week, as nearly every week without fail, the missus would send Mr. Dudgeon to Elmwood's late on a Thursday night to get a few frozen pizzas and peanut butter. Half of the time the customer behind her would exit to a different queue and Alan would never hear from them again, but the other half, well, they would let him know their frustrations. Every five items or so, he would rise on his tippy toes, discreetly trying to get a sense of the temperament of the customer hidden behind the end cap.

The first two times he could only get a glimpse, a slim blur of hair or an arm in between the displays. The third time, he heightened himself up and stared right into the eyes of the person, his face flaring up immediately. She was probably about his age, with dark brown hair and a medium complexion. Her eyes were a deep chestnut and he could have sworn she had ever-so-slightly grinned when he caught them. He must have mis-seen, however, for that was no behavior for the person behind Mrs. Dudgeon.

Exactly 71 items later, Alan totaled the bill and took Mrs. Dudgeon's check as they pushed their caravan away. Now, the moment of truth. Alan prepared for the worst. It was true that those younger in age usually grew Dudgeon-irritated at an inverse relationship to that age, but the Dudgeon virus was always mutating.

Instead, the girl Alan had seen coolly pushed the cart forward and maintained a pleasant expression. She flipped a page in her book and closed it upon a bookmark, then unloaded her groceries onto the belt. She hummed pleasantly, as though she hadn't a care in the world. Alan's jaw slackened, and he didn't blink for a second, in awe at the fortitude of the person who stood before him. As she laid a gallon of 2% on the belt, she caught Alan's gaze and, flustered, he grabbed a box of cereal nearest to him and got to work. She laughed softly.

"So, uh," Alan hated himself for this, "did you find everything with a smile?" He cringed as the last word fell out of his mouth onto the conveyor belt, tumbled along to the crack between the scanner, and let out an awful screeching howl as the *smile* was sucked down below.

She nodded, said, "yep," then returned to her book as Alan continued to scan.

As he rang everything up, Alan tried to perch his head and crane his neck at just the right angle to make out the title of the book. All attempts were without success, however, as the position required for this would have been anything but circumspect.

He decided to risk it.

"That's a good one." He nodded to the book as he punched a few buttons on the register to total the order.

She looked up, beaming. "Oh! You've read it?" She held the cover visibly now, and Alan nearly cursed himself aloud. He had *not* read *Dream Cycle* by H.P. Lovecraft. In fact, he knew nothing about it. *What a despicably ambiguous title*, he thought to himself.

"Yep! It's been a while, though. How do you like it?" Judging by her bookmark, she seemed to be a little over halfway.

"Pretty good so far." She pulled out a check card to pay with, still smiling. "Although, I have to admit, it's not what I'm used to reading."

"Oh. You usually...be reading...not ones like that?" *What the hell was that.*

"Um...yeah. Usually..." She laughed, "Usually I'm reading like crime pulp fiction, but...well, I guess I wanted to try something different."

"Cool." Alan smiled with teeth gritted, stifling a rising uneasiness that his expression was far too stoic. Feathers ruffled, he feigned a sneeze to reset his face.

"Gesundheit!" She chuckled as she took the last bag of groceries and departed. "Well, maybe I'll see you next week and I can give you my final review."

"I'm looking forward to it!"

He averted his gaze to a pyramid of soda and stared blankly, analyzing his actions. It hadn't gone poorly, he supposed, aside from the small dose of pirate dialect and the colossal lie he had dug himself into. Maybe he wouldn't see her next week. After all, he had never seen her before. *It'll be fine. Right? Will it?* His thoughts spiraled further, as he considered how un-cashier-class she probably was, how little money he would ever have to take somebody on dates, and how bombastic the eruption of laughter would be when she saw his Volkswagen 411.

THWAP. Ms. Grayson, a short old lady that lived two houses down from his parents, smacked the register with a folded newspaper.

"Young man!"

Alan turned, startled.

"Oh! You're the Hendershot boy...well, young man, I finished unloading my groceries long ago. Please." She motioned to a five-pound bag of yellow onions at the front of the belt, and Alan sunk back into his work with an apologetic nod.

His day continued as it had before, the next three hours filling his line with an equally distasteful cast of characters as the morning had served. No customer before or after the girl made any attempt at cordiality.

*****

His car started on the third crank, and he fiddled with the radio tuner to pick a station before leaving. As fate would have it, Def Leppard's *Pour Some Sugar on Me* was hitting its climax on 93.3 *The Wolf*, and Alan immediately remembered Miss Etta's promise of a cake.

As he made his way to the bakery counter, he saw no one, so instead of ringing the horrid bell Vick had installed, he found his usual seat and waited.

"Alan!" Miss Etta's voice echoed out from the back of the bakery. "I'm putting the final touches on it right now." She whistled a little, a medley hybrid of sorts combining *Happy Birthday* and *What a Wonderful World.*

"Okay, now close your eyes. I'm bringing it out."

He closed them tightly, avoiding a sure chance of scolding if she saw him peeking. She walked slowly enough that those odd bubbles of red and purple began floating around in the ether of his blindness.

"Open them!"

In Alan's life, he had had a few cakes he remembered very well. For his sixth birthday, his mom had made a Willy Wonka cake, complete with a melted chocolate lake, a golden Cadbury egg, and a singular, fat blueberry. At age 10, it had been *Escape to Witch Mountain*, and although photographs of the U.F.O. cake revealed it to be objectively ugly, Alan had loved it.

This cake would probably make it to that list. It was a flat sheet cake, textured on the top with brown and green icing and decorations for ground and foliage. In the middle sat an enormous boulder with the hilt of a sword protruding from it. He knew that Miss Etta didn't care about King Arthur or T. H. White, but she always made a point to get a "book report" from him when he finished a new book. King Arthur was probably the only name that she had recognized.

"It's so cool," Alan said, walking up to the counter to examine it closer.

"I don't know if this is...accurate to the books you've read, but I couldn't remember exactly how-"

He grinned. "Oh, this is exactly how I imagined it."

She returned his smile. "Good. There's also a special surprise." Miss Etta nodded to the boulder.

"In the cake?"

She smiled and but wouldn't say anything else. Alan looked at the cake for a minute, touching different parts to test the texture. He grabbed the hilt of the pinky finger sized sword and wiggled it just a little. It felt different than he expected, more like moving a straw in a milkshake than a stick in a cake. He pulled on it, and as it came out of the boulder, warm fudge flooded out over the cake.

Miss Etta chuckled to herself. "I don't really know how the story goes exactly, but I know you have to be special to pull the sword out. Happy birthday, Alan."

"I'm no Arthur, but I'm not going to let that stop me from enjoying this. Do you want to eat a piece with me?"

Miss Etta happily agreed, and the pair sat down to indulge in her creation. They talked about Miss Etta's best birthday memories from her childhood in Georgia, how she made the cake, and what their favorite flavors of ice cream were. Alan's was butter pecan and Miss Etta's was turtle tracks, because in the summer there was enough hard stuff in it that even after it melted, it was still all right. She took her last bite, imagining the taste of turtle tracks instead, smiling.

Alan put his fork down. "I think I messed up today."

"How?"

"I told a lie that might come back to get me."

She chuckled. "Honey, all lies come back to get you, eventually."

"People always say that, but I'll have you know, I've told some pretty good ones that are still buried." The two looked at each other, and then both broke into laughter.

"Well, if it was to Mr. Vick, I'm sure nobody will hold it against you. That man—"

"It wasn't. It was a customer."

"Well, Alan, honey, we've all told customers lies before. Do you really think fuchsia-colored icing is impossible?"

"Well, it's a little different from that. It was a girl. She was—"

"Oh." Miss Etta grinned.

"Yeah. And, well, she was reading a book and I kind of told her I had read it. She implied if she sees me again, we'll be discussing the book."

"Okay."

"I haven't read the book."

"Alan." Miss Etta smirked and looked at Alan in faux disappointment.

"What?"

"I see you reading every minute you're not at that cash register. You're telling me you can't finish the book by the next time you see this girl?"

"Oh...yeah, well I—I guess I didn't think of that."

Miss Etta laughed, and although most of the sensation came from warm lava fudge filling his belly, he felt a little less anxious. By the time he was leaving work, it didn't seem out of his purview to read the entire collected works of H. P. Lovecraft while he was at it.

IV. Jack, who loves the alphabet

The alarm clock blared. Regardless of Alan's affinity for the device, a Panasonic RC 6067 he had found at a yard sale only weeks after its starring performance on the McCallisters' night stand in *Home Alone*, now was not the time. He was already awake and in a sweaty panic.

My library card. Alan was pulling out the pockets of the fourth pair of pants that he'd picked up and had still yet to locate it. Typically, it lived in the third slot on the right side of his bi-fold wallet, behind his Taco Tom's loyalty punch card and in front of his third-grade yearbook photo.

There were no more dirty pants or shirts in sight, and he had already ransacked his dresser and underneath his bed. He knew of two books in his car and jogged out to the passenger side in nothing but long johns and a pair of well-worn slippers to check these. Nothing again.

He could pay a $10 fee and get another card, *but* he didn't get paid until Wednesday, *and* he'd become slightly frantic knowing that he had just enough gas to get to the library and back, *and* even that would be a gamble. With what he had left, he could afford a half tank or a new library card, and he wasn't surrendering to selecting between those options just yet.

As he walked into Micah's room, who was still deep asleep on his bed with one empty on the floor and another crushed can next to his head, Alan considered which was more likely: Micah to allow him to use his identity to register for a false library card, or for Micah to let him drive his car, a freshly imported Range Rover full of gas, to work on Wednesday. He knew the answer.

He softly jostled Micah's arm, hoping to wake him without agitating him.

"Hey Micah, buddy, good night last night?"

Over the course of zero parties and one 21st birthday spent with his parents, Alan had consumed two beers and half a glass of wine's worth of alcohol in his life.

Micah groaned and pulled a pillow over his head.

"Good. Good to hear. Hey, listen. I lost my library card. Do you care if I borrow your ID and use it to get a new one? The prices for replacement library cards these days are ridiculous."

From beneath the pillow, Micah opened one of his eyes partway and looked confusedly at Alan. "You want my what to do what?"

"Just your license. I'll be back in less than an hour. Libraries, you know, always trying to pinch a penny."

"If I say yes, will you get the hell out of my room?"

"Yes! Thanks!" Alan turned and headed out. "And just think, anytime you want to read a book, now you'll already have the card."

***

The Ashtabula County District Library was special, not just to Alan, but to many people. A couple of years ago, when they were doing some renovations (the library was *old as dirt*, Alan recalled), there was a fire and thousands of books burned up or got tossed. A man who wrote for a newspaper out in Chicago did a column about the fire, and people from everywhere mailed in books to replace those they lost.

The library was actually quite posh now, whether from insurance-funded repairs or newly befriended Friends of the Library. Everyone from the town had used it a lot more when it reopened this year, as many said, "to try out all the new books."

Alan hadn't been to the library since it had reopened. It had all happened around the time his dad died, and he still wasn't that comfortable being around other people.

As it was a Monday, the middle of a Monday, and the middle of a Monday that was surely a summer camp day, the parking lot was empty. The new signage and addition around the back gave Alan a weird feeling; it was almost like seeing an old friend with a new haircut. Not a mullet or anything wild, but just different enough to throw you off.

Mrs. Youngstown, probably in her 80s now, with white hair, large diamond-framed eyeglasses, and a pale complexion, still sat at the front reference desk, just as Alan remembered. And *no*, she was *not* from Youngstown.

"Hi, Mrs. Youngstown."

She looked up from what she was reading and over the tops of her glasses.

"Alan!" she said, surprised. "I haven't seen you in—" She frowned slightly, having realized what she was about to say. "I was so sorry to hear about what happened. I hope you and your family are doing okay."

"We are, thanks." Alan felt disingenuous, as she'd probably seen his family more recently than him.

"Um, I guess it might be a bit hard to find what I need..." He looked around at the main floor, finding, at a quick glance, many items to be in new places.

"Yes, it probably looks a lot different in here to you." She smiled and waved her arm over the new wares. "Are you looking for something in particular?"

"Yes, Lovecraft. Dream Cycle, I think it's called."

"Okay, one minute." She smiled, punched away on her keyboard, then waited.

"Hmm...nothing on my search query. However," she grinned, "as you might know, we do have a lot of new books. There are some that still haven't been catalogued. Follow me."

She led Alan back behind the reference desk to a set of double doors leading to a long hallway. All the doors were closed, except for the one they passed through, which opened to a large, rectangular room full of book carts. It smelled of old books and coffee.

"Now, we processed most of the children's books first, as that was the high-publicity stuff. So a lot of this is adult fiction and non-fiction. I think that, for the most part, Jack—" she motioned to a kid, probably in high school, with long, black hair, who was kneeling next to a cart marking on a clipboard, "—has only sorted these alphabetically by *title*." Jack turned and waved, though he was out of earshot.

Mrs. Youngstown frowned and pulled Alan to the side, "obviously we would have preferred that he sort by fiction, non-fiction, genre and the like to begin with so that it's a little easier for us librarians to get it to Dewey. But, believe me, it was a hassle and a half getting him to pull out the children's books *before* alphabetizing. What can I say, some kids just love the alphabet." She paused and made for the door. "I'll need to be getting back to the desk now," she grinned, "you never know when someone might come through that door these days! If you find what you want, just come see me and we can get it put in the system for you to check out."

Each book cart had a piece of printer paper taped to the side of it with a letter scribbled in black permanent marker. They seemed to be in a random order, but then Alan realized that the first four carts were J, A, C, and

K. *Of course.* About halfway down the right side, he found the D cart.

He had to hand it to Jack; they *were* very well-alphabetized. Some familiar titles stood out as he glanced along: *Different Seasons* by King, two copies of *The Divine Comedy* (which seemed an odd gift for a library that burnt down), *Don Quixote, Dracula.* At the D-Rs he drew in closer and turned his head to read the title on each. *What incredible luck,* he thought to himself, as he found a copy of *Dream Cycle* right next to *Dreamsnake,* and grabbed it right away. It was a ratty hardback copy missing the sleeve, and the title was written in marker along the spine.

He waited in line behind two parents and their child that were asking about the high point-value books for summer reading. After Mrs. Youngstown pointed them off to the aisle next to the big Curious George chair, Alan approached, beaming somewhat.

"You found it?" she asked, enthusiastically.

"Yep. Kind of a torn-up copy, but it'll do just fine." Alan smiled and handed her the book.

Mrs. Youngstown pulled out an envelope to hold the circulation card and glued it to the back cover of the book. With astounding force, she stamped a barcode to the inner cover, held it under the *BEEP,* and flipped back to the front. As she wrote on the circulation card, she frowned.

"Oh, I'm sorry Alan. Lovecraft, it was?"

"Yeah. What's wrong?"

She held up the inside cover to face him. "This is *Dream Cycle Reimagined: Lucid Dreaming for the Casual*...well, hold on, something is taped over it..."

"Oh." It had felt like much too lucky a find to happen to *him,* Alan thought.

"Do you want to go back and look again?"

"No, that's okay. I'm sure Jack has them all in order."

"Okay," she frowned, and looked back to the book, "I'm very sorry. I can go put in a loan request at another library if you'd like."

Alan looked at the book laying on the counter and felt a strange sense of comaraderie with it. He clicked his tongue.

"How long do you think that'd be?"

"To get it through an interlibrary loan?"

He nodded.

"It all just depends. Could be a week, could be several. It would really be something incredible if they could put all of the books on one of these computers, wouldn't it?"

Alan nodded again, but couldn't take his eyes off of the ragged book that he hadn't meant to grab. "You know what, I'll just take this one. Maybe it's topically related."

She looked at him oddly and chuckled, before filling out the rest of the card. "Okay, we'll do four weeks, just in case you really enjoy it. Do you have your card?"

Alan's face grew red. *How did I think nobody here would recognize me?* "Oh," he said heavily, gritting his teeth, "I actually—"

Her eyes widened, and Alan felt his stomach sink.

"Oh, Alan! You've lost it haven't you?"

He was taken aback. "Um, yeah. I have actually. How did you—"

"One moment!" She exclaimed with a pointed finger and disappeared behind a room divider off to the right of the reference desk. When she returned, she carried a torn yellow envelope in her hand.

Her hand extended towards Alan, and in it lay a library card flipped to the reverse side.

"Is that your signature?"

Sure enough, there in faded blue ballpoint ink was 11-year-old Alan's signature.

His mouth hung wide open for a moment. "Yeah. How'd it end up here?" he asked, as he turned the card over in his hands.

"It got mailed back to us. That *is* why we put the address on all of them, you know. Any idea where you lost it?"

"Not a clue."

"Well, all the same!" She dialed the stamp to the proper date and pounded it onto the circulation card.

"Take care of yourself, Alan."

"Of course. You do the same."

***

It bothered Alan that he hadn't any idea where his library card had been. He supposed that was often symptomatic of losing something, but it still made him uneasy. He should have asked her when they received it, or what the return address had said, or more questions like that, he thought to himself during his drive home. *Of course, they probably wouldn't be able to tell me anything, what with librarian-reader confidentiality and all.*

As he pulled back into the driveway, he found himself so intently pondering what the librarian equivalent was to a Hippocratic oath that he didn't notice Sarah's beat-up red Miata in his usual spot and had to slam on the brakes to keep from colliding into it. Sarah was Micah's not-quite-live-in girlfriend.

She greeted him as soon as he crossed the threshold, though he would use the term "greeting" in the loosest sense.

"Hey Alan," she said snidely, "we've been waiting hours for you to get here so that we can fill our starving stomachs—" She turned from her bouncer stance against the hallway wall back towards Micah's room where he was much more focused on *Super Mario Bros. 3.* "—where for lunch, Mikey?"

He kept his eyes on the TV. "Wherever you wanna go, babe."

She turned back to Alan. "Right, so..."

Alan looked on, confused. "Why did you two wait for me? I don't think we like a lot of the same food, Sarah."

She turned up her nose. "The law, Alan. Micah needs his license."

"Oh, right. Sorry."

"Thanks, bro." Micah's voice echoed out from his room. "Library officially has me in the system now, huh?"

"No...they uh, well they actually had my card there, so it was all good. Thanks anyway though."

"Oh, for sure, for sure." He stopped talking, as the pounding on his controller had sapped his focus momentarily. "What book did you need so bad? You were neck-deep in that textbook-looking one the other night."

"Yeah, it doesn't matter. They didn't have what I wanted. I got a random one but I probably won't read it."

"For sure." Micah's words came out hollow, his attention fully drained now. "Hey, there's a party this Friday at Scott's if you wanna tag along. My dad just dropped off a case so I can spot your beer."

Micah was on the soccer team with Scott in high school, and they were longtime best friends. He was nice, but he charged beer admission for any guys coming to his parties. Alan had never gone, but he was pretty sure they weren't worth the ticket price.

"Nah, that's okay. I'll probably just stay here and do a puzzle."

Micah let out an over-embellished laugh that sounded more like a screech. "For sure. For sure. Puzzles can be cool."

***

Finally alone in his room, Alan tossed the book over to his desk and threw himself back-first onto his bed. He felt frustrated, but more than that, he felt disappointed in himself. He felt disappointed that he had gotten his hopes up, that somehow getting this book would lead to some fairy-tale romance with a girl that only knew him as a cashier at Elmwood's.

Through the thin wall, he could hear the middle of an argument quickly growing louder between Micah and Sarah.

"—seriously, though!? The flag is right across this gap! One minute means one minute."

"Okay, but we already had to wait like two hours for *your* friend to get back from the library when he didn't even need your license there in the first place. I can't just fast for days on end like you!"

"He wanted to get a book. Sorry not all of my friends are heirs to the...what was the oil guy...Vanderbilt! Sorry all my friends aren't filthy rich." He chuckled at his own clever joke. "And I only fast when my body demands it. For fitness."

"It's a *video game*! It's not real! Just turn it off so we can go eat."

"Just...one...more..." Micah's voice trailed off.

"And quit making cracks about how much money my parents have. I can't do anything about that."

"I didn't say anything about your folks."

"This time, sure. How are you paying for dentistry school, hm? Earned all that money yourself? It's not like—"

"But all the money I'll make back will more than—"

"Do not interrupt me, Micah. I don't want to talk about this anymore until I'm not angry from being so fucking hungry. You're always letting Alan walk all over you. We probably could have avoided this argument entirely if we could have left when we wanted to."

"It was just a book."

"Then you invite him to a party that I've been looking forward to for weeks so that we can follow him around the whole time and make sure he's not alone. I don't even think he wants to go! He can't carry on a conversation with anyone after his dad went and—"

Alan heard Micah's door shut, muffling the rest of the argument.

Once the lovebirds had departed, Alan tried to read. He was halfway through three different books at the moment, but every time he laid back against his headboard and started, he felt himself growing restless and angry and had to put the book down.

He wasn't mad about the argument he'd overheard. That was nothing new. But he couldn't shake the feeling of stupidity and ignorance he felt from wanting to find that Lovecraft book so badly. Every time he tried to read a sentence, he reminded himself that he could be reading *that* book, and then considered how dumb he could be for ever believing that one little book was the answer to his social misfortune, that he could just pull a romance like a rabbit out of a hat by having all the answers about *Dream Cycle*. Was the girl going to give him some sort of private trivia hour and then find herself so enamored by his literary prowess that she would ask *him* on a date? Of course. Then he would lose all inhibitions and emerge from his tragedy-built cocoon a social butterfly.

He looked over at the book he had gotten as if it were the culprit to blame for everything. It felt good, in a weird way, to have a physical object to be angry at. Alan sat up and held the book in his hands, squeezing it and cursing it beneath his breath.

He tossed it aside and laid down again with his eyes closed. Alan tried to breathe as slowly as he could, *in* and *out*. He had never meditated before, but he had gotten the gist that slow breathing was the foundation. Instead of reading, he tried to close his eyes and imagine one of his books, trying to remember the words of one he had read before.

It worked, for a minute, maybe a little longer. Then he heard a knocking on his door. It was Micah.

"Hey, I don't know how much you heard earlier, but...well, you know, she was just angry. She didn't mean any of it. It was my fault, really."

"Don't worry about it."

"For sure. Thanks." He slapped Alan on his shoulder. "Hey, she invited a friend or two over to hang out here tonight. Just a heads up. I can slide some pizza under the door and tell them you're not home if you want."

"Sure. Cool. I'm gonna try to go to bed a little early. I got put on that early stocking thing before we open tomorrow."

"For sure. I'll tell them to keep it down."

They didn't keep it down. But Micah did keep his word about the pizza. Alan tried to eat as much as he could to force himself into a food coma. He laid on his bed with his bloated stomach and his lights out, trying to tune out the rattling bass thumping throughout the house.

It might have been the vibrations from the music, but Alan could have sworn the book he'd gotten that day nearly leaped off of his desk in the middle of the night. It fell to the floor, open.

V. Ice shift

The *ice shift*. That's what they called it. Every week when a large shipment came in, one worker from the front (typically a cashier) would have to clock in an extra four hours early to help the night-stocking crew get everything on the shelves.

Today was Alan's day. The name originated from the ice that your spit crystallizes into as you're swearing and spitting on your walk into Elmwood's. Today the illustrative capacity of the name was lost, with a balmy 48 degree low.

The night-stocking manager was Raphl. Miss Etta said that his parents meant to name him Ralph, but his mother found herself too distracted by his right ear and forgot to add the L until the end. His right ear *was* guilty of causing staring, even to this day, when Raphl must have been well into his fifties. The ear shriveled up right into a point at the tip—how you would imagine an elf ear to form. To make it even worse, his twin brother, who'd had the same condition but on both ears, was properly named as Rudolph, and the parents could only afford one corrective treatment, so they picked the worse of the two.

Miss Etta said Raphl could afford the more expensive adult version of the procedure now if he wanted to, but he had grown fond of the ear and would often leave the other covered, hoping to create the illusion that both were pointed.

Raphl, or "raffle," as everyone pronounced his name, was mean, but Alan didn't blame him for it. He was on the eternal ice shift. He only had one other to keep him company at night: Hilda. She had only worked there for a year or so, but everyone already thought she was a touch insane.

As Alan got nearer to the back of the store, Raphl stepped out of one of the freezer doors wearing a beanie pulled over his unaffected ear and a puffy grey coat.

"Hendershot. Good to see you." He held up a gloved hand to his forehead in a half-hearted salute.

"Glad to be here." Alan coughed into his sleeve and rubbed his not-gloved hands together to make some friction.

Raphl led him to the back where they had a few towers of milk and cheeses stacked up, ready to get broken down and put into the coolers.

Once he arrived at work and got busy, Alan actually enjoyed the ice shift. The work was easy, simple, and relaxing. Raphl wasn't a bothersome supervisor and would only cross paths with you once or twice the whole time. It also meant he'd get to leave work four hours early. Waking up at 3 a.m. was a real bitch, though.

***

A few hours later, all the cheeses, from Havarti, to Muenster, to Parmesan, to blue, to cream, to American singles, were snug in their bunks and Alan made off toward the bakery for some breakfast. Miss Etta had just arrived and was hanging her jacket up on the rack behind her when she saw Alan walking up.

"Good morning, Alan." She smiled and flipped on the display lights illuminating each of the bakery coolers. "Okay, looks like I've got a misshapen apple fritter. Will that do you?"

"Hit me with it."

Alan dug into the pastry with tenacity, as he always did at the end of an ice shift. He was already swallowing the last bite before Miss Etta asked, "So, did you get started on that book for the girl?"

Alan felt a heat rise in him, but he wasn't as frustrated as he'd been yesterday. He'd gone the entire night and morning without dreaming or thinking about it.

"Well, not great news there. I have no way to get the book. The library didn't have it."

"Oh, that's too bad," she said heavily, as she shifted around some brownies and pies to put the best-looking ones in the front. "Well, maybe she won't even remember you said that."

"Yeah, maybe." Not that he didn't believe this would be a possibility, but Alan had felt better after resigning himself to no further interactions with the girl and didn't want to get his hopes up again. "You know, I probably won't see her again. I mean, I think she was maybe just trying to be nice, and I got worried for nothing. I'd probably avoid my line if I was her and came shopping here again."

Miss Etta looked at him disapprovingly through the display window she was working in, and her muffled words came from behind the glass. "Well, maybe she didn't see you pull the sword from that cake the other day."

Alan attempted to chuckle and grin, but he knew he was right.

***

The day on the register was always rough on an ice shift day. He could never make himself get up *earlier* than 3 a.m. to have a real "breakfast," so whatever scraps he got from Miss Etta would be all that his stomach caught a whiff of until he left at noon. Cashiering didn't take too much focus, but there were little things like water on the bottom of a cart or checking eggs for breaks that he would slip up on because of exhaustion. Today it was produce codes.

The customer was a shorter man, probably only mid-forties, with thick, ruffled, chestnut-red hair, but bald in the middle. He wore thick-framed black glasses over enormous eyes and a curled mustache. His groceries were all neatly arranged and stacked on the belt, and they were all flipped so that the barcode was on the bottom. Each flew over the scanner rhythmically without a hiccup. Then he got to the avocados.

Every item of produce has a little sticker with a tiny barcode and a number on it, and you punch in that number, the register computer looks up the store price, then the cashier weighs or quantifies the item. At least that's the idea. In practice, a whole lot of items don't have stickers on them. There are the excusables: loose bananas separated from the bunch or a sprig of mint freed from its tie. Avocados weren't an excusable though.

At first glance, Alan had no idea what it was. He knew what avocados were, sure, but the act of holding it in his hand before seeing it (combined with his drowsiness) had him second-guessing himself. *Is this a really old lime? No, limes aren't this bumpy. It might be a bulbous pickling cucumber. 4596. Wait, why do I know the code for pickling cucumbers? No, I don't think it's that. It doesn't smell like a pickle. Oh no, did he just see me sniff it? Eh, probably not. I think it's a kiwi.*

3-2-7-9. Alan put in the code followed by the quantity of 2. Unfortunately, his sleep-deprived thumb slurred across the keypad and depressed the *3* key as it went for the enter key. While the price of two kiwis would in fact get you about a 50% discount on your avocados, 23 kiwis did no such thing.

"Okay, $68.42. Check, card, or cash?"

"No, I don't think that's right." The man pushed his glasses further up his nose and surveyed the cart. "Yeah, there's no way. You've done something wrong."

"Sir, every single barcode went across just one time. I don't think—"

"Son, I know what the total cost of this should be. I buy the same thing every week, and the only items that changed in price were the on-sale avocados."

"You didn't have any avocados."

"What are these, then?" The man held each avocado in a tight fist with his eyes wide and brows furrowed.

"Oh."

"Oh? Who is this kid?" The man looked around the store mockingly as if it would answer his question. "Are you really so incompetent that you—give me that."

He tore the incomplete receipt off of the printer and whispered partial syllables of the products to himself as he moved towards the bottom.

"23 KIWIS!"

"I'm sorry, I can fix—"

"I don't want you to fix my order!" He had a manic stance now, with his legs wide and his eyelids unflinching. "I want this damn county to educate their youth a little better so I don't have to explain to some man-baby the difference between an avocado and a kiwi!" Spit flew with every consonant.

"Look, it was a simple mistake. I can subtract the cost of the kiwis and—"

"Can you?! Can you do that for me? I would *love* that!" The man said, just as angrily.

Alan hurriedly punched in the negative tally and added it to the total, before punching in 3080 followed by a 2. As the man pulled out his wallet to swipe his card, he opened his mouth again.

"This week an avocado. Maybe next week I can teach you what an ounce of common sense looks like. Pfft. Yeah, right." He ripped the card through the machine and left the receipt in Alan's outstretched hand.

***

Alan didn't eat lunch when he got home. His stomach was quivering and his entire body felt hollow, but there wasn't enough energy left in his bones to resurrect Chef Bobby's frozen assets in the microwave. He went right to the couch and flopped onto his back.

Ow.

A crushed beer can wedged in between two of the cushions dug its way into his spine.

"Hey Micaaaa..." His voice faded to silence as the effort to speak his roommate's name had almost done him in. *Probably for the better*, as a confrontation over a rogue beer can was only something Alan would get himself into in his hazy, fast-drunken stupor. But soon, curiosity got the best of him and he sneaked over to Micah's door, peering in. Nobody was there.

Back in the living room, he saw the blinking orange light on the answering machine and he immediately regretted resupplying the tape. "Hi, mom," he said aloud to no one, punching the play button and throwing himself back down onto the couch, hitting the can again.

The static clicked in and, sure enough, he heard his mom's voice.

"Hey Alan. It's mom. New tape, I see. I'm glad you changed it out." She paused, and he could hear the ruffling of some papers in the background. "Hey, so some mail came for you today. You know how I open your mail just in case there's a bill or something you might miss? Well, it's a letter from that school in Youngstown that you applied to. It has your name on it and everything. It really sounds like, well, I don't know, it sounds like they really want you. Well, anyway, if you don't come over in the next couple of days, I'll put it in the mail for you. Just thought you'd want to know." He could hear her turn away from the phone, saying something to his sister. "Yeah....I know, one second...going to ask him. Hey, Alan. We're still going to have that birthday party in a few weeks. I know I'm probably just pestering you at this point...but, well...I think your sister would like it a lot if you were here. I told her we could get Pizza Inn since that was his favorite." She stopped talking again. "Get your...um, your pizza topping orders in soon so I know." She let out an empty laugh. "It's good to talk to you, even if you don't say anything back. I still know you're listening. Goodbye, baby, I love you."

Alan felt a tear running down the side of his cheek and wiped it away angrily. If anything, he wanted to call his mom back just to explain to her what a form letter from a college was. *Yeah, I'm sure any university would be desperate to have the guy that doesn't know the difference between an avocado and a kiwi grace the halls of their beloved alma mater.* He pried the beer can out from underneath himself and threw it at the wall.

He couldn't imagine if his mom had been there at work and had seen all those people talk to him like that. She'd be writing the universities back for him, "Sorry, my son is doomed to scan eggs and milk for the rest of his life. *If he's lucky.*"

The thought of Pizza Inn was practically torture upon his malnourished soul. A few years ago, he'd had a dream he'd fallen into a huge factory vat of their marinara sauce and that his fingers were breadsticks. He hadn't any arms by the time he woke up.

But yeah, wouldn't that be *great. I'm sure if I go to the party they won't ask me a single thing about my plans for school. Better yet, I bet they wouldn't dream of mentioning my romantic life! Nobody ever asks a single, down-and-out guy in his 20s about those sorts of things.*

In his newly agitated state, he nuked a meatloaf and green peas before stumbling to his room to take advantage of his newfound satiation and take a nap. He looked down upon the surface he was about to throw his back onto for a beer can, but saw the book from yesterday lying on his bed, open.

He knew it had been on the floor the last time he had seen it, and he *never* left a book on top of his comforter. He always left it open to the page where he left off and slid it neatly beneath his pillow. But that was only for his current reader. Alan hadn't read as much as a single sentence from this book.

He tossed it over to the desk and let the mystery remain just that, quickly falling asleep.

***

"Babe, I swear to god, that's the guy from Home Alone."

"No way, Mikey. The hair was way different, *and* he had that earring."

Micah and Sarah had gotten home just as Alan finished his dinner, which to his stomach, was more like a breakfast. They had seen *Lethal Weapon 3*.

"I am telling you, they have wigs and hair dye." Micah was in the middle of presenting the evidence to Sarah that Leo was in fact Joe Pesci.

"Okay. Maybe. But that's crazy. And how do you explain the earring then, huh?"

"They have props! It's Hollywood. They have the best props!"

Alan was washing the fork he had eaten with while Micah and Sarah shouted from the couch.

"I just don't buy it. You think all those burns he had on his head would have just healed in that short amount of time? Are you sure you should be going into medicine?" She giggled.

"Babe. These are all movie effects. They have such good effects now, it's like, like you wouldn't believe it. I can't believe the hair is the one thing that stands out to you as not real. Back me up on this, Alan."

As much as he didn't want to join their conversation, his fingers would shrivel up soon if he kept washing nothing.

"Yeah, I mean, they can really do some cool things now. We all saw *Terminator 2* together, right? That was movie magic."

"For sure, for sure. You've gotta see this Lethal Weapon though, man. We would've invited you, but—"

"Yeah, no worries. I was pretty tired. Hey...um, you guys didn't move that book that was on my floor, did you?"

"For sure no, bro. I leave your floor books where they lie. Is it gone?"

"No, it's not gone. It's just...never mind, I think these weird hours are just taking a toll on me."

Micah laughed inappropriately. "Alright, bro. For sure. Hey, do you mind if we push the TV out to the living room? We were gonna get drunk and watch Dateline."

"Nah, go for it."

***

Tonight, Alan could read once again. He took it as an unspoken blessing from his subconscious that he was over the girl who read Lovecraft. He didn't even like Lovecraft. What were the chances they would have gotten along? Slim to none, he bet.

By "watch Dateline," what Micah really meant was, "have Dateline on in the background while we yell and scream at each other in between making out." But even with their rage-fueled romp musically accompanied by NBC thriving in the next room, the reading was good.

He was nearly at the end of *Wise Wizard.* It hadn't been a brilliant book, but you know, it had been a thing. It took him somewhere, he guessed. The writing wasn't awful. Maybe a 3 out of 5 stars? He'd had little choice though with his leave of absence from the library. His stack of yet-to-be-read books consisted entirely of Christmas presents from aunts and uncles that had probably just walked up to the first poor schmuck in Books-A-Million and began describing their weird nephew.

But even then, the reading was good. He was with Undor. He saw the story to the end. Alan fell asleep satisfied *without* a stuffed stomach. Happy and alone, as he was meant to be.

Then, with a loud thump that woke him, the library book fell to the floor once again, wide-open.

VI. A tavern to quench his thirst

Alan's Wednesday at Elmwood's came to a close missing many things, though it could not be said that Alan *missed* any of these things. There were no double coupons, no unlabeled produce, no Dudgeons, and no Mr. Vick.

Once home, he tempered to his preferred habitat right away, pulling a dinner out of the freezer and kicking off his shoes. Today he had two Beast Feasts revolving around each other in the microwave like binary stars. It was clear from the packaging, which showed a boy with a wolf's body holding the tray of food while blasting through space, that their target consumers were, at eldest, middle school boys. Alan bought them for special occasions because each came with a sprinkled brownie. He'd decided that with double the quantity of food, the entrée was just as filling and delicious.

There's no version of Chef Bobby chicken nuggets, but he doubts the caliber would be any greater.

Even though today had been an okay day at work, it wasn't special to Alan yet. He had *decided* to make it a special day, rather, by eating the Beast Feasts. This is a rather charming invention Alan has developed over time, in that sometimes all you have to do to have a special day is simply consume things you have saved *for* a special day.

***

There on the top of his bookshelf, open once again, the pages fluttered as a breeze whisked across them. That's where the autonomous book now sat. He moved to the window, slammed it shut and closed the half-inch gap that had ushered in the wind.

Strange.

He closed the book and brushed his fingers along the cover. It was a faded blue, and the spine bore a piece of yellow binding tape where that disingenuous title displayed itself: *Dream Cycle.* He shook his head, finding it cosmically funny now that he had surrendered that romantic hope he had clung to just the other day.

His fingers came upon a rough patch near the top right corner, like a piece of loose tape or an old stamp. He scraped at it with the tip of his nail and worked away at the blue paper that now revealed itself to be a false cover. Half an inch, then a bit more, and finally he was peeling away a ratty, thick sheet that had closed off the entire face of the book.

The true cover was a deep-crimson shell, very sturdy and unwavering. It smelled ancient, but only of an old book, as if you had boiled down 10,000 books from a library sale and distilled their oils into one essence. The lettering on the front was a golden, modern serif in all caps that read: *Dream Cycle Reimagined: Lucid Dreaming for the Casual.* Then it ended. Next to *Casual* there was a piece of tape the texture of papier mâché that had written upon it in harshly faded black ink: *Adventurer. Lucid Dreaming for the Casual Adventurer.* He scraped off that tape. Beneath it, the correct title's end: *Oneirologist.*

He had to hand it to the book; this was one time where taking the mask off left him more disappointed and confused than he had been prior, as if the book were a Scooby-Doo bad guy. *I mean really, how could you be a casual any kind of -ologist?* Although, he supposed, oneirology wasn't even an important part of the title. It had been last, and using context clues, he determined that it probably had something to do with sleeping or dreaming. But this torn and tattered *Adventurer* that now lay on the floor—now *that* had him interested.

He flipped through the pages gently to prevent any further damage, and his curiosity grew even greater. In the margins of every page were frantic handwritten notes—the same handwriting that had renamed the book.

One chapter seemed boring enough: at a quick glance it was a simple list of tips to prepare for your first night lucid dreaming. But brief notes crept along the outskirts of the pages. One read, "Must make list of characters before dream. Seems to help to look at the drawing or repeat the name before closing your eyes." Scribbled across the page: "Nudity is unlikely. But you must determine what is in your pockets." Further down in the published text there was a list of supplements and foods that would encourage lucid dreaming. Out to the side the ghostwriter had written a recipe for an herbal tea using a few ingredients that Alan had never heard of before.

On the next page there was a tip suggesting that you wake yourself up with an alarm in the middle of the night, that interrupting this stage of sleep would promote lucid dreaming. The footnote here once again clashed with the advice. "This is reckless. No longer set alarms in the middle of the night. If I'm already in the dream, it's too difficult to predict how the alarm sound will manifest. Maybe try bright lights?"

On and on Alan read, and he found more notes on characters, settings, and storylines. Soon the picture became clear to him. Someone had annotated this guide to lucid dreaming with rules for dreaming up a fantasy realm, or at least experiencing one. Near the end of the second chapter where the original author was discussing good jump-off points for your first dream, the mystery penman had written a brief treatise on one's first fantasy world.

Nᴇxᴛ ᴛɪᴍᴇ I ᴍᴜsᴛ ɢᴏ ɪɴ ᴡɪᴛʜ ᴀ ᴄʟᴇᴀʀ sᴇᴛ ᴏғ ʀᴜʟᴇs. Iᴛ ɪs ᴏʙᴠɪᴏᴜs ɴᴏᴡ ᴛʜᴀᴛ ɪғ ᴛʜᴇʏ ᴀʀᴇ ɴᴏᴛ ᴜɴᴅᴇʀsᴛᴏᴏᴅ ʙʏ ᴛʜᴇ ᴅʀᴇᴀᴍᴇʀ ʙᴇғᴏʀᴇ ᴇɴᴛᴇʀɪɴɢ, ᴛʜᴇ ᴅʀᴇᴀᴍᴇʀ' s ᴍɪɴᴅ ᴡɪʟʟ ᴀʟʟᴏᴡ ᴀ ᴍᴀɴɪғᴇsᴛᴇᴅ ᴇɴᴛɪᴛʏ ᴛᴏ ᴄʀᴇᴀᴛᴇ ᴛʜᴇ ʀᴜʟᴇs, ᴏʀ, ᴀᴛ ᴛʜᴇ ᴠᴇʀʏ ʟᴇᴀsᴛ, ᴄʀᴇᴀᴛᴇ ᴛʜᴇ ʀᴜʟᴇs ᴏᴜᴛsɪᴅᴇ ᴏғ ᴛʜᴇɪʀ sɪɢʜᴛ. I'ᴠᴇ ɢᴏᴛ ᴛᴏ ʜᴀᴠᴇ ᴍᴏʀᴇ ғʀɪᴇɴᴅs ᴀᴛ ᴛʜᴇ sᴛᴀʀᴛ. Iᴛ's ᴅɪғғɪᴄᴜʟᴛ ᴛᴏ ᴄʜᴇᴀᴛ ᴛʜᴇ ғᴀᴄᴛs ᴏғ ᴛʜᴇ ᴡᴏʀʟᴅ ᴀᴛ ᴛʜᴇ ʟᴀsᴛ ᴛɪᴍᴇ ᴛʜᴀᴛ ʏᴏᴜ ʟᴇғᴛ ɪᴛ, sᴏ ʏᴏᴜ ᴍᴜsᴛ ɢᴇᴛ ᴏғғ ᴏɴ ᴛʜᴇ ʀɪɢʜᴛ ғᴏᴏᴛ. I ᴡɪʟʟ sᴛᴀʀᴛ ᴀɴᴇᴡ ᴛᴏᴍᴏʀʀᴏᴡ.

Alan sat on his bed, completely entranced by the book. It had at first seemed like a ridiculous prank, but the more he read on, the more earnest the hand-writer appeared. There were notes where he seemed afraid or unsure of what would come next in his dream and notes where he conveyed deep joy that seemed too expositive to be a joke.

He lingered within the first couple of chapters, rarely glancing over to the original text, but retaining every word scratched on the boundaries of the pages. The more he read, the deeper the idea had dug its way into his mind: *am I going to try this?*

The excessive amounts of sodium in his Beast Feasts were wreaking havoc. His tongue felt like stretched cotton balls and his throat cried for water. But he couldn't take his eyes off of the book. He flipped and skimmed, reading as many of the bullet points as he could. The inclination to test the advice had rooted itself strongly now, and he knew he couldn't put the book down.

He had seen a few notes about one's first time, and though he hadn't bookmarked them or written any down, he had a running mental list that was frantically expanding. It was clear he needed a good idea of where he was going and who would be there. That was no problem. Creating his own universe wasn't a foreign thought to him. Characters were a little more shady, but it didn't seem as important to flesh out all the details at the moment.

There was a small note taped in (it was on a page full of text with very slim margins) with a meditative technique listed out step by step.

The writer had put at the top: "consistently the most foolproof way to get there—the tea works wonders but this can do the trick in a pinch." He thought back to the other night when he had tried meditating. It *had* seemed like he had missed a sizeable chunk of time lost in his own thoughts. *That had to be a good sign.*

He flipped through some more, reaching the end of the next chapter, but he was growing far too anxious. Alan didn't want to spend the entire night taking notes on what could go wrong. He closed the book after he'd found one more piece of advice he couldn't argue with: *be sure to go in with a stuffed stomach.*

Alan ran out to the kitchen with the book flopping around in his hand as he dashed. He popped a bowl of noodles into the microwave, poured a good tablespoon of soy sauce on top and dashed back to his room.

The brief intermission had given him some pause. *What am I doing right now?* He looked at the book again in his hand, judging its veracity again as if for the first time. Alan glanced to his desk where *Wise Wizard* sat, no bookmark left in its completed pages. He thought about how long it had taken him to finish it, and how the ending was, well, mediocre. *I only sleep for seven hours, eight on a good night. Wise Wizard took a lot longer than that. What will it hurt? I can't waste time if I'm doing something while I'm asleep.*

He looked at the spine of the book again, at the abbreviated title that had fooled him into checking it out. Alan thought about the girl, the girl that would probably never see him again, *thank god.* He thought about the customers of Elmwood's, their items, their shopping carts, their incessant complaining.

That ratty old piece of makeshift tape still lay on the floor. *Adventurer.*

He lay down on his bed and began the meditation.

***

The list of directions was short and repeated some things from the handwritten notes, like visualizing the setting and repeating the name of the location. There was also a note at the bottom underlined twice: "Must stay uncomfortable. Do not lay in normal sleeping position."

Alan lay flat on his back like a corpse and let every limb of his body remain where it first fell, even though his right foot was a bit too compressed by the sheets and his left arm was bent awkwardly to the side. He whispered silently to himself and tried to avoid crinkling or flexing his eyelids, like a child pretending to sleep in the hopes of being carried in from the car. He wouldn't bother with the conjuring of particular characters, as he didn't have any in mind and was perfectly all right with being alone in the world.

The name of his world wasn't the most inventive, but it was all he knew it as. When he was little, he picked it off an old gas can. Where before there had been a warning label, only two faded label fragments remained with enough adhesive to cling to the can. *Important warning: contents are combustible and, if left near a source of heat or flame, may explode* had become *Imp Lode*.

His world was one that he'd imagined slowly. It began as an imaginary place that he'd often traveled to as a child in the woods of their backyard, and as he grew older, he'd fleshed it out more and more with things he liked from books he read. A conscious construction he'd never intended, but now as he tried to picture it, he recognized these familiar niceties, charms, and characteristics borrowed, twisted, and boiled down from his favorite stories.

The list recommended focusing on a very specific spot or location and picturing yourself there. There was one spot he knew very well. Deep in the middle of the woods behind his childhood home, there had been a clear grassy patch surrounded by a ring of very short trees with wide branches that covered the inside with shade. He and his dad had always traded stories about what the spot had been.

One cool, summer evening when the cicadas, crickets, and fireworks were loud enough to mask their sneaking and snickering, Alan and his dad went out to the woods to partake in a holiday tradition. July 4th Whatchamacallits, a candy bar only to be enjoyed once a year under a firework and star-lit sky with no moms around. Alan didn't know what Independence Day was, but he knew Whatchamacallit day.

They went to the same spot every year, sitting in the ring of trees that had become their hideaway. Every year, a new tale. But this year, his dad told his best story.

Long ago, a giant had lived beneath their woods deep under the ground. He was a giant that ate the berries that grew along the roots of certain trees; Ruteeter, they had called him. The shortest trees had the roots that reached the furthest underground, and in this ring were the trees that the giant had planted himself, very deep. They grew the sweetest berries around. This is where he lives.

"We're right above him, Alan. A giant. He's down there below us—maybe even knows we're here." His dad's eyes widened, and he put a finger up to his mouth. "Be quiet...and listen."

For a moment, as he stuffed his mouth with chocolate and peanut butter, and a cool breeze sent a shiver up his spine, there was a crack and a boom that he swore wasn't a firework. It was Ruteeter.

"But he's your friend, Alan."

Alan had always thought about the giant when he was laying in the ring reading a book or looking up through the leaves at the clouds as he fell asleep for a nap, convincing himself he had heard a soft rumble or felt a tremor from his friend Ruteeter.

He continued to whisper, imagining the ring of trees. His right foot grew faintly numb, but he didn't move it. *Water. I just need something to drink.* But he couldn't get up. He tried to focus in again, repeating the name of the world: *Imp Lode. Imp Lode. Imp Lode.* There he was, laying on the soft grass in the ring. He whispered more, but softer now. His mouth grew tired, and he moved only his tongue against his teeth with his mouth closed. *Imp Lode.* His eyes relaxed and he no longer had to scrunch them. *Imp Lode.* He didn't care about his foot anymore. Alan hardly cared about anything. He didn't want to think anymore. *Imp—*

***

Bump. Ba-dump.

Alan looked around. He was riding in a wagon of some sort, and in front of him was a single horse with a stocky build, trotting along at a leisurely pace. His eyes followed the reigns to the man seated next to him. He was short and plump with white hair and a worn grey tunic. He didn't seem to notice Alan's gaze.

There were several barrels behind them in the wagon's bay, bouncing up and down, as one wheel seemed to kick a bit with every revolution.

Very tall, dense, hardwood trees colored dark green with flecks of creamy snow filled the forest along either side of the dirt road. There wasn't any other living creature in sight, but sounds of singing birds and jostling pine needles filled the air.

Alan looked down to his hands and saw that his clothes were like the driver's, though with cleaner leather pants and grey boots that rode up past his ankle.

"Hi. Um, who are you?"

The man looked over at him and unveiled a grin missing three or four teeth. "You're in *my* wagon, lad. Did ye nod off there?"

"Oh yeah. Must have." He felt in his pockets, half-expecting to find his wallet or keys. "Remind me again, you know, where we are in the world."

"Well, this road here came from Needlewich, ye remember, and goes to Drireford. You haven't been sampling the product, have ye?"

The man shot a cheeky grin his way and urged the pony onward.

"Sampling the what?"

"My, lad? Did ye forget everything I told ye when ye hitched this ride?"

"Yeah, I guess so. One of those bumps must have really—"

"The name is Treog. Pleasure to meet ye, *again.* I've got to take this here poll ale from me cellar in Needlewich, which is where I picked you up, to a tavern in Drireford. Half-Cracked Staff, it's called. A tavern is where I was told I needed to take ye and it was just right convenient I already happened to be goin' to this one."

"Oh right. The tavern. Of course we're going to a tavern."

"Yes. Course." Treog nodded and looked suspiciously from the corner of his eye.

"And this would be Engl—"

"This would be what?"

"I'm sorry. You must understand I'm a *very* weary traveler and I've all but forgotten my name—"

"Yes. Alandriel. I have not forgotten yours."

"Oh...yep. So pretend that I just appeared here. Just tell me everything that I would need to know to not sound crazy."

Treog now returned a very concerned look, but responded hesitantly. "Here? What do you mean, here? Imp Lode?"

Alan nearly woke himself from excitement. "Yes. Well, I mean, of course I knew that we are in Imp Lode. I more meant, you know, region, town, et cetera."

"Et cetera?"

"So forth and so on."

"Well, I don't know exactly what ye mean by region. We are in the region between Needlewich and Drireford, as I said. Have you already forgotten that?"

"No, no. You're right. I'm sorry. I guess for some reason, in my memory of Imp Lode, there were, you know, those towns like Needlewich and Direford—"

"Drireford."

"Right. Towns like those and...others. But, I thought I had been told before that there were sort of larger places that held those towns."

"Like a god?"

"Well, no. But that's a good point. Which god do you worship, Treog, bringer of fine ales?"

"I don't believe in no god." He spat off the wagon onto the passing ground. "Men ain't allowed to worship no gods here. Ye tryna be funny?"

"No. No! I know that I'm not funny. I'm sorry."

Treog relinquished and focused his attention back on the road ahead.

"You're sure ye know people at Half-Cracked? They don't take too kindly to the last stranger I'd seen round there."

"Oh, yes. Of course. I've actually known the owner for a fairly long time."

"You know Vander—"

"Vanderkil? Yes. He actually—well he owes me a life debt." Alan gritted his teeth and held his breath, awaiting to see the fate of his lie.

"Vanderkil. Yes. Hm. Mighty strange. I felt I had another name on the tip of me tongue. Don't know what come over me. Well, any friend of Vanderkil is a friend of mine. Though not a friend of many!" He laughed uneasily. "Pays better coin than most do for me ale. Funny he never mentioned knowin' another man."

Alan exhaled in relief as quietly as he could.

"Yeah. He's a good ole...guy. Fine man."

Treog now returned the same look that Alan had gotten *several* times since coming to in his cart, but said nothing else. In fact, he was mostly silent for the rest of their trip.

The sun that had formerly been high in the sky was now slowly being blotted out by the treetops at the back of them. The forest cleared away, and they passed through one long, open meadow filled with light blue flowers and tall, thorny weeds before reaching an overlook that sat atop a small valley town below.

A stream carved its way through the hillside and traveled down the rock face to the level of the paths in the town. There were several houses dotted along the edges, but the middle of the town seemed to consist of shops and industrious dwellings, for dark smoke billowed out from nearly all the chimneys, and the distant clanging of metal-shaping and woodworking echoed all the way to their altitude.

They descended along the road they had come in on, and the pace of Yuggle (this was the pony, of which the calling and chastising had first led Alan to take it as a swear word) had slowed dramatically as they reached more level ground and ventured into the rows of shops.

It was a town of men, best Alan could tell, as they passed by a few shopkeepers and craftsmen that were doing work outside. A long, slender man with thin fingers and a delicate face was wrapping up fresh boules of bread in a cloth towel and taking them inside. One sturdy, blond-haired fellow covered in a veil of soot was cooling a twisted piece of metal in a small vessel of water. A woman near the end of the lane on the right was picking some fancifully colored herbs and flowers that grew in front of her shop and depositing the pickings into glass jars.

The guide had warned not to dwell too much on the reality of the world when you're there, but Alan couldn't help but consider the possibility of races other than men, though he daren't ask yet.

"Well, looks as though we made it right 'fore closing time." Treog chuckled. "Which means opening time for Vanderkil. I'm sure he'll be wantin' this ale real soon."

The wagon came to a halt on the main lane as a lot of the stores and shops had outed their lanterns inside and locked up their doors. Though some made their way to other parts of town through little roads and paths jutting off to the sides, to their homes, Alan guessed, a small parade of people making for the tavern had formed behind their wagon now. Treog greeted and nodded to a few of them as they hopped off. The man closest spit at the wagon's wheel, and none looked too kindly upon them.

Treog gritted his teeth and halted Yuggle near the door. "Okay, laddy, help me carry these in and I'll consider yer debt paid."

They both took hold of a barrel by either end, and the weight of it nearly collapsed Alan. *This has got to count as one of those dream reality checks that book mentioned.* His arms popped right to the bottom of his shoulder joints, and his legs buckled.

The tavern was built from a dark brown, hand-hewn brick, and some interior paneled wood was visible in places. A scruffy blackbird perched on a rectangular sign fastened with thick rope to an overhang above the door. The sign bore a painted carving of a staff split in two longways, right about down halfway, and simple block lettering:

HALF-CRACKED STAFF, and beneath in smaller type: BOTTOM ALES AND SHARP GINSKEY.

The interior was simple, and the bar took up most of the back portion of the wall, save for a little cubby on the right side. Paneling came down from the ceiling leaving only a gap of about three feet to the bar's surface. There were lamps in the middle of most of the tables, many of which were actually just large barrels with a rough slab of wood on top. None were lit, though the daylight able to infiltrate the inside was waning.

Two men sat at the far end of the bar. One tipped a tankard forward to his lips, and the other slapped him on his back, laughing loudly. They both greeted Treog with harsh eyes and a reluctant toast, and traded hushed whispers about Alan before each dropped their sullen gaze.

From a door behind the bar emerged their host, Vanderkil, and Alan immediately realized his mistake in counterfeiting their friendship. Vanderkil stood taller than either of them, his head nearly concealed behind the upper paneling. From the neck down, nothing stood out except for the hook he had instead of a right hand. He was solid in frame and wore a very dirty and dark apron. When he bent down to rest his elbows on the bar, with his head in full view, it was clear: Vanderkil only had one eye. And no, it was not one eye in a proper right or left place, maybe with an eye patch to match his arm. Rather, it was one enormous eye in the middle of his head.

It blinked, briefly concealing the bright blue iris and deep black pupil.

He spoke, and the voice, both high in pitch and nasal, surprised Alan, though he did his best not to show it.

"Treog." He nodded. "Who's this?"

Treog looked at Alan disappointedly, confirming his suspicions that Alan had lied.

"This is Alandriel. I was—well, I was under the impression that the two of ye had already met." He shot another glare in Alan's direction and rolled the barrel over to the counter. He whispered something to Vanderkil before turning back.

"Come'n lad. Let's get the rest of 'em."

They heaved the next barrel out of the wagon and Treog said nothing about the lie, so Alan decided not to bring it up. There were four more, all at least as full of poll ale as the first. By the time they put the fifth next to the bar counter, Alan's arms were on fire.

"Right, so..." Treog lingered next to Vanderkil, looking down at the goods.

"Oh, right." Vanderkil disappeared for a moment back through the same door, then returned with a small leather pouch. "This should cover me for this moon and the last." He tossed it to Treog.

"Right. Well, I'll leave the two of ye to..." He shot Alan a final dirty look. "Well, g'day, Van."

With that, Treog was back out the door, and Alan could hear his wagon pull away.

"Right. Can I get you a drink, pal?" Vanderkil seemed to lighten up as soon as Treog left and had stooped at the bar again, smiling.

"Sure. I don't know...what all do you have?"

He laughed, though it was much deeper and rumbling than his speech. "Well, I've got a lot of fresh poll ale. There's one or two elder barrels yet to run dry, and there's ginskey, of course."

Either of the ales seemed to be the safest choice, so Alan went with the elder. Vanderkil filled a tankard until it overflowed and spilt onto the bar.

Alan glanced to the other two men sitting near him, who maintained a speculative stare alternating between him and the bartender. They did not seem at all happy, more of a confused anger than anything.

"Cheers." He slid it across to him, and Alan picked the tankard up to his lips, taking a big swig of the ale. It had a pleasant taste, like how freshly bloomed flowers smelled but a little sweeter and with a stronger presence of yeast. It was delicious, and Vanderkil laughed heavily as Alan turned the tankard upwards, nearly finishing it, right as—

***

He awoke in his bed with a yelling bladder and wet lips. His thirst had been quenched.

He looked over at the book, short of breath at the rush of thoughts and questions flooding his mind. It had worked.

He didn't sleep the rest of the night.

VII. The dreaded CIST

It was senior day at Elmwood's, and Alan could hardly keep his mind off of *Imp Lode* enough to scan items properly, let alone greet the customers. He found his thoughts endlessly wandering: to Treog, to Vanderkil, to Drireford, to the taste of that wonderful elder ale.

Alan barely touched his noodles on break, finding the slurping and noodle-chasing to take too much attention from the world in his head. He hadn't noticed that he'd forgotten to microwave them.

Around midday, Vick came to fetch him off his register.

He was sure something was wrong or that he would be yelled at shortly, but even during the trudge up the stairs, he found himself re-imagining the inside of the Half-Cracked Staff, ensuring that it would be the same when he visited it again. He was making mental imprints and maps of every place and person.

Inside the office, he took a seat in a cheap folding chair ripped to hell and patched with packing tape. Mr. Vick sat across from him at his desk, leaving a gap of silence after they had both taken a seat. He pretended to type urgently on his computer, as if he'd forgotten that Alan was there.

He continued to stare at the screen, but spoke up. "Right. So, Hendershot. I'm sure that you know why I called you up here." He punched a few more keys and then turned to face him.

"Um, no, sir. I don't, actually."

Vick chuckled and nodded his head once. "Of course, of course you don't. Well, take a look at this. It might clue you in." He slid a printout across the desk.

At the top was printed, "E.O.E. CASHIER 003, CIST REPORT GENERATED 05-1992." Beneath that were several numbers that Alan did not quite understand, and one of them had been circled in red: 11.73. He looked up from the paper and back to Mr. Vick.

"I'm sorry, sir. I'm still not sure what this is."

"Well, let me enlighten you. CIST is a top-of-the-line software. All the big box stores are using it at their registers. So, of course, I've paid for a trial version for us to try here. That number there—that's your items scanned per minute. Are you beginning to understand?"

"Oh. Okay, I see. So what's the problem with my CI—"

"Your CIST score, yes. Well, as you can see, it's 11.73. I'm sorry to say, but," He held up another paper, moving his finger down it, "that's a bottom-sixth percentile score. As you can imagine, that's completely unacceptable for a store with our standards."

Alan had only heard a few words: sorry, bottom, score, and unacceptable; for in his mind's eye, he was in Imp Lode, trying to recount *exactly* how tall the trees had appeared, smiling wistfully.

"Do you think this is funny, Hendershot?"

"No, sir. I'm sorry. I was...um, a bit distracted."

"Is that so?" He picked up the papers and stacked them together aggressively, staring at Alan. "Well, here's what's distracting me, Hendershot."

Alan did his best to sit up straight and hold eye contact with Mr. Vick, and he realized that this meeting was more serious than his clouded observations had relayed.

"—your sorry attitude. Now, we both know that you don't have a lot of opportunities in life. Even though that's mostly your fault, I've done my best to stick my neck out for you in front of customers, even when it's clear that you've made a stupid mistake or your little *temperament* here brought on the stones. Would that be fair to say?"

Alan knew he had no choice but to agree if he wanted to keep his job.

"Yes, that's true. You've been most...watchful."

Vick returned a skeptical look while he considered whether Alan's sentiment was genuine. "Yes, it is true. Good. I've done that for you for a while now, but, well...the tax man is coming around now."

Alan said nothing, confused by the metaphor.

"What I mean to say is, there's no more room for this sort of communist leniency that I've given as charity. Taxes are due. You've gotta start holding your own. That starts with this score." He held up his flimsy printout again, blocking their eyeline.

"Okay, understood. I guess I can practice at home or something. Do you have any advice on getting faster?" Alan did his best to keep his expression earnest, but he hated everything about this meeting.

"It's effort. It's all in the sweat. I know that seems like a joke to your generation, but you have to put hard work in to see results. Move faster. Work up a little heat. Do you know what I'm saying?"

"Yes. I'll just *move faster*. Is there—"

He held up a hand, cutting Alan off. "Good. I'm glad we understand each other. Now, I know today might be more difficult, what with the..." He pursed his lips, trying to find a nice way to frame the current age skew, "—greatest generation shopping. Slow unloading of items, so on, whatever. I get it. 11.73, now a dead man unloading groceries doesn't even make up for that score. Use today as practice. Move faster. Give yourself a little workout. Tomorrow I'll reset your score, and we'll look at the CIST from Friday first thing the next day."

"Okay, I'll...uh...do my best, sir."

"You do that." Mr. Vick looked away, signaling the end of the conversation, and Alan made for the door.

"—and Hendershot. Don't let me down. I'm trying to help you."

***

If Alan believed in any conspiracy theory (aside from his adamant insistence that extraterrestrial contact was made long ago), it would be that for the rest of the day Mr. Vick was colluding with the slowest customers to go to Alan's line and take as long as humanly possible to place their items on the belt.

Alan would never assert the claim that older people moved slower. That sounded ageist, and he was perfectly happy moving very slowly himself. He would, however, put forth the suggestion that life wears on you, and the more it wears on you, the less appealing it is to prance around like a spry, young buck. After all, there were older bucks like Elmer Nunn or Mrs. Lydia Foster that life had not slowed down a bit; 91 and 86 years of age, respectively, but could get in and out of Elmwood's in fifteen minutes or less.

But they didn't come through his line today.

Today, the wheels on the shopping carts spun round and round with a squeak, slowed by kids and grandkids, two world wars, joint replacements, heart pills, uncomfortable shoes, loud music, and that mantra Alan could not disagree with: *slow down before you miss something.*

Alan never missed Mr. Vick's attempts at covert surveillance. Every time he turned around, he found Vick watching him from behind an aisle while he was checking stock, or looking down from the balcony above outside his office. Every time they made eye contact, Vick would offer a slight shrug and a shaking head, as if he somehow carried with him a live tracker of Alan's CIST score. This only provided further support for Alan's conspiracy theory.

Shortly after 3 o'clock, Mr. Vick was more bold about his surveying location of choice and occupied the empty register right behind Alan's, finding something to clean or bang with a screwdriver every few seconds to ward off suspicion. Alan hoped that he had taken up the post to dismiss Alan to his break at a moment's notice, but then he approached from behind and confirmed Alan's fears that this wasn't the case.

"Hendershot," Vick declared coolly, hoping to draw surprise.

Alan placed the last bag in a couple's cart and put the check beneath his cash drawer.

"Oh! Hi, Mr. Vick. I didn't see you there." *Of course I saw you there.*

"Yes. Well, though it be news to you, I've watched several of your transactions today, Hendershot. All the way through."

"Okay. Did I—"

"And! Luckily enough for you, in watching, I took the time out of my day to take note of your shortcomings and now come offering my advice."

"Oh. Yeah, that would be really great. I'm going as quick as I can, but I'm sure you know the ins and outs of—"

"Please. Do not talk so much, Hendershot. *Listening.* Your generation would be well-served to do a little more of it."

Alan nodded without saying a word.

"Now, as you have, *for once,* aptly observed....I do know the ins and outs. In fact, I have had conversations at length with CIST. Oh, if they were here, what a ride they would have watching your work." It almost sounded like a compliment if not for the snide look on his face. "Now, as you know, each transaction is timed. That total time is then divided by the number of items scanned, and, well a bit of algebra is done...wa-lah, a CIST score. What it seems you do *not* know, is when that timer stops."

"Oh."

"Yes, I saw you move lazily along as you wrote the driver's license number of the last customer upon their check. That entire eon of a time, Hendershot, all of it, it was ticking away at your CIST. The buzzer does not stop until you tender their payment. Again, I've really gone *so terribly* out of my way to help you out again, but I really must insist this time that there will be no more of it. But keep that in mind. Tick...tick...a slow card swipe...tock...oh my, where in good heavens are my coupons...tick...what is today's date for the check...tock..." He backed away slowly, indulging far too deeply in the theatricality of his intervention, and then disappeared back to his office.

The true motivations of Vick were always difficult to decipher. He had a questionable habit of offering poor advice under the facade of *truly* wanting to help. Most often, like in interactions like the pair had just shared, Alan resolved that the advice really was in bad faith. In fact, it was hardly advice at all. There was nothing in his power to affect how quickly a customer paid. Vick had only revealed the intricacies of CIST calculation to inflict mental ire.

For the rest of his shift, every customer grew slower and slower than the one that had ventured before them, and as Vick had now made him painfully aware, the handwriting upon checks grew more tedious as 5 o'clock drew nearer.

***

As soon as he'd escaped the hellhole, all the day's fresh worries seemed to evaporate away with the rambunctious emissions clanging and bonking their way out of his 411. With his eyes on the road and his mind unburdened, now he could truly think.

Rather than darting for the freezer and the siren-calls of Chef Bobby, he went to his room as soon as he got home, pulling out an old legal pad and a pen, and made notes. It was clear from the guide that defining your locations and characters thoroughly was *essential* to returning to the same moment in time on sequential nights, so he wrote everything he could remember right away.

For location, he didn't have a lot. He wrote in large hand at the top, *Imp Lode*, and then three bullet points below that, one for *Drireford*, one for *Needlewich*, and a final dash for *Ruteeter's lair*. With Needlewich, he didn't have much, and although he'd like to be surprised when he saw the town for the first time, he wrote a few things to give some structure and permanence to ensure that it didn't disappear. He suggested the name came from the wonderful trees that he had seen on the path (which appeared to drop needles, much like earthly pine), and hoped that there was an abundance of them within the town. This tangent led him to a few more notes, like *probably a logging or woodworking town*, and *higher in elevation than Drireford*. He struggled to remember the surroundings that lay behind the forest, but he knew that there had been mountains somewhere. He gave a proximal location of west of Drireford, because he had remembered the sun behind them as he traveled (later he would realize the fallacy in assuming that the sun of *Imp Lode* operated the same as our own).

For *Ruteeter's lair*, again, he didn't have a lot. He sketched a quick picture of the circle of short trees best as he could remember it and put a few notes down from his dad's tale. Alan considered drawing Ruteeter, but decided he would allow his adult subconscious to create it rather than his waking mind based on fragmented visions from his childhood. He had no proximal location and instead put several question marks.

Now came the heavy-lifting: Drireford. He realized that this town merited a few sub-categories, so he made one for places, one for people, and one for events, where he would log what happened there. As a brief treatise on the place overall, he gave the proximal location to Needlewich, a picture of the overlook they had crossed when entering the town, and said that most of the people seemed to be men.

Places was easy, as he only knew of one. He drew the sign for the Half-Cracked Staff, described the interior and exterior, then put some smaller footnotes for the owner, Vanderkil, and the menu (though at the current moment in time he only knew what the elder ale tasted like—it had been the highlight of his visit, so he wouldn't allow himself to exclude it). The other buildings and shops could be surprises.

He began the people category with Vanderkil, again completing another rough sketch. He wrote *high-pitch*, *friendly*, and *knows Treog* for notes, and then with a line tracing back out to the side, he wrote *Cyclops?* For Treog, he considered putting him instead under Needlewich, as that's where they'd allegedly come from, but he decided it was just as well to go with Drireford, as he didn't know for sure where he was from and that was where he'd last seen him.

Under Treog he wrote *missing teeth, short, fat, old,* and *brewer?* and a minute later added *not sure if friend or foe.* He spent a moment deciding whether to include the two strangers in the tavern he had not met, but thought including every face he saw would require another three or four legal pads by the end of the week.

Finally under events, which he now transferred to its own page, he put yesterday's date and wrote: *Came to Drireford by wagon with Treog. He was friendly along the way and only asked for help unloading a few barrels in payment for the ride (though they were heavy). He dropped me off at the Half-Cracked Staff, where I met Vanderkil. Vanderkil and Treog seemed to exchange suspicions about me (perhaps due to me lying about already knowing Vanderkil), but he was kind and poured me a pint of elder ale, which I nearly finished before waking up.*

He looked over his notes now from start to finish and decided that they aptly covered all that he knew so far about Imp Lode. Heeding the same advice about an empty stomach, he chose to heat and eat a Beef Bolognese, though every revolution of the microwave's turntable felt like an hour to him. He had spent the entire day restlessly awaiting this: coming home and returning to Imp Lode, meeting more people, exploring more towns, and at the very least, having another pint of ale.

After scarfing down the final noodle, he downed a glass of water, tossed his dishes and trash, and practically sprinted back to his room.

He flipped through the legal pad, reciting the names and staring at the pictures until he'd engrained them in memory of more permanence. He could feel his pulse speeding up as the dream grew nearer, but he did his best to slow down, breathe, and lay flat again. His other foot was numbly falling asleep tonight, as he whispered *Half-Cracked Staff,* picturing the sign above the entrance, the stool that he had sat in, and the pint pulled up to his mouth, nearly empty.

VIII. Hushed whispers in dark corners

Immediately he felt it on his lips: the frothy, floral kick of his last ounce of elder ale, warming his mouth and curling his smile. *Now I'm awake.*

On the other side of the bar, Vanderkil had just finished laughing. Alan had done it. He'd arrived at the precise moment in time that he'd left. He grinned back at Vanderkil and burped.

"That's quite a draw for a man of your size, Alandriel. I'm impressed."

"Thanks. I'm a big fan of elder ale."

"You don't have to tell me twice. Another round?"

Alan nodded right away then felt the blood drain from his face. *I have no money.* He looked around him, as if a gold coin might fall from the ceiling. He caught the eyes of a rough, bearded man sitting at the other end of the bar, one of the men that had been there when he arrived, who quickly averted a watchful gaze and said something to his friend. Behind him, three more now entered, two women of blonde and brown hair, both wearing smith or craftsman aprons, and another man, smaller than the other two with dark black hair and skittish eyes. His clothes were fine and unwrinkled.

Yep, definitely would die if I tried to dine and dash right now.

On a whim, he patted the pockets of his pants and felt a hard bulge shaped like a mess of metallic money. He pulled out three silver coins and one more brown, maybe bronze, he reckoned. Underneath the change, there glinted a color of gold that Alan recognized: his gold cat's eye marble. *Odd.*

I'm definitely writing that I'm loaded before I fall asleep again.

As Vanderkil came back with a new overflowing pint, Alan held out one of the silver coins. Vanderkil laughed boisterously and shook his head. "My friend, Treog said that you might be up to no good, but I didn't think you'd come to buy the tavern from me." Some attention from the other patrons had now shifted to Alan, and Vanderkil lowered his voice to a whisper. "You're not from around here, are you?"

"No, I'm from *quite* far away."

He nodded. "Well, Alandriel, there hasn't been a coin that fine in the likes of Drireford in some time. I'd keep it put away if I were you."

Alan shoved the coins back into his pocket. "Okay. So you can't make change from it, then? I need to pay you for the ale."

"Change?"

"Oh. Um, I can't trade it to you for some smaller coins and then pay with those?"

He laughed. "The ale is cheap, friend. I don't keep enough coins in here to exchange for that one of yours. Just come here whenever you need a drink and someday I might fairly take it." He moved now to a hushed tone, "Truth be told, I don't run this place for the coin." Alan looked at him, confused. "What I mean to say is, this is *not* my chief source of income. I just run the only tavern in town to keep all these men from running me out with pitchforks. They know they'd not have any idea how to order ales from the likes of Needlewich, or even further, say, Yunglin. None of them take too kindly to me, as you can probably see why. Matter of thinkin' 'bout it now—it's a bit odd how friendly you're bein'." He chuckled to himself.

Alan had an idea why the others might fear Vanderkil, but he popped out his bottom lip and shrugged his shoulders.

"Don't play, friend. You might be a stranger around here, but I doubt even you've seen many folk with one eye, and even fewer as ugly as me. 'Specially since...well, y'know." He laughed and moved to the other side of the bar to serve the people who'd walked in a minute ago.

Alan sipped on his elder ale, becoming more aware of every pair of eyes routinely checking in on the local stranger. A few more made their way through the door, nearly filling every seat in the place. Everyone that spoke to Vanderkil or got a drink seemed to treat him with the utmost humility, almost cowardly, but Alan didn't doubt his words that they were a bitter lot. Perhaps it was the ale, but he felt Vanderkil could be trusted.

A small party of men (well, *men* in the sense of human, but by appearance, three men and one woman) had now taken up at the sole table in the back cubby to the right of the bar. Alan sat outside of earshot of their low voices, but as the fourth joined them and nodded over to Alan before taking a seat, he had no doubts what their conversation concerned.

One of them sat very short and wore a heavy tan cloak that concealed most of his figure. His head was free of hair, even above his eyes. Two of them were taller, likely twins or brothers, and both had red hair, though one of them, the one that had joined the table last with a round of drinks, had his cut much shorter. The last, the only woman, was slender, but shorter than the pair. She had silvery hair, but it didn't seem from age, as she would have looked to be thirty or so in good light. Her skin was tattooed with deep purple ink all the way from the tips of her fingers to her upper arm, where her body disappeared beneath a red chainse with torn sleeves. She was the only one that Alan had not seen look his direction.

Vanderkil walked by him on his way to their table, and Alan knocked on the bar to gather his attention.

"Ah, what can I do you, friend? Another ale?"

"Still on this one, thanks though." He sucked air in through clenched teeth. "Hey, is there any reason why the people at that table over there would have a problem with me?"

Vanderkil coyly looked back to the table. "Why do you ask? Have they given you any trouble?"

"No, no trouble. It's just...well, they've looked over here quite a few times."

"Hmm. Right. Well, I can tell you right now that they're not from around here. I've not seen any of them before. Could be how friendly you are with me. Unfortunately, that's na'er do well, round here at least. Though I will say, far as strangers go, I trust you a whole lot more than them. Folks gatherin' in groups never do well to come off as pacifying, if you know what I mean. 'Specially not round here."

"Yeah, I would agree with that."

"Tell you what. I'm about to go tend to 'em. If something seems off, I'll let you know. I'll not have any roughhousing in my tavern."

Vanderkil spoke with them for a minute while motioning with his arms in some elaborate circle, and then as he erupted in laughter as if he'd just told a joke, the three men at the table shuddered and laughed nervously. He left them, returned with three more tankards, then returned to Alan.

He shrugged his shoulders. "Sorry, nothing off about them in my opinion. Your average men, I suppose. If they've got a problem with you, they didn't make it known to me. Maybe flash those coins less."

He left Alan, producing second and third drinks for a few of the patrons at the left end of the bar, including the two men that had been staring at him earlier. They too had resumed their spying, and Alan felt it was not a grand idea to stay in the tavern any longer when he apparently had a treasury on his person and no weapon. He sucked in some air to fill his stomach with emptiness and then poured forth the entire remainder of his ale right down his gullet.

Outside the light had all but faded, and a faint yellow moon was soft on the horizon in front of him behind the closed down shops. The wind was cool, but pleasant, and sounds of critters and insects that he didn't recognize filled the air. The streets were empty, and it seemed he'd just exited the only waking establishment in town.

First, he thought *I need to find somewhere to sleep tonight.* Then he thought *what is this black bag being ripped down over my head, my god!* and then *what the hell! what the hell!* and then *Ow!* as a blunt object hammered down on top of his head.

"Well, well, well. The sheep wandered a bit too far, did'n he, Lorey?" a rough voice asked mockingly before cackling.

"Yes. I'm 'fraid it did. Baaa baaa." The second voice was higher and weaker, but did a fair impression of a sheep.

"I'm...I'm—I don't understand. I think you've got me mistaken for somebody else." He couldn't see either of the aggressors' faces, but could make out silhouettes of their figures illuminated by moonlight.

A sharp boot kicked Alan right in the ass. "Move it, boy! It's too late for mopin' now!"

He walked forward, and a firm hand pressing down on his shoulder guided him to the left or right every now and again when he strayed. He could faintly see the glow from the moon off to the left, but aside from that, he was blind.

After a few minutes of walking, the high voice asked, "this good, Jep? I ain't seen Papa or the others, but we's know it's slow on nights like this'n."

"Yeah, take that lamp and get the spoon hot. I'm be needin' your help. Looks like a squirmer."

One of them ripped the sack off of Alan's head, and it took a second for him to slow his heart down enough to see without the bloodshot fogging up his eyes. His mind was racing. He took in the surroundings between huffed breaths. The man that wasn't busy tying rope around his arms was fidgeting with an oil-burning lamp. They weren't far from the main row of shops. There were a few shoddy houses up in front of him, but the closest was still fifty or more feet away. The lamp crackled on and he could see the men's faces up close in a pale, orange light. They were ugly.

They were the two that had been in the tavern when he'd arrived with Treog. The one close to him yanked on his knot and spit on it, satisfied with his work. "Right, Lorey, you hold this'n legs from kickin' and gimme that spoon. I did'n bring nuff rope."

The bigger one picked him up and tossed him forcefully to his back on the ground, but the soft grass padded some of the fall. He jumped on top of him and licked his tongue all around the edges of his dry, dirty lips. Fat was squeezing out between the buttons where his black overalls were drawn too tight. His face was scarred in more places than it wasn't, and rage filled his black eyes. Below, Alan could feel the lesser weight of the other man now laying belly-down on his legs.

"Ain't you jus a real prim 'n proper clops lover? I ain't seen one this pretty since that damn magic woman we'd throwed in the river, Lorey. Take a look at this face." Jep spit right into Alan's eyes as he felt the other one, who must be Lorey, stand up on two feet, both right below Alan's kneecaps, and he could make out the outline of his face against the moonlight. He bit down hard from the pain of his legs buckling.

"Damn that is a pretty boy, brother. You might reckon we should get one o'them painters from over north to come draw this'ns picture somewhere nice?" He broke into a snorting laugh and fell back onto Alan's legs.

Alan spit up blood and tried to slow his breathing enough to talk. "I...I swear...I don't know what you want. I have money in my pocket. You can have it."

Jep laughed. "Oh, we'll have your money, boy. You might be bout a stupidest clops lover I seen, you should know you can't come into our town and parade your dirty bid—"

THWAP.

A club the size of a hockey stick came out of nowhere and smacked Jep right on the side of the head, and Alan could feel the blood splatter onto his face. Lorey stood up in front of him and pleaded with his hands in the air to an unseen figure behind Alan. A sword came out of the night's shroud and went straight into the middle of Lorey. He fell to the ground as blood dripped from his tongue.

Large hands untied the rope from around Alan's wrists, picked him up, and turned him around.

It was the redhead from the bar, one of them at least, for as the shorter-haired one let go of Alan and examined his sword, the longer-haired one was further away throwing a bloodied haft into the woods.

"Pleasure. Name's Rime. That's Riddle, my brother. What's your name?"

Alan looked to the two lifeless corpses bleeding out at his feet and back up at the man who had saved him.

"Um...Alandriel. Thanks for...that."

"Of course. Clearly you're not from here." He cleaned his sword on the underside of his tunic and placed it back in its sheath. "Or from anywhere nearby, for that matter."

Alan felt his heart rate go back to something closer to normal as he took in a deep breath. "No, no I'm not. Who were they?"

"Ah. Right awful bunch of worms. Call themselves *Two Eyes.* That's the best name they could come up with, can you believe that? If I had a group that hated clops, trust me, I'd have a lot better names up my sleeve than Two Eyes. Give me a break."

"Give him a break," Riddle called out sarcastically from behind him, returning from the woods.

"Clops. Like Vanderkil?" Alan asked.

Rime surveyed the land around them and stretched the arm he'd just run through the man with. "Yeah, well, he's not their ideal version if you get my drift. Can't paint him into a crime scene with the finest oil pastels this side of the ice. Far too nice. Guess it's been an awful dry spell lately for them to be hanging around his joint."

Out from behind one shop, the other two that had been sitting with Rime and Riddle at the table, the hairless man and the tattooed woman, emerged.

The woman spoke first. "I see you've taken care of our guest most adequately, Rime. Get him to grab a leg. Kard, you help Riddle with the other one. Take them to the river we camped on yesterday."

The man with the long tan cloak and no hair picked up the remains of Jep and Alan grabbed one leg of Lorey as Rime took the other.

Alan tried to gather his breath enough to speak a complete sentence. "So, I'm sorry. I'm just now realizing what happened. Why were they trying to kill me?"

Riddle spoke up from behind them, dragging his end of Jep. "Not *kill* you. Well, not unless you're prone to infection. All they were going to do is take your left eye with that hot spoon."

"Oh."

Rime heaved as they pulled the body over a ridge. "Yep, they do that with any folk fraternizing too much with a clops. You see a man with an eye patch around here, Two Eyes probably got to him."

"Well, I haven't done that. I just met the guy today. The uh...clops?"

"So why didn't he make you pay for your drink?"

"I didn't have change, so he just said to keep a tab going."

"Change?" Rime asked.

"Right, sorry. My coins were too valuable, and I didn't have any smaller ones."

Rime laughed. "Let me see one of them."

Alan reached in his pocket and pulled out one of the silver coins. It glinted in the moonlight as he turned it over in his hand.

"Goodness, boy. You're from Reul? When you said he wasn't from here, I didn't think you meant that far, Stell. How did you get here, anyway?"

The woman spoke up before Alan had a chance. "Boys, give him a minute to breathe. He was just nearly gouged if you hadn't noticed." She was walking in front of the group now, leading the way and whispering softly to herself. The trees had become thicker, and they had lost all light but faint streaks still peeking through from the moon. He could hear a faint babble of moving water in the distance.

Alan took another minute, still trying to piece together the details of his situation. "So you all followed them from the tavern? Why did you save me?"

All of them kept walking without saying a word, even Rime, who was sharing the weight of a body with him. After a few seconds, Stell spoke up. "It's not important *why* we saved you, Alandriel. Just that we did. We just...happened to be in the right place at the right time."

"Okay, yeah...okay."

Now didn't seem the time for interrogating their secrecy.

"Yeah!" said Rime, "We really just happened to be walking out that door at the right time and saw them dragging you off. Can't have a stranger in town get mistreated on our watch."

Riddle whispered something to Kard that Alan couldn't make out.

"So you all are from here, from Drireford then?"

"Well, no. Just meant you seem like a stranger to this part of the world, you know." Rime laughed and Stell stared at him displeased. He bowed his head toward her and continued, "We're from...well we're from out west. Pretty far from here."

A bright light came from up ahead, illuminating a path through some underbrush, as the sound of the river grew louder. Stell turned back to the men. "Okay, that's enough chit-chat. We're here. Dump them and let's be gone."

They followed the path under the low trees and slid each body down the muddy embankment. All four of them watched as the lifeless humans bobbed back up and floated downstream. Alan realized he'd just disposed of his first body, and it didn't quite have the impact that he thought it would have. But there were a million other things going through his head. As he reached the top of the bank, he saw Stell was controlling the light that had illuminated their path. Her hands guided it back towards the party, illuminating everyone's faces with a soft white-blue glow. A silence built up, and Alan noticed Rime, Riddle, and Kard all exchange glances, shrug, and then look to Stell.

She looked at all of them, irritated, then turned to Alan. "Right, so, you're from far away, as are we. Do you have a place to stay the night,

Alandriel? We have a room at the Dead Inn & Keep on the edge of town. I'm sure we can put out a blanket."

Surprisingly, conspiring to get rid of bodies with someone doesn't make you fast friends like Alan would have assumed. He still felt weird about them, especially the woman.

"That's all right, we've hardly been introduced and I don't want to be a burden. I can find my own room, thanks." The men all looked at him then back to the woman, who seemed a tad irritated at her assigned role as voice of the people.

"Look, I know this seems weird. I haven't told you anything about me. *My name is Stellis, by the way.* Your first interaction with us is dumping bodies that we've just slain. I'm sure you have a lot of questions. You're probably wondering why Kard is so ugly." The others laughed, and Kard shook his head and kicked some dirt. Stellis grinned slightly. "I can explain more in the morning once we leave here and are on the path again, but there are too many eager ears in this town, as we've seen." She nodded to the river, and Alan pictured the bloodied bodies of Jep and Lorey bobbing along downstream and couldn't help but shiver. "Besides, if anybody here takes your coin as payment, they're robbing you. You might as well stay the night with us for free. If we wanted to hurt you, we would have done it by now." She managed a half-smile and offered a hand to shake.

"Well, I guess when you put it that way, I haven't got much of a choice. I am grateful you saved me, I've just been wary...so long on the road, you know."

Riddle chimed back in, sensing the tension had lifted. "Oh, us too. Don't worry. You're safer with Stellis than anyone in this town." Riddle smiled, and the others mirrored his expression as Stell turned back towards the town with the light traveling in front of her.

***

They would soon arrive at the Dead Inn & Keep, and along the way Riddle had explained to Alan just why it was so named (Alan soon learned that Rid was the better-read out of the two brothers, or at the very least, the more informed). A hundred years ago (or so), the spot where the Inn now operates had been a graveyard for all of Drireford. In those days, the valley had not yet flooded seasonally as it did now, and so all the dead that the town had to offer were buried in rough tombs that the people carved out of the rock. They had named this rock aptly, Dead Rock. Well, a century ago, the river spilled forth for the first time, and the plains above Drireford also found they held too much water to hold back, and so the valley flooded. The recently buried were all washed out into the streets, and it was said that the woman and children wept all over again (while all their food soured in the wet).

To avoid such a travesty again, the townspeople had switched to stilted mausoleums that kept the corpses well above the water level, even if such a terrible flood as the one a hundred years ago were to come again. As he told this story, Rid pointed out a canal dug around the edge of the town that they were now crossing, one measure of flood protection for the shops and homes, he said.

A skeleton by the name of J.G. Billy had purchased the property that contained the carved rock from the town 93 years ago and still runs it today as the Dead Inn & Keep. Now all the rooms are cut with drain-ways and canals in case of a flood.

The cliff was not over fifteen or twenty feet tall, and the round, rock door had been carved just a small step higher than the ground. Streamers of bones linked together hung in front of it, like tacky drapes of beads that Alan expected he could still find in his grandmother's house if he were to go searching (Rid later explained that quite a few bones had been included in the deed to the property). The door slid, rather than swung, with a tiny brass handle on the left side to aid in the heaving.

The lobby of the inn revealed itself to be much more polished and posh than the craggy outcrop of rock that bore its sign. There was a luxurious red carpet running from end to end, several benches, a small bar, and five oil lanterns, though one had already burnt out for the night, and a hallway that led to every room. From some far off place, Alan could hear smooth jazz.

A tiny desk sat in the back left corner, and upon it sat a pair of legs. However, this pair of legs was incomplete, as there was no flesh or muscle or blood attached to them. Just bones. The bones connected to a full skeleton that was reclined in a chair with a brimmed farmer's hat pulled down upon its skull.

Alan now considered why he hadn't questioned Rid when he told him that a skeleton owned the inn.

As he heard them walk by, J.G. Billy lifted the brim of his hat, smiled, and waved at the party. Rid, Rime, and Kard all looked terribly startled, but returned a wave and hurried along to the hall. Stell hadn't looked at the skeleton and continued on.

Their room was sizeable. *Probably was a tomb for a family of...what was it...clops lovers?* The floors were bare stone with channels running along either long wall that deposited into small canal reservoirs at either end. Kard immediately rushed to the middle of the room to a fireplace built of roughly shaped brown brick with a chimney that went through the ceiling. He stoked it while adding fresh logs. There were six beds, all of them the same size, and all of them looking equally uncomfortable. A candlestick hung on the wall next to each of the beds, and a small wooden slat beneath it to hold personal items.

"Take your pick." Rid said, "We ought to leave bright and early before anybody starts looking for those two fine gentlemen now sailing the river."

Alan kicked off his shoes and rubbed his feet, which felt awfully tired. He was starving, but he had no intention of complaining right now. His whole body ached, but the back of his head especially so, as he let it rest upon the pillow.

Just as he closed his eyes—

—he awoke.

IX. The ballad of Willy the hound dog

Alan did not dream of labor. But, he did hunger and thirst like his fellow man, and that required the subsistence only a paycheck would bring. Imp Lode, he conceded, would have to wait for nightfall.

Today, he'd brought with him a list of ingredients for a special tea he'd found in the guide (the handwritten guide, not the boring science gobbledygook). During his first break, he hurried down aisles 6, 8, 9 and 13, searching for the items, many of which he'd never heard of. A few were roots, two were powders, and the others he thought he could locate easily enough, like turmeric, chamomile, and beets. But a couple were more mysterious.

He was squatted down on his knees halfway down aisle 9 looking for something called *droom flume leaf*, scanning all objects within a shelf or so of bay leaves, when a pallet hit him right in the kidney. He wasn't sure, actually, if it had hit him in the kidney, but that seemed to be a better descriptor than the lower right anterior quadrant of his abdomen.

"Ow."

A lift, driven by Raphl, was motoring along with several cases of children's cereal, and Alan apparently hadn't exclaimed loudly enough, for the dull whir of the weak motor persisted, gently nudging Alan but not moving. Alan stood up and faced his vehicular assailant, and Raphl nearly leapt right out of the seat of the lift.

"Oh, my! I'm sorry, Hendershot. Can never see what's in front of you with this mess of machinery. I must admit, I get a bit weary here at the end of my shift." He leaned in for a whisper. "I ran over a stray cat at the loading dock two weeks ago. Threw the remains in with the broken down packaging due for the dump and nobody said a thing."

"Oh...no. That's sad."

"Yeah, well. I feed the wee ones scraps now when I see them because I feel I might have orphaned them, but life goes on."

"Hey Raphl, you stock these aisles too, right?"

"Yep." He moved his eyes to the cereal and back to Alan, who now felt a bit dumb.

"Have you ever stocked something called...droom flume leaf before? We probably don't have—"

"Droom flume?" He was wide-eyed with one of his eyebrows cocked up higher than the other.

"Yeah. I mean it's not a big deal if you've never seen it."

"Oh, I've seen it. Not in here though. What exactly do you need it for, anyway?" He eyed Alan suspiciously.

"Oh, nothing. I just need it for a um...a tea recipe that my doctor recommended I try."

"Ah, I see. Trouble sleeping?"

"Yeah. Yeah, you could say that. So you've used it before?"

"Oh no, I haven't. I've given it to my dog though. Many occasions. Sweet ole boy, but he's got I reckon bout 40% beagle and 90% bloodhound. Now that I'm uh..." He paused and seemed to check the surrounding aisle before continuing. "Now that I'm romantically involved again, I can't have him sleepin' in the bed with me anymore, though it breaks his poor little heart. I had to put him out in the hall and that's one of the only things that'll stop him from howling. Vet sent me all the way out to some sorta natural foods store out in Youngstown to pick a few different things up. I mix it all in with a can of wet dog food and he's out like a light. Didn't wanna drug him, you know, with what happened before and all..."

"I'm...um...what—what happened before?"

"Oh, I might have never told you. The vet I had before, bout a year ago, thought he had cancer round his eye. Real bad, they said. Kept runnin' into things soon as I turned a lamp off. Thought he might suffer worse if we let it spread, so they recommended I put him down." Raphl was sniveling now and his eyes were glistening. "So I took him in, held him real tight, you know. Can't leave a dog alone in a time like that. Doc came in and put the needle in his butt, but it turns out the doc was high as a kite and put the wrong thing in the needle. Not sure what it was, but Willy whined and whined. I never wanna give him nothin' like that again that might scare him, so I found this vet that's real into all the natural things. Only thing is Willy farts like hell when he's gotta chew up the anti-flea supplement. Damnedest thing."

"And the cancer?"

"Oh yeah, cancer was actually a miscalculation too. Turns out he'd just gotten bit by a real sucker of a mosquito right next to his eye. Really dodged a bullet with that one. Literally, I guess. Well...no, not literally, but you know, closer to literally than just a figure of speech, if you know what I'm saying."

"Yeah."

"So...droom flume leaf. Hey, I tell you what, if you need some that bad, I'll just pick it up when I go get Willy's refills. I was actually planning to make a trip out there as soon as I leave. I've got to leave Willy with mom while I go to the lake, and that'd be just the time for him to run out. He'd make her go deaf."

"Oh, yeah. That would be great, actually!"

Alan looked down at the list in his hand with everything marked off that he'd been able to find in the store.

"Hey, I've actually got a few other things I'm supposed to put in the tea. Do you think you could just check if they have any of them at the store you go to? Only if you've got the time, of course."

Raphl took the list and quickly scanned it. "Course. I know for sure they got one or two of these. This is an awful lot for a tea. You oughta make sure your doctor isn't...you know...probably happens just as often as with vets. Anyway. I'll get these to you tomorrow morning before I head to the lake."

"Well thank you, Raphl. I'll look into his drug-use history as well. Good tip."

***

The rest of Friday was an absolute slog, and he found that no customer interaction could outdo what had happened to him last night. More than once during the day he had felt his eyes with a bare palm just to make sure they were both there. *What a night. What an adventure.* Sure, it might be strange to be so enthralled by a near-death experience like that, but he couldn't help it. What was next? Where would he go, what he would do? The possibilities were endless, and the only thing making the day worse was his fruitless effort to keep his mind far from the *adventures* and focus.

Miss Etta had yesterday and today off, and he didn't feel like talking about the dreams with anyone else at work, nor could he, he figured. Instead, he had to keep it all bottled up inside, nearly bursting, and scan each item, deal with each customer, and tender each total with the same amount of patience that was expected under the Elmwood's Standard of SatisfactionTM (not actually trademarked, but Vick has sent out a few feelers into the legal community, he says). He was so doggedly focused on exuding this steadfast patience, in fact, that he had nearly forgotten about his CIST score. *That dreaded CIST score.*

He looked up at the clock and it was 4:13. He'd spent nearly all of his shift in slow-burn mode, and he was sure that his score would reflect the results. A tiny ache grew in the pit of his stomach as he relived the conversation with Vick all over again. *Taxes are due. You've gotta start holding your own.* The words looped in his head.

He surveyed the few customers wandering back and forth between the end-caps, hoping that there just might be another cart full of candy bars or puddings that he could scan fast as lightning.

It didn't matter though. He knew it didn't matter. His CIST score was toast, and Vick would let him have it. He thought of the other cashiers, like Higgy, the 37-year-old pro-bowler wannabe that said he only worked at Elmwood's to pay for his spot on the amateur team two towns over. Even with his "cannon of an arm," Alan found it hard to believe that his performance as a cashier was that much better than his; *come on.* Or Joy; sure, she'd somehow found a way to make a 28-year-long career out of being a cashier at Elmwood's, but could she really be that much faster than him?

The more he thought about it, the more his doubts surfaced and flourished. Maybe he was that bad. Maybe cashiering was just another thing he couldn't do. It wouldn't surprise him. It wouldn't even hurt that bad, except it would've been nice to have that one thing. Even if he hated it, even if he dumped on it every day, to have that one thing that he could get right. That would be nice. That was something he could tell people. It was pathetic, sure, but it was half a ladder-rung above where he felt without it.

Pizza. Pizza would be nice right now. A nice, long, droopy slice at Pizza Inn. With dad. At least *he* didn't have to see him get fired from a grocery store for scanning items too slow.

***

Alan's earliest exposure to idiomatic language was the phrase *a stitch in time saves nine.* Every time Alan's grandfather would put off doing something, like switching out the loose knobs on the kitchen cabinets, or seeing the doctor about his arm being sore and tingly, his grandmother would say it. She even said it to him in his hospital bed after his heart attack. His grandmother very much enjoyed being right.

Alan now found her harping ironic, even ignorant, as a loud, deep pop rang out from the engine of his 411, and the car slowly coasted to a stop as if it were careening down a cheese grater. Sure, he could have taken the car in for a check-up, maintenance even, but when the billow of smoke fuming out from the inside nearly choked him as he popped the hood, he made an educated guess that this was not a problem that had manifested anytime in the past six months since he had gotten the car from his grandmother. *Stitch in time my ass.*

He was only a mile from work, and as much as it pained him, he knew that trying to walk anywhere else for a phone wouldn't make any sense.

Alan found the payphone near the money wire counter without anyone realizing he had returned (there was a phone in Vick's office that he could likely use for free, but Vick would charge another sort of toll). He lingered for a minute after putting the quarter in, trying to decide who to dial.

Sure, his mom would come. She would probably pay for the tow truck, too. But that meant at least a twenty-minute ride in the car with her, not to mention she'd probably want to take him to work for the next few days until he had a new mode of transportation. That wouldn't do.

He rang the only other option he had.

Micah answered. "Heyo?"

"Hey, Micah. It's Alan. Are you busy?"

"For sure. Um, sort of. We're packing up the car and are gonna head over to Scott's as soon as Sarah finishes her makeup."

"Is that Alan?" Sarah whispered in the background.

"Okay. Well, my car broke down. I walked back to the store. Do you think that you have time to give me a ride home?"

Sarah's muffled voice broke in again. "What does he want?"

"Um, yeah. For sure. I got you, bro. I'll zip over there soon as I can."

"Thanks a lot, Micah. I really appreciate it."

"For sure. For sure."

The line clicked. Alan sat. Time passed. Twenty-three minutes, to be exact. He felt every one of them. Somehow, sitting in Elmwood's *not working* was even worse than being in there on the clock. As soon as he heard Micah's Range Rover roll into the parking lot, he jogged out to his rescue party.

Micah rolled down the driver's side window. "Hey, bro." Sarah leaned forward in the passenger seat. "Sarah came along for the ride."

"Cool. Well, thanks for coming out here."

Alan made a bulldozer head with his hands and pushed over a sticky pile of empty cans and fast food bags that were composting in Micah's backseat. As he hopped in, some warm liquid seeped into his shorts, but he didn't want to investigate.

"Thanks again, Micah. This is a lot better than walking home."

"For sure, bro. For sure. Don't worry about it."

"So...Scott's. That should be fun."

"Yeah, bro. It's probably gonna get wild. Scott invited a lot of the crew from back in the day. Those guys really know how to have a good time." Micah smiled wistfully and chuckled to himself. "I might blackout. That would be such a perfect way to end the week. Like sort of poetic, you know? Damn. T.G.I.F."

"Cool. I hope you guys have fun."

"For sure. We def—" Micah's mobile phone buzzed aggressively. "Speak of the devil." He pulled the antenna out and punched the answer button.

"Scotty boy! What's shakin' down, bro?"

Alan could hear Scott's muffled voice on the other end, but couldn't make out any words. By the look of Sarah's strained neck and agonized eyes, she too was suffering the same dilemma.

"Oh. Yeah that would be a huge bummer, bro." Micah looked innocently at Sarah and then back at Alan. "Yeah, I will definitely come through for you, bro...for sure, for sure." He hung up and looked in the rearview at Alan with puppy dog eyes.

"So, we've got a slight change of plans. Scott has to go pick up the keg and was hoping Blake would get there soon enough to let people in. Blake isn't answering his phone though, so like, huge party foul already, but yeah...there's no one to let people in."

"So?" Sarah truly didn't know where the preamble was going.

"So...I told Scott that we'd watch the house until he gets back and let people in. On the bright side, he's letting the beer admission slide. I'm sorry, bro. I know you didn't wanna come, but I'm sure he'll be super quick at the liquor store and I'll take you home as soon as he gets back."

Sarah nodded, but didn't seem thrilled with the development.

"No worries. A few minutes at a party won't kill me," Alan tried to say with confidence.

Alan couldn't protest. He had no right, anyway. Micah was just trying to be that dependable friend, the same quality that got Alan this ride.

Scott's house was actually not Scott's house at all. Well, it was Scott's house in the sense that he lived there, ate there, slept there, and damn sure partied there. But he didn't pay for anything. His parents had bought the house for him after he dropped out of a junior college he'd gotten a soccer scholarship to (most people knew he didn't dropout, but was actual dropped after three semesters of academic probation), and they paid the utilities, landscaping, and HOA fee. Yeah, it was in that kind of neighborhood. Alan was sure all the retirees and families that lived on the same road loved when Scott's goons took up street parking all the way to the "Evergreen Hollow" subdivision sign.

The front of the house was Tudor style, with well-manicured hedges running along either side of the driveway and three crabapple trees guarding the path to the front door. Scott greeted them wearing a paneled green and purple windbreaker and black jogging pants. His hair had more product in it than Elmwood's moved in a week.

"Sup, fellas. Sarah. Make yourselves at home. Pizza is coming in an hour, but I'll be back before then. Really appreciate this, Mike. You always come through, bro."

"For sure. For sure."

Sarah immediately found her way to the kitchen and began rummaging through cabinets, as Micah and Scott did a two-fold handshake, forced to combine their greeting and goodbye rituals into one awkward charade.

Before Micah and Alan had even taken their shoes off in the foyer, Sarah had already slammed down two shot glasses on the kitchen counter.

"If we're here, we're doing shots!" she shouted in a playful voice.

"Babe, I gotta drive Alan back. You take mine for me and I'll catch up as soon as I get back."

"One shot? C'mon!"

"Baaaaabe. I'd rather wait and rally." Alan could already hear the fattening tone of defeat in Micah's voice.

"Just one! Alan's not going to have one with me." She barely glanced over at Alan. "Micah, please." She grinned mischievously.

"Fine. But I'm doing coconut rum with a soda chaser. Don't tell Scott."

"Ha-hah! You're such a softy when your *bros* are gone. It'll be my secret." She looked at Alan, not entirely signaling for him to leave, but not entirely not, either.

Alan left in a hurry in search of the bathroom. He sat down on the toilet and felt remarkably better after discovering that the well-insulated walls of the home completely silenced their rapid inebriation.

The quiet was the first peace he'd had all day. With a clear mind, his dreams were on his mind again, and he stared blankly at the *love, joy, peace* cross-stitch hanging across from the toilet. He imagined picturesque locations that were surely hidden away in some corner of Imp Lode, eagerly awaiting him slipping into another deep sleep.

Soon his *feet and thighs* were asleep from the imprint of the porcelain toilet seat, and he withdrew from his private retreat without the time to consider why Scott had a 'Fruits of the Spirit' cross-stitch.

In the kitchen, Micah slumped over the counter with three empty shot glasses in front of him, and Sarah wrapped around his leg and across his shoulder, whispering something in his ear. Three more guests had arrived, and though he could probably guess their names by going through a list of boy-band lead singers' first names, Alan didn't know any of them. One of them was mixing up a dark red punch, and the other two were trying to get toilet paper to stand on its thin side hoping to create a makeshift pong net. The punch craftsman looked at Alan and his eyes lit up.

"Hey bud! It's uh...you're Micah's roommate right? I haven't seen you at anything in a while. How have you been? How's life?"

"You know. Not great, I guess."

"Yeah, bro. I feel that." He turned to Micah. "Hey Micah, this is the genius you always got answers from in high school, right?"

Micah burped loudly and nodded, grinning. "Yeah, that's Alan. He's sooo smart."

"Damn. Alan Hendershot? Shit, I didn't make fun of you, did I?" He laughed. "Oh well, I bet you're the one laughing now. They always say guys like you put guys like me on their payroll. Wait, Hendershot... you're not...damn. I'm sorry about your—"

"Yeah. I'm that one. No big deal." Alan scooted around the guy and his newly solemn face as he poured more vodka into the punch bowl.

As Alan approached Micah, the whiff of coconut rum overwhelmed him.

"I'm gonna guess you can't drive me home."

"Alan, bro," Micah let out a burp he tried to hold in, "I might have had a few shots more than one." He looked at Sarah. "I probably shouldn't—"

"He probably should not drive, Alan." Sarah jumped in, more sober sounding. "I'm sure there's somebody we could link you up with here. There's a lot of friendly people." She looked around but didn't make a move or resume eye contact.

"No. I wasn't asking him to drive me. I know that's not—"

"Bro. For sure, I would drive you if I could." He looked down sadly at the shot glasses. "I got carried away." He looked back at Alan, and his eyes softened as he considered his friend's predicament.

"I'll let you drive the Rover, bro. I know you don't wanna be here. I'm sure Scott or one of the guys can drive us home in the morning if we crash here."

Sarah looked at Micah, disgruntled, but said nothing.

"Thanks, Micah. I can come pick you guys up in the morning if you need me. Just ring the house."

Alan was out the door before anyone else could try to strike up a conversation.

X. Paint me like one of your skeletons

"Yep, this is Sulley Coffey. You've reached Coffey Towing. You been towed or need to get towed?"

"I need to get towed."

"Yep, all right. And your name?"

"Alan Hendershot."

"...Hendershot...okay. Where is the vehicle?"

"It's on Elm Street...maybe a mile from Elmwood's."

"You got a mile marker?"

"Um...no, I just—"

"Okay, southbound or northbound from Elmwood's?"

"...um...southbound I think."

"No problem, I'm coming down from the top end so I'll pass both. Okay, do you have Triple A or roadside assistance included with your insurance policy?"

"No, I don't."

"Okay, what's the destination for the vehicle?"

"1227 Eversley Circle."

"...okay...boy, that's a big circle."

"Yep."

"All right, looks like that's gonna be about six or seven miles. Final charge...I'd estimate somewhere in the ballpark of $80. Good deal?"

"...um...sure, I guess so."

"All right, give me about an hour and we'll have it there."

The line clicked off and Alan returned the phone to the mount. He opened up his billfold and whistled aloud. *$80, no new sneakers for me anytime soon.* Alan looked down at his wiggling big toe visible through the top side of the shoe. *Duct tape will have to do for now.*

He called the towing company immediately after getting back from Scott's, because he wanted to prepare as quickly as possible for his dream tonight. Alan had the late shift at work tomorrow, which meant he would have time to sleep in. He wasn't sure yet exactly how the math worked out, but he figured that meant more time in the dream world.

While he was scooping up bites of Chef Bobby mac-n-cheese with his left hand, he was writing the notes from the previous night as quickly as he could with his right. He added the Dead Inn to local places, added Jep, Lorey, Riddle, Rime, Kard, Stellis, and J.G. Billy to people, added Reul to world places, and recounted the events of the night, including the double murder (though he notated that it was, in fact, self defense) and began a new list titled *Secret organizations/ factions,* which for now only included Two Eyes. Alan looked everything over once or twice, was satisfied with his work (though he made a mental note to use less flowery language next time, as it hardly seemed academic), and began his pre-dream rituals.

He encountered a problem right away. Last time, he had recalled and conjured up a specific moment in time, drinking the elder ale in the tavern, and that was the moment in time that he woke. But when he last left Imp Lode, he'd been falling asleep. Should he go back to the moment right before he felt himself lose consciousness, or should he cut to the morning? Could he cut time like that? He flipped through the book, scanning for any notation on the topic.

Near the middle, *Time jumps* written in marker caught his eye:

OUT OF NECESSITY AND NOT A DESIRE FOR EXPERIMENTATION, I WAS FORCED LAST NIGHT TO ATTEMPT A TIME JUMP. A FRIEND WAS IN NEED OF MEDICAL AID, AND I MUST ADMIT, I COULD NOT STOMACH THE CONDITION OF HIS SKIN FOR ANY LONGER. WHEN I PREPARED TO ENTER THE DREAM, I INSTEAD ENVISIONED A MOMENT IN TIME APPROXIMATELY 12 HOURS FROM THE TIME WHICH I HAD LEFT, AND ALSO ATTEMPTED TO SET THE FACTS OF THE TIME TO STATE THAT HE'D ALREADY RECEIVED THE AID HE NEEDED AND WOULD BE FINE WHEN I ARRIVED.

THIS WAS NOT THE CASE. I HAVE NO FURTHER DETAILS ON THE RULES, BUT IT SEEMS THAT TIME-JUMPING LEAVES THE TIME THAT YOU ARE JUMPING UP TO CHANCE OR FATE. IT COULD HAVE BEEN OWED TO A FAILURE OF MY OWN SUBCONSCIOUS, BUT I HAVE NOT FAILED TO ARRIVE AT THE ENTRY POINT THAT I DESIRED IN SEVERAL MONTHS, SO I FIND THIS POSSIBILITY TO BE UNLIKELY.

Alan reread the entry twice just to make sure he understood it completely, but concluded that he would attempt a time-jump anyway. He did not wish to attain any improved status or circumstances during the lapse, he merely wanted to skip the night. It made little sense to lucid dream of yourself sleeping. That seemed like it could get messy.

The safest arrival seemed to be the moment immediately after waking up, so that's what he focused on: sitting on the uncomfortable bed, looking down at his feet, a yawn beginning to wake in his belly, and the sleep not yet wiped from his eyes. He whispered *Dead Inn, our room...Dead Inn, our room.* Alan lay flat, this time an incompletely extended arm as the reason for his uncomfortable disposition. He continued to whisper, taking slow, lengthy breaths, and soon he awoke.

***

Much to his relief, he awoke exactly where he hoped to, both in the sense of the transition from sleeping to dreaming, and the transition of sleeping to waking. He found his body, however, riddled with many aches and pains that he had not hoped to bring along, but as he examined the thickness of the mattress (it was not) and the bedding that had covered him, he could not argue with this fate.

Only one of the other beds was yet occupied, that which nestled Kard, and the others had been made and tidied.

Alan sauntered across the room to Kard, who wore a blue and white striped cap upon his head and was snoring, musically at that. Alan jostled his shoulder just enough to wake him without bringing a fright, and Kard awoke in a hurry and reached for a sheath that lay on the floor before he even opened his eyes.

"Aye...aye! Who is it?" He opened his eyes now, with his blade half-drawn, and realized it was Alan. "Oh, I'm sorry, mate. Not a kind dream I was having just then. Pray you never have to fight a gnome who reckons you had sticky fingers 'round his stash of gold. They can be right nasty little beasts."

"Sorry, didn't mean to frighten you. Do you know where the others have gone? I suppose I must have slept in. Last night was a bit exhausting."

He grinned as he switched his nightcap out for a feathered day variety adorned with a purple flower. "Mate, you earned a long sleep. Two whitnecks runnin' at you like that. I woulda needed a drink 'fore bed for the next two moons. I'm sure the others have gone to get a bite to eat. Skeletons are known for their bottomless pantries, as I'm sure you know."

"Oh, no...I didn't know that, actually."

"Hah! I'm pulling your leg, mate. I've never known a skelly to keep more than a scrap of food in his house. We've brought plenty of food with us. I'm sure the others didn't bother waking us before digging in. Come, mate. Let's rustle their feathers a bit."

He followed Kard out to the lobby of the Inn and watched as he contorted his face into a twisted, fuming mess of a frown. He marched with intent and purpose out to a long table at the far end of the room where Rime, crouched next to a fireplace, scraped something from the bottom of an iron pot. Rid and Stellis both sat with half-empty plates of toasts, cheeses, and salted meats, and a platter with some of all lay between them.

"Well, well, well. If it isn't the early breakfast club tried to sneak off and leave me and the kid with nothing but crumbs. Some way to treat a recruit on his first day with the lads."

Rid at first turned with an earnest expression, but quickly drew up a smile and tossed a scrap of toast at Kard.

"Give it a rest, you old git. We knew the smell of hot meat would have you out of bed faster than a bell ringing." He pulled a stool out next to him. "Have a seat Alandriel. Better take your pick of the plate before that one has his fill." Kard gave Rid a playful shove on his way to the other side of the table, taking a seat next to Stellis.

Rime returned with a plate renewed with a heap of egg scramble and sat on the end. "Have at the pot, as well; caught good luck and found a nest of slickbill eggs not too far out this morning."

"Hunting is one of your...few talents, brother. Well done." Rid held up a mug of tea in a mocking toast.

"What a surprise that all talents requiring physicality and a spry body were blessed upon me rather than you." Rime grinned after his retort, and everyone chuckled.

Rid turned to Alan. "So, you didn't sneak out in the middle of the night? I'm glad. I'll have someone to tell stories to on the path today. Everyone here has heard well more than half of them, I'd wager, but hopefully they'll fall on some fresh ears."

Alan was halfway through a delicious cut of ham...or, at least, some meat that tasted an awful lot like ham, and spoke with a full mouth. "Of course, I'm always ready to hear a new story. Where are we headed today, anyway?"

Stellis looked at him slyly. "That's your first question? So eager to be alone last night, and you're off on the path with us just like that? I feared it would be quite a trial to bring you along."

"Well, I figured since you didn't slit my throat in the middle of the night, and—" He felt his pockets; the coins were still there. "—didn't rob me, then there must be a halfway-decent reason you want me to come. That or you're just kind folk."

Kard chuckled to himself. "Why's it got to be one or the other, mate? The kindest folks have the best reasons for dragging other people along into their troubles." His belly shook as he laughed again.

"As promised, I do not wish to tell you much more until we are on the road, but so it is fresh in your memory, I must do something before we go." Stellis turned over to the desk where J.G. Billy sat, playing with a wooden puzzle. "Keeper Billy, would you come here and take these bags to our mounts as we finish packing up?" As Billy's bones cracked, he stood up, popping nearly every joint and stretching his neck to one side. Stellis turned back to Alan. "Right. I would like you to pay attention to Billy. Remember every detail of his appearance that you can."

The skeleton ambled over to their table, and it surprised Alan how well his body moved without a single bit of muscle or flesh. He was surely much quicker than Kard. He bowed, tipped his hat, and said, "I do hope your stay was acceptable. I also hope you found the parchment this morning to leave any review you might have of the Inn. As you know...business has been...well..." With that, he returned his hat to his head, took the bags, and retreated to the stables through a rear passageway.

"Well, I mean, he looked quite like a skel—"

Stellis held up her hand and coyly surveyed the room. "Not here, Alandriel. Just keep it in your mind's eye for the time."

It was a weird request, but luckily, not one foreign to Alan. His preparations the past two nights in which he would go over all the people, places, and events of the past, which included intensive visual memorization, now seemed to be the perfect dress-rehearsal for this very task. All that being said, there weren't a lot of "details" he'd need to remember. J.G. Billy, for the most part, looked exactly like a skeleton. He'd seen enough skeletons in his life, whether it be in a textbook, a school video, or *Raiders of the Lost Ark* (although those were really melted faces), that he didn't need to remember much. He just needed to remember: skeleton with eyes.

J.G. Billy's eyes were sort of beautiful. Around them there were tiny flaps of skin, not too dissimilar to eyelids, which ensured you saw no more of his eyes than you would a normal person. This was the only skin on his body. His eyes were a very pure white, with no visible blood vessels (probably because he had no blood), and an iris the color of the sky. As this was the only unique detail, this is the image that Alan held in his mind for the next few minutes.

The group gathered up their bags, and Alan, Kard, and Rime returned to their room to get what they'd left and make sure that nobody had forgotten anything (a frequent habit of Rid, claimed Rime). It was then that Alan realized he had no possessions other than what was on his person. He had no bags, sacks, or slings and no clothes other than that which he wore on his back. He was now, once again, thankful that he had wandered into the company of this party, for at this point he did not wish to barter for food or lodgings with his coins that were apparently altogether foreign to this place.

*****

At first sight, Alan could not believe his eyes. In the stables, which were just a carved chamber that opened to the left side of the hill out into the air, there were several stalls on either side of the room. There were three mounts, which to you, might seem an awful low number for such a party, for you do not know the nature of these mounts. To Alan, three seemed to be a gracious plenty, and he supposed they could have even added one or two more to their number and been all right.

At first glance, the creatures were simple, large birds, not much stranger than an ostrich or an emu, however it was easily apparent that they were much larger. They were birds in the sense that they were feathered (very fine and soft), had beaks, and, of course, wings. However, the number of wings would have immediately thrown a wrench in the quickly complexifying work that a taxonomist of our world would be faced with, were they presented with one of these. They had four of them, all in pairs, and the two rear wings were very slim and extended back behind the birds rather than to the front.

The second thing that Alan noticed was the tail. It wasn't entirely unnatural, he thought, for a bird to have a tail. After all, most of the prettiest birds he knew had lovely tail *feathers*, and, if considering dinosaurs, it didn't seem too outrageous. But the tail was very long and thin with a tiny little barbed bit at the end. Now that he got closer to one (following the lead of Rime, who was placing a saddle upon its back), he could see over the edge of the stall and their bright orange webbed feet.

They also smelled terrible, though he could not be sure if it was the fault of the birds or the stable, but their beautiful feathers of periwinkle and light blue nearly made up for it.

"What are they?" Alan asked, momentarily forgetting that he was supposed to be from this world.

Rime laughed. "Really? You've never seen an avimu?" Alan shook his head.

"My, my. Well, you're in for quite a treat. I still remember my first ride. Your bum, on the other hand, may not enjoy it as much. The leatherworkers claim that water-resistance severely limits the comfort of the saddle. I don't know if I believe them."

"Water? We're going in water?"

Rime laughed again and whistled. "You will see, Alandriel. I guess Rid was right. You probably *haven't* heard any of his stories."

They loaded up the provisions, putting about twice as many on the darker-feathered avimu, which Rime explained Kard would ride on alone. Alan took the rear seat on the double saddle behind Rime, and Stellis took the lead on the third with Rid behind her.

They had already discussed a riding order and fell into line with Rime's avimu in the front, followed by Stellis, then Kard bringing up the rear. In that order, the names of their mounts were Mina, Drake, and Dazzle. All had been named by their drivers.

They made their way to the lane that ran through the straight of Drireford, the same that Alan had come in on with Treog, but they took the path out the other end of the town, heading west-southwest, with the sun shining upon their faces. After a brief treatise from Rid on the normal path of the sun (which Alan tried to provoke without appearing too ignorant, and was fortunately aided by the misinformed Kard who believed that the sun reversed paths after so many moons), they were a mile or so from Drireford, with red-capped mountain peaks growing on their horizon.

The sides of either path were again filled by tall trees which were of the same species as the ones on the road from Needlewich. The snow left on the needles was quickly melting with the rising sun, and the land grew more sparse. It was not uncommon for a small, red, bushy-tailed critter to dart out in front of their party every few minutes. They had not passed a single rider, whether it be on horse or avimu.

As for the avimu; they were punishing on one's lower back and rear end, just as Rime had promised. Their steps were smooth and graceful, just a touch slower than a horse's, but their backbone was rigid and had several points at different intervals, none of which the saddle seemed to neutralize properly.

Riddle had just opened his mouth in preparation to tell Alan the first story of his journey, when Stellis felt the ingestion of breath brush past the nape of her neck (which was not nearly the finest of sensations Stellis could perceive that the others could not), and she held up a hand to silence him.

She instead spoke now to Alan, in a soft voice, as the riding order had slackened and Alan was near to her. "It is time to answer one of your questions, Alandriel."

Alan was in the middle of re-situating his left butt cheek so it sat less on a point and more on a slope, and turned to her awkwardly.

"Oh. Yes. Good, I've been curious for quite some time. Do I get to pick the question?"

"I'm afraid not, though we will be able to discuss things in more detail when we make camp tonight and I can retrieve my books. For now, I must only tell you what you ought to know."

Alan nodded.

"You wanted to know why we saved you, among other things of course, but that was one of chief importance to you, yes?"

"Yeah. I mean, I do trust you all more now, but—"

"Of course. I asked you to remember what J.G. Billy looked like, yes? Every detail."

"Yes. I have him fresh in my mind."

"Good. If you would, please describe him aloud. Everything that you can remember."

Alan gave her an odd look, but obliged. "Okay. Well, he looked like a skeleton, really. Just a skeleton. His eyes were very nice-looking, I thought. Very nice shade of blue. I suppose he probably stood about six feet tall—"

"Feet?" Rime asked from in front of him. "Does Reul really not use witchits? I thought that the imperial—"

"A witchit?" Alan cut in.

"A witchit. You know. I'm probably four and a quarter witchits, Kard, maybe three...maybe." He laughed.

"Well, how long is a witchit?"

"I dunno, I guess about sixteen or so switchits? I mean how do you even...that's like trying to say—" Rime stumbled, quite confused how to answer the question.

"Alandriel, please continue." Stellis looked at Rime exhaustedly.

"Okay, well he was just a bit taller than me. Maybe a switchit or two taller."

"Ah...yes," Rime mumbled, now able to concur with the declared height.

"And that's about it. Really just bones. Like you took a body and took all of the flesh, muscle, organs, all that out. Left just the bones. Except for the skin around the eyes, I supp—"

"You're sure, Alandriel? Describe him exactly as you remember." Stellis appeared more confident now and was reaching for something in her pocket.

"Well, yeah. I mean it is strange. Seeing just bones walking around, but I guess...I mean, you all are familiar with skeletons, right? I don't understand." Alan felt very unsure about himself now, and was looking to the others for help to answer the question, but they all showed varying degrees of surprise and shock.

Stellis handed Alan a folded sheet of paper. "Before you awoke, I asked Riddle to draw a sketch of Billy, as this is something that he does often for people and creatures he meets. Unfold the paper, Alandriel."

Alan unfolded it and looked upon the horrific drawing. Instead of a set of bare bones, Riddle had drawn fragments of a man. In places you could see bone, but in others, hanging, ripped flesh, deteriorating muscle, and limp blood vessels. It was awful, unlike even the most gruesome injuries that Alan could imagine or had seen on television. It was like Billy's corpse had been fed to rats, but then removed after they had only just gotten a sizeable taste. More bits of scarred flesh and skin now surrounded his formerly pleasant blue eyes as though his face was hardly held together with more than tacks or staples.

"This...this is *terrible*. I don't understand. Why would you draw him like this?"

Rid spoke up now, nearly at a loss for words. "Because, that's what he looks like to me, Alandriel."

Alan looked from his face, to Kard's, then back to Stellis. They all seemed sincere, but he didn't understand the meaning.

"You see, Alandriel, they look different to you. The innkeeper is not the only one. I can only assume that you see Vanderkil much different from anyone else as well. Your behavior and interactions with him are what first caught my eye. It is a gift, though I do expect it is difficult for you to see how, as I think we have all begun to realize how little you know or remember of this world. As I said before, I can tell you more once we make camp, but I think I speak for all of us when I say that, especially with this confirmation, we are very glad that we have taken you into our company."

"Aye!" Kard shouted, grinning.

"Absolutely, friend. It's good to know you travel with us." Rime said from in front of him.

Riddle took the drawing back and returned it to a small book that he carried in his coat. "I never doubted you, Alandriel."

***

As the day drew on, so too they all grew more sore. Casual conversation to make the ride gentler and quicker sprang forth now and then, but for the first leg, they were all deeply consumed by their own thoughts.

Kard was thinking of breakfast, how he had not gotten nearly enough of one, and how he could feel his stomach quivering with every step the avimu took. He thought back to the mattress that he had left behind, how much better it would have felt on his bum at the current moment in time, and how he had *nearly* gotten enough sleep. He was also having quite a time trying to come up with a decent joke to play on Alandriel that night to welcome him in.

Rime was scanning the surroundings for any sign of life or enemy, especially as the great woods of Kolosso due west in front of them and all the beings that lived within drew nearer to hearing their footsteps. You see, although the others knew the way (except for Alan), only Rime knew every detail of their route and was holding each piece in his consciousness, bringing each to the fore when that quadrant drew nearer. For example, right now he knew that the River Mere lay just to their left, behind the cover of trees, though the others could not hear it, and he knew the river would continue to draw nearer to the party (or, in reality, vice versa) as they gained distance upon the forest. He knew what grub or game he would need to gather up in a pinch, and was prepared, perhaps even delighted, for a situation to arise where the others relied upon him for their survival. In all of this, he held a satisfaction that not even his brother could draw a map of the land as accurate as he.

Riddle was not at all thinking about how poor in quality a map would be that he drew of this place. He had, in fact, never drawn a map at all, at least not that he could remember. Riddle preferred words to pictures (unless it was a person or creature he was likely to meet again) and would use them sparingly to describe the world in its current state. He much preferred to chronicle anything at least a day old, but the older, the better. But right now, he was carefully studying the faces of those in front of him, and Kard behind, whenever they turned and he could get a look. *Was now an appropriate time for a story?* He had a wonderful one that he had been saving all morning, but it seemed no one was in the mood for talking once the temperature had picked up. As it were, Riddle rarely spoke *unless* he was telling a story. He was not much for letting others know how he felt or what he thought, unless he considered the information pertinent to their safety or wellbeing (which it often was).

Stellis focused entirely on Alandriel. She'd been apprehensive about telling him about this little trick that he seemed to possess, and it worried her that he would not react to it well. Stellis has always preferred to take all options into consideration before the execution of any action, but she knew that Alandriel needed to know as much as possible as soon as possible, and because of this, she was already pre-meditating upon how she would explain the rest of it to him tonight once they made camp. Well, not *the rest*, for that would take much more than one sit around a campfire, but *enough*, she hoped.

Alan's mind was not too far separated from this train of thought. After learning that he was *innately blessed*, he considered the gift for a while, though he understood that now was not the time to press Stellis for more information. He had spent a long while picturing Vanderkil and wondering desperately how he could be more fearsome than that, as that indeed seemed to be how his view had been warped from those around him. *Less fearsome. He* was less fearsome, he reckoned, as he glanced upon the scars and bruises of his new friends. He would not be shy to wager that he was one of the least fearsome people that they had ever met.

Far ahead he could see trees much more dense and drawn together, and though the sun was already nearing its apex, he hoped they made it to the edge by nightfall. It seemed much safer than the nakedness of the road.

Now Riddle had decided that his story was overdue, for if they continued any longer on this part of the road *without* hearing it, it would not fall on as interested ears.

"This road...Rotte, do you all know why they call it such? Why the old men of Drireford named it such an ugly name?"

Rime laughed at his brother, as he knew Rid had reached the point where he could no longer hold it in. "No, I do not. But I trust that you will tell us, brother."

"Well, many years ago, when there were more chep deer close by that lived in harmony with the men of Drireford—"

"What's a chep deer?" Alan whispered to Rime.

"It's the deer that gives the best cheese. They are quite rare nowadays. Don't be ashamed of having never heard of them."

Riddle had paused mid-sentence, waiting for his brother's attention, and then continued.

"When they lived close by, before the men began to hunt them out of desperation and drive them out of these lands, there was one cheese-maker in the town by the name of Blacklin Marbiter. Many say that he had a more-skilled hand at cheese-making than any for miles, and a few of his varieties gained such notoriety that after not too long, everyone began calling him Stink. Stink Marbiter. It was a name of respect, but it's tough to say whether or not he took it as such."

"He was a friendly chap for the most part until his wife died in the middle of the night. The circumstances were suspicious to say the least, and he became wary of all the other men in Drireford, any that had ever lay an eye on her or so much as said hello when they walked past together. Because of this, he grew quite bitter and isolated, only communicating with people as much as it took to sell his cheese. Well, this necessity for solitude combined with the recent death of his wife soon had some rumors brewing in town. After no more than a month or two, there wasn't a child walking down the lane that hadn't heard of Stink Marbiter, the deadly vampire."

"As even we've seen, some folks in Drireford are awful drawn to mob-mentality and hating those that they don't quite know enough about, and one night they hatched a plan to force Stink out of town and exile him, and if he refused, kill the poor man. They came knocking on his door in the wee hours of the morning, after all the folk had already gotten their fill of drink, no doubt, and pointed dull blades and farming forks at his throat the moment he opened the door."

"Even through all his suspicions, Stink had never been one to start conflict, and that night was no different. He obliged, according to their wishes, but asked only that he have the rest of the night to fix things up in his shop and gather some provisions to take with him. The more aggressive folk of course thought this was a ridiculous notion, but in those days, the reasonable still outnumbered the radical, and they allowed him the night to make amends. The men that were a bit more on edge about the whole ordeal returned to their homes to guard their wives and children, some with fake silver they'd hid under their mattresses, in the hopes that the vampire would be dissuaded."

"Well, Stink took the night to stash some of his smelliest cheeses in some very choice locations, notably those well-prone to moisture and hid away from keen eyes. The next morning, when the townsfolk drew him out to the woods, right near to the edge of Kolosso, he got straight to work. With the cheese he'd brought on his person, he trained and raised a whole mess of rats to fix their attention upon the town, slowly releasing more and more near the town's borders under the cover of night. The records of Drireford still claim that was the worst plague that the town's ever faced, and many died of starvation, if not from rat sickness, for they got into *everything*."

Riddle took a deep breath in, his mouth parched from so much speaking, and Rime laughed. "Brother, I think you've forgotten one little detail."

Rid was taking a swig from a bladder tied to his avimu and wiped his mouth. "What's that?"

"Why'd they name the road Rotte?"

"Oh...yes. Well, I thought it had been well-implied by the story. This path here that we're on, this is the road that they took him out on. This is the road that all the rats traveled on, to and fro, or so the story goes. That's why."

Everyone laughed, even Stellis cracked a smile, before Kard spoke up.

"Aye, that was a mighty fine story, mate. You always do tell them better than any drunk bastard in a tavern. I must say, though, all this talk of cheese has made me mighty hungry. Do we wish to picnic for a midday meal?"

Rime spoke, but kept his face ahead on the road. "I've grown hungry, too, however, I think that our pace must quicken to even make it to the edge of the forest tonight. I do not see the affordance of a snack in our future, but if you will look to the south, the River Mere runs much closer now. How say we fill up our bellies with water now and make quickly for the forest? I will set fair traps tonight, I swear it."

With that, the party deferred to the wisdom of their hunter, and they hastened to the forest before they had sight of the night's moon.

***

They had just drawn their avimu entirely under the shade of the canopy as the last bit of the sun was disappearing behind them, leaving little light on the path. They settled on a small clearing only twenty or thirty feet to the north of the path, on the other side of the Rotte than the River Mere, as they made camp.

Kard and Riddle unburdened the avimu, removing all the packs and bags that they had no reason to continue carrying, and laid out woolen blankets for each of them. Stellis was pre-occupied with the path ahead, and decided that she ought to scout out another few hundred paces in front and behind of them, both to ensure no stalkers or danger ahead.

Rime unfastened several ropes and metal contraptions from the back of he and Alan's avimu.

"Would you like to come set traps with me? It will at least get us out of hunting for kindling or hearing another one of Riddle's tales."

It pleased Alan to receive an invitation to do anything the slightest bit exclusive, and he quickly nodded his head.

"Good. Take these two lengths of rope and go see if you can find a hunk or two of cheese in the saddlebag hidden away on Kard's avimu."

She snorted softly as he came nearer, but purred lowly as he slowed and gave Alan a welcoming nod. He shoved his hand into the leather bag and felt many things, some sticky, some warm, some wet, and one or two that felt like cheesecloth. As he unwrapped them to inspect the contents, he decided these could be cheeses of Riddle's lore, for the stench nearly made his eyes water. He returned to Rime, and the pair made their way across the path towards where the river ran through the forest.

"Have you ever laid a trap?" Rime asked, as they walked to several tall trees that stood very near to the bank.

"No, I can't say I have."

"Okay, well, I might not be the best teacher, but I have a lot of luck with it. First you want to find two pretty solid sticks, if you're out on your own, of course. I bring hook sticks with me. You'll take the sticks and carve the same size chunk out of each one, maybe halfway to the middle of the stick. I always carve mine out three fingers from the end of the stick and three fingers long for the notch itself."

He pulled out two of his hook sticks and laid them on the ground.

"Before you bury the base stick in packed soil, you want to find the tree that you're going to use to tie the rope to. It needs to be young so that you can bend it well enough. See any around here that look good?"

Alan surveyed the bank and spotted one that stood maybe six or seven feet tall. It looked bendy enough, he thought.

"How about this one?"

"Ah. Not a bad choice, but look at the ground beneath it. There's a lot of growth there, so no animal is likely to take that path. Look for a sapling that has a bit of a beaten path running nearby."

Alan walked further along the bank and soon came upon another sapling, nearly the same in size, but with a worn game trail that went all the way to the river's edge.

"Perfect! This will do splendidly. Now, we pull the top of the sapling down like this." Rime grabbed the top and pulled it towards the path until it was nearly bent parallel with the ground. "Now hand me one of those lengths of rope...maybe the shorter one."

Alan handed it to Rime, and he tied a knot around the top of the tree and stretched the rope out until he had seen where it met the ground in a straight line.

"Now, we put the first hook stick in the ground here...then we tie the middle of the rope around the second hook stick and work the grooves into each other so that the stick is just held by a thread, see? Now, the next bit is up to the hunter's discretion. How big of an animal do you want to catch?"

"What were those bushy-tailed creatures that crossed our path often earlier today?"

"Ah. Vosvudu, yes, they would be tasty. They often stay high in the trees at night, but we might be able to get lucky. That is a good size though. We do not want to carry its meat forever."

He tied a snare at the end of the rope and arranged a few rocks in a circle to keep the edges of the snare just off the ground.

"Now, with the cheese...there! A mighty good toss for your first trap, I would say. Good eye on this game trail. Excellent spot. That's all you need to know about your prey as a trapper...well, *one* of two things: a sweet and a spot. This cheese is far from sweet, but it's a figure of speech, as my brother would say."

With that, the pair walked along the river further west, placing traps whenever they found a suitable spot. They didn't return empty-handed, either, for they had come across several footberry bushes on their way back to camp. Rime was not too interested in explaining the name, at risk of the subject devolving into a story, but he explained to Alan that they were the best berries to stomp and ferment, if you're drawn to the vices of good drink.

Back at camp, a fire was already burning, sending red and orange sparks high into the trees above, which were nearly black if not for the stars that gave some life to their leaves. Kard was stirring a spoon in a pot that they'd suspended above the fire, and both Riddle and Stellis were staring down at books that sat on their laps. As they approached, she shoved something small in the pocket of her cloak.

"Well, the party has started without us, I see." Rime jested, as he peeked at the inner bounty of a pot. "Don't have too much fun or someone will hear us from a chit away!" He laughed to himself.

Stellis drew up an absent face, as she was not nearly satisfied with the amount she'd recalled from her books, and was hoping to have more to explain to Alan. "Oh, do sit down, boys. I think it is time that we talk about the path ahead. Alandriel has traveled this far with kidnappers for all his knowledge."

Rime took a seat on his blanket and nearly leapt into the air as he yelped in pain.

"Why you sneaky bastard!"

Kard had broken into laughter and almost fallen off his chef's log. Rime reached to the rear of his pants and pulled out a ball, spiked and pointed all around. "Really!? A thumbdrum ball? You couldn't come up with anything more clever to prod my ass with?"

Kard was still laughing, trying to draw himself back from a hysterical sob now. "I thought it was mighty clever, mate. But I suppose you're right, there are a lot of other things I could have stuck up your ass. Woooo." He wiped the tears from his eyes and stirred the pot again, still chuckling softly to himself.

"Well, now that we have that display of courtship out of the way, can we get on with it? Yes?"

She pulled out another book that lay beside her and flipped to a marked page.

"Right. To the problem at hand. Where we are going and why we must go there. Why *you* must go there, Alandriel."

Alan too was stifling laughter and took a seat beside Riddle, trying to conjure up a solemn expression upon his face.

Stellis took a deep breath before beginning.

"Though the others have not lived long enough to truly see it happen, they are aware of it. Somewhere between sixty and seventy years ago, something strange began to happen all across Imp Lode. We did not know it at first, and even as it happened and became more and more clear, very few wanted to talk about it. This is, of course, only in my order, for the men of Imp Lode were altogether ignorant to the change, and nearly all of them have died off as it is."

She showed a page to Alan with a drawing on it he immediately recognized as the same style as the one they had shown him earlier today; more artwork of Riddle.

"This is Vanderkil, though you might have quite a time recognizing him. It is not old, nor outdated, but rather, reflective of how all living things see him."

It was a horrific sight. Instead of the soft, kindly man Alan had met at the Half-Cracked Staff (who was only abnormal in that he was quite large and had just the one eye in the middle of his head), the creature on the page was gruesome. His skin was rough and cracked, a horn sat atop his head, his ears were pointed and gnarled, and he had a bloody row of bottom teeth that tore into his upper lip.

Stellis watched Alan as he took the image in, quite discomforted. "All living things...all, except for you, Alandriel. The gift that you have is deceptively referred to as such, for it is more the absence of a curse, a spell, a plague. Whatever you wish to call it, it did not begin to blind the eyes of men, and all talking beings for that matter, until that time not too long ago. Too long, however, for your companions, as there has never been a day they can remember where they saw the true face of a creature like Vanderkil. Even still, it grows stronger every day."

She flipped to a new page in the book she had been reading when they had approached the campsite. "Those in my order are not yet sure of the purpose of the curse, nor the source or creator. But we have good reason to believe that it is malicious. Some say that it is the reversal of an old ancient magic that has lingered on the land for long. Those say that the sight men gain now is the sight they had long ago, but that some other force had blinded them. Even if that lore contains the truth, I do not see the ill in it. The way men see other creatures now has only brought evil and hatred into their hearts. Our land has been desecrated by this hatred. I'm..." She faltered, but quickly regained her composure. "I can provide no guarantee that your path will be safe. Our destination will not look kindly upon one who sees the world differently."

Alan was contemplating all that she had said, though found himself very short on words. "Is that...well, what do you need me for? I mean, what good is my gift, really, if you know that the curse exists? It's not like I can give my eyes to someone else..."

He was silent for a moment.

"You don't intend to rip out my eyes just like those men last night, do you?"

Stellis laughed quietly, burdened by something. "No, Alandriel. We do not wish to rip out your eyes. It is true, we do not know of a way to give your gift to another. Instead, I have volunteered to my order to seek a being that has not been touched by the disease. Initially, we thought it to work in a manner not completely ignorant of geography and distance, for those in the city that we are from, Oognysse, were effected earlier and with a heavier hand than those further out. It is for that reason, that I, along with Kard, Rid, and Rime, left our home in the west and traveled as far to the other end of Imp Lode as we could. It is true, though you may not believe it, that we have been on the road for many moons in search of a being with your gift. Our destination was the lands much farther east of here, with the land of Fyrestire being at the end of the road and, because of this, our last resort. After we surveyed the folk there and found even they had been touched by the sickness, we'd resolved to return home, empty-handed. Drireford was merely a place to lay our heads on yet another night of drear on the long path home. Then, I saw you in the tavern. We had contacted several of our order who were in Reul, but they only returned bad news. It is a mystery to me how you have remained untouched, but here we are."

She paused, and then upon remembering Alan's original question, added a suffix to her statement. "Our order searches for one untouched by the sickness in the hopes that the same wool that has been pulled down upon our eyes also covers the source or creator of the sickness, which we hope to find in Oognysse. We hope that with you there, our investigations of both the city and those that live there might reveal something that we cannot see with our own eyes. At the very least, the presence of yourself, of *one who can see*, well that might be enough to draw out whatever is causing this." She paused again, gazing at the path ahead. "I do believe the cause to be intelligent in nature. You or they will know of the other soon enough. This is our hope, for if things continue as they are, and conflict continues to bubble up from the hearts and arms turned foul, then the world over may soon be ravaged by war."

Alan looked at his company with a new sense of their journey, a genuine one, for the first time. They all smiled at him as he met each of their eyes around the campfire, though he could sense their exhaustion and weariness, even though it now seemed that they were much closer to an answer.

"Well, thank you for telling me all of that. It is good to know. I am sorry to all of you for how hard you must have searched without any luck, but I am glad that you have found me. I will continue with you until we find some sort of answer, I promise."

Alan felt a welling bit of joy in his heart, even though the circumstances he had just become aware of were most grim. For the first time he could remember, he had something to offer to people that he liked. They really *needed* him.

After the silence lingered for a moment longer, Kard was the first to rise, dispensing some of the stew they had been cooking into a copper bowl. "Well, that was a fine story, Stell. But, Alandriel, what the lass has failed to mention is all the bloody trouble she's gotten us into, as well as how many times I've had to save everybody's rear end. The road has not been easy." He laughed and took a long slurp of soup.

The others chuckled, and Alan took another bowl from the provisions and poured some stew as he spoke. "If you don't mind me asking, how do all of you know each other? I guess, aside from Rid and Rime, whom I'm assuming have known each other since birth."

Rime laughed and was the first to respond. "Well, yes, I can say without a doubt that Rid and I have known each other the longest. It's a relationship that offers many fruits, I'd say though. You've seen his pretty pictures, right?" He laughed. "But, yeah, I'd only met Stellis once we were on the road. Rime knew her much longer than that. You see, our mother, well, I'd not like to get into all of it right now, but she was killed. By a group of rats not too different from Two Eyes back in Drireford." He spat upon the ground. "The sickness had a sworn enemy of the two of us since that day, and when Rid asked me about being...well, I guess being the muscle to accompany he and Stell to the other side of the world, I knew I couldn't do it on my own. I asked Kard to come along."

Kard had a mouth full of stew, but grinned widely. "Aye, you did talk me into this, didn't you! Yep, me and Rime have been mates for a long time, no strangers to shared adventures between the two of us, but I'm also his butcher. I reckoned with him out of town, half the meat I carve will be gone with him, so I decided to come along. I'm 'fraid I don't have much muscle to speak of." He laughed with all of his belly.

Riddle, who hadn't spoken in quite some time, but seemed to enjoy such, now chimed in. "Yes, I suppose I'm the missing link. The order that Stellis belongs to...well, many of them have lived much longer than any men. There's no greater source of stories and wisdom. One day, Stell came to help me rid the garden of some magically inclined pests, and since then, I'm sure I've annoyed every bit out of her asking to hear tales of old. One day I might stop growing vegetables forever if I'm able to sell my stories. Seems like a rather impossible quest at that, so I suppose that's why I had no inhibitions about coming along on this one."

Stellis smiled, though she had not eaten a bite yet. "I'm afraid all of them…well, all save for Kard, speak much too humbly of themselves. After all, Riddle has knowledge that even few in my order possess, if any. As well, it is a highly overlooked gift to not only have wisdom, but the ability to share it in a way in which others will pay attention."

"Your order…well, again, tell me if this is too prying of a question, but what is your order?" Alan asked.

"Do not hesitate to ask me a question that lies on your heart, Alandriel. Though I doubt this is one of grave importance to you, I do wish you to know that in the future."

Alan nodded.

Stellis continued, "My order is that of sortiars. You might know us rather as witches, for that is what many call us, though it is a name most foul. There are ever fewer and fewer of us left, so, no less than 300 years ago, we came together. Though we had formerly acted upon our own desires and morality, since then, we have hoped to act in unison when it allows for the survival of us all. I do not wish to appear as though I am hiding something from you, but I would rather you heard the rest of our history from Riddle when he is willing to share it. He knows it at least as well as I do, and it would not befit my ego to go on about trials we have overcome or evils we have faced. For although our history is short, it is thick and dark."

"Well, I am sure that I have bothered all of you quite enough for a night. I don't mean to ask so much, it just seems that there is so much I do not know."

Rime put down his bowl and pursed his lips before speaking. "Do not sour your memory of our first camp together with such humble regret, Alandriel! Finish your stew and we will sing and be merry. We are all too doggedly aware that times like these are in short supply."

He slurped down the rest of his soup and was off to the avimu. Rime returned with a stringed instrument that Alan did not recognize, but if he had to describe it, it would be the gnarled child of a banjo and guitar.

"This ballad is one we're known to sing on a sour night in Oognysse, when the air is thick and black with the smoke from the rock mine—the eyesore of the city, it is! An ode to a time before such pollution of the soul. A dandy tune, if I do say so myself."

For the rest of the night, Rime sang for them, with Kard often joining in, though he knew less than half of the words. By the time the fire was dying and Riddle nodded off, Alan figured he had learned at least as much of the songs as Kard.

He lay down on his blanket with a smile and quickly fell asleep to the lively sounds of the forest and the good warmth of friendly company, hardly concerned that he was the hope of their world.

XI. The only sound within the room

Raspberry jelly squirted out from the donut and onto Alan's face and neck, startling him out of a half-nap.

Even though he had slept in until 11, there was something draining about staying in the dream for that long, and he'd asked Miss Etta for the most sugar she could provide in a small package. Luckily for Alan, raspberry donuts were his favorite. Days after Miss Etta came back from a "weekend" were always something special, as she always had a lot to throw away.

For the moment, he was grateful he hadn't wrecked Micah's car on the way into work. Footing the bill for the tow truck already had him worried.

"So...let me get this straight. You're doing all this in your sleep? But you're still controlling it in some way?" She was putting some newly assembled pies into the oven, a customer-favorite on Saturday evenings.

"Well...not exactly. I mean, yeah, I am asleep. I don't have complete control over all of it though. Well, I guess I do, somehow with my subconscious. I don't know, it feels like it's all happening on its own, you know? I guess all dreams feel like that. But the only control I really have is where I try to take myself when I fall asleep."

"You go somewhere new every time?"

"No. I mean, this book, the one I was telling you about with the notes in it, it kind of focuses a lot on keeping the same story going each night. You know, like if your dreams remembered the dream from the night before, and everything carried over. Kind of like a TV show. So I've just been picking up where I left off."

She smiled knowingly at Alan as though she didn't believe what he was saying. "And you swear you're not pulling my leg? I'm old. You gotta tell me if this is just some joke. I can't tell."

"No. No joke. I swear. It's weird. Being here, everything just feels so empty."

"Well, I'm sorry that—"

"No, I don't mean it like that. I mean, this is nice, of course. It'd be great if you were there in the dream and you could just see it all."

Alan felt a bid odd for suggesting that he'd like Miss Etta to be in his dreams, but was momentarily distracted imagining how she would manifest. A person? A fairy of some sort?

"I just...it's not like other dreams, you know? Everything there is so real. I can't explain it very well, but there's hardly any difference in it and real life. Maybe all dreams are that detailed; we just can't remember them well enough to know it."

She laughed and shook her head. "Okay. I believe you. Just don't get too wrapped up in all that and forget about your real life."

Alan nodded, but he didn't agree with the sentiment. These five minutes, that was one of the few bits of his life that remained tolerable. The dream offered so much more than that. How could she understand, though, after all? *I mean, she has no problem smiling here, there's nothing in life that could drag her down.*

This Saturday was a mixed bag. The customers were just as intolerable and insufferable as usual. Not a single friendly face had come through his line yet, and it was nearly the time that he would get off on a normal day. With late shifts, anytime after 5 o'clock drags on like a half-lived eternity.

Everything about the day wasn't bad, though. Mr. Vick wasn't there, and the gossip going around the store was that he'd gotten pink eye. This was only particularly volatile gossip because Higgy, the soon-to-be-professional bowler, had also come down with pink eye a few days before. Alan decided that this rumor was more reflective of how boring and dismal working at Elmwood's truly was, rather than anyone's interest in Mr. Vick having an extramarital affair.

It wasn't until Alan went to the break area seeking confirmation for his own eyes of Vick's absence that he saw the note taped to his office door:

To all under my employ: I will not be at work on 5/25 (tomorrow). I am running a slight fever and have felt very nauseous all night. Work harder in my absence as a courtesy. Thanks. -V.

The implication of Vick lurking around the building late enough at night to type up this note *after* having had nausea all night had nearly stolen all of Alan's attention from the direct effect the situation had upon him. He wouldn't have to discuss his CIST report, after all!

Alan had nearly forgotten about the thing. He discovered that with the dreams came a not-so-great side effect (although it was perfectly all right with him), in that after taking in information and creating memories during both your waking hours *and* your sleeping hours, the memories of your waking life faded and grew hazy.

As he walked back down the stairs while whistling from the unburdening, he considered the future implications and felt nauseous himself. Sure, he didn't have to talk about the score today, but he was sure that the minute Vick returned, their little conference would be one of the first orders on his plate. The day grew even drearier now. At least if he'd had the meeting, he'd already know the outcome.

He should start saving coffee cans so he had a decent tin with which to beg for change.

Unfortunately for Alan, another one of his grandmother's favored expressions would prove true on this day: bad news prefers to arrive in pairs.

On his 7 o'clock break (which wasn't an assigned break, but he'd decided no one was left that might rat on him) he returned to the break room to try reading. He didn't want to read anything in particular. Instead, he was operating on the sentiment that reading anything, anything at all that was some sort of fantasy, might make him feel like he was back in the dream. Not really, of course, he was sure that it wouldn't have the same depth. But he was desperate and itching after dealing with his fourth double-couponer of the day (he really wished that Vick would make the sign larger).

In his work locker, he had a stash of books for just the occasion. They weren't new books or ones that he wished to read; rather, they were his favorites: stories that he had read cover-to-cover more times than he could keep track of. For a moment, just a small, weaseling five-minute break in the middle of a terrible day, he could trick himself into forgetting his own reality. Just for a moment.

As he reached for *The Hobbit*, intending to read one of his favorite passages where Gandalf reveals himself to Bilbo before the final battle, he saw the bag that brought his spirits down even further.

There was nothing wrong with the bag. It was a normal, ugly, smiley face plastic bag — the cheapest, and, therefore, the only Vick would order, but it was the contents of the bag that made Alan aware of yet another grim tiding Saturday had brought with it. Inside were the ingredients that Alan had procured from the store for the tea, the tea that the book recommended. They were fine even though they'd been left there, and although he was glad he chose canned beets instead of fresh, another error he made ruined it all.

He'd forgotten to tell Raphl that he worked the late shift today. Now he was off at the lake for who knows how long. Who knew if he'd even gotten the stuff? They were probably out of it. Maybe he'd dropped it off and somebody had already taken it. Maybe Higgy took it to recover from the pink eye. There didn't seem to be any outcome where Alan would get the ingredients anytime soon, and that just *did it* for him.

If he couldn't wait to get back home before, he'd fly home now. He shoved the book back into his locker, too frustrated to read, and returned to his register to serve the rest of his sentence.

The hour before closing was always a lull, and where before he'd loved it, now he cursed it. Time went slower and slower the longer between customers he went, and after the last woman had gotten laundry detergent and plastic forks at 7:12, he'd spent the next fifteen minutes trying to stay awake, listening out for the begotten sound of squeaking shopping cart wheels or a voice asking, "is your line open, sir?"

None of it came. His eyelids grew heavy, and his legs quivered beneath the weight of a drowsy body.

Then—

A carton of eggs bumped into his right hand. He had been slumped over the register, trying to get into a comfortable position to take a standing nap, and he hadn't even heard the customer approach. He must have bumped the belt switch, and the carton scraped in a low, flat-noted skid against the belt as it could not overcome the barrier of his hand.

"Hi. I'm glad that you're working tonight."

Smiling back at him was the girl from a week ago. She carried no book, nor pushed a cart. She stared down at the eggs.

"Oh, hi. It's good to see you, too."

Alan opened the carton of eggs to check them for cracks, a response more because of muscle memory than anything else. Every egg in the carton was cracked. All of them, save for one egg on the top right corner. Alan picked it up and examined it in disbelief.

"Um...these eggs...they're mostly bad. Do you want me to go grab another dozen?"

She laughed. "No."

"Are you sure?"

"Yes."

"Okay. Well, it's your choice. I'll ring them up at a discount, anyway. They go bad...wait, these went bad on the 17th. You're really sure—"

"Did you read the book? Dream Cycle?"

"Did I...I..."

The whole egg cracked from the pressure of Alan's nervous, clenched hand. The yolk poured forth, covering the scanner, dripping down onto his shoes. It went in through the hole and soaked his toes through his cheap, worn socks. It was warm.

—then he jerked his head up, wiping the drool from his face. It had dripped all the way down to the floor. The clock read 7:54.

Alan went home.

***

I must admit, that even as the bearer of Alan's tale, I have often found his routine monotonous. Every day upon arriving home, he kicks off his shoes to the same spot, opens up the same freezer door, is greeted by the same Chef Billy, and does little of interest until it's time to sleep and do it all the next day. Thank goodness for the events of the past few days, for otherwise, I don't know how much longer I could have written about him.

This evening ritual did not at first have any inclination to differ from the rest. He only desired to lose waking consciousness as quickly as possible, so he was rushing through the usual routine. Halfway through a *Thanksgiving Feast* variety of Chef Billy, his phone rang.

It had been a while since the phone had rang and Alan was around to hear it. Like the tree falling in the forest, the instigation of the process startled him a little. It was nearly 9 o'clock, Micah and Sarah were still gone (or, more likely, they had already left again), and there was nothing in the house to dampen the sound.

It rang. Brrrrrrrng. Brrrrrrrrrng. He realized he had no idea how many times the phone would ring before it went to the answering machine. Brrrrrrrng. His mom would not be calling this late. *Who could it be—oh shit! My car!* He hadn't even clocked it in the driveway as he had pulled up.

He darted to the phone and picked it up.

"Hello?"

"Hi...um, this is Sulley Coffey for Alan Hendershot."

"This is Alan."

"Hi, Mr. Hendershot. I'm glad that I was able to reach you. Completely my mistake that I didn't get your phone number the other day. Unfortunately, I spilled chili on your order form...and...well, I had to have Lisa look you up in the phonebook. We got in touch with a...Theresa Hendershot...anyway, I'm sure she'd already told you all of this, but I'm just reaching out as a courtesy."

No, my mom hasn't told me anything.

"I'm sorry, I haven't been able to get in touch with her since yesterday. What happened?"

"Oh...no. Well, I'm...I'm awful embarrassed, Mr. Hendershot. She gave me an address to bring the vehicle to and said that they'd get the vehicle repaired. Paid for the towing bill. You do know Theresa, don't you? She knew the model of the car...that's all I could think of to verify. Didn't want to leave the car out there...I—I can give you a phone number for a friend who is an officer here in town—"

"No, it's okay. I know her, I just wasn't aware of any of this. It's completely fine. Thank you. You said she already paid you for the towing?"

"Yes, sir. Everything is squared away here. Are you sure there's no problem?"

"No, no problem. Thanks for calling."

He walked outside to his car. There it sat, in the spot that he always parked it in. He looked under the back right floor mat and found the spare key right where he always kept it. Right where his dad always kept it. There was a note taped to the steering wheel.

HEY HONEY. I KNOW YOU'RE PROBABLY REALLY MAD AT ME FOR DOING THIS, BUT I KNOW YOU STILL DON'T FEEL LIKE SEEING ANYONE, SO THINK OF THIS AS MAKEUP FOR NO BIRTHDAY DINNER. THEY FIXED IT IN A RUSH, SO PLEASE CALL ME IF ANYTHING SEEMS OFF. YOUR REAL PRESENT IS IN THE TRUNK. YOUR DAD PICKED IT OUT. I LOVE YOU. -MOM

He walked around to the rear of the car, put the key in the trunk and popped it.

Inside were two huge cardboard boxes. In the one on the left, he found a brand new record player, still in the box. He knew the model. All of his savings had been stashed away for it over past year and a half. He'd talked about it with his dad a lot.

The second box had a note on top, as well. *These were all your dad's (okay, maybe a couple of the corny ones are mine). I know he would want you to have them.* This box was deeper and wider, and inside he found every single record his dad had owned. He recognized almost all of them.

He felt his eyes watering a little. Of course that's what it was. It was cold tonight, after all.

He unboxed the record player in his room and sat on the floor, staring at it. It lay inside its own wooden cabinet and had the amp and speakers all built in. It looked just as good as he hoped it would. He took the cover off of the needle and plugged it in. A soft, warm buzz came through the speakers. It smelled like wood you'd just gotten from a home improvement store. It smelled new.

He pulled out his favorite record from when he was little: *Gunfighter Ballads* by Marty Robbins. He still knew right where to drop the needle for his favorite song. The needle cracked, hissed, and then the guitar melody he knew so well started. He didn't know why he liked it so much. It'd been forever since he'd listened to it, now that he thought about it. He had never really understood the words, but he'd always loved the sound. Now that he looked at the case, he didn't think he'd known the title before either: *They're Hanging Me Tonight.*

He wobbled on his knees and let his eyes close. Tears got hot in his eyes. He really missed his dad. Damn, he really wished he was with him right now. He knew every single word, but he heard all of it for the first time now as he sang it to himself. Alan had never killed two people out of rage and unrequited love, but he was sad tonight. He and Marty had that in common.

Alan pulled the needle back and played it again, then again, then again. An hour went by. He felt a little better. There was something cathartic, he thought, listening to the same song over and over. The longer it went on, the less he listened to it and the more he paid attention to his own thoughts. His mind felt clearer. He wanted to go back to Imp Lode.

Alan pulled his journal out from under his dirty laundry and went through his notes. He updated everything from the day before and read it all back to himself, imprinting the events and places to his memory. Alan didn't want to be alone right now. He wanted to see his friends. The friends that wouldn't ask him about his career plans or his dating life. The friends that needed him for his gift. *Or absence of a curse, whatever.*

He went back to the kitchen and shoved the cold turkey and cranberry sauce down his throat, ensuring he was truly stuffed, then finished it all off with a glass of water.

Back in his room, he lay down and started the ritual. He did a mental check on whether his body was uncomfortable enough (tonight he had been so eager that his pants and belt were still on, which did plenty to make him feel weird as the guide deemed necessary). Alan took deep breaths, closed his eyes, and focused on the last moment in Imp Lode while whispering all the details to himself.

He knew he needed to skip through a night once again, so he imagined the sun rising in the forest, illuminating a wet dew on the ground. The trees smelled strongly of maple, and he could even smell the dirt beneath him. He could hear the birds waking as songs were being shared back and forth from up high in the canopy. He could see all of his friends around him. Kard, the prankster. Rime, their dedicated survivalist. Riddle, ever the storyteller. Stellis; who knew what thoughts she held within her mind. He imagined them all asleep still, for he wanted to wake up before all of them and have a few moments in the forest by himself to take in the morning air and, perhaps more importantly, have a first go at the breakfast provisions. He wasn't sure if he could just imagine other people the way he wanted them, but he might as well try.

The bed beneath him faded away, traded for a rough woolen blanket and bumpy undergrowth. He took another deep breath in and then out, as his eyes relaxed on their own, not squeezed at all. He fell asleep.

XII. Forgotten tale of Follis

"Oh, the wee lad musta been exhausted. Think I see his eyes crackin' open...yep! G'mornin' mate. Slept like a baby, I see."

To Alan's disappointment, not only had Kard woken up before him, but so had everyone else. The smell of eggs and meat frying already filled the air of the new day while Stellis and Rid warmed their hands over the crackling amber fire. Kard was rummaging around for some more cheese, no doubt.

Rime's voice came from behind. "Oh good. You're up! Gather yourself quickly. We need to go check the traps before any waking beast has a chance to rob us of our bounty." He was chewing on a piece of hard bread and spryly packing up some of the camp off behind them with the avimu.

Alan groaned and stretched. "Yeah, I guess I was more tired than I thought. My butt is *really* sore."

Kard laughed. "Yeah, those birds will do that to you. If only we had a horse that could swim."

"A good walk and stretch will do you good then! Come on, let's go!" Rime was tying up their bags impatiently, but Alan appreciated that he'd waited for him to wake before going to check the traps.

They walked back across the path to the other side of the woods and down to the river where they had set them. As they approached the first trap, they saw it was empty, and twenty feet upstream the second bore the same fate. As they got to the third, there was a squeal of something awful, like a rat met with an upset cat, and they saw a red-orange flurry of fur squirming and dangling about five feet off the ground.

They ran to it, and Rime unsheathed a large hunting knife mid-stride, which Alan decided was quite a dangerous maneuver.

"Okay. Of course, we don't want it to suffer any longer than necessary. I need you to hold it firmly around the belly while I cut it. It won't be able to bend up enough to bite you."

"You're sure that's the only way we can do this?"

"You don't want to touch it?"

"It just looks...really angry. I have a hard time believing it won't be able to hurt me."

As Rime lingered in front of the vosvudu, which was now screeching desperately and snapping its jaws at the nearest moving thing, they heard another scream from further off.

They both lingered for a moment, confused, and then jogged towards the source further south in the wood. With Rime in the lead, they soon came to a bend in the river as they heard the scream for a second time. There was no doubt in either of their minds that it was coming from the other side, but the water that lay between them was at least thirty or forty witchits, and it was bubbling and frothing ferociously across the jagged rocks that scattered the path. A thick morning fog lay on the water like a curtain, blocking their view of the opposite bank.

"Hello!" Rime shouted with his hands cupped to his mouth, projecting his voice across the river. "Stellis...Rid...Kard! Who's there? Are you hurt?"

No response.

"You think that was a person?"

"Yes. I know of no animal that makes that call, even though I've only come through this wood once or twice before." He looked around himself and walked to a knotty tree closer to the bank. "I'm going to climb up this for a better vantage point. Stay below and spot me."

He grabbed the bottom-most branch and pulled himself up with a laborious heave. The next was easier, the one after that, closer still. In a matter of minutes, he was so far from the ground that the sunlight nearly blocked Alan's line of sight to him.

"What can you see?"

"Well, the trees make it diff—hold on!" He shouted out, "You there! Are you okay? Do you need help?"

Alan looked in the direction that Rime was shouting but could see no one. Two minutes later, he was back on the ground next to him, his breathing hardly increased.

"I saw a woman. She's not too far across on the other bank."

"On the other side of that?"

They faced the water again, and the rapids roared so loudly now Alan was nearly trembling.

"Yes, don't worry. I'll go across. She looked as though she was hurt badly...she also—well, it doesn't matter. I'm going across."

"Are you sure you can make it?"

"No."

He threw off his tunic and shoes and leapt from the sheer bank into a headfirst dive. Alan could hear the crash and see the foam below, but had no sight of Rime. A moment later, he surfaced, nearly fifteen feet in front of where he'd entered, but nearly twice that downstream.

Stell arrived swiftly behind Alan, followed by Rid and Kard.

"Curse us all," she whispered and walked to the very edge to get a better sight.

"I tried to get him not to go, but he seemed—"

Riddle was breathing exhaustedly from the run. "What did he go in after? Don't tell me he saw a beautiful woman?"

"Um...well, he didn't say she was beautiful, but—"

Riddle moved ahead of Alan and shouted, "Brother! Turn back! It's not real. There's nobody over there!"

They jogged along the edge of the bank to keep up with his drifting path, but even though he wasn't yet halfway across, he was out of earshot.

Rid was prancing nervously along the bank, his eyes fearful. "There's no way he makes it across. He's a fine swimmer, but this River...I shouldn't have let him go off alone..."

Stellis's eyes were closed as she moved her hands in a circular motion. "He is out of my reach. The river holds him now."

"Surely there's something we can do?" Alan felt truly helpless, but was having a hard time holding himself back from jumping in, even though fear filled every bone of his body. Anything seemed better than waiting. They only caught glimpses of him now between the crashing rapids. Alan couldn't tell if he was still making for the other side or had given up.

"I've always got rope on me, but I can't swim well at all, much less in that raging beast," Kard said.

Rid shook his head anxiously. "Neither can I."

"I cannot touch this River, or I'd suffer a worse fate than he." Stellis looked at Alan.

Alan thought back to the two summers he had spent in his aunt's above-ground pool with his swimming teacher, Miss Maxwell. Yeah, he could swim.

"I'll do it. Hand me the rope." He didn't know what came over him, but the adrenaline had filled his body with an electrifying energy. Alan took the rope and jogged further downstream with the others fast behind him, both to get away from the rocks and give himself some headroom as Rime continued to drift.

He jumped off of the shoulder and landed in the river in poor fashion, legs and arms sprawled, though he hit nothing on the way down. Immediately he felt the full force of the water against his right side, pulling and pushing him with a ceaseless rage. He struggled and stretched to get his head back above the surface and finally caught a breath of air after a brief lull took hold, just for a moment, at a straightaway.

He gathered his bearings and cleared his eyes of the water long enough to see across the river. Rime now looked back at him, steadfast, but in a panic, no doubt. He did his best to show the rope that was tied around his arm, and Rime seemed to receive the message—that, or he had already given up. He made sweeping motions with his arms toward Alan, but the strokes didn't seem to move him.

Alan knew he'd have to bridge the gap. He dived beneath again to pull himself away from the river's tug, and it seemed to work. He pushed forward tenaciously and could feel his legs and arms crying for oxygen. Alan surfaced once again and could see Rime no more than ten feet away.

"Come—" A crash of water hit him in the face and he fell back under, his lungs filling with water.

He came up again, struggling for air, and Rime was nearly within reach. He stretched out his body flat again, and with one last push, he held Rime's outstretched hand in his. Rime grabbed hold of the rope, and immediately Alan felt a tug from behind him as Kard pulled the rope in.

He was far too drained to swim in aid, but Kard was making fine progress on his own, and soon they touched the northern bank with their own feet.

"Brother! Have you forgotten everything I told you!" Riddle was scrambling down the bank, with a small fury growing in his eyes, though he was much relieved. "I am glad that you have both escaped alive, though. We only grow greater in your debt, Alandriel." The water had irritated and fogged his vision so that Alan could not tell if Riddle was crying, but it sounded like he was.

"That was mighty brave, mate." Kard wound the rest of the rope around his arms.

"Yes, Alandriel. I echo the others. We are grateful to you."

Rime was still spitting up water and stumbled up the bank after Alan, his body bloodied and bruised from the gnashing of rocks and limbs. "What are you talking about, brother? How could you ever," he coughed up more water, "ever expect me to remember everything you've ever told me? That's not possible for a library, let alone one man." He coughed again, though it was more of a laugh this time, and the others joined, though nearly all were in a hysterical state of mind.

"What...what did he forget, Rid?" Alan had nearly caught all of his breath now as they were nearing the path.

"The River Mere. It is cursed. Always has been. Men go in hoping to help a beautiful woman and are never seen again. More bones lie on its bed than any graveyard. I've only told the story of Follis the Tragic twenty or so times."

And so it was that on the journey back to the camp, and during the next leg of their travels through Kolosso, Riddle told the story of Follis the Tragic for the twenty-first time.

Follis was one of the first men to leave the east, to leave Fyrestire in search of new land in the west. He took a company of four men with him, in hopes of finding a place where they could prospect for gold, for it had all but run out in their hills. The men were rugged, strong, and stalwart, and the camps that they wrote back to their families about became a lot of the towns of men that still thrive today.

They first caught sound of the River Mere in what today is Blackpool, a town south of Needlewich. They had all trained in the hard work of mining for gold deep beneath the surface of the land, in caverns as lost and dark as night itself. However, the gnomes that once thrived in Blackpool didn't take too kindly to strangers, and they already knew the curse of the River.

To keep them out of their holes and caves, they told Follis and his men about a new way to mine for gold, where you would take a pan or pot and sift through the sediment until the gold fell to the bottom, heavier than the rest. The gnomes knew the river carried no gold, but in a matter of days, it had soon carried away all the men, and the gnomes were free of strangers once again. The fieldbook of Follis was all that remained.

So it was that the five travelers continued through the forest, with two of them dripping water onto their avimu, Mina, who did not appreciate their sopping cargo in the cool shade of the trees. She had appreciated, however, the raw, wriggling giblets of vosvudu she'd been given by the same pair. They'd cooked up two whole from their trappings and only carried less than a day's worth of meat after they'd all engorged.

When they were nearly halfway through the forest (according to Rime), Alan asked aloud what type of tree he was looking at it. For they were all the same, except for a random pattering of outliers, but even those might have been more dead versions of the others. They had patchy grey and white bark that grew lighter and lighter closer to the top of the tree. They all had many branches, and the leaves were green or yellow, but there was no in-between. The canopy allowed the sun to peak through on rare occasion now that they were in the thick of it.

When he asked, Rid spoke up right away, beginning the preamble to a story he thought would be delightful. Rime cut him off and gave Alan the bare bones of it.

"These are sombra trees. They grow taller than any trees you'll find for a far travel. Kolosso is the only forest in Imp Lode where these are known to grow."

Alan appreciated the answer, but found it a bit dry. It didn't answer several of his questions, and even then, what a boring way to describe such a magnificent phenomenon: the tallest trees in the world! In an attempt to spur Riddle back into a story without directly offending Rime, he nodded his head curiously and gave little more than an affirmative grunt.

Just as he'd hoped, Riddle cleared his throat.

"As I was saying…the forests of Kolosso hold much more than my brother would let on, though not all believe it. They are tall for a reason. Before men had traveled this far into the world, long before any of their settlements had begun or their cheese had been stunk, explorers have found traces that giants once walked here, on the surface."

He paused for dramatic effect, but by the lulled reactions, it seemed Alan was the only one who was new to this tale.

"Well, not much is known about the giants in those times. But it's said that Kolosso was a place of great importance to them. Every now and then artifacts are found scattered in and around the forest: trinkets, smooth stones, even parts of tools and weapons. We know they belonged to giants, for example, because the head of one shovel was larger than our friend Kard here."

Kard looked down at his belly and laughed.

"It is said that the giants buried their dead in what is now the forest you see around us. Each one of their dead bore a seedling of the sombra, and their souls are said to live within the tree, ever-reaching for heaven."

"Well, that's kind of sad. They never go to heaven?"

"Well, I suppose everything you or I have ever lived is just a path leading to the after, whatever lies beyond," Rid said. "They just go about it a different way. It would be silly to say that it's sad that a man who has lived a long time hasn't gone to heaven, for we do not know the giants will never get there."

"Well, yeah, but trees can't feel."

"Says who?"

Alan could think of a lot of ways to explain *why* trees couldn't feel, but Rid did have him there. He couldn't name a single *person* who said that. A cool breeze brushed their faces, and Alan looked up at the crowns of the surrounding trees, swaying ever so slightly in the wind, grasping for the sky. It seemed sorrowful now, but the further they rode, the more he felt at peace.

As they traveled on, the sky began to smell wet. The wet smell that you notice as the grey clouds darken and soft rumblings bellow out from far away corners. The air felt heavy and soggy, and the temperature suddenly warmed and then chilled in tight patches. A storm was fast upon them.

For as long as Alan could remember, he had loved storms. He had memories of sitting in front of the floor to ceiling window in his childhood bedroom, sticking his face on the glass as the rain started, slowly falling asleep to the soft pitter-patter against the glass. The energy in the air during a good storm, well, there was nothing else like it.

His friends seemed to be of a different persuasion, for as distant thunder rumbled louder and louder, and the skies grew dark enough to relax one's eyelids, they grew uneasy. Riddle was whispering quietly to himself, no doubt recounting a comforting story about what folly it was to fear storms, though his face betrayed him. Rime held steadfast, but often quickened his pace out of nervous agitation, leaving the others to catch up. Stellis remained mostly calm, but Alan saw her look behind them once or twice, for that was where the sky was most ghastly. Kard had taken up an anxious whistle, a melody Alan had never heard, but it was soothing.

Rime broke the silence. "We should get to the edge of the forest before it hits. We don't want to be stuck in here if trees start falling."

Riddle looked at him, aghast. "Do you really think that out in the open is better? You do know Flour is west of here? There's no shelter to be found there."

"No, I do not think out in the open is better. That is not what I said. I said the edge of the forest, where we still have the shelter of trees if we need it, but cannot be betrayed by it."

"Yes, I agree with Rime. We should look for any sort of dugout or burrow we can find near the edge. Even a small pit will do in case of high winds." Stellis patted her avimu, signaling for the others to match her pace.

"Is it really going to be that bad? I mean, it's just a storm, right?"

Kard laughed from the rear. "Mate, storms out here must be a lot more unbroken than the storms up in Reul. Just like the horses, I reckon. She'll be fierce, I can promise you that."

Alan's blood warmed as another crack of thunder shook the surrounding trees, and the first drops fell. They were huge. Each water drop was no smaller than a golf ball. Alan's clothes were soaked through within a matter of seconds, as were the avimu.

Mina released a sharp shrill, almost playful, and ran along, bouncing as she went.

"I thought she didn't like water?"

"What made you think that?" Rime asked.

"She seemed awful mad at us when we got on her wet earlier today."

"That wasn't because she was wet! That's because we smelled like river water. This storm is from the ocean just over the Funus Mountains up ahead. She can smell the salt."

"I thought you said there was no cover up ahead?" Alan was nearly having to shout now, for the sound of the rain had grown too loud.

"Yes! First, mountains cover nothing but evil things! Second, the Funus are still a day's travels, if not more. Between us and them lies Flour. It is a flat meadow, but you will see it soon if you do not believe me!"

Rime quickened Mina's pace drastically now that the excitement spurred her on. Every few paces she would flap and flutter her wings, spraying a salty mist up into the air. Alan had trouble keeping his hair, which was now drenched, out of his eyes, and had quite a thrill speeding through the downfall nearly blind.

A few minutes later, as the wind picked up even more, Rime slowed and turned back to face the others. "I can see the edge, not far up ahead. A hundred itchits, no more! Keep your eyes out for depressions that haven't yet flooded with water."

They moved slower now, while Alan kept lookout to the right, northern side of the wood, and Rime to the other. He had very little hope that they would spot a depression like this, or at least that he would, for he did all he could to keep his hair from his eyes, yet still felt blind.

To his surprise, Rime abruptly directed Mina to turn on a dime, and he shouted back, "I've spotted something! Looks promising! Southwest. Stay close to the path and I'll send Alandriel if it's suitable."

They both dismounted and Alan jogged after Rime into the woods, thankful to get under more cover from the bombardment. Up ahead now, he could barely make out a shallow hole, no more than fifteen feet in diameter and bedded with leaves. Behind, a dirt wall with protruding roots acted as a wall against the wind, and Alan could now see that it was just the bottom of a tree that had fallen, likely the cause of the hole.

It seemed dry enough inside, as the water drained through the leaf covering. After Rime stomped around in it for a moment, he motioned for Alan to get the others. Alan ran all the way back to the path, waving for them to follow, and led them back to the hole.

Rime had spent the interim pushing more leaves (only those which lay underneath others that were still dry) into the hole, and there was no longer any bare patch of ground.

"All right! I'm not saying this is the best case, but we'll be safest lying flat on our bellies next to each other. Keep your hands over your head! The winds are picking up now!"

One by one, they entered the burrow and lay down. Kard had lay down first and was on the far end. Alan got in next to him, then Riddle, then Stellis, and after throwing a couple of blankets in after them and securing the avimu, Rime took the left flank.

It was quieter now, in the hole, and much warmer, though Alan still felt wet to his bones. After only a moment or two, they had all decided that laying on your face was not the best of ideas, and they turned their heads to the side, everyone facing to the left to avoid any intimate shared breaths.

Kard had stopped whistling and now hummed in a less-frantic rhythm, as the company of his friends calmed him. Alan could feel his warm breaths on the back of his head and tried to avoid doing the same to Riddle, for each one sent a shiver down his spine.

"Hey, Alandriel." Rime shouted out in a hoarse whisper from the front of their queue.

"Yeah?"

"Thanks again for saving my life earlier. If you hadn't, I wouldn't have gotten to hear the story of the trees once more before dying to this storm."

Alan could feel Kard laughing behind him. Riddle answered, "Sod off! I'm allowed to tell stories if someone has never heard it!"

"Brother, don't take it as mockery. I know that's about all I do, but that's one of the only stories I like. I just couldn't let you know it, or I'd hear it all the time."

"Oh. Well, yes. It is a good one."

The wind howled like a banshee, and the rain smacked the trees and ground around them like bullets hitting tin.

Rime mumbled, "Do you think we'll be trees if we die here?"

"Yes. Yes, I think we will, brother. Do not take too much sunlight from me if it happens, though!"

"I wouldn't dream of it!"

The wind screamed, ever the more loudly. The clouds beat down with a ferocity and persistence Alan had never seen. The thunder rumbled through the whole of the ground when it struck. And yet, Alan was calm. The storm did not bother him. He was not alone, and he did not need to run to another hole to hide.

He closed his eyes and took deep breaths. Then—

—he awoke.

XIII. Losing my religion

When Alan woke up, he could barely remember the previous day. Not the day in Imp Lode, no; he could remember every detail of that—the near-drowning, the torrential storm, all of it. Even as he rang up all the trimmings of an Italian feast for Mrs. Lombardi, his idle legs felt as if they were treading water in the River Mere.

He hadn't forgotten a minute of that. What he struggled to recall was his waking time. It had all been a blur. He knew he had come into work for a late shift, that Vick had been gone, and something about the girl and some eggs, but other than that, he hadn't the slightest inkling.

Now he wasn't sure if he *had* actually remembered Vick had been out, or if he had only known about the absence from the patch that Vick now wore on his left eye as he walked by carrying a brown bag from the bagel place down the road.

"Good morning, Hendershot. I hope you've prepared your offering."

He did little more than glance at Alan as he glided by and ascended the stairs to his throne room. *What a strange guy.*

After a few more customers, Vick appeared next to him once again, this time with a puffed-up sneer and both shirt sleeves rolled up. In his hand he held a slip of paper, outstretched to Alan. He stunk of Irish Spring and bacon.

PLEASE SEE ME IN MY OFFICE @ YOUR 12:00 BREAK.

Alan put the note in his pocket and stared at him, expecting some disparaging commentary. Vick only snarled and turned up his nose before leaving once again in dramatic fashion.

For a moment, Alan was ignorant. A babe in the woods. But, I'm sure that you already know for what Vick beckoned Alan. I do, too. After a moment, so did Alan. His heart dropped and his throat dried up. He got a strange feeling, right at the end of his tailbone, almost like a stomachache, but more immediate than that. It was as if his bowels felt his fear more intensely than any other part of his body.

The tax man was coming to collect, just as he'd said he would. The pauper stooped to his station, absent of any hope for reprise. He knew his CIST score was abominable. He had no doubt. Who knew if this head of cabbage, this bunch of bananas, or that tube of toothpaste were making the score higher or lower? He sure as hell didn't. He thought he'd be lucky to be at five items per minute. Who cared though? He was sliding groceries across a piece of glass with a laser behind it. If people want to shop at the busiest time of the week, they could wait five damn minutes to pay. What was the rush?

Soon, 12 o'clock arrived, and Alan felt like Ebenezer awaiting the arrival of Christmas Future. Only, his ghost was a man dead of spirit that was equally cheap as Scrooge. His mind drifted into imaginings of Vick in a nightgown, made to realize the wrongdoings and misdeeds he had wrought upon those beneath him. Alan couldn't picture the characters in any other style than that of the Mickey Mouse version.

He knocked on the door.

"Come in, Hendershot. Please, take a seat."

Vick's white button-up was nearly glimmering in the harsh fluorescent light of his office. Behind his head hanging on the wall, he had one of those motivational posters—the ones where there's an image surrounded by black, and then at the bottom there's some bland, vanilla anecdote about GOALS or SUCCESS.

DISTANCE was the title of this one, and beneath it read, "Sometimes you have to separate yourself from the lazy and uninspired to reach your true potential. Do not be afraid to go too far to get what you want." This was all below a picture of the moon, which yeah, Alan had to admit, was pretty far away. The creator definitely knew what distance was.

Right now, the moon was silhouetting Vick's enormous head in a way not unlike some depictions of Christ. As Alan took a seat in the cheap chair that ensured any visitor sat lower than the boss, he recalled everything he had ever learned about worshipping false idols. For Vick, it was success; a success that he hoped would bring him more money than he could reasonably spend in a lifetime, and all those who had it. But here in Elmwood's on Elm, Alan couldn't decide who was more blasphemous: Vick, or the world that made him think his was an envious ambition.

"Well, I do hope I've given you enough time to prepare a repentance in my leave. I trust—"

Alan would normally never cut Vick off, but today, it didn't seem like such a bad idea. He reckoned right now there wasn't much left to lose.

"Why were you out, again? I hope everything is okay. Your eye?"

Vick twisted his face indignantly, surprised at the interruption. "Yes, everything is okay. I'm wearing this patch to prevent touching it and spreading it to you." He snarled his lip. "Although I'm sure you cretins are capable of developing such...maladies without my aid." He laughed shortly to himself.

"That's very kind. How do you think you got it? Someone else not wearing a patch?"

"Anyway, Hendershot, my personal health is not the reason for our meeting, although, I'm sure it would do you good to discuss yours. We're here to address this."

He laid a paper down, just like the one before: a new CIST score. Alan's knee started bouncing, and he tried to hide his angst with a heavy arm. Any confidence he'd come in with had vanished.

"Oh, yes. That."

"Yes. Go ahead. Take a look at your catastrophe."

He scanned the page until he found the number he was looking for: 6.67.

He laughed nervously. "Well, that's good. At least it wasn't a 6.666, yes? Number of the beast and all that."

"No. The system rounds to two digits."

"Oh."

"Do you have anything to say for yourself?"

"I did try to speed up. I really did. Are you sure that's the right number?"

"Yes. I am sure that a successful company knows how to calculate simple arithmetic. So, nothing? *I tried?*"

"I—I...maybe there's...I don't know. I'm not sure what happened." Alan felt his lip trembling and bit into it hard, angry at his tick.

"Very well. As I expected. I don't know why I thought that you would be capable of self-correction, but I suppose it's the inordinate amount of grace I offer to all of you. In that same reasoning, yet again, I offer you a chance to find a new path. There are consequences to your actions, however, and that is why I have been forced to remove you from the front staff."

"What—what do you mean?"

"Beginning tomorrow, you will be taken under the wing of the night staff. As Raphl is currently on vacation, Hilda will be taking you under her wing. Perhaps she can make use of your tediousness."

"I'm going to be a night stocker?"

"Yes. Beginning tomorrow, as I've already said. I would have you start tonight after your cashiering shift, but unfortunately, due to dictatorial workplace laws, I cannot do that. Your first shift will start at 8 p.m. tomorrow."

"I'm off tomorrow."

"Yes, you're off from 8 a.m. to 8 p.m."

"But...that's...are you sure there's nothing—"

"Enough. It's already been decided. Now go down there and enjoy your last day at your register. Your last day in the sun."

Vick smiled a twisted, perverted smile and stared at him as he left. Alan left with a grey feeling in the pit of his stomach like he'd just knelt at the altar of a cheap god that couldn't afford his own sacrifices.

***

There were three minutes left in his break, and Alan spent them with Gandalf, Bilbo, Balin, Thorin, and all the other dwarves in the house of Beorn. It was another part of the book that always seemed to cheer him up, when Beorn recognizes that even though he's not a huge fan of dwarves (by any measure), they can find common ground in their hatred of goblins. That, and the feast they enjoyed had been deliciously written.

He skimmed through it now, not reading completely, but just hitting the highlights to remind himself exactly as it was told. Initially, it had the intended effect. He thought about his dreams, about Imp Lode and his friends there, and how much better it was to experience all of it rather than just read it in a book. He knew the cheer from reading of such tales would soon be dwarfed by experiencing it himself.

But then, the more he thought about it, the more it upset him. He would be stocking groceries at night now. How would he sleep? Sure, he'd probably get shut eye during the day, but what if it wasn't good enough? What if it was only a half-sleep, too warped and fractured from a neglected circadian rhythm to provide him the zen he needed to dream, to really *dream*? The thought was annoyingly persistent.

The dream had been...well, it had been all that he had lately. If you, like most people, don't particularly enjoy your dreams (sure, you have a neat one now and then, but mostly, they're chases and deaths and all that nonsense), then imagine if all you had left was your dreams. No more waking life. That's how Alan felt, here, stuck in his head, considering the possibility that his adventurous nights might be over.

He returned to his register, but his mind was elsewhere. As a young man no more than thirty came through his line with a lot of baby food, cheese sticks, and milk, Alan considered the prospect of homelessness. He had enough money for another month of rent. He could probably afford some frozen dinners and peanut butter for all that time, too. What if he just slept on the street after that?

He swiped some pureed green beans and pureed butternut squash over the scanner.

No, that didn't make any sense. If he was only leaving his job to get better sleep, he doubted that a sleeping bag on the street corner would provide that. But, maybe it would? What if he drugged himself every night to fall asleep? *That could do it.*

Drugs seemed easier to come by once you were homeless, and Alan let that thought become a blanket, slowing his tailspin, if only for a moment.

***

"But you don't *have* to keep it, Mikey. Do you really think you're going to buy a Frosty and three large fries anytime soon? It expires in a week."

"Well, that's not the point. Look—maybe Alan might need it. Alan, do you want a flyer of Wendy's coupons? There's over $37 of savings inside. I haven't used a single one."

Micah and Sarah were at the kitchen table sorting through the mail that had piled up in the cardboard box that sat next to the front door.

It was really just a dump box. Neither one of them opened anything unless it had URGENT stamped on it in red ink. Sometimes more than just mail made its way in—really any paper that was in your hands when you entered the house and needed to put somewhere.

"Nah, that's all right. I don't usually use any coupons unless it's something for free."

"What about a free order of chicken nuggets with two bacon cheeseburgers?" Micah asked naively.

"Well, then I would still be buying the two cheeseburgers. I don't think I should make any purchases bigger than a kids' meal anytime soon, anyway."

Micah dropped the ad, devoting his full attention. "What do you mean, bro?"

"It's nothing. Don't worry about."

"Well, for sure it is. But tell me anyway."

"I got moved to night stocking because I wasn't checking people out quickly enough. I guess I don't have the greatest job security right now."

Sarah smiled pompously. "Well, you can't really expect job security in an entry-level position for high schoolers, can you?"

"Yeah, thanks for the advice."

"Bro, don't worry about it. You're like the smartest guy I know. They'd be crazy to fire you. I bet you know more about...cashiering and stuff than anyone there."

"I mean...I don't know. There's not a lot to know."

"For sure, see? You don't even think it's that big of a deal. Sort through some mail with us, it'll get your mind off it. Zen, you know? There's already a pile for you right there."

"Eh, that's okay. I think I'll just go—"

"What else do you have to do? Come on, we haven't really gotten to talk in days."

"All right."

"For sure."

Alan took a seat next to his pre-sorted stack, which he soon realized was most of the junk mail, any stray trash from the box, and then a couple of things addressed to him. He rifled through the first twenty items and sent them all to the graveyard pile on the floor.

"So, Sarah, how is cosmetology school going?"

Alan wasn't exactly sure if that was what her school was called. He really wasn't even sure if she was still going. He was bad at talking to Sarah, not least because he did not like it.

She stuck a finger in her hair and twirled a strand around it, as her eyes widened how eyes widen and glance down when you don't really want to respond to something. "Oh, yeah. It's going like really great, I guess. You know, all of the teachers seem to think that I'm like top of the class or something, but I'm like *I'm really not that smart, it just comes naturally to me.* But they don't even believe me."

"Yeah, I bet that would be hard. Are you going to start cutting Micah's hair for him?"

"Oh...well, I think that I could totally do it, but like Micah is sort of a girl when it comes to his hair. He won't let me near it." She cocked her head and looked at him playfully.

"For sure, for sure." Micah was distracted by a leaflet that he held in his hand. He looked up at Alan and slowly slid it across the table to him. "Here."

In Loving Memory, Howard J. Hendershot, 1944-1992. Ugly cursive across the top with a cartoon cross on one side and a dove with an olive branch on the other. Below the text was his dad's high school graduation photo.

The funeral program was wrinkly and shedding from a soaking. Not from tears, but from snow. It had been cold as shit that day, Alan remembered. They buried his dad at the church cemetery two days after he'd died. Closed casket. They were in such a hurry to get him in the ground before the blizzard that Alan hadn't even seen his dad after the hospital. It's hard to say goodbye to somebody fifteen minutes after you found out they got hurt. Suppose there wasn't much they could do though; the coroner said the accident had done more damage than was worth the mortician's effort. They still tried to charge his mom a rush fee to do it anyway. What a load of bullshit.

He remembered it all. He'd been at work when it happened. Can you believe that? He was getting yelled at for the garbage bags being the wrong price (really the customer had gotten a 48 count instead of a 20 count), when Vick came to tap him on the shoulder. What a thing to be doing while your dad is dying in the back of an ambulance. Explaining the price difference in bulk fucking garbage bags to some schmuck paying with a metal bank card that couldn't give less of a damn what his final cost is anyway.

That was the only time Alan had ever seen Vick let someone use a store phone for a personal reason. He was still an asshole about it though. He handed the phone to Alan and then tapped his wristwatch (a velcro, workout-banded one for middle-aged men convincing themselves their life will improve with a gym membership).

"Hey...Alan...is that you?" His mom was crying between every word.

"Yeah, what is it? What's wrong?"

"It's your dad," she breathed hard here, and he wasn't sure if she would say anything else. "There was...an accident at...at his work."

"Is he okay?"

"They...his boss called...I'm not sure."

"Okay. Okay, where are you? Are you with him? I can leave, just tell me where to go."

"We're going to...to St. Giles...I have to let you go now so we can leave the house."

"Okay, I'll be there as soon as I can."

Alan hadn't told Vick he was leaving. He just dropped the phone on his register and abandoned it, his lane light still on. It was surprising he didn't get fired for that, or at least reprimanded. I guess even guys like Mr. Vick have a small soul left. Kind of like the Grinch.

The hospital was weird. Alan walked into huge sliding glass doors on a side of the building that he couldn't tell was front, back, or side.

There were people sitting all around in uncomfortable chairs, talking quietly to those next to them. No one was laughing.

Now and then a nurse would walk through two swinging doors on the left side with a clipboard and mumble somebody's name. Nobody was happy to go in. They'd just say well here we go. Let's do it.

On the back wall, there were a few plexiglass windows with people behind them. They all wore scrubs, too, but they weren't taking blood or fixing hearts. They just sat there typing away on keyboards without letting their eyes wander anywhere else. One woman looked a little less intimidating than some others.

"Hi, I'm looking for my dad. Um, Howard Hendershot. He came here on an ambulance."

She offered tired eyes and no condolences. He couldn't blame her. He was just another customer coming through her line.

"One minute."

He stood there biting his tongue and tapping his foot. He got tired of that and tried to breathe slow. It didn't work.

"We don't have a Howard Hendershot in a room. You're sure he came here?"

"This is St. Giles?"

"Yes."

"Yeah, can you check one more time? Please."

She pretended to type in the name again and waited long enough to act like the search had failed.

"Sorry, hun."

"Well...do you know where to look? Where I can look?"

"Maybe the ambulance hasn't gotten here yet. Outside those doors and to your right, that's where they unload."

"Okay, thank you."

Outside there wasn't anything but a whole lot of cracked concrete and dead plants. No ambulances, but he saw the sign where they'd pull up. He sat on a bench that was covered in bird shit and laid his elbows on his knees again to keep them from tapping too much. Alan felt like he had to poop, like that feeling of something looming you get in your stomach that makes your body want to empty itself. He felt his heart, just as fast as when he'd hung up the phone.

Then he heard the door slam, far away, but within earshot. He found the car, an old GMC Jimmy, the family car. His mom got out and faced him. She was crying. She was walking slow. Why was she walking so slow?

He ran to her and held her. He didn't want to let her go. Through sobs she told him that his dad was already dead. They walked to the ambulance. It's weird seeing ambulance EMTs taking it easy, moving slow. It makes you feel bad. They patted Alan on the back and opened up the doors.

He stepped up into the cabin. His dad lay there, mask on his face for air, cords all plugged up into his arms. He didn't look good. He looked smashed up and broken. Alan cried really hard and didn't care that the EMTs saw him. They closed the doors just a little and left him alone. He buried his head in the pillow next to his dad and bawled his eyes out. He said he loved him more times than he could count, but it didn't feel the same. It would never feel the same again. He would have traded a million of those times just to say it to him once more when he was still there, still looking, still hearing.

The next day a lot of people brought casseroles and crock-pots to their house. That was the last day he'd been home. None of them tasted too good, but he wouldn't have felt right enjoying food, anyway. What a stupid time to eat something that tastes good. He wanted to eat dirt and dishwater and never feel anything again. Guys from his dad's work came and just looked at them. They said nothing and stared at their shoes if anyone talked to them. He wasn't mad at them. He didn't know what happened. It was ruled an accident. Who gives a shit. He just wanted his dad.

Everyone stayed for way too long. They all asked him stupid questions about life and his plans, like any of that mattered. Like the last date that he went on mattered, if he'd gone on a last date. They told him how great his dad was like he didn't already know it, like he didn't know it better than anyone else. He hated it all.

The funeral. The snow fell like God had ripped open a pillow and was just throwing the stuffing down. Everyone was freezing. He was glad. Everyone should be miserable at a funeral. Their pastor spoke like his dad went to church all the time and read his Bible every day. He didn't. Why'd he have to lie like that? Couldn't he just say that he believed there was a God, and that was that? Everyone acts like the dead are so holy, he hated it. His dad would have hated it. His dad was great regardless of whether he spent every Sunday in a church pew.

"You okay, Alan?"

He put the funeral program back down on the table.

"Yeah, just didn't expect to find that."

"I can't imagine what that's like, but you know I'm here for you, bro."

"Yeah."

Alan stared at the photo of his dad on the front. That guy knew exactly what he wanted to do. He went to his trade school, got the job he wanted, met his mom, and started a family. Then it all got taken away from him anyway.

"Hey, me and Sarah are gonna hit the hay. Don't worry about cleaning any of this up. We'll get it tomorrow."

Sarah scowled. "Really? Micah, I do not want to clean tomorrow. That's why I told you we had to clean today."

"For sure, babe. For sure." The pair walked to Micah's room, and he turned around right before he closed the door. "Seriously, don't clean any of this up."

Alan retired to his bedroom and reflected upon how awful the day had been. *Really.* That's how he'd classify it. *Really awful.*

The loneliness crept in again, and he wanted nothing more than to be laying in that pit, next to his friends. He couldn't dream alone, definitely not tonight. Who knew how many more opportunities he'd even have to visit Imp Lode. He was on the night crew now, the permanent ice shift.

He updated his notebooks again. The note-taking and recounting of events had become one of his favorite parts of the day. It was as though he were making all the dreams real. If he saved them in his journal, then they existed, they became real. At first it had seemed like a chore, but now, as he wrote how he had saved the life of Rime, he felt such a deep satisfaction that he went into way more detail than necessary. It was like saying I love you when the person is still alive to hear it.

He talked about how the water tasted in his mouth, how his wet clothes felt on his body. It was strange, writing something so fantastic, so other-worldly, that he had lived and experienced. It made everything count.

He laid in bed in a bumbled shape, closed his eyes, took a deep breath, and he was there—

—awake again.

XIV. Imp shit

The ground was wet, slimy even, beneath the heavy, webbed feet of the avimu. Even now, well outside of the tree shadows' grasp, they were hopping and fumbling over fallen limbs and debris.

The storm had come and gone. Although he didn't mean to skip the time, it had happened anyway, as a grey, depraved landscape was surely the last thing Alan's subconscious yearned for after the day he'd had. He wouldn't have tried to skip it if he had really thought about it. It seemed like quite a risk to do a time jump during something so dangerous.

Everyone's clothing was wet and clumpy, full of mud and drying rain, and they were all nearly as filthy and smelly as the birds. They'd spent the night in the ditch, fetching wet blankets from the avimu when the rain slowed, and woke cold and soggy, for there was no dry wood to light for a fire. Nobody was particularly happy as they rode out, hardly thankful to be alive, but the fresh sight of Flour was sure to be medicinal for their stale eyes.

The budding ridges of Funus were not far away in front of them. At least it seemed that way. But at their bottoms, and running all the way to the treeline, was a grand meadow of a beauty few of them ever saw, especially Alan. The grasses were a fresh green all lulling in a light breeze at the height of their calves, whisking chilly drops of dew upon their pants and shoes. The flowers stood taller still, their new buds just breaking over the horizon of grass. In their palettes were born the finest colors of autumn, some a golden-orange the shade of a sun ray shining through a nearly expired leaf, others a cardinal red flittering about like a juicy strawberry or ripe tomato. Among the vibrantly colored were some others, dull, but magnificent in shape and artistry. They were white, unfurled and pointed on each petal, with yellow spots like drops of paint scattered upon their broadsides.

As they traveled through, bending and brushing the flowers as they went, sweet perfumes joined the visual splendor, and for a moment, they were all thankful for the storm.

"Hey Riddle?" Alan looked behind him to their avimu, where Riddle was grinning ear to ear and picking flowers within his reach.

"Yeah?"

"Do you know why all these flowers grow here? Like, is there a story about it?"

Rime groaned from in front of him, wringing out a knit cap in his hands still soaked from the rain. "Of course there is." He paused. "Wait, is there? I don't think I've ever heard it."

Riddle smiled and crossed his arms. "Hm. I truly don't know. Wouldn't it be nice to have a companion that knew of things such as these?"

Rime rolled his eyes and turned back to the front. Kard was far behind them, and not on his avimu either, for he had been running along at the level of the ground, picking some flowers and putting them in a bag he wore on his waist. He shouted up as he hopped back on the bird, "I know this one! Shall I tell it?"

He was with them now, panting. "Did you hear me, should I tell the story?"

"It's up to Rid, he's the master and keeper of tales." Rime said.

"When has it ever been up to me? If it was up to me, you would have heard many more stories than you have so far. Go ahead, Kard."

"Right...well, I'm not the best at this sort o'thing. Long time ago, I guess it was...what, maybe a few hundred years?" He looked at Rid expecting help. Rid grinned.

"Ah, forget the whole thing. I'm sure I'd not tell it right as he'd tell it. Was a good one, though, too. Lots of magic and little dainty things of that sort."

Rid struggled not to snicker. "No, do go on, Kard. I only found the experience amusing, not your struggle to recall the date."

"Well...that's not really the—hold on."

"Kard, I humbly submit to your narration. Please, go on."

But Kard was not listening anymore. He was nearly hidden from their eyes, knelt down in the grasses and flowers, examining something that lay within.

"Kard, let's get a move on! We can't keep loitering for you to catch up with the group." Rime had not slowed their avimu.

"Ye all should really come over here. Stell. Rid, maybe. I d'know for certain that this is what I think it is."

Stell looked over Kard's shoulder as Rid was having a trifling time removing his left foot from a loop on the saddle.

"I'm afraid that's exactly what you think it is."

"And what's that?"

"You tell me."

"Well, to me it looks an awful lot like a bit of imp dust, but I don't know that I've ever seen..." His voice trailed off and he watched Stellis nod damningly. "It's a legend, idn't it, Stell? Or, mighty rare at least?"

"It's difficult to say. I do not know the area well enough."

"But I can't hardly believe it. We came this way east not that long ago. An imp...I mean—I never in all my years would have expected to see..."

Rime had dismounted now and was lingering near the pair, just in front of Alan.

"I don't believe it, but sure as I'm Rid's pretty brother, that's imp dust. You and I both know there's nothing else it could be."

There, in the grass, some of it painted along the blades, some on the ground, some seemingly suspended in the air, was a golden power, reflective and metallic like gold but far more enchanting. The air smelled sour and acidic, like the taste in your mouth right before you vomit.

"What's imp dust?"

Kard, nearly bewitched, looked up at Alan. *"What's imp dust?"*

The others shared Kard's disbelief and gave him the same look they had produced every time he had asked a question he quickly realized he shouldn't have.

Riddle joined them now, nodding silently at the specter. "You really don't know what imp dust is, Alandriel? I mean, even in Reul, I would have thought they surely would have—"

Stellis calmly cut him off. "It is not our duty to inspect the extent of his knowledge. He does not owe us a biography. There are far reaches of our world where things like this are not known." She nodded to him, but he got the feeling that even she wanted to question him.

Rime patted him on the back. "Well, bud. Do you know what a groot bear is? Or...any kind of bear, really."

He didn't. "Yeah."

"Okay, so if you see a heaping pile of groot bear shit in the wood, you know a groot bear is nearby. You know that you should probably tread quickly and carefully, aye?"

He nodded.

"Well, this ain't exactly imp *shit*, but it's the same idea."

Kard shivered and hopped back upon his avimu. "How are you at tracking imps, Rime?"

"Well...tracking imps is a bit of a...what's the word, Rid? Ah, ironic. It's a bit of an ironic statement."

"That's not the word."

"It's not all that right, you know, not possible? Ironic. I've never met a man that can track an imp. Course, imp dust is really most contained within fairytales nowadays, so I don't suspect many I've met have ever had the opportunity."

"Do you think it's nearby?"

"Hard to say. I'm told they move bloody fast, but the dust don't hang around too long. There's no way of telling which way its headed, though I'd assume the way we came. Stories say they can smell men. All the more reason to quit staring at it and make for that mountain."

Alan had fallen absent from the conversation, distracted nearly to hypnosis by the color of the imp dust. He *knew* that color. Absent-mindedly, he felt for the gold cat's eye marble in his pocket to see if it was still there. It was. He began to pull it out to compare the colors, but decided against it.

Alan followed Rime back to the avimu hesitantly. "If they came from the mountain, won't there be more there?"

"Not over the mountain, friend. Not if we're quick and lucky. In the pass that we'll take there's an old keep. More of a tavern these days. If we get there, we'll at least have some walls. Besides, if anybody knows a thing or two about imps, it's Dard."

Stellis nodded, providing silent approval for Rime's suggestion. Alan could see that she was shaken though, as she took several more long looks at their surroundings before continuing on.

He had more questions that he wanted to ask about imps and mountains and Dard, as well as questions he was afraid to ask about the marble in his pocket, but he decided they could wait. Instead, they rode. Rime pushed the avimu with a fury that Alan had not yet seen, and the others did their best to keep up.

The breeze of Flour grew more pleasant the deeper into the meadows they got, and soon they found themselves equidistant from the forest at their backs and the red peaks looking down on them from the front. At least, that's the way it seemed. Their ride had been so intense that he could taste the hot, salty sweat on his upper lip just from the struggle to keep a grip on the bird, and he did not understand how Rime had endured.

It grew quieter now with only the sound of hard breaths—from Rime, from Alan, and most of all, from Mina, who did at the very least seem to enjoy the change of scenery. Every few minutes during a slow in the pace she would lift her head and inhale sharply before chirping. It was the sea breeze in the air. She could feel it, and so did Alan, though none of them could see it.

It was odd. The mountains seemed to be knowingly concealing the sea. Or, maybe not the sea, but something. Even from their great distance, they could see little flitters of movement across a ridgeline. It could have been a falling tree or a herd of goats climbing a cliff face, but there never seemed to be enough detail available. The mountain kept its distance, and with it, its secrets.

Not too long after when the sun was beating down on them hard, they took rest near a small stream that ran off from the River Mere. Rime and Alan, of course, arrived first and unloaded some provisions. They were running lower on supplies, but had some vosvudu and fresh breads they had taken from Drireford. Today would be the end of their *finer* dining.

They laid out a blanket where the grasses were lower, and they could hear the sound of the stream running. It was wet from the night before, and the damp felt good on their hot, sore butts. After a moment of privileged meat selection, Stellis and Riddle arrived, followed in tow by Kard, who was breathing like an iron lung.

They tossed the rest of the giblets to Mina, Drake, and Dazzle, the latter of which, not unlike his master, hogged the bounty. They all ate slowly, both to regain some energy and take in their surroundings, for this was a beautiful part of Imp Lode, and they were all aware of it.

In the midst of one hearty bite, Riddle said, chewing, "Well... Kard...if you're not gonna...tell the story of Flour," he swallowed loudly, "then I will."

Kard had already finished eating and was reclining on his back, peaceful and lulling. "I would never take that joy from ye, mate. Have at it."

"So, Kard was not far off with his time. It was a few hundred years ago. In those days, the men of Vissen held much more land than they do today. It was not uncommon for them to fish all the way to the boundaries of Kolosso. Now they keep themselves further north, where the fish are just learning to swim, and there's no danger of other creatures fighting them for their haul."

"I'm sorry," Alan said, "not to interrupt, but are all the great stories from long ago? Nothing happened recently?"

"Well, the answer to that is two-fold. First, yes, all the stories describing how something got the way it is, most of them did happen long ago. But no, nothing much has happened recently, anyway. Or, that is to say, not much has been written about it. But I suppose, just because not much has been written, does not mean not much has happened. I have written about a great number of things that nobody has read."

"Perhaps," Rime began, "the length of your answer to that short question is reason for such."

"I do not disagree with you, brother. If your attention span is any indicator of the rest of men, my stories may often fall on fatigued ears." Rid smiled and continued. "Now, as I said, their lands stretched to the very ground that we walk on today. The stones that held up their houses could be found today, in many cases, with just a little digging, and in some, none at all. They were wiser men, wiser than they are today, and knew that fishing this far south in the River was still dangerous, though not as dangerous as Blackpool. So the men that lived here tended to crops in the fertile ground more often than they ventured to the water."

"Chief among those crops were malts and grains. It is said that the fresh bread from Vissen could fill an empty belly for three days. Although their crop was bountiful, and the ground sympathetic to their wishes, it too required rest, just as we do now. In the offseason, the men would fill the plots with flowers, beautiful ones the colors of crimson and the Sun, quite like the ones you see around you today."

"Then, one day the men left. All the buildings were torn down or destroyed. No one recorded the why, only the before and after. If any survived what happened, they did not make it to their northern brothers alive to tell the tale, or if they did, they have kept their secrets well. It was a time of rest when they were vanished, and no grain or malt lay in the ground, only the flowers. So they spread, left untouched and unhindered by hungry men. It became beautiful in the absence of people."

***

They all agreed that it had been a good story, even Rime, begrudgingly, and they packed up their things and mounted their birds once again. The plan they had all agreed upon was to get as close to the base of the mountains as they could by nightfall, and during the next morning they would venture northeast along the foothills until they found the path for the pass.

They rode nearly as hastily as before if not for their full bellies, Alan thought. There was silence once again between the riders, as all had become separated nearly out of earshot by their driver's paces, and Rime was not much for small talk along the path.

He thought about his other life, the one he did not want to go back to. It was strange, thinking of it here. That life seemed like some far-off place. It seemed like a dream that he would never have again if he didn't want to. But he knew that wasn't the case. He knew that the opposite was more likely, what with the new schedule he would have. Sure, maybe in a week or two his sleep cycle would be back to normal, but what would he have missed in the meantime? How big of a time jump would that be? Would his friends here forget about him? Did he have any control over it?

He felt hopeless, there, in one of the most beautiful places of Imp Lode. How was he carrying around a dark cloud? He'd lost the sense of joy he'd had when he first came. Leaving it all behind, what was the point? There was one person he wished he could ask for advice, but he knew that was an impossibility.

After a while of thinking without thinking anything that he liked, their shadows had grown long in front of them. They searched for a clearing near the small hills which were no more than a chit away, according to Rime. Alan still did not have a good idea what this distance was, but unless his eyes deceived them, they were very close.

Soon they came upon a barren patch where the ground was not too saturated, with quick access to a stream. The red peaks loomed on their western horizon, and they assembled kindling for a fire and cleared out a patch for sitting and sleeping nearby.

Stellis arrived, with Riddle tending to Drake, both of whom were utterly exhausted. Not far off, Kard could be heard whistling a tune that Alan recognized as a slower ballad of the one he had whistled in the ditch during the storm. This version was equally pretty, and surely more calming. On arrival, he immediately opened the cold pot that hung above the newborn fire and stopped whistling.

"Ye boys got here so fast, I would have thought there would be a fine stew ready for my lips once I got in." His belly shook with laughter.

"Your gut may not be too happy with you, tonight, friend. We are low on provisions until we meet a good tradesman or post. We've got not much more than breads and roots. If you can lend some of the flowers you picked today, I reckon that we can render a stew, though it might not be the best."

"No vosvudu left?"

"Not any. Though it would have soured by now, anyway. Do not kid about your ignorance if you want to keep customers, silly butcher."

"I will go fetch us some water," Riddle volunteered. "If all else fails, we can fill ourselves with that. We've gone to bed on less."

And so they had. But the stew was, perhaps, slightly worse than Rime had wagered, though slightly better than the rest had imagined by the color. But it was hot, and it was something. They ate it in big gulps and soaked their breads to chew them. It seemed quite alright once they had their fill, but Alan would not have minded a frothing pint of elder ale.

They all reclined to resting positions. Kard, on his back, as usual, Stellis looking up at the stars and scratching notes in a book, and the others involved themselves with the fire.

"So, Alandriel," Riddle said, "is it everything you dreamed that it would be?"

The wording caught Alan off guard for a moment. "Is it what?"

"The land south of Reul. Is it everything you hoped? Has it quenched your reasons for leaving?"

"Oh, yes. I suppose it has. The land here is unlike anything I've ever seen."

Alan looked out along the starlit meadow, feeling the wind flick his hair back and forth.

Rime glanced at him through the high licks of flames. "You spend some more time here, I'd be keen to have you on a hunt with me. If that's ever something you'd consider after this is all over."

"Sure, I would. I do hope it all gets there." He fiddled with a pebble in his hand. "Over."

"Well, it will end one way or another. All things do. I just hope it's the end of the right things and not the wrong."

Riddle was fishing a long stick around in the embers, making sparks dance higher than the flames. "It's strange, living during this. It almost doesn't feel real."

"Do you think it'll be dangerous?" Alan asked. "When we get to where we're going?" He did his best to hide his fears and said the words slowly.

"That's hard to say, friend. It was bad when we left. If things have gone like they have elsewhere, it'll be a whole lot worse when we return. There's a big mix of folks in Oognysse. Usually a good thing, until this." Rime stood up and walked away from the fire to relieve himself.

"So Rid, I don't mean to make you tell another story, but what is the deal with imps? And their dust? That's bad?"

"Oh, it's bad, yes. I don't know how much you already know about imps, but the dust is an absolute sign that imps have borne from the mountain. If you see the dust, they're out. They're wandering."

"That's just it. I know next to nothing about imps." He watched Rid's face reflect the orange hues of the firelight, deep in thought. The others had nodded off or lost interest in their conversation. "Rid, could I show you something?"

Riddle looked at him curiously, recognizing the change in key of Alan's voice. He nodded.

Alan pulled the gold cat's eye from his pocket, angling it in front of the fire to pass the light through its beauty, creating a glimmer. "Have you seen anything like this?"

Riddle beheld the marble with great curiosity, forgetting to breathe as he watched the sparks float up around the marble.

"I—I can't be sure. I feel as though I have, but…" He stopped in the middle of the thought, devoting all attention to the marble.

"Could I—erm, could I hold it?" Alan nodded and stood to pass the marble over the fire. Riddle's hand shook as he reached for it, knocking the marble into the embers. He gasped, but Alan acted quickly, kicking it out with his feet. The stirring of the smoke irritated his eyes, but as he wiped away the tears, he swore he saw the gold inside the marble begin to swirl as though it were liquid.

"I'm so sorry, Alandriel! This is why I am not the hunter! I hope I did not damage it."

Alan felt the marble gingerly with a finger, wary of heat, but it had cooled. He picked it up and held it out in an open palm to Riddle.

"Not a worry at all, I think it would take much more than that to hurt this guy!"

Riddle nodded apologetically, not entirely convinced.

"So you've never seen anything like it? The imp dust made me think of the gold inside it, see?"

Rid took the marble in his hand and looked it over cautiously. "I can see why. Would you…" He lowered his head. "Would you mind if I borrowed this tomorrow? Purely to make a drawing of it in my book."

"Of course. I doubt it's worth much. I've had it for a long time."

Riddle slipped the marble in his pocket and nodded graciously, but kept an air of uneasiness about him. He returned his attention to the fire and stirred the embers again with a stick. "They're devils. Imps. Mean, nasty, and not a good part to their soul. At least, that's the way the stories go. A few strange ones here and there. I think there's a lot about them we don't know. I've recorded a few of the tales. Well, not tales per se; many of them are niltlore."

Alan could see the glimmer of lore talk smothering Rid's guilt of nearly destroying his marble. "Niltlore?"

"Old word. Really it just means a scary story that's supposed to teach you something. Some people," he nodded over to Rime, "think they're all a hoax. Or, maybe a little bit of truth, but mostly for mothers to keep their children well-behaved. I'm sure none of us have ever seen an imp. Now we tell ourselves that they're just stories to tell around the fire; stories that man made their morality from."

"But you don't think that?" Alan asked.

"I think every story starts with a truth. You just have to decide how deep that truth is hidden."

Rime came back to the fire, yawning. "You going on again, brother?"

"I asked him. About the imps."

"Ah." Rime's face was stony and quiet.

Alan waited for another minute, enjoying the fire and the company before he interrupted it all.

"I don't know the best way to say this to you all, but I don't know if I can continue."

Stellis put her book down. "What do you mean by this?"

"There are...obligations, from where I came from. They might pull me away. I don't want it to happen, but if it does, I don't know how to stop it."

Alan chose his words carefully, intentionally avoiding any mention of night-stocking or sleep schedule.

"What do you mean?" Rime asked, frustrated that he could not understand. "Someone is hunting you down?"

"Sort of. I—I don't know how best to explain it. I just don't want you all to be surprised if it happens."

"If what happens, mate?" Kard was sitting up now.

"If they take me. If I disappear."

"I'd like to see them try." Rime pulled a knife from his belt and held it close to the fire. "You are not in danger as long as we are near to you, Alandriel. Are you indebted to these men?"

"No. Not quite. They just...well, I'm sorry. I shouldn't have brought it up." He felt angry with himself for even mentioning it. "I just...you all have come to mean a fair amount to me, though it's been only a few days. I wouldn't feel right if I didn't let you know. I will do all I can to stop it."

Stellis looked at him, solemnly, but almost knowingly. "As I have said before, you do not owe us explanations to your past. But I will not stop you from sharing it. If you are being hunted, we will stand together with you. Even if your eyes were not as special as they are, you have proven your heart. *You* have come to mean something to us."

"I may not be the best with a blade," Rid said humbly, "but I will slice and dice any who try to harm a friend who listens to my tales."

"Though he might do more damage than good, my brother does mean well. We will keep our eyes on your back." Rime smiled pleadingly. "Do not lose sleep over this."

"Aye, Rime is right." Kard's ugly teeth glimmered in the firelight. "If all goes well, in a day or two we will have fresh ale in our stomachs. That will lull you."

Alan nodded and laughed with the others and felt a warmth, even though the fire was dying. When he lay down after sharing some more tales and jokes, his mind was unburdened. They did not understand what he was trying to tell them, but, who knows, maybe they could fight it off. Maybe he was just exhausted. But it made sense to him, there, beneath the stars, surrounded by the flowers and quietly babbling stream, that this place, the people here—they could fight off an eternal ice shift. They could.

XV. The ice age

Upside down. The world seemed that way to Alan Hendershot.

His car was driving better than it ever had. He had spent all of his waking hours at home, rather than Elmwood's, making detailed maps and bestiaries for a world that he only traveled to in dreams. Even his arrival at work had been twisted.

The moon was out, not the sun. The parking lot was practically empty. Inside, the last cashier on shift, Renee, was counting out the coins at her register. There was little sound but for the low hum of neon lights and display coolers and soft jazz coming from the store PA system. He didn't see Vick, nor did he want to, and instead followed the trail of bright red popsicle juice to the back of the store, where he assumed he would find Hilda.

It felt as though he were following the blood trail of wild game, probably the tomfoolery of a child without a keen eye watching over them. He thought back to the traps he had made with Rime. It was strange. It had only been a few days ago, but here, in the real world, it all felt so far away and unreachable.

"Oy. You must be the new meat."

Hilda stood before him, or over him, really. She was a towering six and a half feet tall, pushing seven. He wondered how many witchits that would be. Or itchits? Maybe. Her hair was the color of dirty carrots just pulled out of the ground, and freckles covered her face. She wore an Elmwood's polo, but had cut off the sleeves at her shoulder, probably, Alan assumed, to sport her tattoo: a tire tread ring around the arm with *P23* and a cross above it.

She was already talking before he realized he'd been staring at it for too long.

"Psalm 23. Shadow of death. My MC. You got a cage or you ride?"

"Um...I guess a cage? I have a Volkswagen."

She laughed. "That's good. You're young. Less squids on the road never been a bad thing." She dropped the box of shredded cheeses she'd been holding and pulled out a folded piece of paper. "Hendershot, Alan. I'm sure Vick's been riding your ass. Says you're kinda slow. I guess you know Raphl already. This work isn't for speed. It's for putting shit where it goes and in the right way. You do that, we won't have any problems." She looked him up and down. "You own a jacket? Hoodie?"

"Yeah."

"All right, well unless you've got warmer blood than Satan, you're gonna want to bring one next time. Spend a lot of time in the back. We call it Laska. Guess that came from Alaska, but that's a lot of syllables. You hear that?"

"Okay. I'll bring it tomorrow. Sorry, I didn't know."

"Right. I'll have you doing baking, bread, and cans tonight. That'll keep you warm as much as possible. Course, Vick usually cuts the heat off at night, so I can't promise a whole lot." She led him into the back towards a smaller warehouse room on the left side. "Most of your dry goods will be in here. Bread comes twice a week, Monday and Thursday. Most of the stuff is obvious. Put it where the other shit is. There's a sheet on each pallet with the inventory. Highlight it after you stock it, then throw it in this bin. If it's a new product, it's already underlined in red. Don't worry about those yet, just leave them. Raphl will have to show you how to do the labels and all that other shit. Hear that?"

"Sure. So just do everything that goes on those aisles?"

"Yep. New stuff goes behind the old stuff. All common sense really if you've ever shopped in a store. And kid?"

"Yeah?"

"Take it easy. It's not a big store. Vick ain't here at night, so we don't need to be breaking our necks to get cream of mushroom soup on the shelf. You smoke?"

"Nope."

"All right. Go out and look at the stars or something every couple hours. Get some fresh air. Makes it easier. You'll be tired for the first week or so until you learn to sleep when the sun is up."

***

Alan started with the breads since they were closest to the door. On top, there were a few loaves of whole wheat with seeds. The brand sported a grandmother figure with an electric guitar - Granny's Grains. He spotted the other neon purple bag tips easily enough, slid the older bread forward and put the new stuff in the back. Not too bad.

After Texas Toast, two different types of Italian, English muffins, 12 grain (which differed from multi-grain, but he wasn't sure how), rye, honey wheat, honey oat, thin-sliced honey oat, white, giant white, country white, soft white, and finally, a "Mountain Man" sourdough that had a blue man playing banjo (maybe the son of Granny Grain), the first pallet was done. He'd never bought any of them. He hardly ever shopped for bread, but when he did, it was plain wheat. No frills, seeds, wholesomeness, or old-fashioned charm about it. Plain wheat.

Without even realizing it, after finishing the aisle with some more bagels, breads, and a lot of buns, an hour had passed. Seemed mighty fast to be a third done with his day's work. He figured that as much as Mr. Vick wanted to turn the front of the store into a "big box" style speed machine, there wasn't a great way of doing the same with stocking. You couldn't stock more unless you sold more.

Heeding Hilda's advice, he went out back with a pastry that Miss Etta had left in his locker and sat on a pile of broken-down pallets, staring up at the stars. They looked a lot like the stars in Imp Lode, he decided. Stars never seemed to change, even in fantasy stories. Sure, now and then you might see a couple of extra moons or something in a movie, but stars were stars. Even in the wildest imaginations of authors and movie-set designers, a sky filled with stars was something they kept.

He thought about how there must be something to that. Then about how delicious the pastry was. It was a raspberry danish.

He licked some jam off his thumb and thought about the girl. The girl with the book. The girl that somehow started all of this and didn't even know it. He hadn't thought about her in a while, hadn't even cared, and he was proud of himself for giving up so quickly. But looking at the stars, he felt sentimental again. He'd never see her again. There was no way they'd cross paths. He was locked away now, in *Laska*, kept out of the public eye where no one could see how slow he scanned groceries. Had she ever thought about him again? Probably not, he figured.

He sighed, hoping for a shooting star or something that seemed good for wishing on. Something that could tell him what he wished for. That seemed more valuable. Who needs one wish? *I'd just like to know what my one wish should be.*

***

After two-and-a-half hours of sorting through canned peas and another two and a half or three of all the different salt and paprika, he realized he had underestimated the true chore of his task. When one company makes 37 different spices and seasonings, it's as if you're doing an issue of *Highlights* for every row you fill. Trying to find the reduced sugar form of the butter-flavored maple syrup was a challenge. But other times, his thoughts were free to wander, like when he had a whole case of the same brand of white flour to shove onto the bottom shelf, five-pound bags by five-pound bags.

What if I never see Imp Lode again?

He stowed his final empty pallet in the graveyard somewhere in the frozen depths of Laska, next to a white tub of long fish deep in a block of ice and another pallet fresh from the night truck stacked floor to head-height with different varieties of peanut butter.

He opened the door to the loading dock to take another brief reprise before offering to do anymore work. Hilda was already there, smoking a cigarette and looking at a magazine she held in one hand with the cover rolled behind it. He wasn't sure how she was reading it under the glow of the faraway security light. He could hardly make the cover out during a quick flutter of wind: American Iron Magazine.

"Done for the night?" She took one last draw and tossed it to the ground, smooshing it beneath a black boot.

"I finished those three aisles. Do you have anything else for me to do?"

She cracked a short laugh. "Kid, take it easy. Nobody will be at the store for hours. You can head home, or if you're really paranoid, hang out until quittin' time."

"Okay." He looked around and needed to break the silence. "Good magazine?"

"What? Oh. Yeah, it's fine." She took a long puff and eyed Alan thoughtfully. "I want a bonnie, but I have my buddy's old hog for now. I really just look at the pictures, myself."

"Is a bonnie a motorcycle?"

"Oh. Yeah, a real beautiful Brit. Hard to find around here. The British. They do a lot of things right. You hear that?"

"Hear what?" He looked around in the dark.

"Sorry. I mean, do you agree with my statement?" She coughed and laughed again.

"Oh, yeah. I guess so. I usually like British authors more than American. I think it's just easier that way with fantasy books, you know?" He shrugged. "I mean, hear that?"

She smiled. "You mean like how they write it?"

"Yeah, like it already sounds sort of fancy and far-off just because they describe things differently than we do."

"Hm. Never thought about that. Maybe that's why I like their bikes so much." She closed the magazine. "Hey kid, you any good at making things look pretty?"

"What do you mean?"

"I'm no good at it, but I'm supposed to make some sort of pyramid or something with all our overstock soda with the summer contests on it."

Summer soda sweepstakes. A contest where 1 in 10,000 win a new *Super* Nintendo Entertainment System when they began shipping in the fall. Half of the remaining contestants get diabetes, a sugar addiction, a mouth ulcer, rotten teeth, or some combination of the above. The pyramid felt like a temple built to these gods—living off humans having access to more sugar than their biology had planned for.

Their finished marvel was fifteen cases high with Yoohoos at the top since there were no gold-branded sodas. Vick had typed up the signs advertising the incredible deal, and with one plastered on each side, their creation was complete, ready for a mummified Pharoah of caffeine and carbonation. It was a simple design, just like every pyramid you've ever imagined or seen in a grocery store yourself.

Alan figured Hilda probably didn't need his help, unless she really didn't know the fundamentals of three-dimensional geometry, but he was glad she asked. It had occupied his mind more than stocking, and her "war stories" from her motorcycle club were real nail-biters.

They both took a great big step back and cracked open Mountain Dews that they had pulled from a smashed up case.

"Looks like those big ones."

"Like in Egypt?"

"Yeah, like the one the big cat lives in."

Alan took a big sip. "Yep, we definitely nailed the shape."

"Thanks for the help, kid. Oh, completely slipped my mind. Raphl left you a bag of some stuff when he was by before he left for vacation. Come grab it off the desk and you can head on home."

It was a brown paper bag with *Ronnie's Remedies* written on a paper tag stapled to the top. Inside, Alan found cellophane wrapped around a bunch of leaves that looked like basil (droom flume, he hoped) and a couple other cannisters with what he assumed to be some other odd items from the list.

For several reasons, Alan got home faster than he ever had before. First, he was wired on the caffeine from the Mountain Dew; second, his car was driving better than it ever had before (relative to his past experiences, an exotic sports car); and third, his excitement was at such a high level it was tangible. He'd spent the past 24 hours or more worrying about his sleeping arrangement and how he would ever return to normalcy with a night job. Well, if it worked for Willy the hound dog, surely it would work for him.

Once home, he emptied the contents of the bag onto his bed and found every item from the list accounted for. He was so happy he skipped to the kitchen to retrieve the rest of his ingredients and spread them, along with a plastic bowl and an old teakettle, all out on the table, shoving the forensic postal investigation remnants to the floor.

The amounts were crudely written, sometimes just numbers, other times *1 T* or *3 t*. He didn't know a lot about cooking, but translated these to the letters on a set of measuring spoons Micah's mom had dropped off at the house. After doing some mashing and cutting of more tedious ingredients, he had a bowl filled with his stock, which was certainly more than one batch of tea's worth.

The author had written *Freeze extra* at the end of the recipe, so, following those instructions, Alan stored away about 95% of the batch in the capable hands of Chef Bobby's Laska, and threw the rest in a steel strainer he found in a bottom cabinet. He didn't have any other way to infuse the tea, so he boiled water in a small pot just high enough for it to cover what was in the mesh strainer, and after five minutes he had a deep red, bubbling soup. It smelled strongly of dirt, chamomile, and maybe lavender.

He was in such a feverish state gathering up all his supplies to begin his usual regiment, that he nearly forgot his exhaustion entirely. Ever since he had started the dreams, every waking hour had become less and less cohesive.

By now, the sun was already warming up the dew drops idling on the grass outside. Soon it would breach the horizon.

Alan wanted to know the time (only to know how long he dreamed), and as he stuffed some noodles into his mouth, he ran back out to the living room to check the clock above the phone. But something else had him transfixed: a blinking light on the answering machine. His heavy eyes tracked from the light to his room door behind him, sleep-deprivation nearly making the decision irresolvable beneath a layer of fog.

He mashed the button.

"Hey baby." Guess who. "How are things going at work? I hope it's all going well. Please tell me if anything seems weird with your car after the repair work. I'll take care of it for you." A pause. "We decided on a day for dad's party. We were thinking two weeks from now, on the 9th. I have choir practice after church. You can just meet us at Pizza Inn if you want after that, or we could have cake and ice cream at home...or something like that. I really hope you think about it. It would mean a lot to your sister...and me. I hope your record player sounds like you imagined it would. Play one of dad's records on it for me. I love you."

A fifteen second pause where she forgot to hang up.

Then, muffled, "dagnabbit, I can never tell with this thing." *CLICK.*

The noodles tasted sweeter and blander in his mouth the more he chewed each bite: slowly, thoughtfully. They were missing a lot: fresh marinara sauce, a whole lot of that full-fat mozzarella cheese, and the warm buttery crust that was crisp on the bottom but tore apart like a cotton ball. Something in him, a very tiny little twinging inclination, was itching to go. Maybe it would be okay? He could talk to his mom and sister for an hour. He had saved a guy's life just last week, matter of fact. That would be a delightful story for dinner, right?

It wouldn't. Alan knew it wouldn't. He couldn't tell his mom he was enjoying his time asleep more than his time awake. He couldn't tell her he hadn't thought about colleges in weeks. He definitely couldn't tell her he got demoted to the night shift at work; he'd barely let himself believe it. The only way he would have made it through his dad's birthday was if his dad was actually there.

Boy, his dad would love to hear about Imp Lode. He'd love to go there.

He poured the tea into a *Branson, Missouri, You'll never want to leave!* mug, another of Micah's, and popped it into the microwave to heat it back up. It came out just as fragrant as when it was boiling on the burner.

There wasn't really any advice next to the recipe in the book, but he assumed the effects would be like those in the original section of the text. It would just help him dream better. If that was the case, he decided he should take it as close to falling asleep as possible.

He prepared his notes and read through the most recent events, iterating the campsite in Flour, as well as Rime, Rid, Kard, and Stellis. He took long sips of the tea in between the whispering, which at first interrupted his lulling, but soon became a catalyst, the tonic warming his belly and relaxing his muscles. It tasted a lot worse than it smelled, almost muddy, with sharp floral notes that would have belonged in a cold elder ale, but not something hot.

He kept sipping and continued whispering, reaching the bottom of the mug and laying himself flat. His mind felt hazy, muddled even, and when he closed his eyes, he couldn't withdraw his attention from the warping, fluid shapes on the inside of his eyelids. They were faster and warmer now, maybe vibrating, and danced like shadows of moths behind a lampshade.

His thoughts were more frantic, squirming back to the urgency of the remedy, of whether he could continue dreaming or he had seen his last of Imp Lode. The shapes grew faintly golden on his eyelids now, and he knew the Sun had found its way through his bedroom window. He felt like everything in his body was growing hot, burning from some old coals sitting at the bottom of an hourglass. It was all so abstract, but he didn't recognize the ethereality. The sleep hormones were already smothering the quickness and sensitivity of a waking mind, clouding his thoughts in ambiguity.

Beneath it all, there was still that pang. Like a small, bloating stomach ache plaguing your meal while you're trying to eat something delicious like good fried chicken. It was worry. It was anxiety. It was a longing, a sad yearning. A ghost that was buried in some deep grave down there at the bottom of the hourglass, somewhere beneath all those hot coals. If he only had a shovel, or a pick, even.

He needed water for the coals. Water to put them out so he could continue standing on them without burning himself. The stream, the one that had been so close to where he had fallen asleep last. It was cool and fresh. It was alive. He could hear it, whispering and mumbling, ever so faintly. Or was it crying?

XVI. Valley of the shadow

Alan awoke to continue the same thought he had explored the previous night. That the stream, somewhere nearby, was actually a flowing fount of elder ale, coming from some divine place up high in the mountains. Here, with his eyes closed and his mouth parched, it made sense.

Stellis was the only other one up, he presumed, but he didn't see her. After a bit of walking around in the still dim light of infant dawn, he found his way down a small hillside which sloped alongside a babble in the stream and saw her sitting at the bottom on a barren patch of ground.

As he approached, she didn't turn or raise alarm, but faced away from him towards the harshly red-dyed orange that was bathing the grass in the northern divot. There was a small breeze in the air, and Alan felt the dew brush onto his pants, cooling his legs through the fabric. He walked softly, not trying to surprise her, but not wanting to disturb anything important.

When he was still twenty or thirty feet away, she didn't turn, but said, "Good morning, Alandriel. Come, sit next to me."

He sat to her side, within arm's reach. "What are you doing up so early?"

"I could ask you the same, but I find it likely that we both know that answer and would feel better if it was left unspoken." She looked at him from the corner of her eye and beamed gently. "I am here to gather myself. There is more energy in the air and the ground when most creatures still sleep."

"And what do you gather?" Alan looked in front of him, but found the growing glare too sharp to stare at directly, so he looked down at his lap.

"What do you feel, Alandriel?"

He looked at her unknowingly.

"Place your palms on the dirt, flat and spread. Take deep breaths of air. Forget that I am here. What is it telling you?"

Alan did as he was told. The dirt was damp and warm, but the cool air felt fresh in his lungs. "I don't know? I don't think it's talking to me."

She smiled softly. "It is always talking. It has never been quiet. Listening is the difficult end of the bargain. It's hard to hear something that's been there all along, just as you are deaf to your own breaths or the beat of your own heart." Stellis took her hands, already muddy, and pressed them against the ground again. "I can hear it, but I do not like what I hear. Something. Too close to us. We must move with haste today. It is not happy with whatever moves. It is foul."

"You heard all that? From the dirt?"

She chuckled to herself. "It is not the dirt, Alandriel. It is all that the dirt once was. The flowers, the trees, the birds, you and I. All that life doesn't disappear like the changing of seasons. It's just used in other ways."

He saw her eyes and nodded. The two sat in the dirt as the Sun rose, higher and higher, brighter and brighter, peeking through more cracks in the mountains, until their shadows were not as long and more solid, and they could not hide from them any longer. He returned to camp for breakfast with the others and left her alone there for a little while longer.

Their breakfast was sorry, as were they about it. What little cheese they had left were varieties that none were too keen on consuming, the hardest, of course, and they filled the rest of their bellies with nuts they did not like too much and berries they had foraged. None was more vocal about their displeasure than Kard, who grunted after every other bite and chomped upon the nuts meticulously like a grindstone.

Their mounts had only grain-meal; no giblets or scraps were tossed their way. But they did not falter on the path and carried on towards the mountains with persistence equal to yesterday's. The closer that they drew, the flowers and lush grasses gave way to harder ground, less fertile and more like stone than soil.

"I do not wish to second-guess you, brother, but are we sure that we travel true to the path?" Riddle did not speak too loudly, for they were keeping a closer pace to Rime and Alan today.

"Do you mean to say that this land does not look familiar to your eye?"

"No, it just seems like a much greater feat to find a small hole through the mountain than it was to come out of it. If the Bruder Pass is oft used as you say it is, I would only expect that the ground crawling to it be beaten down. I am no tracker, though."

"No, you are not. I must agree with your judgment, though. It will be difficult to find, even for I, for Flour offers no landmarks to mark your way. I could not be sure, even with a map at hand, at what point we will meet the mountains."

Stellis pondered after a long breath, "Menace grows in the air the closer we draw to Funus. We do not want to be stranded at her feet with little defense."

"I have considered it. I think that there may be a way to avoid such a circumstance," Rime said, "but as the plan already lies in my mind, it seems foolish to argue about it now. Let's see what we find when we get there, and if it's as we fear, we can resort to other measures."

"What is your plan, brother? We have time. Why not share it now?"

"Because there is no point. Come up with your own plan in the case that we can not spot the pass if that will ease your mind. I see no reason that we need to concern ourselves with possibilities when we are not yet lost, just unsure if we are on the right path."

"Aye, some would call that lost!" Kard shouted up from behind, chuckling. "But I agree! It is not as if we can turn back and retrace our steps. If we shiver tonight, Rid will sing us a ballad by the fire, I'm sure. Hah!"

"Fortunately, we made good pace yesterday. We should know our fate by midday, I hope."

Alan assumed Rime was right, for firstly, the group declared him the best with navigation, and secondly, the mountains were looming above them now like great beasts, grumbling and groaning with ferocious might and deep thunder, moving through the frame of their eyesight just enough to be alive.

They rode hard without stopping to eat, over the thinning grasses and cracking ground. The sun beat down on them from in front, and none were too keen on wasting their energy to talk to one another. The slope of the ground became indiscernible until sometime when the Sun was very high in the sky, and Rime turned them around to the east, facing the way from which they had come. Stellis was fast behind them, resolute and unwavering, and Rid behind her was fading once again from exhaustion. Kard was not seen, though not due to slowness or lag in pace, but because of a large boulder which lay in the path. From behind it, he was now emerging in a heavy sweat.

"That was a lot of work, mate," he heaved, "are we taking a breather now?"

"That's funny," Rime said, "you were not the one doing the work. Dazzle was."

"Aye, doing a hell of a job, too, at throwing me on my arse down the hill. Are we not on the mountain now? I could trip once and tumble all the way back to Flour."

"We are as close to the ridge as we want to be, yes. And, unless any of you have sharper eyes than I, I think it is just as we feared. I do not see Bruder Pass."

"I would volunteer Stell," Rid suggested, "for she has the best eyes of any of us. Well, maybe of any but Alandriel. Do either of you see anything?"

"I don't," Alan said glumly, only blocking the sun from his gaze for a moment to scan the face.

"Nor do I," said Stellis, "but I have felt the same presence, though its shadow blocks even more light now. It is nearly at hand. Whatever your plan was, we should move hastily, Rime. I do not want to linger. I hope everyone is agreed that we would be better served with a hearty meal at The Ferryman tonight than take a meal in the sun in front of eyes surely watching."

They all nodded in approval, though Kard grumbled more than he nodded.

Rime dismounted and pulled a map from a bag latched to the avimu. "Very well. Our daylight is burning, but I believe that we have enough time. Does everyone, aside from Alandriel, remember what this side of the pass looked like?"

"Yes, perhaps because of the terrible stories, I cannot forget its image." Rid mumbled.

Stellis nodded, "I do."

Kard spit. "I'm afraid I wasn't much payin' attention to the scenery last time."

"No problem." Rime handed the map to his brother. "You take this, along with Stellis and Kard. Travel northeast, trying to keep the same elevation. I will go southwest with Alandriel, as I can keep the map in my mind. It might not be much use unless you get very lost, however, for I do not know where we are on it."

Riddle looked nervously from the map back to Rime. "We're splitting up?"

"Yes," Rime chuckled, "has your heart grown so fond of me when we no longer share an avimu, Rid?"

"Make your jokes. It just seems like a lot could go wrong."

"I agree. A lot could go wrong if we don't find the pass before nightfall. Unless you feel confident that you can place us on this map, then neither of us has a great idea how far away that is. If we both cover the same amount of ground, that doubles our chances. If the mountains went more than two ways, I'd reckon it'd be a good idea to split again."

"I think Rime is right," Stellis chimed in, "but I would like to know how you see this working if one of us finds the pass. Surely you know that I cannot send thoughts as well as I can read them, and certainly not over a distance such as that."

Alan had spent enough time with Rime to have a good idea of where this was going. "I think I see a way." He looked at Rime. "I don't know if this is what you had in mind, but if you find the pass, stay there. If you don't, come back to this spot. When dusk approaches, if we all arrive back here, we've failed. If one group comes back here and does not find the other, then they can continue on until they arrive at the pass."

"Exactly as I imagined it, Alandriel. I knew there was a reason that I brought you trapping with me. Does anyone have a problem with that plan?"

Kard had already started trotting to the northeast. "I'm on board with any plan that gets us to the tavern faster, mate. If this puts ale in my belly, you've got an endorsee out of me."

Stellis and Rime nodded, though not as confidently.

"Good. Keep each other safe. I'd say once the sun is mid-way to the tops of the forest behind us from where it is now, then if you haven't found the pass, come back to this spot. That boulder there shall be our marker, if anyone would like to adorn it with a fabric flag or sash. The losers should have enough time to dash to the pass if they hurry, assuming it is not too far. Agreed?"

They all did agree, and so they all set off from the boulder at the foot of the Funus Mountains. As they rode, hurriedly and not altogether different than a jog, Alan felt the darkness that Stellis had described earlier. It was difficult to bear on his mind in its entirety, squirming around like a worm, but there was certainly wickedness in it. The shiny, hot rock on the sheer faces, still cracked and jagged in many spots, made their shadows dance up and down across the surface as they moved alongside it. It felt like a whisper, watching the display, and he wanted very much to run away from it back to the comfort of the forest.

Rime slowed the avimu to a walking pace as they came upon a spot with more growth, little dashes of green and sprigs of grass peeking out between the cracks of the rock. The ground grew wet, and further up ahead, they saw glimmering trickles of water rolling out in a slow, meandering way from up high that would no doubt join up with others of the same to feed into the River Mere.

"I feel a strangeness. Do you feel it, Alandriel?"

"Yes, I think I do. What does it feel like to you? To me, it's as though a cloud has been over us since this morning."

"I feel that weight, but there's something more to it. Sinister almost. It's odd. I don't know why, but I could surely use one of Rid's stories right about now. Maybe he's got something cheery about these mountains, but I doubt it."

"I would like that, too."

"Alandriel?" He looked at him, almost hesitantly.

"Yeah?"

"I know...well, I know Stellis keeps saying that you don't need to tell us any of your story, and so on."

"Mhm."

"But...well, I agree with that. I don't want to make you say anything. But I am mighty curious how you are so unfamiliar with all of it. All of…well, all of the world, it seems." He looked at Alan with a contorted face, as though he feared he had made a mistake by broaching the topic.

"Well, to be perfectly honest with you, Rime, I myself don't really know how I ended up in Drireford. It's a bit foggy for me."

"And before that?"

Alan did not look in front of him, for he did not want to risk showing any fear that might be in his eyes as he decided what to do. Telling the truth was not an option. But what was the truth? Sure, he was dreaming right now, but that would be a lie in this world, wouldn't it? He could not tell Rime that he was actually a figment of his own subconscious. The implications of that hurt his head, and he realized he had been silent for nearly a minute.

"I—I don't know exactly how to put it, Rime. It feels as though I lived an entirely different life, as though it didn't even happen in this world. I only have little glimpses of memories, only when I try very hard to remember them."

They were stepping over a stream now and guiding the avimu on foot, as one trickle had spread quite wide, flooding the ground in front of them. Behind, Alan had no sight of the boulder, nor did he recognize where they were, even though the ground remained level.

"You must know something. I don't want to pry, it's just gotten me concerned—what you said the other night. That someone might be hunting you."

"Oh, no. I shouldn't have brought that up. I think a small twinge of fear got the best of me."

Rime's eyes betrayed his dissatisfaction with the answer.

"Maybe someday I can try to explain it all to you over a pint of elder ale. I think you are better off not knowing, for now, anyways."

"I will take you up on that if we are ever to drink together, Alandriel."

They rode on at a pace that had continued to slow since midday, but they did not have any sight of the pass. Rime described it to him as a huge, gaping crack in the rock, at least fifteen witchits high and half that across. It grew wider and higher once one was inside, and after you'd walked far enough to forget about the daylight, the ceiling would break open to the Sun.

Unfortunately, they saw nothing of the sort. They had traveled far, and both of them were aching, for the terrain here was much harder. It hurt to even sit upon the back of a beast as you went. Alan was just about to point out the sun's position in the sky, and that they should probably turn around, when Rime fell off the avimu like an invisible rope had yanked him to the ground. He lay there, writhing and groaning in pain, flat on his back.

"What is it? What's wrong?"

"I—" His face was red and strained, and the blood vessels of his neck had sprung to the surface. "My side, something has pierced—"

He squirmed more intensely, kicking up more dirt, until he was still. Alan could not see any movement in his chest, nor could he hear any breath.

He opened his eyes and gasped in furiously. "Riddle! We must fly, Alandriel. I am hurt, so you must lead. Get on!"

Alan frantically took the reins and swung his body up on top of Mina. He reached down a hand to Rime, who seemed to be in a pain greater than death, and with all his might, he pulled him onto the rear.

"Fly! Back to the boulder, or further. We must find Rid!"

Alan did not ask questions, nor did he have to issue any command or catalyst to Mina, for she was already dashing as though from a ghost, kicking up rocks and leaving a cloud of dust behind them. The wind came at him so fast it was impossible to take in a full breath. Rime was digging his hands into Alan's waist, a grip like an alligator death-roll. His breaths were slow and labored.

They went faster still, and the water from the teeny streams splashed across their faces, enacting every stimulus they could conjure. He'd no idea how far they had gone now, but he could have sworn that he saw the boulder pass by him in a flash on the right side, though the repetitive nature of the landscape gave no decent indicators.

Rime's head was resting on Alan's back now, a clenched jaw hard upon his shoulder, the growling breaths still eking out. Suddenly, some far way off and barely visible in the newborn dusk, sparks flew high in the air. They were red and frantic, sputtering out high and then in an orb, like a silent firework.

He thought to point Mina toward them, though it was not a different path than that they were already traveling. She shrieked at the sight of them, but did not slow, rather bearing her head now and picking up even more speed if it was even possible.

Up ahead, the rock on their left jutted out nearly ten or twenty witchits from the steadfast face, and they turned a sharp path around it back to the east, Mina nearly slipping as she veered back to the west at the pinnacle. In front, Alan could now see the hazy figures of people, two of them, maybe kneeling.

Yes, they were kneeling. He could see better now.

One was shorter, Kard, and one taller and sleek, Stellis. They arrived in a flurry of dust and scattered ground, and Kard turned to face them, his face wet with tears and his hair matted against his head with blood and sweat. He got up and stumbled over to the avimu, his lower lip trembling.

"Rime's out, I expect." He sniffed and wiped a dirty sleeve across his face. "Bloody bastard already high-tailed it out of here. No doubt he's at least a chit away by now."

Over Kard's head, Alan could see a pale, bloodied, limp Riddle lying on the ground, face-up. His face hurt to look at, for it showed no emotion or life.

"Is he—is—" Alan felt short of breath and stumbled to the ground. His stomach was in knots and he felt as though a warm heat had just risen through his spine and hit a block of ice at the nape of his neck.

"Aye, mate. He's already passed. Imp musta come outta nowhere."

"How...how did it—"

"How'd it happen? Yeah, we'd like to know the same thing." He blew his nose on a filthy handkerchief he pulled from his pocket, which really may have just been an ordinary filthy piece of fabric, and growled as if he was trying to ward off despair. "We was goin' in that pass there." He gestured behind him, where beneath the faint light that was left, Alan could make out a hole of the size described. "But see, we didn't know whether it was the pass or not. Lotsa dangerous holes round here. We thought we was saving him trouble by leaving him to watch the entrance while me and Stell went in. A minute later we heard a yell—and then..." He was nearly whimpering with his last words. "I just caught sight of it for a moment, but the face of that imp is burned in my mind. I'll kill it in a heartbeat if I see it again, I swear."

Stellis was still examining Riddle but withdrew her shaking hands, and as she turned to face him, Alan could see dire exhaustion in her face.

"I've done all that I can. If I'd brought more provisions, perhaps I would have had something that—"

Kard held up a hand. "You've done all you could, Stell. You can't bring that back. I don't know nobody who can bring that back." He looked up at the sky, new tears welling in his eyes, and nearly howled, for his cry was so pained and loud. "I can't believe it. I can't believe it. Why'd we leave 'im?" He looked back at Rime's slouched, unconscious body on the avimu. "And—and poor Rime. It's gonna kill 'im, the news. He'll blame himself, he will. Splitting up was his idea, but, oh it don't make a difference. Imps kill so fast, we might all had been dead if we'd been out here."

Stellis approached Rime now, not crying, but trying to hold back emotion with a firm grip on her composure. "Was he hurt, Alandriel? Rime? I'm sure that he felt it when he happened."

"I think he's hurt. It was his side. He said he felt a piercing or a stab, I think. He collapsed from Mina when it happened, I guess. How exactly...how did that—"

She immediately tended to Rime's side and began whispering quietly to herself. "I do not have time to explain. Night is falling fast, and we must not leave Riddle here in the open. Hasten."

XVII. The Ferryman

Riddle's head hung limp next to Drake's hip, jostling slowly and passively with every pace, like a bounty that none of them wished to have. Alan could not help looking into his eyes every so often, hoping for some sign of life even though he knew that none would come.

Mina, leading, carried the still-unconscious Rime under the guidance of Stellis, who was walking Dazzle and Drake by hand, or maybe by spell. Mina's head swung low, and she whined every time she looked behind her and saw the party's burden.

"We must get to The Ferryman before all light is ushered out of the pass. I expect we are no more than an hour away on foot. We will not be able to bury Riddle until we arrive," Stellis said.

Alan and Kard took up the rear, frequently glancing behind them to check for stray imps, though all they saw were streaks of water crying down harsh black rock walls and a tiny pinpoint of light far behind them where they had entered. It smelled musty and sour, like a wet towel shoved to the bottom of a suitcase. Up ahead, Alan thought he saw signs of light where the ceiling opened up once again, but he couldn't be sure.

"Who is the ferryman?"

"Not a who, but a what," Stellis answered. "It is the tavern Rime spoke of. It is the only shelter we will find on or in Funus. Though now it seems we are in between."

"How is his breathing, the poor lad? Quickened?" Kard asked in an unsure voice.

"It seems to have steadied. I've done all I can. He may wake before we arrive, although I almost wish that he wouldn't."

"I will talk to him," Kard grumbled, "after all, I've known him the longest. Best mate o' mine, he is. I shan't of left his brother. Delivering the message is not even the start of my debt. Aye." He fidgeted with his cap in his hands, folding it and rolling it back and forth. He had spoken little in the pass, but muttered insults and disappointments to himself every few minutes.

Alan tried to hide his anxiety, a task made easy, for the sadness overwhelmed the nervousness every time he looked in front of him. "Will you tell me what's happened to Rime once we get there? You're sure that there's nothing I can do?"

"You are doing it, Alandriel," Stellis said, "We cannot move any faster with such delicate..." She sighed. "We are going as fast as we can. You are watching our backs. That is all we need right now."

His breaths quickened as they walked. The air felt thinner and thinner the further they got from the light behind them. He felt like tearing his own head off so that he could scream all the louder from his open neck. Why was there nothing they could do? How had it all happened so fast, and they hadn't even gotten to swing a sword at the creature that did it?

"If I carry him, would we go fast—could we go faster? If I carried Rime?"

She did not turn to face him and said nothing for a few moments. Then she lowered her head and said, "Alandriel, I swear to you that there is not anything for us to do. He will be all right and you cannot carry his—"

He felt rage boiling in him and the tears in his eyes growing hot. "How do you know what I can't do? Have you seen that, too, Stellis? You've seen how much weight I can carry? You know that I can't carry him?"

Kard laid a hand on Alan's shoulder. "Mate, it's gonna do no good. None of us can carry a grown man any quicker than Mina or Drake. It'd only tire you out."

"What's the point of me not being tired? What good will that do?"

"Well, lad, for starters, you can still swing a sword if another imp comes round a corner."

Alan kicked a rock the size of a baseball as hard as he could, back towards the light behind them, and grunted.

"Have it your way."

The anger compressed and twisted inside of him, but there was nothing else to say. He felt foolish for letting it rile him up as it did, but also regret that he hadn't erupted enough at the lack of action.

"Do you know how far away we are?" Alan shouted to the front. His words resonated off the walls and generated a long echo that traveled in front of and behind them. Stellis said nothing. Up ahead, she reached her hand into her robes and dropped something on the ground. It glowed in the dark of the cave and illuminated a crooked post of wood fixed against the rock. Words were roughly burned into it:

IF THE BEYOND HAS YE WARY, AND YE NOT GRIMFOLK OR IMPFOLK, MAKE YER WAY TO THE FERRY, FOR A PINTE OF ALE AND A PIPE SMOKE. (YE ALMOST THERE)

There was something cruelly ironic about the crude poetry written on the sign. Alan almost wondered if it had been a trick of the eye or an enchantment, for it had showed at such an opportune time in their path. If things had gone normally, the sight of it would have livened his spirits. His waking thoughts had been oft-plagued with the trappings of another pint of elder ale, and although he hadn't smoked a pipe, that would have sounded just as good. A tavern after all of this walking and riding, and to be there with friends, that would have really been something.

But things hadn't gone normally. They hadn't foreseen their arrival because their navigator lay slumped over and passed out on the back of an avimu.

There was no story being told about why the pass was called the Bruder Pass, but Alan was sure that there was one. *He would have loved telling a story here,* Alan thought to himself. In the dark, that's where people pay the best attention to your stories. In the dark, or in front of a fire. There're no rumblings or charades to distract them from your words. Scary stories—those hold men's hearts tightest in the dark. In the dark, anything can happen, and they'll hang onto every word while searching the shadows behind your voice for any sign of the monsters you breathe into being.

But there's a contract with a scary story. Unspoken, but it's there. People only want to hear a scary story when things are decidedly not scary. When things aren't sad, glum, terrible, or horrific. It's the only way to enjoy them. Things now seemed to be all of those things at once.

In front of them, Alan was sure that he could see a beam of light coming down from above. The light drew on, blanketing the path, and he knew they were reaching the opening. It was a cold blue, like how you imagine the night sky appears in fairy tales before you're old enough to understand that it's all black. It was a welcome sight after their trudge through the cave.

But once they got there, and he looked up at the stars, he felt the emptiness inside of himself aching harder than it ever had.

They walked on, past small, delicate ferns grasping for the light out of cracks in the ground and tiny crustaceans just brave enough up to slip from a puddle or come clicking out of a hole to see the new passerby causing the hubbub. The signs of life grew in number, and after not too long in the light, up ahead, they could see the ceiling close off again to darkness. Just at the lip of the black a torch was lit, sending dark smoke out of the shadows and up to the moon.

"Thas the Ferryman, it is." Kard grunted from behind Alan. "Dard'll be truly shaken, I expect. Let us take the lead, lad; he don't take too kindly to strangers."

They reached the cave, and as his eyes adjusted, he could see the tavern. Carved into the cave, rather than a structure of wood or brick built up from nothing. From the main channel, there was a rough rectangular hole in the right wall curving upwards, fitted with a rotten door that bore rope for an axle instead of traditional hinges. A small square window, if you could call it that, a few feet to the left of the door, outfitted with rods of iron crossways. Up above the door there was a slab of wood that bore the same handwriting as the sign before, *The Ferryman*. A boat helmed by a tall figure that looked not unlike the grim reaper burned into the heart of the door.

He could hear some talking inside, but it didn't sound like many people. One or two old friends at the bar, some shuffling of food preparation and beverage conjuring, and maybe an order being voiced. They tied up Mina, Drake, and Dazzle at a post that came right up out of the middle of the cave, which was considerably wider now, and Alan and Kard supported the dead weight of Rime on their shoulders to take him inside. Stellis pushed the door open with great effort as it heaved and whined against the rock floor.

The Ferryman was not like the Half-Cracked Staff, not in the slightest. Its smell hit him first, which was one of malt and wort, and perhaps vomit. The volume was immediately louder. Off to the side of the bar, if you could call a long piece of wood hanging by rope from the ceiling a bar, there were two men equipped with more daggers than either of them would have needed to commit a gaggle of murders. On the wall behind them, which was in fact some decaying paneled wood rather than naked rock, there was a round board, not unlike a dart board. One dagger went whizzing by and stuck into the top left underneath a symbol of a lightning bolt. One man yelled with fury or happiness and immediately chugged the rest of his drink, leaving a mustache of head above his lip. They both turned as the door closed shut again and looked unkindly upon the strangers.

There were a few others seated at a table in the back corner, barely illuminated by a single candle, and the only other being was the bartender, Dard, who was busy attempting to replace a barrel on the second-shelf with one he held half with his gut and half with his hands. He was round in profile, and with his back turned to them, his pants fell well below the level anyone would have preferred. He grunted and stumbled, and with a painful yelp he shoved it into its place.

"Oh, hello, there. I didn't see you guys come in." He wiped the sweat from his bald head with his apron. "And what's this? Has my friend Rime had a bit too much at the pub down behind the abbey?" He cackled dryly. When none of the newcomers reciprocated, he furrowed his brow.

"I'm afraid that we've got some heavy news, Dard. Do ye mind if we take a seat?" Kard motioned with his hand to the only other table, close to the front and well out of earshot of the other patrons.

They all drew up rickety and sticky seats, and Dard brought several full pint glasses from behind the bar and set them on the table. "Is it bad news? He's not...he's not fallen ill, has he? I was only jokin' 'bout the abbey. My sister, see...she's gone quite religious in the past months and humor is—"

"No, Dard, he has not fallen ill." Stellis pushed the ales from her view and rested her hands on the table. "We do have unfortunate news, however."

His eyes widened. "Your fourth; it wasn't this rascal?" He nodded to Alan dismissively. "Where's Rid? Has something terrible happened?"

Kard took a gulp of ale and spoke. "An imp. Bastard musta snuck up on him when nobody was near. Rime, well, you know." He exchanged a knowing glance with Dard, but the plump man did not return the same, instead twirling the end of a badly cared for mustache as his enormous eyes darted between them.

"My stars. I'll split the varmint from head to tail if I see him round here. He's really dead?"

"Aye. We've brought him here to bury...or burn. Suppose it doesn't make much of a difference." Kard had finished one ale and was pulling another one to his lips.

"And Rime, what is the matter with the man? Shock?"

"No..." Kard exchanged a wary glance with Stellis. "Wait, do you not know?"

"Know what?"

"They were...well, they were doppelbrothers. Rime never told you?" Kard looked at Dard in a state of shock which Dard mirrored. Kard paused after he said it and looked at Alan, knowing that he too was hearing the information for the first time.

"No...oh my. That's dreadful. Will he be okay?"

"Aye, he's a fighter if he's anything. Stell did what she could."

The five sat in silence around the table, one because he was unconscious, and the others in a silent, mournful observation. Kard sipped his ale and shook his head, cursing himself.

"Well, I know it isn't much to offer, but you lads...and lass...are welcome to find quarters here tonight. Rime—is he...well, not to put it too bluntly, but do you have the body?"

"Aye. With the avimu outside. Obviously we'd like to send him off, but...well, seems like Rime should be here for it. I'm not sure when he'll—"

"He can be woken now." Stellis said. "Do you have any peppers? The further south they're grown, the better."

With that, Dard released a high-pitched, enlightened grunt and dashed off to the kitchen. The kitchen in the Ferryman was in fact not a kitchen at all, at least, not by any standard that you may commonly find or possess. Like the rest of the Ferryman, it was a hole where a hole shan't of been, and sinks and stone ovens jimmied into nooks where they ought not to have fit. But, because of this dark and dank disposition, the Ferryman did have one thing going for it. Dard could preserve food here with little ice or salt for much longer than any man on the surface could have. Folks came to the Ferryman for the ales and drink, but they stayed for the snacks. Rarer foods were hard to find, for anywhere else, they would have rotted itchits away.

In one tiny cellar beneath the floor, he had an assortment of peppers: red ones, green ones, purple ones, curly ones, straight ones, short ones, fat ones, and even some ugly wrinkled brown ones that weren't old, but just grown by a farmer quite bad at his job. He pulled some crinkled bright orange ones out and could already feel the heat on his hand as he ran them back to the table.

"These ought to do. Can't remember the man I've bought them off of, but they're spade peppers, no doubt about it."

Stellis took them in her hand and mashed them up into a puree with a stone roller and a bowl. Alan leaned over and felt the hairs inside of his nose curling up. Kard took a bit on his thick index finger and licked it.

"Aye, they are a bit shaped like spades, but they taste more like the devil himself."

"Aren't named spade for the shape, lad. Named that way for how they're liable to bury ye."

Stellis finished mashing and poured the contents through a cloth so that only a liquid remained. "Well, we hope to do the opposite of that now, don't we? Kard, pour this into his ale and then to his lips. Make sure it goes down."

Alan held up Rime's heavy head with his hand and tried to prevent the front of him from sliding down into the chair with his other. Kard took the glass and pulled his lower jaw down, spilling most of the concoction on his clothes, but a fair amount trickled into his mouth.

Rime coughed like a man drowning and gasped for air. He opened his eyes, which were bloodshot and frantic, and grabbed one of the half-full ales from the table. He chugged all of it in between hot heaves and then slammed it down.

"What in the hell was all that? I feel as though I've been killed and brought back to life." He examined his body, noticing the wrapped wound on his side and the dirt and sweat that covered the rest of him in a thin layer of grey filth.

They all stared at him, not sure what to say, and none of them very well-prepared for this moment. He looked confusedly at each of them, and just as Stellis began to speak, he said, "Wait a minute; where's Rid? He taking a leak? We're in the Ferryman, yeah?" He grinned wearily at Dard. "Dard, my friend. How are you?"

Dard offered a small smile, and Kard stood up, placing a hand on Rime's shoulder.

"Take a walk with us outside, mate. There's something you've got to see."

A bumbling Rime lifted himself slowly out of the seat, groaning and grunting as he went, and followed behind Kard with Stellis and Alan in tow. Up ahead, Alan could see Kard push open the door, taking the entryway torch in his hand and illuminating the cave with Rime just beside him.

He heard nothing, but he knew the avimu were right outside the door. They were looking at Rid, there was no doubt.

Stellis and he shuffled out the door, and the sight took him back at first. Rime was on his knees beside Mina cradling his brother's head in his hands, and tears were flowing down his face making clean streaks where the dirt was turning to mud. He cried, but it was quiet. Rime didn't breathe hard or make a big show out of it. He just cried.

Kard stood off to the side with his hands crossed in front of himself, and tiny glimmers of tears fell down his cheeks, too. It was only then, after a minute or two, that Alan now realized that he, too, was crying. He tasted the tears in his mouth, salty, like the humid air in the forest before the storm. He looked at Stellis, but she had turned her head so that none could see her.

Kard knelt down and whispered in Rime's ear, asking if he'd like to be alone. He shook his head. They waited, filling the cave floor with more salty water and cleaning their dirty faces. It was hard to look at Rid, though Alan felt he ought to. That's respect for the dead, isn't it?

To look at them and tell them it's okay, that they're not too strange or sad to see. To acknowledge them.

After a while, Rime stood up, slowly but strongly, and looked upon his friends.

"Kard has told me all that I need to know. I blame none of you more than myself. I—" He paused, trembling with his breath, "—I should not have left him alone. Not there."

He turned back around and took his brother up in his arms, cradling him like a child. "Will you all come with me to bury him? His body is cold." He looked at Riddle's eyes. "He should not be cold tonight."

The agreement was left unspoken, and they all followed Rime wherever he chose to go. Kard passed one of two shovels to Alan, and they trotted behind, quiet and still, trying not to disturb the stillness of the night.

They walked back the way they had come, back to the opening in the sky where the moonlight shone down. Rime lay his brother down gently upon the ground, and felt along a rock wall on the eastern side, whispering quietly to himself with his eyes closed. After a moment, he turned back around and took Riddle in his arms again.

They followed behind him as he made his way back to the spot, somehow entering a chasm in the wall where the rest of them had only observed the solid face. Down this tunnel they traveled for some time, and it was narrow and dark, for it did not open to the sky.

Soon they came out to an opening, full of even more moonlight than the other, but there were no other visible tunnels leading to this courtyard. They walked out onto soft ground covered in wet moss, where small purple flowers grew that seemed to glow upon the dark green undergrowth. They could hear water flowing somewhere, but they could not see it.

Rime lay his brother down again, this time on a pillow of the petals, and took a shovel. He dug without anger or haste, and he did not ask for help, though they gave it anyway. Soon they had a pit, large enough for a brother, and Rime lay him down one last time.

"I would like to say something, if I could. At the very least, it will make him laugh if I try to tell a story here." He looked up at them, his eyes glistening and wet, and laughed softly.

"When our mother died, I was too dumb to understand it. Well, we were the same age, but you all know Rid. I cried and I cried for so long that it felt like I didn't have anything left in my body. My throat and head hurt, and I didn't understand why anyone would have killed my beautiful mother. If I didn't know more of angels and winged things, I would have said she was one of them."

"Rid knew why they killed her. He didn't want to know, but he knew. That sort of evil, well, I guess that it was young then. But he knew it so well. He saved me the ache and the confusion though. He covered my eyes so I wouldn't see the words men had written in blood. I couldn't read, but he could. He read them. *She-elf came from Hell.*

He told me a story that I could handle, one that wouldn't drive me to a fury stabbing every man in town I could point a finger at. He said that *It*, whatever made it all, had run out of beauty and kindness to put in other things, and that she had volunteered. That she would be the paint that It needed."

"When I was older, he told me the real story. I was full of anger, but many of the men had died. Rage had gotten them all, one way or another. I could scream at the sky and weep all night but it would not change that."

He took a handful of dirt and laid it gently on Rid's chest, where his hands were clasped together. "Now I'm less dumb, here, burying my brother. I know that the first story was the real one. Or, at least, it had the most truth in it. So tonight, as best as I can figure it out, It did not need more beauty. For that, It would have taken Kard." He sniffled and chuckled. "It has run out of stories to tell and needed to borrow some more. I'm sure that my brother went happily."

Back in the Ferryman, the four of them all sat at the same table, all nursing drinks (except for Stellis, who had juice). Dard insisted that everything was on the house, including the rooms, and would bring them new pints the moment he saw any below half-full.

Rime was quiet, but now and then would start to tell a story about Rid or their childhood, which he would make it only a minute or two into before his face grew stony and he took another swig from the glass. Kard and Alan were doing their best to keep spirits up, but neither of them was having any luck coming up with jokes. They decided it was best to join Rime in drinking and quiet. Stellis was making notes in one of her books, flipping back and forth between pages with urgency and jotting down more things as she went. Occasionally she would look up and offer a small smile before burying her head in the pages once again.

After a long period of silence, Alan could no longer restrain himself from asking a question. There were two things plaguing his thoughts: he needed to know a lot more about the imps, and he wanted to know why Rime had gotten hurt. Neither one of them seemed particularly appropriate, but it was late, he had been drinking, and he had to have closure for something.

"Rime?"

He took a sip and burped. "Yeah?"

"If you don't mind me asking, what are doppelbrothers? Is it something to do with why you got hurt?"

Rime paused for a minute, examining his ale as if the answer lived somewhere in the bubbles coming to the surface. His eyes were still red and glistening, and Alan hoped that this question hadn't asked too much.

"Well, doppelbrothers...they're brothers born at the same time from the same woman, you know? We both were there at the same time."

"Like twins?"

"Like what?"

"Never mind."

"Well...that's it."

"So why were you hurt?"

"I just told you."

Kard looked at Rime and then back to Alan and could see that he did not understand.

"Lad, that's what it means. Doppelbrothers, they feel everything that happens to the other. Rare as a shooting star, many say. Rime and Rid, they were the only two I'd ever met."

Alan watched as Rime poured the last drops of ale onto his tongue and laid the tankard back down on the table. He looked at Alan, solemn, but proffering a small beginning of a smile, not out of happiness, but because he was being looked at.

Behind Rime, Alan now caught the eyes of a man with several others at a table in the back, barely illuminated by the glow of dying candles. His face was dirty, and the beard was the same, but Alan felt it deep inside of himself when he looked into his eyes.

Dad.

All the commotions of the tavern, all the noises, faded away to a low hum. The world moved slowly around him. He saw the dancing of the flames in steps like a stop-motion movie. The shadows played on the walls in time. He got up from the table and took steps toward the man.

He could not see the man. There was only silver smoke where before had been candlelight. He kept walking, across what felt like an endless sea of nothingness in the tavern, as if he was wading through a current pushing him the other way. As if he would never get there.

Then he got there. There was nobody at the table. It was silent. He looked around the tavern, but there was nobody there. Alan was alone. He could hear his own breathing, slow, but tired. It was nearly morning now. He did not know it by sight, but by heart. His heart slowed. And then—

—He awoke.

XVIII. The keenest child

Alan had never been hungover in his quarter-century of life on this planet. He'd often interacted with Micah during this state, but had never experienced it himself.

As he lay on his bed, watching the last amber rays of a setting sun, he felt like he'd been hit by a bus. His head ached with a rhythmic panging that seemed to be both plagued and fueled by consciousness. Even the soft orange light hurt and made his stomach twist into knots. It felt as though his brain was a sponge that had been dried out on hot concrete instead of properly quenched with water.

He gathered himself up into a stumble and let his momentum carry him into the kitchen where he could get a cold glass of juice. It felt like a vomiting was inevitable. His head thumped like a timpani drum. But then he began to feel the effects of the hydration, and his thoughts didn't seem as scattered or pained.

The tea. He knew it instinctively, not only because that was the only variable that had changed last night, but also because the mere idea of it rattled his insides like the idea of a vodka shot on New Year's Day. The cause of the hangover; he knew it. But it also did something else.

He had dreamed *a lot* longer last night. It was nearly a full 24-hour period in Imp Lode before he had woken up. In his short tenure of experience, that was unheard of. As he reminisced on the dream, the final details that had been so fragmented and hazy when he awoke in pain now flooded back to him.

Dad.

A rush of adrenaline coursed through his body when he remembered what he had seen. Without a doubt, it had been his dad sitting at that table in The Ferryman. But what did it mean? How did he get there? How did *he* get him there? He thought back to the guidebook and the rules for bringing characters in.

Could it be that simple? Could he just follow the rules, dot all the lines for the "procedure" for falling asleep to bring in specific characters, and bring his dad into the dream just like that? If he'd brought him in once, he could bring him in again, right?

His confidence mounted as he scrounged up assorted snacks in the pantry for a breakfast before work (which was really dinner), and he began to formulate in his mind the plan for bringing his dad into the dream. He'd referenced the book so many times, he felt confident that he knew the protocol.

Would it be his dad though? Would it be the same person, or just some half-dimensional caricature of him—the best that he could bring in? He would know who Alan was, right? He would have all of his memories?

His train of thought was interrupted as Micah's bedroom door swung open. Micah slunk his way from behind it, trodding quietly on the carpet like a cat burglar.

"Hey, bro. You're up."

"Yeah."

He was speaking at a volume between a whisper and a *very* quiet inside voice. "Sarah's taking a nap before we go out on a date tonight." He paused for effect as a smile curved its way up to his cheeks. He pulled out a small black box from his back pocket. "I'm proposing tonight."

"Really?"

"Yeah."

He was grinning with his mouth open wide now and Alan couldn't help but succumb to some suffocating remnant of his own humanity and return a small smile.

"Like to marry you?"

"Yep. I called her old man on the phone earlier day. He's kind of a dick, but he's loaded."

"Well, that's really exciting. I'm happy for you."

He lingered for a moment and allowed his grin to retire to a modest size. "Are you really?"

"Yeah, why?"

"Eh, I don't know. I know you don't think she's that great or whatever, or maybe you think that we're both stupid. It's just...you know, it's one of those things you gotta do, right? You gotta find a wife. And I really think a lot of her."

"Yeah, no. I mean, sure, I don't think that Sarah and I get along very well, but we don't have to. I'm not marrying her, you are. If she makes you happy, that's what matters." Alan did feel some conviction behind what he was saying. Sure, it wasn't *all* that mattered. But you don't tell a guy that's already bought a ring that.

"That...that just makes me really happy, bro. To be honest, I've been worried about telling you. You know? I mean, we've been buds for so long, now I've gotta pack up and move out...go start a family, you know?" He chuckled to himself.

"Oh...yeah. Of course. You're moving out?"

"For sure. I mean, not right away. Sarah has already wanted to start looking at houses together, though, so I'm sure that this will speed that right along. You know, maybe the down payment comes from her old man, who knows."

"Well...that...that's just great, man. I'm glad that all of this is falling in place for you."

"For sure. But hey, really don't worry about how it affects you. I'll spot rent through the end of the lease so you don't have to pack your bags up right now." He looked at Alan earnestly, and he knew that Micah really did mean well.

"Well, thanks for the heads up. Where are you going for dinner tonight? Somewhere fancy?"

"I figured I'd pop the question at Bambino Viziato, it's a pretty shmoozy Italian joint in Cleveland. It's where my dad proposed to my mom. Figured that's good luck or something."

"Well good luck. That's a crisp white shirt. Don't get any pasta sauce on it."

"For sure, bro. Hey, I'll try to bring back a doggy bag. Their breadsticks will make you lose your freakin' mind." He laughed and went back into his bedroom, adjusting the tie that hung loose around his neck.

***

It was torn at the little holes where the pull strings come out, practically worn bare on the right elbow, and had a peeling Dark Side of the Moon album art iron-on that might as well have been taped on at this point. But Alan was glad he had it, the only hoodie that he could find when he scrounged around in the open lockers when he got to work and realized that he had forgotten a jacket.

In Laska, it was cold. Hilda hadn't been there to greet him when he got there, but there was a piece of notebook paper taped to a pallet of beer:

SQUID, ANOTHER JOB FOR YOUR ARTISTIC SIDE. MAKE A DISPLAY IN FRONT OF REGISTER 3 WITH THIS BEER. I'LL BE IN AROUND MIDNIGHT - RIDING. -H.

It was a lot of beer. Some light, some lite, some natural, some crisp, and all of it packaged in red, white, and blue. *Do people really start stocking up on alcohol for the Fourth of July this early?* He maneuvered the pallet out of Laska, through the backdoors and lay it to rest in the front near an end-cap.

Upon a closer survey of the aforementioned gallery space, he struggled to decide on a way to arrange the cases. Another pyramid would come off as derivative since you could still see the altar to the soda gods off near aisle 11. He stacked a few on top of each other as a test (most of them were 24 packs) and decided that they were pretty sturdy. Alan figured he could stack them at least as high as himself without any risk of injury or catastrophe.

He thought of other structures, perhaps something to the American god himself, Uncle Sam. A flag? No, too simple. He'd seen that at other stores a million times. A firework mid-explosion? Too complicated. He didn't have the artistic training. The Statue of Liberty? He didn't have enough green to work with. It was a limited palette, after all. How about the hat of the man himself, Uncle Sam's red, white, and blue top hat?

Alan found a piece of paper under one register and sketched out the plan in box form. He broke the drawing up into rectangles and marked which ones he would leave the red side showing, which ones the blue, and which ones he would double up for the smaller silver sides. Once he was satisfied with the integrity of the blueprints, he started to build it from the ground up.

The bill was easy enough, as all the tops were silver. It just looked as if someone had laid a bunch of beer on the ground in a jagged circle. He started to add the walls of the hat, and second guessed himself as to whether the hat had red stripes. It didn't matter, he decided, because he was going to use all the colors whether or not Uncle Sam liked it.

When he got to the top, he realized a disastrous fallacy inherent to his design. He had implemented no way for the top of the hat to be supported. He stepped off of the step ladder and looked up at the top of the hat.

No one would be able to tell. You couldn't tell that there was no roof to the hat. We don't actually know if Uncle Sam's hat had a roof. You can't see it in the drawing, after all.

The time had flown by, but for Alan, it felt like minutes. He kept going back to adjust this case 10 degrees to the left, or turning this one to the other side to hide a dent in the box. He grabbed a broom from the back and swept around the foothills of Mt. Tophat, ushering a flock of dust bunnies over to a bin. It looked pretty good, he thought. It was no Mona Lisa, but it was geometrically sound, and making a circle out of cubes is not an easy feat.

He saw a Whatchamacallit in the checkout display in front of him and smiled. He dropped the broom and grabbed one of the candy bars. Inside the top hat, he ate it in secret.

They sure don't make them like they used to.

***

He had just gotten started on some cured meats: various salami, pastrami, country ham, and pepperonis, when he heard the back door open and close. He had lost track of time entirely. The clock in the front showed that it was almost the next day already.

Hilda came shuffling down the aisle with a leather jacket thrown over one arm and a clipboard in the other.

"Hey, kid. How's it hangin'?"

"Not too bad. Figured these meats were good to go out? I finished up the display, so I thought I'd start on these."

"Jee, squid, I gotta start puttin' you on all the artistic, expressional jobs. You really get it done that fast? I can never come up with any ideas."

Alan felt a grin coming on, but tried to hold back to maintain some sort of semblance of hating his job. "Yeah, it wasn't too bad."

"Well, what're you waiting for! Lead the way, Michael Angelo."

Alan dropped a fat salami log in the cooler and led Hilda to the end of the aisle where they could see the display area in the front of the store. There, twenty feet away, a beautiful, patriotic top hat stood proudly beneath the flickering fluorescent lights.

"I didn't have a lot of inspiration, so this is what I went with."

Hilda said nothing, but approached the hat with childlike wonder. Alan could have sworn that her mouth hung ajar. She was close enough to reach out and touch it, which she did, before she said anything.

"So you really do love the United States of U.S.A., don't you, kid?"

"Well, not like that. I just couldn't come up with—"

She snorted. "I'm just messing with you. It's your colors, you ain't got much of a choice."

Alan walked up and joined her in the reflective glow of red, silver, and blue. The light was real damn bright here.

"What do you mean by that?"

She gave the sort of grin that you give when you know you're going to have to explain something, but you make the person ask anyway. "Your colors. You know, like the colors you sport. You didn't pick to be born here, did you?"

He thought the question rhetorical, but she paused and stared long enough that he shook his head.

"Exactly. The colors picked you. You didn't go around asking mommy and daddy for pictures of Uncle Sam so you could make this one day when you're older. You know what he looks like because he's your colors."

"Yeah, I guess you're right."

"I know I'm right. If you ask me, these colors ain't been right since Jimmy Carter. You know him? Or are you too young?"

"Uh, ye—"

"Don't answer that. I shouldn't get political. Professional workplace and all, you know. My colors, Psalm 23; I don't know about all that. They just picked me, you know. You don't go trying out for the biker gangs you want. You just kinda fall into one."

"Yeah, I see what you mean. It's sort of like getting picked for a Little League team. You don't really choose the team. Sometimes you don't even wanna play in the first place."

"I know that's right." She cackled. "There's other things though, you know. Colors you get to pick. Like being in a motorcycle club, I picked that. I call that a shade."

"A shade?"

"Yeah, real smart of me too. See, cause shades are there no matter what. You take a black-and-white photo of this hat, all the shades will still be there. You can see what's dark and what's light. Some people think a biker is dark by default. Some of the kindest people I know are bikers, though. We just like to ride."

She took a step back and laughed again.

"Me and you both know we didn't pick the colors of Elmwood's on Elm."

"I don't know, I think it suits your eyes." He gave Hilda a playful glance, and she elbowed him before laughing quietly to herself.

The rest of the shift wasn't so bad. There was a lot of salami though. Apparently, it only gets ordered every so often when the store is down to their last leg, quite literally. Hilda told him that it can outlive humans if it's kept in a refrigerator. Alan wasn't so sure if he believed that, but he didn't have any reason not to.

***

He got off early again, which meant that he drove himself home in the pitch dark. It was nice, driving in the dark. There was more space to think, and he needed all of it.

Alan rolled his driver-side window down and felt the cool air rush in. He turned up his radio a little bit louder. *Losing My Religion* by R.E.M. was on. The incessant chirping of the crickets nearly fell in time with the song, and the rush of wind around his left ear provided a sturdy rippling of bass.

He second-guessed himself. *That was dad, right?*

It seemed so far away and so long ago, even though it had been just last night that he had seen his dead father sitting in the other end of a tavern buried beneath a mountain in a land he visited in dreams. But it had happened. It could happen again, couldn't it?

In the driveway, he left the stereo on and the windows rolled down. He hopped out and sat on the trunk of his car. The stars looked so bright at four in the morning. Everything was quiet and still. He started to whisper, just to himself at first, but then to his dad.

"Are you one of those stars? That's what people always say. I've always thought it's kind of weird. The sentiment of it, at least. Why would you want someone you loved so far away? I don't want you to be some star a million light-years away. I'd be fine with you being this rock. This one, right here in my hand. If that meant that you were here next to me, it'd be good enough."

He felt his eyes getting hot and wet. The chill of the night.

"Were you there last night? I want to find you. Will you come back again? I miss you, dad. Thanks for the record player. Mom gave it to me with a bunch of your old records. Maybe you knew that already. I wish I knew what the end is or where you are. Are you really there in my dreams? Sorry for so many questions."

Alan shut his car off and rolled up the windows.

"Good night, dad. I love you."

***

At the kitchen table, Alan had it all spread before him. Off to the corner, he had a fresh, hot mug of tea. He was sipping it, slow and sweet. It wasn't bad this time, though his cheeks and tongue still squirmed in between swallows. In front of him he had his guide and his notebook.

At first he thought it odd. But he decided it best not to leave anything up to chance, and he made a page in the persons section for his father. He drew him, to his best recollection, as he had been the night before in the Ferryman. It was crude and not at all an accurate depiction of his memory when he'd finished, but it would have to do.

He read through the section about bringing certain characters into the dream a second, third, and fourth time until he was sure that he had seeped every detail there was to gain from all the tiny footnotes. One stood out to him:

If there is something in the physical, natural world that you possess that may remind you of this being, bring it into the space that you sleep. It should trigger one of your senses, but strongly. I have found in order of least to greatest strength in this capacity the following ranking: sight, touch, sound, taste, smell. This may change depending upon the dreamer.

He searched around the room for something that would smell like his dad, though nothing jumped out at him or came to mind. It wasn't that there weren't any smells that he associated with him; it was that he didn't possess the means to create those scents. He didn't have the combination of rising dough, warm milk glaze, and cinnamon sugar pecans to create the smell of the sweet rolls his dad used to make on Christmas Eve, nor did he have a bucket full of hot motor oil and a rag covered in grease and sweat to remind him of a Saturday morning spent with him in the garage.

He was searching every last crevice of the bathroom, considering resorting to taste or sound, when he found it. It must have been Micah's, but it would do. Aqua Velva Ice Blue. He'd know that bottle anywhere. It sat on his dad's dresser and was only opened on special occasions and Sunday mornings. He breathed in a whiff, and further inspiration struck.

Alan grabbed the aftershave and hurried to the kitchen. He'd rifled through almost every drawer, when in the last one he found some instant coffee powder. He microwaved a mug of hot water, made the coffee, and put the aftershave on his own neck.

That was it. The iconic scent of Howard Hendershot on a Sunday morning drive to church.

He did the normal recitations like he'd always done and took up the time-proven position in his bed with one foot tightly wrapped in the blanket so that it felt numb and uncomfortable. He whispered and took deep breaths to calm himself.

For a moment, he was in the backseat of their red Ford Taurus, adjusting his clip-on tie. He had a nervous stomach ache, too. About Bible verse memorizations in Sunday School.

"But can I maybe go after communion out to the playground if I get out before nobody sees me?"

Alan was talking, but he couldn't hear anything.

"Honey, you know that someone will see you. You have to go to children's church just like all of the other kids. It'll be fine."

"I just...I'm not sure if I know the verse." He felt sick. "What if I don't know it when they ask?"

"It's not a big deal, Alan. You'll do your best and that'll be that."

His sweaty fingers fidgeted with the tie a little bit more. He wanted to wear a real tie like his dad, but he was too small. They all went down to his feet.

They pulled into the church parking lot and got out of the car. His mom went ahead, and his dad tapped him on the shoulder and told him to wait a second.

"Hey, buddy. So you've gotta do verses today, you think?"

"Yeah." He rolled his eyes. "They call it a *surprise*, but it's always the same day as communion."

"And you don't think you can remember it?"

He shook his head no and looked at the ground, still fidgeting.

"You know what? We're gonna need some extra help for the fish fry at lunch. Do you remember how to put two pieces of loaf bread on every plate?"

He looked up and grinned a little.

"Yeah, and three for Mr. Collins cause he doesn't eat the crust!"

His dad smiled. "Well, I'm glad to hear I've got another set of hands. I guess...well, jee whiz I guess we'll have to pull you out of church during communion so we can get started."

Alan smiled up at his dad. He patted him on the back as they walked up to the church. "And Alan, the smartest guys in the world don't like reciting things in front of adults. I bet you're one of those guys."

The church started to fade away in front of him like they were walking into heavy fog. He didn't hear his dad's footsteps next to him anymore. He didn't hear anything anymore. The fog got thicker and thicker and then he walked through it like he'd walked through a cloud.

The world had flipped itself over, or at least a quarter of the way. He felt the gravity change, and he was looking up with a scratchy quilt laid over him and a wet, rock ceiling up above. He took a moment to gather his senses and let his eyes adjust to the dim light of a single candle in the corner of the room.

Rime was sitting up in his bed with a book in his lap, and the candle in his left hand was throwing dancing shadows on the wall.

He whispered across the room, "Is the light keeping you up? I can go to another room."

"No, no. I'm up." Alan wiped some of the sleep from his dry eyelids. "Do you know what time it is?"

"No idea. I've been, well…"

Rime got up from the bed and sat at the foot of Alan's. He laid the book on the quilt. It was Riddle's journal.

"I've been reading this. Or, trying to at least. Are you any good with reading?"

His eyes were red and strained. He was only flipped to the second page of the book and had his index finger firmly placed against the page to hold a spot.

"I'm fairly good at it, yeah. Do you need…um, help?"

His eyes lit up as his cheeks turned light crimson. "If you wouldn't mind. I can't read many words, I'm afraid. I've been trying to make the sounds, but I've only gotten through the first bit."

Alan nodded and held the book closer to Rime's candle. On the page there was a drawing of a vosvudu. It was an abstract interpretation, to say the least, but Alan knew what it was from the bushy tail and the red and orange wax that he had melted upon the page. At the top, there was a title: *The Keenest Child.*

"Is this a children's story?"

Rime grinned. "Oh, yes. When he first learned to write, he started to fill it with the first stories he'd heard. This one is one of my favorites. Could you read it aloud?"

"Sure." Alan cleared his throat and began to read.

THERE WAS ONCE A GREAT, LARGE VOSSY THAT LIVED IN THE DALE ALL BY HIMSELF. HE ATE ALL THE RATS THAT HE WANTED BECAUSE THERE WAS NOBODY ELSE AROUND TO HUNT THEM. HE WOULD CHASE THEM UP TREES, ACROSS RUNNING RIVERS, AND DOWN INTO DEEP BURROWS THAT ONLY HE KNEW. HIS NAME WAS FRODEN.

MORE THAN ANYTHING, FRODEN WANTED SOMEBODY TO SHARE HIS FOOD WITH. ONE DAY, A PRETTY VOSSY NAMED LILA HAD WANDERED INTO THE DALE. SHE WAS A STRANGE VOSSY, WITH ODD STRIPES AND A TAIL THAT DID NOT FRIZZLE. BUT FRODEN DID NOT CARE. HE WAS GLAD TO HAVE THE COMPANY.

FRODEN AND LILA WOULD SPEND THEIR DAYS TOGETHER, RUNNING AND FROLICKING ABOUT. WHEN ONE OF THEIR BELLIES BEGAN TO GRUMBLE, FRODEN WOULD SNIFF UP A FAT RAT AND THEY WOULD FEAST TOGETHER. ALTHOUGH THE DALE WAS BEAUTIFUL, THERE WAS NOTHING MORE PLEASING TO EACH OF THEIR EYES THAN THE OTHER.

IT WAS NOT LONG BEFORE LILA WAS WITH PUP. SHE SPENT THOSE DAYS RESTING DEEP IN THEIR DEN AND EATING ENOUGH FOR TWO. SOON, HER BELLY WAS QUITE SO BIG THAT FRODEN KNEW SHE MUST HAVE TWO PUPS. HE WAS TWICE AS HAPPY.

THE PUPS CAME, DOLDEN AND DRYSDEL. AS SOON AS THEY COULD OPEN THEIR EYES, THEY HAD BECOME THE BEST OF FRIENDS. BUT THEY WERE NOT THE SAME. DOLDEN HAD BEEN GIVEN THE GIFTS OF HIS FATHER, AND

COULD HUNT LIKE NO OTHER PUP. BUT DRYSDEL WAS A BIT STRANGE AND DID NOT LOOK QUITE THE SAME AS THE OTHER VOSSIES. HE WAS BEST AT SINGING SONGS WITH HIS MOTHER, BUT HE KEPT THIS A SECRET FROM DOLDEN AND FRODEN.

AFTER MANY WINTERS, FRODEN HAD BECOME QUITE OLD. HE BROUGHT HIS SONS INTO THE DEN AND SAID THAT IT WAS TIME FOR HIM TO MAKE AN IMPORTANT DECISION. HE MUST DECIDE WHO THE KEENEST OF HIS SONS WERE, FOR THAT VOSSY MUST WATCH OVER THE DALE WHEN HE WAS NO LONGER WITH THEM. A DAY WOULD BE SPENT WITH EACH SON, AND THEN HE WOULD DECIDE.

ON DOLDEN'S DAY, HE SAID HOW KEEN HE WAS AND SHOWED IT. HE TRACKED FAR AND WIDE, THE FATTEST RATS THAT HIS FATHER HAD SEEN, AND HE COULD CHASE AND RUN THE RATS WHEREVER HE PLEASED. HE KNEW THE BURROWS EVEN BETTER THAN FRODEN, FOR HE HAD TAKEN SOME BLINDNESS IN HIS OLD AGE. FRODEN DECIDED THAT DOLDEN SURELY WAS KEEN.

ON DRYSDEL'S DAY, HE DID NOT KNOW WHAT TO DO FOR HIS FATHER. HE DID THINK THAT THE SONGS WERE KEEN IN THEIR OWN WAY, BUT HE WAS TOO ASHAMED TO SING IN FRONT OF HIM. INSTEAD, HE TRIED TO HUNT FOR RATS AS DOLDEN HAD, BUT THEY WERE TOO CLEVER FOR HIM. THEY LOST HIM IN DARK HOLES AND HE COULD NOT CATCH THEIR SCENTS. FRODEN KNEW WHAT HIS DECISION WOULD BE.

THE NEXT WINTER THE TWO SONS FACED ALONE. THE DALE WAS DOLDEN'S NOW, BUT HE STILL HAD LOVE FOR HIS BROTHER AND ASKED HIM TO STAY THERE, TOO. HE DID, AND HE ENJOYED THE FRUITS OF DOLDEN'S SKILL, EATING ON HIDEAWAY RATS EVEN THOUGH THE WINTER WAS CRUEL AND MEAN.

THOUGH IT WAS BAD, THE NEXT WINTER WAS WORSE. IT BROUGHT SUCH A DEEP CHILL TO THE BONES OF THEIR MOTHER, THAT SHE COULD BE NO

MORE, AND WENT TO BE WITH THEIR FATHER. THEY MADE IT THROUGH, ALIVE, WITH THE SPOILS OF DOLDEN'S HUNTS ONCE AGAIN.

BUT THE THIRD WINTER WAS THE WORST OF THEM ALL. THE RATS HAD ALL STARVED OR BURIED THEMSELVES BENEATH THE SNOW. THEY COULD NOT EVEN FIND ANY BERRIES OR ROOTS ON WHICH TO FEED. IT SEEMED AS THOUGH THEY WOULD STARVE.

DOLDEN AND DRYSDEL LAY DEEP IN THE BURROW, SHIVERING AND SHAKING FROM THE STARVE AND THE SNOW. AS THE KEENER BROTHER, DOLDEN KNEW THAT THEY WOULD NOT MAKE IT. HE ASKED HIS BROTHER TO SING FOR HIM, HERE AT THE END OF THEIR TIME IN THE DALE.

DRYSDEL WAS SURPRISED AND DID NOT KNOW WHAT TO SAY! I HAVE LISTENED, HIDDEN AWAY, SAID DOLDEN; I HAVE HEARD YOUR SONGS. IT IS ALL MY HEART WOULD WANT, HERE IN THE COLD. PLEASE, MY BROTHER. SING FOR ME.

SO DRYSDEL DID. HIS BROTHER SMILED AND WARMED THE BURROW WITH HIS CHEER. THE WINTER WIND DID NOT FEEL AS COLD ON THAT NIGHT.

IN THE MORNING, DOLDEN WAS NO MORE. THE SPRING WAS FAST UPON THE DALE, AND DRYSDEL HAD MADE IT THROUGH ON SKIN ALONE. HE WANDERED UP TO A HIGH HILL, TO LOOK UPON THE DALE THAT HE WOULD SOON LEAVE.

IT WAS BEAUTIFUL FROM THE TOP. HE HEARD A VOICE SINGING TO HIM, AS IF CARRIED BY THE WIND.

THOUGH I WALK WITH THEE NO MORE, AND THE LONESOME SHADOW GROWS NEAR, 'TWAS NOT YOU WHO WAS WELL-CARED FOR, BUT YOUR BROTHER WHO WAS FILLED WITH DREAR. FOR A RAT FILLS THE BELLY FOR AN HOUR, A FILL THAT SURELY SOON WILL SOUR. BUT A BROTHER'S SONG

WAKES THE COLDEST HEART, AND OF THE KEENEST LOVE I AM NOW A PART.

Alan laid the book back down upon the quilt and looked over to Rime. There were tears in his eyes, welling up as the candlelight glinted atop them, but he quickly wiped them away.

"He knew a good story when he heard it. He knew how to make 'em, too." Rime sniffled. "Have you ever lost anyone, Alandriel?"

Alan was doing his best to keep tears from his own eyes and coughed before turning away. "Yes. Yes, I have."

"I thought it would be easier. Losing someone again. It probably would have if the someone hadn't been my brother."

Alan looked at Rime, who now seemed so meek and exhausted sitting here without any sleep.

"Maybe it will one day. Just maybe."

"Thanks for reading that, friend. You can hang on to the book if you want, so long as you tell a tale from it every now and then. I think he would have liked if you had it." He smiled falsely. "Besides, Kard and I can't read worth a lick."

He picked up his candle, but turned back to Alan after a half-step.

"Oh, and I nearly forgot—" He placed a closed hand down on the bed. "—this was in Rid's pocket. It must belong to you." He lifted the hand to reveal the gold cat's eye.

Alan fumbled with the marble and looked up at Rime quite confused. "Do *you* know what it is? I have no idea. Rid wanted it to draw—in his book, you know."

Rime stared at the marble with a furrowed brow, not as though he were trying to recall what the item was, but contemplating what Alan had just said. "I'm 'fraid I do not. I would have pointed you to Rid." He met Alan's eyes. "He truly didn't know? Or was he foolin' with ye?"

"And pass a chance to tell a story? You'd know better than me, but I believed him."

A small grin passed over Rime's face and he tapped the book with a pointer finger. "Aye. Well, you find out, you put it in there."

The others began to stir, and Rime briskly gripped Alan's shoulder with a friendly smile before preparing for the morning departure.

They gathered their belongings from the corners, chests, and nooks of the room they had slept in, and soon they had all migrated back out to the dining room of the tavern. There was no smell of breakfast frying or bacon sizzling upon a cast-iron skillet, but Dard was waiting for them with a medium-sized leather bag and a tankard.

"G'morning to you all. I hope that your night provided some rest and security. I've put together some cures and wares—hardy for the road and all that. Take a swig of ale before you go. It'll limber up your legs."

The others graciously accepted the gift and gathered around the bar, each of them touching base with Rime and offering seventh and eighth condolences. Alan stayed back and crept around each corner, but he did not see his father anywhere. The tavern was empty, quite like you'd expect a tavern to be in the wee hours of the morning.

After a moment, he caught Dard's eye and must have looked awful shaken, for Dard discreetly left the group and made his way over to Alan.

"Can I help you, my sir?"

"I hate to pry and all, but...well, were there any other guests staying here last night? I'm looking for a man that was sitting at that table over there."

Dard looked around and scratched the top of his head. "No, I'm 'fraid not. I only have the one room. Course there's also my bedroom. Only I slept in there though."

"I thought as much. Well, thank you anyway. And thanks for your hospitality."

He bowed his head and began to walk away.

"Why are you looking for the man? Is he a friend or foe?"

"A friend."

"Aye. Well I've always heard that the roads of two good friends never fail to cross again. Good luck to ye."

With that, the party left The Ferryman and joined the path once more.

Well, except for Alan. Alan would not have it. He was feeling overcome with emotion, a precious material that his body had produced at such a rare interval he nearly confused it for a stroke or high blood pressure at first.

Alan could not just brush it off. He loved his party of adventurers, but he had gotten the briefest of glimpses into what the dream world *could* offer him. Imp Lode was something else entirely to him now. Imp Lode was a place where he could bring back the dead.

He lingered in the threshold of The Ferryman, feeling tension rising in his body like a wild electricity. It was a tension of indecisiveness. He wanted to continue on the path, to have another full night of dreaming, of adventures, of ale, of kinsmanship, but more than that, *yes*, he finally decided, *more than that, I want to see my dad.*

He spun on his feet and walked briskly back to their room, passing by Dard before he even had a moment to take in a full breath and announce his confusion. Alan was already out of his sight by the time he asked, "Forgot the old umbrella, have we?"

Alan knew what he had to do. He got back into the bed he had only just left, pulled the quilt up to his chest, and began the rites and rituals of the guidebook. He didn't know if this was the way to cancel a dream, but as I know, and as you might have guessed, it didn't actually matter. The intention of exiting the dream, the germination and growth of that in Alan's mind was enough to pull him out of it.

He awoke and immediately leapt from his bed. His mind was operating on a single track.

Alan drank his tea. He read his book. He consulted the journal. He did everything that every annotated note which mentioned bringing a specific somebody in to the dream told him to do.

He did this, and he went back to sleep.

Dard gave him the same news. There was no man in the tavern. His father was gone.

He repeated the steps and went back to sleep.

His father was not there.

Again.

Again.

Soon, it was afternoon. Not the pleasant type of afternoon you experience when you have the queen's tea and scones and cakes and finger sandwiches and cakes and sweet cheeses and cakes. No, this was an afternoon where the only tea to be had was a chalky, muddy, odd bastard of a tea that can put a man to sleep but not raise the dead. A tea had time and time again as the day drug on and the hours were warped into a mess of jumbled time. Alan had lost any sense of it from all the waking and sleeping, waking and sleeping.

But even so, his father was not there.

The empty bottom of his tea mug stared back at him. His own faint reflection barely etched out in the wet ceramic mirror. Mirror, mirror, in my mug, something, something, sedative drug.

Alan wiped a wet streak from his cheek and breathed slowly until the room stopped whirling.

Who do you miss the most? Everyone misses somebody, even if you are fortunate enough to have all the people in your life that you love the most still living and breathing by your side. Pick that person, the one you miss the most, and think about all the wonderful things you did with them. Think of the stories that you told them, the stories they told you, the jokes you shared, the memories you have with them that have only grown finer with age.

Now, imagine you've seen them. You were sitting down at a cafe with a lowly plate of dry chips, and you saw them, just a glimpse, as you got up to leave. You couldn't believe it. There were so many things you wanted to ask them and so many stories you had to tell them. What luck, you thought! What a twist of fate!

Would you turn right back around and go into the cafe to look for them, or would you wait for another day and hope they'd be there again?

Of course you'd return.

But what to do when you find nothing but empty tables?

XIX. The devil went down

The sheets stuck to him like Glad wrap on a stick of butter. He lay in it, steeped in it, even.

Frustration. Hopelessness.

Outside, out there in the real world that whether he liked it or not, he still lived in, it was afternoon. Maybe a quarter till 5. The sunlight was just warm enough to continue pulling those beads of sweat to the surface of his arms.

He'd exhausted himself. Falling asleep. Waking up. Sleep. Awake. Pass out again. Get up. Do it again. Again.

Again.

It turned out two minutes of sleep followed by two minutes awake over and over again was more tiring than being awake the whole time. But still he did it. He had to. Alan had to find his dad.

He would be there one of these times.

But there it was in his clammy mess of starchy sheets. His eyes aimlessly staring at the book on his desk. The feeling of no hope that cleared his mind up just enough to bring a little bit back to him. A little bit of hope.

That book he was staring at—it dawned on him like a divine epiphany.

It may not have the answer within, but there were secrets tied to those pages that weren't yet visible. *Someone* had mailed this book to the library. Somewhere out there in the world, there was the author of *Lucid Dreaming for the Casual Adventurer*, annotations and all.

He knew what he had to do. He felt the charge of energy surging through him as he jolted out of bed.

The library closed at 7 p.m. As Alan stumbled around his house, electrified by the new possibility and looking for a matching pair of socks, the clock was ticking. A mismatched pair would have to do.

***

To his unfortunate realization, Mrs. Youngstown was not seated at the reference desk. Instead, it was a man, probably in his 30s or 40s, with bright ginger hair and thick-framed lime glasses. Alan had never seen him before.

"Um, hi."

The man looked up from his book and smiled pleasantly. "Hi, how can I help you?"

"I have...kind of a strange request."

The man returned an uneasy nod, and Alan wondered if it would be better for him to just come back another time. But he couldn't wait.

"I recently checked out a book here. I believe that it was one of the donated items from the fire that happened a while back."

Alan could already see the story forming in his mind as he spoke. He usually wasn't this apt to lying on the spot, but he had no choice, and the man's expression was disarming.

"And...well, the book has really sorta changed my life. In a good way." Mild intrigue grew on the librarian's face. "I wondered if it would be possible...for me to get a mailing address for the donor, so that I might send them a thank-you note or something of that sort."

The man's eyes were now cheery and bright. "Oh, I don't see why not! Let me go grab the file with all of the information that we recorded from the packages. I'll be right back!"

Alan lingered at the desk and looked around the library. All the new leather furniture and modern shelving basked in an orange glow from the setting sun. There wasn't anyone else in the library except for a boy and his mother who were browsing in the section of drawing books. Alan knew the spot well. He never followed the steps though, he would just put a sheet of tracing paper over the finished product and trace it exactly. Saved a lot of time. He had the slightest urge to go take a look at what new drawing books had come in with the donations, when the man returned.

He smiled again and held up a snot-green accordion folder that looked beat to hell. "I'm Alex, by the way. Sorry if you come here a lot, I just started here about a month ago. Still trying to learn all the faces in town."

"Oh, yeah, no worries. I'm Alan. I come here quite a bit...well, I used to anyway."

He grinned with a hint of disappointment. "Well, I hope you start coming back more! Let's see here...okay, this spreadsheet has quite a few of the donors on it. What was the book?"

"It was *Lucid Dreaming for the Cas—*" Alan's cheeks reddened. "Sorry, it was *Dream Cycle Reimagined: Lucid Dreaming* or something like that. I can't remember the whole subtitle."

"Nonfiction?"

Alan nodded.

"Lucid...lucid...lampoon...legal...liquidation...ah! Lucid, here we are. Do you have something to write with?"

Alan felt at his pockets even though he knew they were empty. "Nope, sorry. Do you have—"

He slapped down an index card and a Bic pen. "Keep it! It's one of my things. I always have pens to give away."

"Oh, cool. Thank you."

"Alright. Street number is 1892 Ridgeway Pass. City is...oh, my. City is Athens, Georgia."

Alan looked up at him. "Georgia, you said?"

"Yep. Must've read about it in the paper. I heard they came in from all over. A couple from Alaska, even. Zip code is 30607."

"Okay." *Athens, Georgia. Jee whiz.* "Was there a name?"

"Yes! You can make it out to a Warnie Tollers, says here. No phone number, though."

"Well...alrighty, then. Thanks for the help, Alex."

"Anytime! Glad you liked the book so much. Maybe I'll give it a read when you're done!"

Sure. Give it a read. You have no idea, Alex.

***

He had to get to Elmwood's early the next morning to beat the Saturday rush. He knew that he would regret it the minute he had to leave his house again later that night to come in for his actual shift, but there was only one person he knew to talk to right now.

Miss Etta stood over a steel table in the prep area of the bakery removing the aluminum foil from the edges of her pecan pies. They were sort of famous around here, and Alan knew why. There was a shot of Jack mixed into the filling. That, and she put a healthy spattering of salt on the top, the real big flaky stuff that's hard to find. Like you shaved it right off the floor of the ocean.

She hadn't noticed him yet. He sat at one of the two-person tables close by with a pad of paper and an atlas he'd found shoved deep in the glove compartment of his car. The panel of the atlas with Georgia, Alabama, and the top half of Florida was stained with dark brown coffee cup rings. Half the town names had gotten muddied and blurred from the wetness like water colors.

"Oh, Alan!" She laughed and came around the display case to his table. "Were you just gonna sit there all morning and not say anything to me? I haven't seen you in a while."

"Sorry, you looked busy with those pies."

She had, but Alan was also still trying to come up with just how he'd tell her this crazy idea.

"I'm a night-stocker now. Sort of living the life of a vampire, I guess."

She laughed and then offered a dispirited half-frown. "Oh, Alan. I'm sorry. Vick's a little rascal. You're not the only one either. I've heard a few of 'em complaining about some stupid score he's checking now, like he's some little runt at a baseball game with one of them stat notebooks. Think they're gonna be a major league scout or something."

"Yeah, it's okay. I guess I was kinda slow. I'm actually not hating the night shift, though. Vick not being here at night doesn't hurt."

She smiled. "That's the spirit. Well what in the world are you doing in here on a day off then?" She looked at the atlas he had opened in front of him. "You planning some kinda road trip?"

"Well, not exactly. That's sorta what I came here for, to ask you about something."

Miss Etta looked closer at the page. "You gonna go see Rock City?" She cracked herself up and sat in the seat across from him.

"You're from Georgia, right?"

"Born, raised, and harvested, you could say. Georgia got the best of me, that's right."

"Well, there's somebody I need to go meet in Georgia."

Her eyes were puzzled, and she tapped the table with her index finger. "In Georgia?"

"Yeah, it's pretty important to me."

"Honey, you're gonna have to tell me a whole lot more than that. You've never mentioned Georgia one time. I know your family isn't from there."

Alan took a deep breath and dove into his spiel.

"It's...well, you remember that book that I was reading? The one about the dreams?"

"The voodoo dreamcatchin'? Yeah, I remember."

"The book I got where I found all that information, I think the person who wrote it all and sent it to the library...well, they live in Athens, Georgia."

"Okay, I'm following so far. Now why do you think you need to go meet this person?"

He looked in her eyes and could see that she did truly want to understand. "Well, it's hard to explain." He felt a rumbling in his gut, like what he was about to say aloud would be crazy and nonsensical the minute the words were real and out of his mouth. "But, I saw my dad in one of the dreams. It wouldn't be that big of a deal, but like I told you, the dreams are just as real as this right now. It's like I saw him alive again, and I could remember it just as well when I woke up. The problem is that I can't find him again. I don't know how to make him show up in the dream again. I've tried everything. I even made a special tea, but it only makes me sleep deeper."

Her face had softened, and a sadness was coming through as she stared back at him. "And these dreams, these are the ones that were kind of like your stories? Magic and all that?"

"In a way, yeah."

"So what makes you think this person is gonna know how to make your daddy appear there?"

"There's notes all throughout the book. They're not the original author, they just marked it up with everything...well, I guess everything they learned as they were trying this stuff out. They've got notes about making a particular person appear there, but those just haven't worked. If anyone knows, it's this person. Some Warnie Tollers."

She sat for a moment without saying anything and looked hard at the atlas on the table between them. She tapped a spot, somewhere in the bottom half of Georgia, and said, "See this little town right here washed away with the coffee? My mama died there when I was twelve years old. She let herself starve and waste away so we'd have something to eat." She paused again and looked at Alan. "I'd go to the other side of the world if it meant I could look at my mama again and see her smile."

"I—I never knew that. I'm sorry."

"Yeah, well, you and I both know sorries don't do much but people still don't know nothing better to say. So that's right. If your daddy might be there, in some roundabout kinda way I don't understand, then I ain't gonna be the one to tell you not to go. I gotta better mind than to say something is foolish that I haven't tried myself."

Alan didn't know what to say, so he just smiled and nodded.

"So Mr. Alan, if I remember right, your car ain't too hot. I still hold the right to tell you that you probably shouldn't try to drive it all the way down there."

"Well, that's just it. I was gonna take a bus. I think I've got enough to pay for a cheap ticket. But I don't know the first thing about taking a bus to Georgia. You've gone back down a couple of times, haven't you?"

She nodded. "I have. My daddy's sister's kids all live there still. Well, most of them. But for buses, there's really only Greyhound. You can get a cheap one if you don't mind sitting your suitcase on your lap and your legs falling asleep. God knows I've done it. Helps if you're willing to go at night, too. Course kinda hard to fall asleep with luggage on you, but you can make it. You've made it here." She winked at him.

"Where do you go to get a ticket?"

"Well, if you want cheap, I'd get somebody to take you to Cleveland. Or take yourself there. I'm sure the address for the station is in this atlas here. Might catch one coming down from Buffalo on 90, but Cleveland'll probably be cheaper, yep. That's right. They might put you on one of them connecting buses or something, but I've only had to switch once. If you're worried about it, call them before you head up there, but I think you'll be fine. No one wants to spend a summer in Georgia." She laughed dryly and turned up the corners of her lips.

"Okay. I think I'm going to do that. You wouldn't happen to know how to get from where it takes you over to Athens would you?"

"Well, it'll probably drop you in Atlanta or Macon. I'd choose Atlanta, myself. Get a cheaper bus there. Shouldn't take more than an hour and a half to get over to Athens. College town, so most people gonna be going the other way right now. Kids comin' home to mom and dad. Shouldn't be too much."

He nodded and tried to take as many notes as he could with the Bic pen that was already running dry. "Thanks, Miss Etta. I owe you one."

She grinned. "Just come back in one piece, Alan. Georgia can be mean. Don't blow all your money either. We've got just as good of pie up here."

"Oh, I won't. You know I'm not picky. A few turkey and tomato sandwiches will do me just fine."

She got up as the first few customers were walking in, and Alan spent the next hour planning out his trip on paper and calling the bus stations to ask about the price of tickets. If he'd added everything up right, he was looking at somewhere between $60 and $70 for his trip. He had the money.

Barely, but he had it.

What he didn't have were the days off.

***

Raphl didn't really have an office. He did have a storage closet, though. Inside, there was a beat-up workbench in lieu of a desk and some sort of rolling mechanic's chair that he sat in. In front of him, he had six or seven crossword puzzle books with the cover curled around to the front and half-finished puzzles on every open page. Above the desk, there were a hundred printed order receipts and inventory logs attached to a cork board with a hundred pink and green pushpins. As Alan knocked and wandered in, he took a peanut M&M out of a C3P0 coffee mug and popped it into his mouth.

"Oh, how you doin' Hendershot? Hey, I been meanin' to tell you, real good work on them displays. Hilda says you went to 'em like dern

Picasser or something like that." He snorted and Alan could smell the peanuts and chocolate on his breath.

"Oh, sure. Glad I could help out. If you've got another display that needs orchestrated, just throw it my way."

"Will do. Will do. Hey, did Hilda give you that bag of goods? I dropped it off—"

"Oh!" Alan pulled a ten-dollar bill from his wallet. "Yeah, thanks again! Does this cover it?"

Raphl looked at the bill and waved his hand in protest. "Oh, no. I can't take your money, Hendershot. Look at me. I'm living the life."

There was an odd moment of silence as the two looked around the dimly lit closet and then back at each other.

"So, what can I do you for? Comin' to the new boss for some tips?"

"Well, not exactly. I've—well, I really need some time off, if it's possible. I didn't know if you'd made the schedule for next week yet, but I could really use a few days."

Raphl pulled a wrinkled sheet down from the cork board and furrowed his brow. "Okay, let's see here." He slid his index finger down along the page. "What days do you need?"

"Well, if it's not too much trouble—and I know this is short notice, but it would really mean a lot—could I not work again until Tuesday night?"

"Hmm...I'm not sure if I can make that worrr—" He paused and looked grumpily at Alan before breaking into a grin. "I'm just messin' around. Yeah, me and Hilda can handle it. What you got planned, if you don't mind the boss man asking?"

"Going down to Georgia, actually. It's a pretty long story, so I'll save you the details. Leaving on a bus tonight, though."

He looked at Alan strangely. "You're not in some kinda trouble, are ya? Not that I have any idea why ya'd go to Georgia if ya were, but..."

"Oh, no. No, not that at all. I'm going completely of my own volition. Sort of one of those self-discovery type of things I guess you could say."

"Okay." He grinned, revealing his horrid dental work. "Hey, I don't know if you need any snacks, but there was a case of trail mix that got all smashed up. A lot of it's loose, but you're welcome to whatever you can gather." He pointed to a large box just outside the doorway. "Ain't any of them attendants they have on flights to bring ya little bottles of booze and cookies, least there wasn't last time I took a bus. Course that was about ten years ago."

"Sure, I'll take some. Thanks a lot, Raphl." He turned for the doorway, but stopped in the threshold. A glint of gold on the wall had caught his eye. *Employee of the Year, 1989.* There were two other ribbons, one blue and one green, and a mug that read *I'm an Elmwood MVP.*

"Hey, can I ask you something?"

"Shoot, kid."

"Do you think I'm an idiot? A screw-up, I guess you could say?"

"Well why would ya say something like that?"

"I don't know, just with getting moved to stocking and all that. I guess Vick thinks I'm kind of a little shit. I'm really not doing any of it on purpose though. Is cashiering actually a skill?"

"Close that door for a minute, Hendershot. I gotta tell you something."

"What is it?"

"Vick's a mighty strange man. I've worked for him a long time, but it wasn't always Vick. It's been other strange people before. Kinda comes with the territory, I suppose. Thing is, you're not a screw-up and Vick knows it. That's the problem. Vick wants, maybe more than anything in the world, for all these skills and power plays he's got inside these walls to translate to the outside world. Sad thing is, they never will. Sure, you can learn a little about talking to people or maybe something about prices of consumer goods, but for the most part, you're here to be bossed around. Ain't real skills in cashiering because the job ain't really fair. People treat you like doggy dookey because they wanna believe the same thing as Vick, that you just haven't got the skills to make it yet. Those skills aren't real and they don't mean nothin'. You wanna know something else?"

"Okay, shoot."

"I asked for you. Sure, you mighta had a slow whatever score or somethin', but I asked for you long before that. Vick wanted to crush your self esteem, because that's his currency. Your cashier score, or whatever it is, that's what he's made of. A whole bunch of that. I asked for you because you don't miss little things. You got a real good eye. Only one on the ice shift that always has the labels turned to the front and pulls the expired stuff. Sure, that might make you a little bit slower, but that's a real skill. That's real currency. You go get a big fancy job as a sales rep for some slick tennis shoe company. You think they gonna give a rat's dirty behind how fast you can scan items at a cash register? But I get on the telephone with 'em, tell 'em how you'll notice more things about a person, more cues, more ticks, than the best of 'em...yeah, that'll mean something. Vick hates that the world ain't making him king."

"How come you decided to do this, Raphl? Did you ever want to do anything else?"

"Hell, I had dreams, sure. I wanted to go down to Hollywood and be a big shot movie actor. Shoot movies with ole Jack Nicholson or Bill Murray. Thought I was funny and good lookin'. Then after one of my improv classes one night, I just started crying and couldn't stop. Woman called me ugly, tried to say it was in character. I knew she meant well, but all the same, it was like I all the sudden knew I was ugly, too. Just been hiding it. Same time, my mom got prescribed her fifth medication, couldn't barely tell the pill bottles apart. I realized that was my currency, spending time with her. She thought I was beautiful and I've always been too nervous to be in movies anyway. I got a job that I could do at night cause that's all that I really cared about anymore—takin' care of her during the day. Now...well, now my mom's doing a whole lot better than she was ten years ago. She laughs at my jokes, too. You know they say that's the best medicine."

He winked at Alan and cackled softly, as if he was another minute or two from crying.

"Well, I guess I'm still trying to figure out what kind of currency I got. Maybe I'll find out down in Georgia."

"I wish you luck, my friend."

XX. Beyond the sea

He was still fidgeting with the radio knob by the time he got to Cleveland and had conjured nothing from the tuner beside white noise. He'd fought the urge to fall asleep with every fiber of his tired body. Finally he pulled into the bus station parking lot.

The cityscape around the station was all higher. There were brown and grey office buildings, some huge skyscrapers thirty or forty stories tall, still with a spattering of lights on, and a few shorter ones that had already gone dark.

The station itself was futuristic, crafted with long curves and rounded corners. It had more windows than obtuse walls. At the front, there was a large vertical *GREYHOUND* sign with the letters stacked atop one another in bright, glowing neon, something you'd expect to see in Vegas or New York, vertical to save space. But here, there was plenty of room.

There weren't any buses in the front, but he could see a couple pulling around the back, splashing up either puddles of sewage or rainwater, though it hadn't rained in days. The heavy smell of gasoline filled the stale night air, and as he walked, a light fog lay on his clothes until it beaded into water droplets.

At the information desk, he gave the trip number he'd written down to a blonde lady wearing too much perfume, and she punched a few keys before taking his wad of cash and giving him two tickets: one to get there, and one to get back. She offered a ten-dollar protection package in case he had to cancel at the last minute. He said this was the last minute.

Alan found his bus idling in station 7 around back. It was a long aluminum beast with a red, white, and blue paint arrangement peeled off like a lottery ticket. It would have made an okay display for the Fourth of July beer sale, he thought.

The driver took his ticket with powdery white gloves, punched it, and shoved it back without saying a word. He'd gotten the cheap seat as Miss Etta had advised, and he knew it too. The denim duffel bag his parents had gotten him a few years ago barely fit in between him and the seatback in front. Determined to make the best of it, he thought of it as a pre-inflated airbag.

The bus growled lowly in place for another ten or twenty minutes as the other riders piled on board. An older woman with sunken eyes and a bright pink knit cap pulled her way up the steps at the front of the bus. She smiled at every person she passed and told two or three that she was visiting her grandson in one of the Carolinas, but she'd forgotten which.

There was a couple. Maybe the age of Alan's parents. They seemed nice and excited, probably taking a vacation. Their clothes were starchy and the woman's white trench coat showed fading from too many cycles through the laundromat. When they sat down, she pulled out a fifty cent Florida travel guide which had a fistful of fast food coupons pressed in the middle. The adjustable magazine holder on the seat in front of them had the husband's full attention.

More and more came, and soon, an older, mustached man with a Browns shirt on sat next to Alan and grinned at him until he stuck out a hand to shake. He wore thin-framed glasses and old Reeboks.

"Roger, nice to meet you." He said, "I know young guys don't like to chat, so I'll leave you alone. If you need to go to the bathroom, just elbow me."

"Alan. Nice to meet you. I don't mind chatting, but to be completely honest, I'm exhausted. If I start snoring, you elbow me."

He chuckled softly and faced ahead. "I like a good quid pro quo."

Alan pulled out a thermos from his duffel bag. It wasn't warm anymore, but it would do the trick. He rested the side of his head on the window and took a sip of the tea. He didn't have to worry about arranging himself in an uncomfortable position tonight, he thought, as the broken zipper of the duffel pressed into his chest.

With a lurch, the bus rolled forward. Out of the back lot, out onto the street, and soon they were on the highway. The passing lights of the cars going north came rhythmically. He took a sip. The light was a soft yellow, and now, just as his eyelids were growing heavy, he could see faint streaks of rain illuminated in the next set of headlights. He whispered *dad* one last time, and then fell asleep, heavy.

***

He awoke just as he had before, on the scrappy bed in the back room of the Ferryman. And again, just as before, he jumped from the bed and dashed to the dining room of the establishment, checking for the weather-worn, bearded man he had seen before. Checking for his father. But once again, he had failed to bring in the person he wanted to see the most.

Alan had not failed, however, to populate his dream with the recurring cast. He met Kard, Rime, and Stellis just outside the threshold of the underground tavern in a cavern, and they were all under the assumption that he'd just gone back in to grab a forgotten item. The hours for Alan resolved to only a few seconds for them.

The party gathered their belongings onto the avimu and loaded up once again. Although their number was one fewer, Alan still rode with Rime, both to keep him calm company and because he still had no idea how to control the mount. He had only ever been on a horse one time before in his life, and his memory of the event is one solely lent from photographs, for he was far too young to record it. Besides, he hadn't held the reins, his dad had.

Before long on the path, the ceiling opened up before them again, and little by little the cave floor gave way to green vegetation and soil. By the time they no longer needed the additional light of a torch, the salty brine of sea air filled their noses, and the avimu were bouncing and squealing every time one of them caught a dense whiff of it.

No one had said a word since they left. There was no need for guided direction in a one-way cave, and the party was still unsure how to converse after what had happened. It would be up to Rime to initiate a discourse, and so he did.

"We're close now. This is what I told you about, what felt like so many days ago, Alandriel. The sea. You will soon see why we chose avimu for our journey."

Alan stretched his limbs and took in a heavy breath of the fresh, saline breeze. "I could use a change of scenery after being under this rock for so long. What's after the sea?"

"Thorne Sea will carry us all the way to Oognysse, friend. That is, to where we are going."

Kard's avimu trotted closer to them now so he might join in the conversation. "Aye, lick your lips lad. You can nearly taste it. The salt, ye, but also ole Nyssey. She beckons, she does."

"Will it be long on the water?" Alan asked. "I mean, it is an entire sea, yes? How do we sleep on the avimu?"

Stellis grinned. "It is long in only one sense of the word. The Sea pulls east or west depending upon the season. You can feel it in the air. It is pulling west."

"She's right," Rime agreed, "our birds will have no trouble crossing the Sea before night falls upon us."

Alan furrowed his brow. "An entire sea?"

"Suddenly the lad wants to be the expert on geography!" Kard laughed. "You didn't know what Oognysse was a moon ago and now you wish to tell us its speed and appetite? He might be from Reul after all!"

"Take it easy on the boy," Rime said. He nudged Alan with an elbow and whispered back to him, "If you really want to outsmart Kard, dig around in that book of my brother's. That'll shut him right up."

Soon they were gathering distance between themselves and the feet of the Funus Mountains behind them. More and more, a fine sand dusted the grass, silver and pink like fancy salt, and the land lay in front of them as flat as a desert.

The legs of the avimu sank into the sand further with every step, and they grew exhausted as the party neared the middle of the flat. With tight eyelids and a covered brow, they were just able to glimpse the flat mirror of the sea far ahead of them. Kard recommended that they take rest to have one last meal on solid ground, and Alan followed he and Rime to a small pool.

The water of the pool was also clear like glass, and the depression lay between a few skeleton-like trees. They had no leaves or life about them, and the bark shone polished like a smooth arrangement of ridges on a hand-carved coffin. Some of them twisted or turned in abnormal ways that made Alan question whether their roots had ever known the warmth of the ground. He'd seen trees like this before but couldn't remember where.

As the others unpacked their snacks from Dard, Alan realized he hadn't brought his pack and went back to the place where they had tied up the avimu. Stellis sat there, leaned up against Drake, who appeared to be (and sounded like he was) taking a nap. She held a peculiar object in her hand and seemed to whisper into it, frantic, but quiet.

Alan cleared his throat to make his presence known. She put whatever it was back into her pocket and formed a thin smile on her face.

"Alandriel."

He spoke slowly. "Hey, Stellis. Just came back to grab some food. Were you gonna come eat with us?"

She looked down at her lap, where a wet pen was holding one of her books open, before looking back up to Alandriel with genuine concern in her eyes.

"Alandriel, I think it's best that we talk."

"Is it about that thing that you just shoved back into your pocket?"

Her face relaxed, and she laughed uneasily. "This?" She pulled the object back out from her pocket, and Alan could see now that it was only a shell. Or half of a shell. But not from the ocean, rather, from a very large nut.

"This has something to do with it, but there's nothing mischievous about it. You might as well know it by its name. This is a heren-nut."

"Wait. Were you eating it?"

She laughed again. "No, no. That would not be a good idea." She held it out closer for him to see. "They are quite prized, however. This one was a gift from a friend. A wonderful friend. Her mother grew a heren tree, but she had long passed before it bore any fruit. Klio picked this and another from that tree. She possesses the other one. It is a great gift, to give one the nut of the heren tree, for most trees must be slain after it is done—for the heren-nuts to be properly used, that is."

"Does it tell you your future?" Alan asked, considering what he knew of sorcery. "Like a crystal-ball or something like that?"

"No, not quite. The heren-nut by itself has no power. Its true value lies in the relationship between any picked from the same tree. You see, if I speak into this, the other heren-nut will hear my voice, no matter how far I am from it. Therefore, whoever holds the other can hear me."

Alan recalled the walkie-talkies he'd gotten as a present for his sixth birthday. The range was long enough that he could hide at the edge of their woods and talk to his dad back in the house. A guard, he thought himself. Guarding the edge of their kingdom.

He smiled at the thought.

"I've heard of magic sort of like that, I guess. Who has the other one?"

"Klio, the one who gave it to me."

"So, Klio—that's who you were talking to, just now when I came up?"

"Yes, and I'm afraid that's what we have to talk about. You should take a seat, Alandriel." Her face betrayed a sense of worry.

Alan sat down on the sand across from her. "Okay, what is it?"

"My friend, Klio—she's in my order. She is also in Oognysse. She stayed behind so as to not rouse suspicion and also to inform me if anything goes awry."

"And?"

"Things have gone awry. Faction warfare has broken out in the city between men, many of those that work in the mine, and the other inhabitants, those that look like Vanderkil or the Innkeeper. The men have called themselves the *Poliserd*. They walk the streets at night, and Klio fears that they've even taken one from my order. Alandriel..." She stopped for a moment, and was moving the sand around in front of her as a child drawing shapes in it. Her voice sounded as though she might cry, but Alan didn't believe she could. "I am telling you this in case you wish to leave. Once we are on the Sea, there will no longer be any chance of turning back. I cannot embark from here, not in good faith, without letting you know the situation in which you might arrive. The others know the risk. The signs were there when we departed that the people of the city were prone to this desperation."

She stopped and stared off to the Sea, and Alan thought for a second that he saw a tear streak down her cheek.

"If you wish to leave, you can take Mina back to where you come from. She has taken a liking to you I think."

Mina sat a little ways away with the bottom of her head resting on the ground. She purred softly as they both diverted their attention her way.

"I would not leave you all, not now. I don't know how much you still need me, or how much help I can give, but I don't have anywhere else in this world." His voice trembled slightly as he took a deep breath in. "You probably know that better than them."

She looked at him, coyly and knowing, but silent. He felt her gaze reach every part of him, as though there was nowhere else he could hope to hide his feelings or his concerns. They were all worn on his skin.

"I also have to be honest with you, Stellis. Since last night, or maybe longer for me—it's hard to explain—I've been searching for someone. This someone means a lot to me, and I never thought that I would find them here. But Imp Lode has surely not failed to surprise me. If I haven't run into them yet, even though my eyes have been peeled, maybe they're across the Sea."

"These aren't the people who were hunting you, are they? The ones you thought might take you away?"

"Oh, no. That turned out to be a false fear. I guess I'm doing the hunting this time."

"Rime said you were a good hunter."

"He did, didn't he?" Alan lingered on the thought.

She warmed up to his smile, and the two carried their lunches over to Kard and Rime to enjoy the rest near the pool. Kard had already finished eating and had stripped down to his undergarments, as he was wading playfully through the water in a place where it was not more than waist-deep. They all joined him for a brief respite after they too had finished their provisions from Dard, and before the Sun had begun its descent, they were all in the Sea atop the avimu.

The speed with which the avimu moved through the water was exhilarating. The salt spray misted Alan's arms and legs even though he sat behind Rime. With a sudden jolt, the bird leapt out of the water in an arch and stretched each wing as far as it would reach. As they touched back down to the surface of the sea, the water splashed up all around, and Alan could feel the cool shock of it on his face.

***

He woke up in the bus to a dribble of drool running down his face and onto his duffel. When he picked it up to readjust, he felt the moisture on all sides of the bag, wet from stray rain water that had trespassed through the window he'd left open.

Next to him, the man in the Browns shirt, aided by a book-light mounted to his glasses, read through a well-worn library book. It was apparent how long he'd gone without blinking from the redness and sugar glaze coating his eyes, and after a moment, he felt Alan's gaze and turned to face him.

"Is my light bothering you? I can turn it off."

"Oh, no. I don't mind." Alan looked around at the other riders. His seat buddy was the only other one awake. "What's that you're reading?"

"Southern Food. Very detailed and well-written."

"Oh, that's neat."

The man nodded politely.

"It's like an annotated cookbook or something?"

"Hmm." He looked carefully at the cover and back to Alan. "Yes, I suppose. I think it is a guidebook."

"Is that why you're going to Georgia?"

He chuckled. "Yes, it's a foolish dream." He closed the book and sighed warmly before sitting back in the bus seat. "It's funny. Have you ever had Brunswick stew?"

Alan shook his head.

"It's a stew commonly served with barbecue in the South. You know barbecue?"

He nodded.

"There's quite the debate over where the stew first came from. There's places called Brunswick in several southern states. They all want to be the one that made the stew, just like Hollywood made the movie star." He chuckled loftily. "But it is not their food."

"What do you mean?"

"The food the south always wants to claim. Most of the good came from slaves. The slaves did not choose to come here and make food. The other is British. Guess what?"

"What?"

He smiled again, but with sadness. "They stole just as much. Steal, steal, steal. Then fight for who stole it first. Curry powder, what a marvel!" He laughed.

Alan looked at him for a minute in the dim glow of his book-light. He appeared older now. "So what's your dream? Why are you going to Georgia?"

"I am very hungry." The man looked at Alan as though he had just told him everything he could possibly want to know, and with a twinkle in his eye, he flipped off the book-light.

Alan stared out the window of the bus until it pulled into the station.

***

The bus ride from Atlanta to Athens went by in a flash. He woke up to amber rays of early sunlight stretching across brick walkways and old town roads in the heart of the downtown area near the bus depot. It was a young Sunday morning, and there was hardly more than dew on the sidewalks.

As he wandered his way through the nearly labyrinthian streets named after old markers of the South: Jackson, Clayton, Thomas, and Pulaski; he passed bagel shops and used bookstores just beginning to buzz and hum to prepare for the Sunday crowd. He could smell breakfast hams and eggs frying. At the turn of every corner, there was a student in a groggy rush to a serving shift at a restaurant or a well-dressed couple in their Sunday best.

No taxis though. He walked to the north side of town where there were more churches and one or two parking garages—that seemed to increase the odds. Just as he was about to bother an elderly woman in a periwinkle dress carrying a Bible case that shook with her trembling gait, a pale yellow cab nearly passed him by.

He held up his left hand and waved it frantically and then scrambled across the road. The taxi slowed at an intersection between a magazine press and a vegetarian restaurant. He jogged as quickly as he could with his duffel and tossed it in the trunk before sliding into the backseat.

"1892 Ridgeway Pass," he asked, nearly out of breath from the run. He looked up from the crumpled note in his hands to the driver, a bald, chunky man with a nice smile and a fuzzy black jacket. The man nodded, and they were off.

Out the window, the storefronts and lively shops soon gave way for more dispersed gas stations and liquor stores, which gave way to foot doctors' offices and small grocery stores, and finally there was little out the right window aside from railroad tracks and silos, though it didn't seem that they'd been driving for too long. The city had vanished in a blink of an eye, and Alan felt he was getting his first glimpse of a real southern countryside.

After a few more miles, they crossed the tracks on the right and drove through a few more spiraling turns and twists before he saw it on the other side of the road: Ridgeway Pass. The green marker was bent over and the paint was peeling, but he had goosebumps up both arms.

This road twisted too, but less so, as the edges were closely guarded by thick oaks and dense brush. Now and then he thought he caught glimpses of a river or maybe a creek, but he couldn't be sure. Then the taxi slowed, and he felt his weight shift as they turned onto the driveway.

It was long and shrouded by turns as everything seemed to be here, and around the sixth or seventh curve (he'd lost count), they came upon the house.

The trees opened up here to the sky, and the grass was the better for it. It was bright green with patches of yellow here and there from being well-used, and it led to a curved stone path that went all around the brick foundation of the house.

Its color was a pale green, though there were so many windows you'd hardly notice. It was old and flat. The gutters seemed to be from a different time: long black pipes that would come right out of the middle of a face. The chimneys were the same; four by his count, and they all came out of precarious spots where he questioned the practicality of a fireplace.

He handed two folded bills to the driver, gathered up his duffel, and stepped out upon the path. No one came, though he wasn't sure if it was good or bad. He couldn't hear anyone either, and wondered for a moment if Warnie Tollers was the church-going type.

As he approached the front door of the house, receded into the brick beneath an archway, he gauged the height of the sun against the horizon. Too early for church, he hoped. As he knocked, his thoughts drifted away to Imp Lode and the path of the Sun. It was his check; he realized. If he was ever unsure whether he was in the dream, he only need a compass and sight of the Sun.

Is that east or west, he wondered.

It had been sometime since his first knock, so he reached out his fist again and wrapped in rhythm three more times. He paused and put his ear close to the pine wood to listen for footsteps.

Instead, he heard a sharp creak and the slamming of a latch from somewhere off to the side of the house, and then an old, melodious voice hollered, "In the garden! Come around. If you're lookin' for Leddie, she's in the bath!" A moment later, the voice mumbled, "Probably shouldn'ta told you that."

Alan followed the path around the west side and saw a garden around the bend. It was small but charming. There were rows of well-manicured hedges, less-cared for thorny ones, blooming lavender petunias, several large sunflowers, and some elephant ears adorning either side of the front gate that the man had just closed behind him.

He was a normal height, Alan supposed, though he was slightly hunched over. He wore a brown scally cap, a sportsman's jacket to match (which he soon left hanging from the fence), and had just returned a wooden pipe to a concealed vest pocket as Alan approached. He furrowed his brow, looked him up and down, and then knocked on a post with a fist as if he were deep in thought.

"I don't know you, do I? Or have I lost my mind?" He scowled and quickly breathed in. "Don't answer that. I have lost it somewhere around here, but I'd prefer to find it myself."

Alan stood in front of him dumbly, still not knowing what to say.

"Well, you're not the milkman. Unfortunately, I have to go into town and get that myself. You're not a peddler, are you?"

"A peddler?" Alan asked.

"No, no. I suppose you aren't. You are very clearly lost, though. What's in that bag, there?"

Alan looked at the duffel he'd forgotten about. The zipper had come open and one of his socks was hanging out.

"Just my things, nothing much. You wouldn't happen to be Warnie Tollers, would you?"

He leaned onto the post and offered no more than a wary gaze. "I suppose there might be justifiable reasons for you asking that," he said after another minute. "Why do you ask?"

"Well...well—if," Alan stammered," if you are, then I'd really like to ask you a few questions." He pulled *Lucid Dreaming for the Casual Adventurer* out from his bag, again freeing the sock. "Is this your book?"

His leery face turned to a tiny grin which grew a bit larger, and then he said, "Well, I might have just as many questions for you, I reckon." He turned and opened the gate again. "Let's have a seat in the garden."

Warnie Tollers, if it was indeed him, led Alan to a small courtyard in the middle of several rows of hedges. There, in a well-arranged hexagon of red bricks, sat a wooden bench. Once seated, they were facing one of the largest butterfly bushes Alan had ever seen. It was swaying as if in a breeze from all the wing flutters and takeoffs happening within its laurels.

The man suddenly had a cane, though Alan was not sure where he had conjured it from, and he hunched himself over it as he spoke. "So, you're a library user, I see. I knew I wasn't as bad a judge of character as my wife thinks."

"Yeah, I am. I guess you did mail it to our library then. So you are Warnie Tollers?"

The old man nodded. "I've never heard it spoken so many times in a minute. And who are you?"

"My name is Alan Hendershot. I'm from Ashtabu—well, I guess you already know where I'm from."

"Alan Hendershot," the man said, as if he was reminiscing. "Tell me about yourself."

"Well, I'm 26. I uh...well, I work at a grocery store." He looked over, but the man sat perfectly still, nodding slowly. "I like to read. Fantasy mostly, I guess. I have a mom and a sister...and my dad passed away earlier this year." Alan took a deep breath in and tried to think of something else to say about himself.

The man's eyes closed as he said, "Tell me about the world, Alan. Tell me about your world."

"Do you mean, well, the world from the dreams?"

"The world you go to," Warnie Tollers said, "show it to me."

"Well, I call it Imp Lode. That's kind of a long story. I've gone there every night pretty much for the past couple of weeks. It feels like I've been there so much longer, though. Everything is so familiar, but still so...well, strange. There's towns and rivers and mountains and cheeses. I've made friends there. I have a job to do with them, sort of. We've had adventures, I would say."

The man smiled, eyes still closed. "What are the trees like?" he said.

"The trees?"

The man was silent.

"Well, they're cool I guess. I haven't noticed them all that much, to be perfectly honest with you. They're comforting though. I heard a story about them, from someone who lives there, something about them being alive." Alan paused. "Well, I mean I know that trees are alive...but, *alive*."

The man nodded and squeezed his eyes tightly as though he was trying to remember. "It's a beautiful land, isn't it?"

"Imp Lode?"

Again, the man said nothing, but the smile remained on his face.

"Have you been there, too?"

"No, not to your world."

"But you said it's beautiful?"

The man opened his eyes and looked at Alan. "Well yes, why else would you go there every night?"

The two sat in silence for a while longer, quietly observing the butterflies and the honeybees flittering and buzzing among the blossoms. There was a cool breeze and the fine perfume of ready flowers filled the air. To Alan, it felt as though there was no civilization for hundreds of miles.

"So, Alan Hendershot, creator of *Imp Lode*. You have questions for me?"

Alan nodded. "Did you write all of the notes in this book?"

The man didn't look. "Yes, I know that my handwriting is horrid. Unfortunately, those are all my god-forsaken scrawl."

"So I guess that you have a pretty good idea how all of this works?" Alan asked, "Did you use it the same way?"

The man took out the pipe from his pocket and packed it. "Well, now that depends. What way is that?"

"To live a story, I guess. More or less. As if you're a character in a book. Going on great quests and chosen to conquer great feats, those sorts of things. Is that how you used it? Or, I guess, is that what you made it for?"

"Made it? Hmph." He rested his chin on the cane. "It was a fantastic world. Not too far from yours, I suppose. Now quests, I cannot say for certain, for I do not quite estimate my own sincerity as sufficient if I were to answer. It would be many days spent on this seat for you to hear all the tales I've taken, and not all would be true, mind you."

He lit the tobacco with a match and took a few priming puffs.

"So you were an adventurer, as the title says?"

"If the hand is ugly, so be it writ by me. Yes, Alan Hendershot, in those days I thought myself an adventurer. Bold and fearless. Hoo-rah!"

"Okay, good. Well, yes. Good. But now I think I've gotten off-topic. Truly I have one main question for you. Though I promise, I would like to hear all of your tales."

The man cracked a short laugh and nodded.

"I need someone to show up. I've followed all the notes and guides you wrote about bringing in a particular person, but I can't make it happen. But it's very important that I see this person. What...well, what do I do?"

The man fixed his gaze on Alan once again and looked at him for a long while. It felt longer to Alan because he was not very fond of being gazed upon, though he could see the man was thinking of other things. After a breeze stirred up the scents of summer once again, the old man drew himself back to his hunch.

"The person is dead, yes?"

Alan nodded blankly.

"Yes. Hrmph." He hunched deeper and closed his eyes. "The answer to that question...I'm afraid, is quite a long story." He took a draw and blew a puff of smoke into the breeze. "I'm quite old, as you've gathered. There was a time when I was not. During this time—the time when I was not—I had a big head full of big ideas about what it means to be a *patriot*."

He laughed dryly and knocked on the bench.

"There was a great war, before your time, no doubt. Before my children's time at that. I thought it best to enlist to rid Leddie of the sleepless nights. Seemed something inevitable in those times, anyway. I was assigned to a cruiser. Radar. Juneau, the ship was named."

He paused and drew another pull from the pipe. "Leddie and I have always wanted to go to Alaska."

"Anyhow, we got into a rough bit. Happened on Friday the 13th of all days. True literary irony, isn't it? We were left out on the water just trying to float and hide from the sharks. They got nearly all of us. I didn't deserve to make it out of there. I knew it, and I told it to myself every night shivering in my bunk on the boat back to Hawaii."

The man stared at the embers in his pipe.

"So, Alan Hendershot, I tore myself to pieces. Even when I got back on dry land, there was a part of me that wanted to go back out there—swim off the Solomon Islands and find myself in the water and let my heavy body sink down to the bottom to be with my mates. Didn't seem right that I was here. But life drug me on. As it does. I moved far away, but I still wanted to be within a day's drive of the ocean. Something still twisted up inside of me, rotten and stinking. Then one night I had a dream. Nothing special about the contents, but this fellow from my desk job—Paul Hoffman—he was there. But it felt so visceral, you know? We had a conversation and I could remember every word when I woke up."

He took a few quick puffs to liven the pipe back up.

"I spent the next three years trying to get my best shipmates to show up in my dream. Something inside me—I needed to apologize, or just see them smile again. I read every book that was ever written on dream journals, hypnotism, lucid dreaming. That's when I found that book. I knew right away that it was something special. I could control the dreams if I wanted. I made a whole world there, like you did. Like we all would, I suppose. It was the best of vices. Beat whiskey, running, even this pipe."

Then, he didn't say a word for two full minutes.

"It was a land of my creation, but a creation you cannot make sober or conscious. Bedtime became a ticket to a faraway land. The grass was greener than any I've ever seen with my waking eyes. I lived in a small stone cabin perched upon the side of a hill. A stream ran in front of it, and my garden was wonderful. There was a small pub a short walk and one bridge away where I could get a pint whenever I dreamed of it. But I soon found the peaceful life rather repetitive, and that's when the adventures began."

He looked at Alan with a curious eye before he continued.

"Dragons, brimstone, thieves, and hexes. But I knew what I was truly looking for. I searched all across the lands, asked every beast and friend I met, but none of them had seen my mates. The world there had not seen them. Not a soul."

"Did you ever find them?"

Alan looked at the old man, hopeful, but the two remained silent. The only noise that filled the air, yet again, was the flirtatious breeze of summer. It seemed too full of life, Alan thought.

"It's a mighty peculiar thing, isn't it? Curious, I'd say, Alan Hendershot. It's right there in the title of the book, the part that I didn't mark out. But I never saw it. You didn't either, it seems."

He laughed softly. His pipe was hardly smoking now, and ash covered his right armrest.

"In a lucid dream, you have control. That's the whole idea of it. That's the rage of it, really. But the world, Silva aeternalis I called mine, it seems to be out of your control, doesn't it? Perhaps that's why we forget. Everything becomes cloudy. It all just happens like the passing of time."

Alan pondered the words for another minute, but couldn't make any sense of them.

"Well, I'm sorry Mr. Tollers, but—"

"That was utter enigmatic rubbish? I agree with you, Alan. You see, the harrowing truth of that quest I'd never reached the end of, well, there wasn't any evil hiding my mates from me, no great, hideous beast who'd locked them up in a watchtower. Do you see?"

He looked at Alan as though he knew he wouldn't. He laughed again.

"I was hiding my mates from myself. My own sleeping heart couldn't bear being unfolded in front of them. I was too ashamed. A beautiful contraption, the mind. The only thing in this world that can truly hide something from itself—if it wants to, that is."

He turned his pipe over above the ground and emptied out the rest of the ash before returning it to his pocket.

"So you think that I'm hiding my dad from myself?"

"Your father, is it? Well, Alan, I reckon that you know the truth to that question much better than myself."

Alan nodded, then asked again, "Did you ever find your friends? In the end?"

The man nodded. "I did. Tenth wedding anniversary. We went out to Hawaii. Frequent flyer miles from work and that bit of jazz. I'd given up dreaming for the trip—to be more *available* mentally. I woke up in the middle of the night to seawater up to my waist, still in my pajamas. I'd sleepwalked right out into the ocean. I just cried. Felt like the ocean was giving me more saltwater to keep making tears. But somehow, that did it."

"They'd never let me grieve. Or I'd never let myself grieve. I'd just held it all in, every year since I'd come back. It seemed so clear to me then, like I'd been a fool for ever feeling the burden of guilt, even though I knew that I wasn't. But I felt them there. Their spirits, whatever you want to call it. And they weren't the least bit angry with me."

"On the plane ride back to Atlanta, I slept the whole way. But do you know what?"

"What?"

"I wasn't sleeping at all. In fact, I was downing pints at the wee little pub in Silva with my best mates egging me on. It always sounds silly to say, but it was a dream come true."

"That's great! I mean, I'm happy for you. That's wonderful that you found them, in the end at least."

"It was, wasn't it?" The man said, more joyful now. "Alan Hendershot. If I remember the proper cost of that postage, you've come a very long way. And that was your question, was it?"

Alan nodded.

"Well, I've got faith in you. That's always a good start, someone having faith in you, isn't it? Just remember the title of that ratty old book—you've got the control. It doesn't take trousers and underwear soaked in saltwater to gain it. It did for me, but I'm a stubborn git. You'll figure it out."

The two got up, and after Alan explained he had already booked his return bus ticket home for that night the old man insisted that he at least have tea or a lunch with him. As it was a beautiful day, they had both in the garden. To this day Alan has not had a better pimiento cheese sandwich.

XXI. Salted underwear

Trying to fall asleep in the sub-economy class seat of a northbound red-eye bus, Alan Hendershot, for once, felt that he was headed in the right direction.

The old man's story had not gone from his mind for a moment; how the man's salty underwear had somehow reassured him that his friends were not angry at him for surviving. Alan knew that there was a reason he could not see his dad, but he had not allowed himself to endorse the thought until now.

Until this moment, Alan has feared very little. Although it might seem as though he has plenty to choose from: lifelong job insecurity, crippling debt once his healthcare costs increase, or that he'd just spent his second-to-last dollar on a bus ticket, none of that had bothered him. He'd figure it out.

The one unspoken fear, unthought even, that possessed Alan was the idea that his father was disappointed in him. That the moment they began talking, his dad would ask him the full gambit of questions that every aunt, neighbor, and cousin at his funeral had asked him.

Are you dating anyone? Will you be going to college soon? Do you have any idea what you want as a career? Do you make good money where you work? That upon hearing the resounding cacophony of nos to every one of these questions, his dad would see his son, would see him, as a screw-up.

But perhaps even worse than all that was the notion that he would be right.

The traffic whizzed by on his left side. Car after car of more travelers going down to Georgia to receive their sought-after fate. The glass on his cheek was wet from his warm breaths. No one was moving on the bus. The driver was hardly even awake, Alan reckoned. But he didn't care. He needed to sleep.

It was almost instinctual now, the ritual. There didn't seem to be any good in going to sleep and *not* going to Imp Lode. What a waste of time that would be.

So he crunched himself up a little tighter to ensure the circulation loss would do the trick it always did. He thought about where he had last been, on the avimu surfing upon the crest of the sea—how powerful it had felt. He whispered the names of his companions, the steadfast friends he had always been able to conjure. The ones he'd had no trouble bringing in to the dream. Just as he was slipping off into it, he thought *maybe there's something to that.*

***

There in Imp Lode, it was morning. A cloudless sky greeted Alan as he awoke, covered in sticky sand and drooling on his hand. There was something above him, a shadow swaying back and forth like a piñata, but the sun was too bright to see it.

He stumbled to the shore where quiet waves were crashing on the beach and wet his hands in the water to refresh his face. When he turned around, he saw the gallows. Three bodies were hanging from them, right above where he'd been sleeping. They hung limp, wrapped in some black fabric soaked in what was surely blood.

Kard was next to him then, appearing from nowhere.

"Welcome to Oognysse, lad. Land of opportunity. If ye aren't a frek of course. Then you'll be one of these fine ornaments."

"Sorry, a frek?"

"That's what they call 'em here. All those that look different now. Freks. Ugly word."

"And they just murder them? Out in the daylight for all to see?" Alan asked, looking uncomfortably at the bodies as he gathered up his things.

"Not quite for all to see. That's why we camped here, see. It's not safe for us here, not to ruffle yer feathers, lad, but Stell has heard from her sisters that the townsfolk got an eye out for you. They know somethin' sour is in the air that don't like them hangin' ornaments round town like these. They know the sisters don't like the killins and they know the sisters want you here. That ain't a good recipe for you. Didn't we talk about this last night? A low profile will keep your divinely blessed ass in one piece." Kard held up a pointer finger in a shushing motion and winked.

"Wonderful. Is everyone here so kind?" Alan asked, "or they must hang creatures in secret so most of the town doesn't catch on?"

"Eh, hard to say, really. Seems to me they do it where nobody can see so that nobody has to say anything about it. Turn a blind eye and all that, see."

"Right. Brilliant. Good to be in the land of opportunity. Where did Stellis and Rime head off to?"

"The two of 'em got up before the sun to go scout ahead. We've got friends here, but as I've said, word's gotten around as to what we were doin' all that time we've been gone. Most important thing now is to keep you hidden, I reckon. The stables, that's where they were off to first. We're to meet them in the forest on the northern edge of town, Fortis. Locals call it Frek Forest now. Lotta strange magic about that place. It's keeping the undesirables safe for now."

"So we have a plan?"

Kard laughed. "Well, plan is a very strong word. Having you here, it'll give everyone a lot of confidence. Lift the troops' spirits, so to speak. After that, it'll be up to you, I reckon. You or whatever might be hunting for you. *Aside* from the townsfolk."

They walked along the shore, staying on the outside of the rocky outcroppings that reined in most of the town from the sea. Alan felt sick from nervousness, but the rhythmic crashing of the waves kept his nausea at bay. He pondered what Kard had said.

"Up to me to do what? What do you mean by that?"

"Well, it's *you* lad. You're the only one who can do anything. All those in Stell's order, they've tried and tried to find the source of the sickness. They've read more scrolls and books than even Rid, I reckon. The answer isn't in the books. That much is clear. You're the best answer we've got. Something in this town is hiding it, gotta be. That's why it all started here. Some more strange magic. I don't wanna scare ye, but yer quite nearly all we've got. We aren't just gonna go diggin' up random graves and knockin' on doors, but we've got to get you around. You've got to *see* it all so that maybe you see *it*." He snorted and shook his head. "I feel right foolish speakin' in riddles like this, but I know little, Alan."

Kard looked up at him as he hopped over a rock, and there, for just a second, Alan could see it.

There was a reason he'd never had any trouble getting Kard to show up in the dream, or Stellis, or Rime and Riddle. From the moment he'd met them, they'd needed him. They'd needed him to do this thing, this thing that he still didn't quite understand, and that was why he could bring them back. He didn't have any worry that they thought he wasn't enough; he knew he was enough. Alan was their only enough.

As he felt the water wash over his feet and turned to look out upon the sea they had come from, standing there in his salty underwear, he knew what he had to do. If he could fix this for them, that was something. For his stubborn, insubordinate mind, that would be something it couldn't ignore. That would *really* mean something. That would bring his dad into the dream.

Now they were passing closer to the heart of the city, the one part of the vast shoreline where you could see through to the bustling market and the sea of people that hummed and buzzed through the streets. Closer to their side of the town on the east, the land was split wish a huge gash that grew wider and wider the nearer it got to the ocean. It looked like a mouth breathing cold winter air as smoke billowed out of the massive crevice and into the hazy sky.

They waded out into the ocean as they got nearer to the feature, per Kard's instructions.

"What is that thing?" Alan asked, trying to make sense of what little detail showed itself on the flatness of the land.

"That, laddy," Kard said, "is the rock mine. The scar upon Oognysse. We used to call it the Sticks River, see, because the craftsmen would float lumber from the forests down it into the heart of the milling district. Only, it's not a river at all, just more of the sea. Only now it's nothing. They put up the wall keeping the sea out so that they could mine down there. Ain't much of a market anymore either. Most of the craftsmen worth a damn are those freks I told you about. Sure, the new men pull out lots of precious rocks, but the smoke is enough to make a small child choke. *Industry* they call it in town. Aye, enough to make you sick."

The distant sounds of chains running on pulley systems and mine cars grinding on steel tracks carried up out of the crack all the way to them. It was a ghostly echo, for the clouded grey air mostly kept the mine hidden from view. Only occasionally would Alan glimpse the great steel staircases running along the broad side of the ravine down into the depths, or ash-covered men piling into a queue at the top, all carrying full rucksacks.

Soon the smog dissolved into the same cloud of blurry air and haze that sat atop the whole of the city, and after a while, Alan could no longer tell where the great big crack had been.

The further north they got, the shorter the trees on the shoreline grew. Soon they could see the red and brown of faded roof tile through the leaves, quick glimpses of the wealthier residential district, Kard said. The bark changed too, from the black and dark browns close to the gallows to a rosy grey with chalky white flecks peeling off. The houses had walls of the same wood, and were quite tall, some stacked three or four stories right on top of each other, but they were all narrow.

"Stay low." Kard said, "Most will be out and about in the middle of town or the market, but there's always a few stragglers keen on spying from their high perches. Everyone's on edge now."

"Who all...well, is it mostly *people* who live here?"

Kard stumbled beneath an overturned log that was too high for him to climb over. "Now what do you mean by that?"

"I mean to say, how many other types of creatures are there? The freks, cyclops, skeletons, gnomes, all those ones."

He laughed. "Mighty diverse town, Oognysse is. Lot more than what you've seen so far. Lot more than you'll see in Reul too, I reckon. But mostly people, aye."

Alan watched the upper windows of each house they slunk past with a close eye. A time or two, he could have sworn that he saw something catch the light or a shape move to the side, but the sunlight had become too bright to see well enough.

Once they had gotten well enough away from the last house, leaving it a few hundred itchits behind them, Kard said that it was safe to turn to the west once again and make their way into the forest. It was an awfully drab forest, with no undergrowth or pretty ferns, and not a wildflower or wet moss in sight. The trees were just as grey as the rest, and Alan would have done nearly anything just to see a squirrel or rabbit cross their path, or a vosvudu even. It was desolate.

"So this is Frek Forest, is it?"

"No!" He shook his head. "No, my lad, do not mistake this sorry land for Fortis. We will see her beauty soon enough. You will know it. Does the silence chill you?"

"The silence?"

"This forest, it's made no noise in ages. No life stirs here. It's said that it can drive a man crazy if he goes in alone. We're sure not to pass anyone here."

"It is a little uncomfortable, I suppose. I never knew silence could be so *loud*. What do they call it?"

"Synn. Don't even call it a forest no more. Just Synn. Here—"

Kard began to whistle the same melody that he had whistled before, what felt like months ago, as they were searching for cover from the storm. Alan had liked it well enough then, but here in the absolute silence of Synn, it multiplied like a gas occupying all the volume it could. It swelled and swelled, and even the grey trees seemed to sway with the song.

Alan couldn't whistle, but he wanted to join in. He began to hum along, off-kilter at first, and then he caught hold of the rhythm.

"That's it lad! There's words to this song, y'know? I'll teach 'em to you one day."

The pair whistled and hummed on and on in the brevity of solace. There was a hidden whisper beneath the melody of the song, maybe, Alan thought, the story. Whatever the words were, he could feel them, like a faint breath lets you know the presence of someone that you love. There was a breeze too, but warm, and it flowed through the leaves, whistling around their sharp edges. Oddly, he felt Riddle in it, and so he grabbed the book from his pocket—the one that Rime had given him. All of Riddle's stories. As the leaves twirled around, up high in the canopy and right above his head, he plucked one from the air and stuck it in the pages of the book.

When Alan closed the book, he saw a glimmer of gold in the brush—the gold cat's eye had fallen from his pocket. The ink in the core was fluid again, swirling around as though it had come to life. As he snatched it up, he couldn't help but recall the night that the marble had fallen into the fire as he tried to pass it to Riddle.

And suddenly, Alan had a very dangerous idea.

"Kard, how quickly can you get a fire going? Doesn't have to be big."

Kard spun and peered strangely back at Alan. He gritted his teeth and spat. "A butcher who loves smoked meat? Fast, lad. Fast. But a mighty odd request from ye who rarely snacks. Havin' a grumble?"

"I just want to test something out."

Kard bugged out a single eye and nodded hesitantly. "Aye, but smoke might draw some..." He paused, taking a moment to observe the thick layer of haze obscuring the town from them. He shrugged. "O'course. Why not?"

Kard furiously scrambled around until his fist was full of springy twigs and dried grasses and needles. Moments later, he was knocking two stones together, and Alan watched as the spark took to a sprig of needles, shriveling them into spirals. Soon, the bundle was aglow.

Alan took a forked stick and gently lay the marble on the split until he was sure it was stable. Slowly, he lowered it until the flames were close enough to tickle the sphere. Kard watched silently, mystified by the object.

That's when they heard it.

Up above, an incessant, tiny scratching, like a single fingernail sliding across a chalkboard. What happened next was a blur.

Kard, still knelt at the fire, shouted a variety of expletives that Alan had never heard before and seemed to be diving towards him and telling him to get out of the way simultaneously.

Next thing Alan knew, he was twenty or thirty feet in the air—and had no time to convert those feet to witchits or itchits. He felt something sharp like barbed wire or claws wrap around his arms, and his stomach had decided not to make the trip up into the sky with the rest of his body.

He looked above himself at it, but saw just a haze. A black, fuzzy, barely humanoid shaped cloud—glitching in and out as if it barely existed within time itself. The only well-defined feature were its eyes, glaring and yellow. They had no pupils or irises, but they were looking at him, he could feel it.

"I'll kill ye, ye no-good, shit-eating imp! Put my friend down!"

Kard was still on the ground and seemed almost toy-like from this height. He had unsheathed his sword and was bracing it against his forearm, but he had nothing to hit the beast with.

In a blink, two more black shapes had arrived, seemingly suspended above him. The one that grabbed him was still holding his arms tightly, and he could feel blood dripping down to his hands.

They were talking to each other, or at least they seemed to be. It was more sinister than a whisper, almost as if a growl had words in it and all those words could be dispensed without taking a breath in between.

The second one looked at him now, unflinchingly, and Alan felt a deep sadness within him, but could not take his eyes away from the yellow of theirs. In a flash and a crackling pop, one had darted away, back down into the trees and out of sight. A second later, it was back. It was fuzzy for a moment, like the other two, but then a terrible fizzling sound came from it and Alan could see the full detail of its body.

The imp hung there in the air, just for a moment. It was humanoid, hardly, but there was nothing else to call it. It had arms and legs and a long, barbed tail. Its wings glowed now, suspended of their motion and left still for all to see. They were a luminescent gold and shed a vapor of dust that lingered around them.

In the middle of the creature, there was a blade, though Alan had just noticed it. Its point had gone through from the back, no longer than a dagger, and it dripped a slimy, tar-like ooze from the end that had come through its chest. Alan knew that the dagger was responsible for its freezing in mid-air.

The imp whimpered, and just before it fell down to the ground below, Alan felt sorry for it.

Though he hardly had time for such niceties, for just as it dropped, so too did he. Still in the grasp of his kidnapper, he looked down to the fast-approaching ground to see the skyward-facing portrait of a woman he had not met, though a second later, he tumbled into her as the three of them rolled across the damp floor of the forest.

She was hardly fazed by the altercation and sprang forth again to her feet, pulling tightly on a white, silken cord that she held in her hands. At the other end, the incapacitated imp grasped helplessly at the binds that were tightening around its ankles and swarming up its legs.

In a scratchy, black animation, not unlike stop motion, the imp lashed out with a gnashing jaw and dark, inky blades of teeth that made a mess of cutting through the cord. It was frayed and shredded like a dog's chew toy. The imp fluttered back into the air now, but in a frame of motion just like every other move it made—it was as if you were only seeing part of it, as though the flashes in between were happening somewhere else. With a horrible grumble, it took off, high in the sky and over the trees.

"*That*," the unknown woman said, "was the damndest bit of luck you'll ever have in your life. You must be Alandriel."

She smirked and flipped a stray curl of black hair away from her eye as she reached down to pull her knife from the chest of the fallen imp. Her skin was dark like mahogany, and at the moment it was splattered from head to toe with the black tar that the imps bled. She replaced the knife in a fold of her scarlet cloak and was now standing directly in front of him.

"I am. Thank you for saving me." Alan stuttered, still trying to compose himself. His heart raced. "Who are you?"

"That's Klio," Stellis said, as she jogged into view from within the dense trees. "She's much better at beaming than I, I might add." She chuckled.

"Beaming?" Alan asked.

"Yes, making oneself disappear from one place and appear somewhere else. Beaming."

"My god, is that really what you call it?"

"He's from Reul, you said?" Klio asked, grinning smugly.

Just then, Rime came around the same bend, his face red as a beet and breathing heavily. "You..." He took a big breath in, "moved so," and another, "fast." He spit onto the ground and took several more deep breaths. "What in the hell was that?"

As Alan drew himself back into reality, he considered what had just happened. He still held the marble tightly in a balled up fist, and looked at the others, contemplating how to explain his theory.

Just as he opened his mouth, Rime interrupted in a befuddled grumble, "is that—" He pointed down at the corpse, having just seen it. "That's what an imp looks like?" His face flushed back to white as he stumbled back.

Stellis nodded but drew her eyes back to Alan. He could sense her keen perception as he met her eyes. She did not look at his closed fist, but Alan felt that all her attention was on it.

"Come, we must make for a safer location. Alandriel, I think we have something to discuss on the way."

As they traveled deeper into Synn, Alan couldn't help but jump every time he heard a rustling or scratch in the trees up above, but the company of his friends helped to calm him down. His arm was sore, bleeding, and bandaged, though he knew it could have been much worse.

Once they had made it safely for some distance, Stellis decided that it was now okay to speak, but that they must be quiet about it.

"May I see what you hold in your hand, Alandriel?"

Alan slowly unwrapped his fingers, which were white from squeezing tightly onto the marble with all that his hand could manage. Stellis did not touch the marble, but looked at it with great reverence. After a minute of silent observation, she nodded.

"Place that in your pack. Do not lose it."

"What is it?"

Stellis looked back at the others in the group, eyeing Rime keenly. "There are very old things, and then there are things that must seem to be very old because nobody has laid eyes on them in a time that we can remember."

Alan nodded.

"This, I believe, is both. I understand as much of the magic of this world as I am able, but even my knowledge has gaps that I must only guess at. I do not know the way in which the imps have followed and found us. But I do know of the ways that the ground works to speak between us, as I showed you before." She stared intently into Alan's eyes to verify the impact of her words. "I do not know exactly what that object is you hold, because I have never seen one. I do know that I have also never seen what has protected you from the blindness. I did not know the image of an imp, not truly, until this day, but I did know the image of imp dust—the color, the shine, and the glimmer."

She looked back at his hand as she spoke of the dust.

Alan nodded slowly, considering what she said. "Okay, go on."

"Furthermore, there is a reason that most people, even a tracker and hunter as skilled as Rime, only really know what imp *dust* looks like, but not the imp itself. In all that I have read, I can find no one in recent times that has seen an imp. There are only those who pretend to know, and they pretend based upon what they read in *very* old stories."

"So people used to see imps?"

"It stands to reason, yes. There is a reason our world is named thus, though the reasons for naming things are often lost to time. However, there are certain people who ensure that these reasons are not lost." She looked at Rime, and he nodded knowingly. "Alandriel, did Rid carry this object you hold when we were last attacked?"

Alan's heart sank as what he feared to be true clawed its way into his reality. He felt a hot flush come over his face.

"I gave it to him. Is it my fault? Is this thing the reason they went after Rid?"

"I would not blame that death on you just as I would not blame his death on his overwhelming sense of curiosity. The evil that we owe Rid's death to is the very same evil we aim to drive out, and it does not live in you, Alandriel."

She held her hands over Alan's, with the gold cat's eye marble within.

"For now, we do have one thing we did not before. I believe we know the minds of these creatures. Or, at least, something they seek. I believe this is why you can see, Alandriel. I believe they want to take that from you, or whoever else may carry it. I believe there is a way that we can use that. But I think that for now, we must get to safety."

Alan did not know what to feel. But he knew that he did feel a lot. He felt scared. He felt empowered. He felt terribly anxious. And overwhelmingly, he wished for a story from Rid.

Rime patted Alan on the back as they all got back on their way. "Aye, onward. Kard is a nasty beast, but I'd rather be safe within a shelter."

Kard nodded in half-agreement, but did not possess the levity to make a joke about the degree to which he could intimidate the imps. "Hm, and don't take this the wrong way," he mumbled, "but how did ye get there so quickly?"

"Check your pack, Kard." Stellis grinned. "I knew that it would blend in with your snacks."

Kard rustled around in his bag and pulled out the heren-nut that Alan had seen Stellis with before.

"What the hell is this?"

"Magic that Alandriel and I know about. I had faith that you would announce the arrival of any aggressor, Kard, and I am thankful that you did. But you no doubt would have been insulted had you known that I had hidden away a heren-nut in your bag, would you not have?"

She smiled and Kard's eyes widened. "A...a heren-nut? I thought... well, I thought those were rare as imps."

"You knew that we would be attacked?" Alan asked.

"Knew? No. Feared, yes. But not from imps. I still think our greater danger in this town is from the men who have no doubt already heard of your arrival, Alandriel—of the one who can *see*. I do admit a small part of me wished we had left the imps beyond the sea. Now that I know they are here...well...it only complicates the situation."

"Well, that's just the thing, Stellis. This situation—what are we to do? If this marble is the reason I can see, how do we use it to end the blindness? I didn't make it. I don't know how to make more of it. I don't—" Alan stumbled over his words, "I don't even know where it came from."

"Do you remember the night that we found you, Alandriel?"

He nodded.

"That night, we were out of hope. When we found you, a little bit of that hope came back piece by piece. It has less and less to do with your sight and this *marble*, but so much more to do with your resolve, Alandriel. The *plan*, if you will, in having you here, is that the answers show themselves. Sometimes it is less about looking in the right place, and more about one's ability to *see* at all. I do not know if there is one being behind this, or several, or none at all. I suspect that whatever is behind it, whatever is behind the curtain, will want to come for the one man that can see behind that curtain. I know that there is no place safer for you to be than here, surrounded by your friends and my order, and all of the creatures that have been cordoned into the forest, when that being comes. After all, Rime said you were not a bad trapper."

She took a deep breath in and looked up at the tree tops. The trees were changing up ahead. There was life in them.

"If you wanted a great plan to be revealed to you here, I am sorry. I do not have it. We have you, and because we have you, we have hope. I hope you do not feel used. My first intention has always been to keep you safe. If you do not feel safer here, I will take you wherever you wish to go."

"No, don't be crazy." Alan said, thinking for a moment. "The best hunter in the world trained me, and he trained me right. There's two things you gotta know about your prey: a sweet and a spot."

Alan looked at Rime, who was grinning ear to ear.

"It all started here, right? People are batshit crazy here, chasing after anything they think is ugly? Well, yeah this seems like a good spot to me. We know they're here, after all." Alan held up the marble for all the party to see. "And this—this is a pretty good sweet, I'd say.

I wouldn't take a bite of it, but those imps looked awfully hungry. I think you were wrong Stellis. I think we do have a plan."

The trees ahead were as full of life as they were of leaves. The breeze that had followed them through Synn lingered, warm and calming as it had been before. At first, Alan only saw the small birds fluttering from branch to branch and the rodents darting from one burrow to another. But the closer he got, the greater the sense he had that others were watching.

Soon there were eyes. Peeking out from around the base of a tree or barely visible from behind a bush. Pairs of eyes. One here, another there, two over there. Then he could see the faces, all different in shape and size, of many different creatures. Some wandered out into the open, cautiously stepping along the trail, others, no doubt, stayed hidden.

There were three that seemed to overcome their fear enough to face them.

In front, there was a short, old man with a pointed purple cap. It was tall, like a wizard's, and so Alan thought he must be one. He was not, however, a wizard at all. He was a gnome, and his name was Lucas. His nervous hand emerged from the flowing locks of white beard that hung from his chin, and he held it out to Alan.

As he shook Lucas's hand, Lucas immediately went off on a rambling story about his bead business. He would make wonderful necklaces before the Blindness. He pulled out a smaller one, a bracelet for Alan, placed it on him, and kissed his hand.

There was an elf, at least, he thought she was an elf. She had ears like Raphl but was much prettier. Her name was, "Elouise, but not in a snobby way," she said. She had taught archery to the younglings of Oognysse with her sister, Ariadne. When the townspeople had murdered Ariadne, Eloise had gone into hiding.

Next to her was another shorter man, just taller than Lucas. He was dressed like a pilgrim, Alan thought, except his hat was wrapped in vines and grasses, and was the only article of clothing that wasn't black. He did not offer a hand to shake, but looked on cautiously.

Later, Elouise would tell him that his name was Forty-Two, and that he was, quite unquestionably, a mean, old sprite. Alan did not feel a meanness from him though, and he would later learn about his "Lifting" services, wherein he would lift the spirits of any person feeling a bit down. His Lifting shop had been burned down a week after Stellis and the others had departed Oognysse.

There were others behind them, but none that he would learn the names of. There were more elves and gnomes, perhaps another sprite or two, and some other creatures that did not look like any of those.

They flanked the party of adventurers and scanned the surrounding forest as they drew nearer to the crowds hiding in the bushes. There seemed to be an awful lot of hiding spaces, surely many for imps, and Alan was glad for the aid from those that appeared to know their way around.

By now, he had been in several forests in Imp Lode and had a good sense of their personalities. But there was something strange about Fortis.

For one, there were different fungi spotted all about the ground. Some were brown with white spots and tall ivory trunks; some were the color of marigolds and sat flat on the ground like stools. But wherever he stepped, there was a new mushroom or prickly coral-looking thing. And the moss, the moss was everywhere.

The trees were normal. Well, most of them were. But now, as they walked through it, being trailed cautiously by several of the gnomes, he noticed that some trees were bigger than the rest. Not a marginal difference either, for the circumference of some trunks was so gigantic that if they had all gone up to a different side and hugged it, their hands would not have touched.

Stellis and Klio led the group, but took turns looking back and grinning at Alan as he looked around at Fortis. The expression on his face was that of childlike wonder, and though he too did not say anything, he grew more and more curious about so many things.

The answer to one of his questions arrived shortly, as they crossed in front of one of the large trees and heard a noise inside. It wasn't one of scratching, clawing, or pecking; the noises you'd expect from critters that had crawled up inside of the trunk. Rather, it was speaking, the voices of people.

"They live in these trees?" Alan asked, loftily.

"They do," Stellis responded, "and that is why the trees were grown. That is the magic that you feel in the air. Stories tell us that the security of Fortis has not failed. Many have sought refuge within Her trees as they do now. As we will tonight."

"We're going to stay in one of these?"

"It's the safest place in Oognysse." Kard shouted. "Especially for you!"

"I didn't mean any disrespect...I just...there's enough room?"

Klio laughed. "You were right. He is from very far away."

Alan stopped to examine the tree closest to them now. He laid his hand on the bark and pulled it back with a startle, for it was warm. He touched it again and left his hand there for a little longer. There was something very calming about it, though he couldn't quite describe it. But he didn't want to leave the tree's side.

As they drew near to the center of the woods, which was marked by several things, but most obviously an old sign on a post that read, "Fortis Middle," the crowd of creatures that had skirted along the shadows of the woods, spying them as they walked, had now started to emerge. One here, two over there, soon there was an overwhelming amount, and Alan was not sure that he even knew the races of half of them.

A buzzing started then, one of whispers and tiny, exasperated gasps, as Alan caught sight of several of the creatures, mostly gnomes again, pointing in his direction. They gathered closer now, a crowd forming as if Alan were about to deliver a sermon on the mount.

To his surprise, Stellis pulled him into the middle of the circle and threw a hand up in the air, quieting the building rumble.

"I know that the nights here have been long...and restless." She spoke loudly, projecting her voice for all to hear. "And that you have had to keep a watchful eye on the edge of the wood. Waiting for the moment that the wicked men that drove you to this place find a way to infiltrate these trees that protect us."

There was nodding throughout the crowd and several anxious glances behind them, as if she were foretelling the future.

"I know that my party and I have been gone long, and we do not return without loss." Stellis nodded to Rime and paused for a moment.

"But we also return with hope." She smiled and held Alan's hand. "It is true that this man has the sight."

The whispers in the crowd grew louder and one tall, blonde elf at the front outburst, "then it is true, there are those that have not been blinded?"

"My heavens! I would not believe it were it not you, Stellis," shouted a short, silver-haired creature that was probably a goblin.

Stellis nodded and waited for the commotion to subside. "There is much yet we do not know. But there is now far less that we cannot see."

Many of the creatures nodded in agreement and some spit on the ground, perhaps also in agreement.

"We still have much to consider and evaluate, but for now, we ask that you only remain calm. When we know where and how to move, we will do it, but to act preemptively would be foolish. Our priority now is to lock down the forest, even more so than we have already done, and to keep Alandriel," she motioned to Alan, "as safe as our own. For he has taken great risk in coming here, and it cannot be in vain."

There were more nods, but some uneasiness had also sprung up on a few pale faces scattered about the group.

A red-haired gnome wearing overalls shouted, "I've heard there were imps! On the edge of the forest! Is that what we are to defend against?"

Now there was a cacophony of frantic murmurs and mumblings across the gathering. Several spoke louder now, and Alan could hear snippets of their conversations: placing blame and insinuating their responsibility.

"There were two imps," Stellis said, "but we have neutralized them. If they return, I and several members of my order will be prepared and will neutralize them as we did those that attempted to ambush us in Synn. But for that reason, I must insist that you all lock down in your dwellings before the last light of day. If you want our protection, you must help yourselves as much as you can."

The same blonde elf that had spoken before spoke again, quieter than before. "The imps...are you sure that's what they were? That they're real?"

"We are sure," Stellis responded. "There is naught else it could be. They come for—"

The red-haired gnome hopped upon a stump and pointed at Alan. "They come for this man! Why don't we just hand him over! He's not one of us. He's not our problem!"

More creatures murmured and several nodded in agreement. Rime approached the gnome from behind and snatched the little being by the top of his overalls and roughly placed him back on the ground.

They watched the crowd for a minute as the echoes spread throughout. At first, only a brave few would offer their agreement that Alan should be handed over, but as more spoke up, more nodded and agreed. There were vile grunts and fists thrown in the air, and not less than a few beginning to advance towards Alan to take him.

Rime stabbed his sword into a crevice in the rock that he now stood on and shouted angrily, "Silence your ignorant tongues!"

"Now I want all of you to listen and listen good. You all know me. You knew my brother. You...many of you knew my mother. If you think Stellis, Kard, Klio, Rid, and I are all a pack of fools, then go ahead. Take your man. Hang him up as bait out on the same posts outside of town that they hang you from. See how long that wards off the imps."

He took a breath and scanned the crowd. No one said a word.

"But if you don't think we're as foolish as Rump would like you to believe, then listen for a moment before you all keep shouting over one another. This man traveled with us all the way from Drireford just to come here and help you wolves who would be so quick to offer him for supper. He saved my life. He did not choose to have the sight that he has, just as none of you chose to look the ugly way that you do. If you abandon him and toss him out, you're no better than the men that have pushed you into these woods. If there is anyone here that would still like to betray my friend, speak now."

He looked at all of them hard and sincerely, and glared long at Rump, the red-headed gnome. Again, nobody spoke, but their demeanor had softened and a few nodded apologetically to Rime.

"Good. So we've settled that then. Now, as we've already said, none of you is in more danger than Alandriel. We will be heading up a guard in and around the tree that he will sleep in tonight. If there are any volunteers that would like to help, come see us. Yes, you will be defending against imps, but their thirst is not for you. Yes...good, then."

He nodded and walked away from the middle of the circle as the crowd began to disband. He approached Alan and gave him a great, big hug that he held for at least a minute. Then he patted him on his back and said, "I will not let anything happen to you tonight. You have my word. If the imps come for you, they go through me first."

"And me, second, though I do not lack faith in Rime's defenses." Stellis had approached from the side with Klio walking beside her.

"I would love to get another piece of that imp that got away earlier," Klio said, sneering.

Kard leapt up on the stump defiantly. "Well the lot of you can get in line behind me. The first swing will be mine. I will not sleep a wink tonight."

Alan smiled, briefly reflecting upon how awfully cliche it was for an adventuring party to *get in line* and claim rank in the order that they would protect one of their friends, but he was quite too happy to dwell on it any longer.

As the daylight was dwindling now, the party made their way through the wood to the spot where Alan would sleep for the night, protected by everyone else. It was in a small clearing, a depression surrounded by tall trees on all sides. It was wet and muddy at the bottom, not unlike a swamp, and in the middle of the puddle of clay and grime grew a very large tree.

Its bark was jagged like broken glass or ice, and there was a faint sense of deep red or brown within the worn tones of grey, almost as though the tree still wore old wounds and scars on its surface. It was wide, as all the lived-in trees were, and the entrance sat in front of the one spot of ground not wet and clumped with mud, not wholly undue to the cobbled paver stones that lay in front of it.

The door was just like any old door. Curved at the top in a semi circle and made of paneled wood painted with a coat of deep emerald green that had faded well with time. There was no keyhole, but there was a sound of unlocking as Stellis laid her hand upon it and whispered softly. The door opened.

Inside, it was warm and welcoming, like you would imagine the reading den of an elderly, well-read author might be. There was a hearth on one side adorned with a homely, curled mantle that displayed odd little trinkets that appeared to have no function at all. Next to the hearth was a rack for a cooking pot and a very old square table and three chairs next to that. In all the corners, there were things stacked in piles that seemed to be the comforts of the place: well-worn books in one, blankets and coats in another, and in the far corner, the bed was tucked away into a little cubby in the wall. There were several candles on the table next to the bed, along with a few more books, and above the bed the most jarring of all the decor: two mounted swords and a crossbow.

Rime followed Alan's eyes around the room. "The bolts are under the bed."

"What's that?"

"The bolts—for the bow. There's a panel in the floor that lifts up. Best pull out ten or twenty before you tuck yourself in to bed."

Alan considered the gravity of defending himself in this tree, which before had seemed to be such a comfy nook, and was beginning to feel more and more precarious by the minute.

"I'm to shoot that bow at someone, at an imp even, if they come upon this tree?"

"Well, yes…" Stellis said, pausing briefly, "but we hope that it does not come to that. And you'll not be alone."

"I won't?"

Rime patted him on the back. "I can't let you loose in here by yourself, no matter how much I trust you." He laughed. "This was Rid and I's treehouse. He was the only kid that Fortis ever let in. I think the forest has always hated him for bringing me along."

Alan looked around at the room again as if seeing it for the first time. There were some drawings and writings plastered to one wall. The handwriting was more ostentatious and free, but was clearly Rid's, though probably as a child. The drawings were much too good, and he knew that they were Rime's.

"Right, so it'll be me and Alandriel in here. Kard, are you still good with what we discussed this morning?"

"Aye, ever at your service."

"And Stellis," Rime said, "you'll be patrolling the ridgeline around the pit with the order and whoever else has volunteered?"

She nodded. "We will. Klio will be in the tallest tree nearby. She'll take the heren-nut and let me know if she spots anything. The signal we discussed earlier?"

"Yes, burn it bright. The night will be black."

"Wait, what are we burning?" Alan asked.

Stellis pointed up out of one of the crudely hewn windows. "On that side up on that hill there are several bushes. If one of those is lit on fire, you and Rime will know that an attacker has come."

Alan gulped audibly. "You mean an imp?"

"I do not know if I would fear them or the townspeople more."

Alan's face flushed.

"But not to worry. This is the safest place for you. These trees will watch over you better than I or Rime can."

"And Kard?" Alan asked. "Where will you be?"

Kard stomped his foot upon the rug and it made a hollow, thumping noise.

"What do you mean by that?"

"I'll be beneath ye, lad. I'm the only one who can fit down there all night. Wee little cellar for when these boys—" He elbowed Rime playfully, "—when they were young and green. I reckon he couldn't fit if he tried now though."

Rime nodded solemnly, not adopting Kard's light demeanor. "Yes, Kard will be our last defense. It is imperative that you and I sleep. If we are awake, the imps are less likely to try an ambush. At least, that is what I believe after they fled Rid when they saw Kard. If we are not woken by their entry, Kard will hear from below."

"And we want them to attack?"

"That was your idea, friend. Though I must admit Stellis may have had whisperings about it before." He winked. "A sweet and a spot, right? We can only hope that the imps lead us to whatever the hell sent them here if we catch one of them. Don't worry. Kard can scream loudly."

"Aye. Don't worry lad. I'm goin' to bed hungry tonight so I'll be wide-eyed till morning."

They talked a little longer, some about swords and crossbows and traps, but Alan pushed the talk to stews and cheeses and ales and did not want to think about what might happen that night. As the sky grew darker, they put a bird on the fire and ate fast and hot with little more time for casual conversation. He could feel the tension at the table as they all hunched over their helpings, but he did not wish to talk anymore about it either.

After much insisting from Rime, Alan laid out his blanket on the bed and helped Rime fix up a spot on the floor next to it. The crossbow, loaded and pulled, sat next to him, and Rime made Alan put a sword in between the mattress and the frame of the bed at the front.

Per Alan's suggestion, they held the marble over a candle flame, just long enough to warm it and let the fire kiss. Kard insisted upon laying on top of the marble on the ground floor of the cellar, but after a series of loud flops and groans, Alan took it back to put in his pocket. He felt better with it on him anyway, rather than risking someone else.

There was little talking now.

They both could feel it, but they did not say it. Kard was no longer stirring below, but waiting, quiet as a mouse.

Alan laid down his head and closed his eyes.

XXII. The sabbath

Alan Hendershot was driving northeast on I-20 towards Erie. He'd be in Pennsylvania soon, but he'd probably turn off before that. He wasn't too sure where he was going, but in a weird way, he was very sure of where he wanted to end up.

It was Sunday morning. He'd not showered, washed his face, put on deodorant, or brushed his teeth since he'd gotten back from the bus station at 8 a.m. He had eaten a pop tart. It was cherry, but it was also expired.

He'd had a glass of orange juice, too, and that's when he thought of it. There was something special about the taste of orange juice with something sweet and sad like an old cherry pop tart.

When he was growing up, Alan's breakfast habits were much different from the other children his age. You see, Alan had an awfully nervous stomach. Every morning before school, he would try to eat a bowl of cereal, and every morning there would be a bowl half full of frosted wheat and milk fast growing warm while little Alan had run off to the toilet.

It was because of this that he had never tried to eat anything else. There was something calming about the frosted wheat. Sure, it made his stomach upset, but it was the same upset every morning. He could time it. He could take his seven bites, put his spoon down before he scooped up number eight, and run to the bathroom right on time.

If he tried to eat or drink anything else: a piece of toast, a bagel, even a glass of orange juice, the results were unpredictable and usually quite dangerous. For this reason, Alan only had orange juice on Sunday mornings. On Sunday morning, he would get up with his dad and have a bowl of Honey Smacks, take one sip of his dad's coffee, and drink a full glass of OJ to get the taste out of his mouth. Then they would go to church.

To church. That's where Alan was driving. He didn't know what church, nor did he care. Churches were mostly the same, he reckoned. He wasn't going for a particular flavor of sermon from a certain pastor or denomination. He wasn't going for the curriculum in a Sunday School class. In fact, he wasn't quite sure why he was going at all.

Now he was driving on a road that hadn't been repaved since he'd been alive, and it showed. There were cracks wider than a baseball running through the heart of the lane, but he didn't care. He knew he was getting close.

The sun was bright now: shining right into his eyes so much that they started to water. It was warm for an Ohio morning. Maybe even hot.

Then, just for a second, the sun was gone. Blocked out by nothing less than a steeple, reaching high into the sky like a sword. This would be the spot.

He pulled into the gravel lot. It was mostly full. Beat-up SUVs and small sedans that could use a new paint job. Nobody here was driving a brand new Lexus. He pulled around to the second row and passed by a couple with two young daughters walking up to the front steps. There on the end of the line there was a spot between a red Ford Explorer and a Geo Tracker.

He waited in his car for a minute, watching all the strangers walk by in his rear-view mirror, greeting each other and waving to friends they hadn't seen in a week. He felt strange, but he didn't want to leave.

As he walked up the steps, the moment he saw the greeter in his pressed church-grey suit with cufflinks and all, he realized how disheveled his own appearance was. He wore a yellow and brown plaid button-up shirt that was torn on the left sleeve and a pair of black slacks that had become so faded they were nearly grey.

But the man didn't notice. He smiled and held out a firm hand to shake and put a crisp bulletin in Alan's other hand.

"How are you today, sir?" The man grinned and Alan could see the glimmer of a silver tooth. He was probably 60 or 70 and smelled strongly of aftershave.

"I'm doing well, thanks."

"First time with us?"

"Oh...um, yeah. First time."

"Well we're awfully happy to have you." He leaned in closer. "I'd avoid sitting on the few rows of pews in the back left. That's the Ladies of Joy class. They can get a little feisty."

Alan nodded as the man winked, and then he navigated through the narthex of the church into the sanctuary. Deep in his stomach bubbled the same strange feeling he had in the car, but it was stronger now and less uncomfortable. He took in all the sights and smells as he quietly scooted into a seat on the back of the right side. There were strong breezes of perfume as an older lady walked by, the hubbub of kids running up to a dad with outstretched arms on the right, and the shuffling of feet as people everywhere were taking their seats.

Then the organ started, and Alan knew why he had come. As soon as the music began, the same walkup song that all the churches use to bring in the preacher, he felt it. He felt his dad. He felt it so strong that he looked over right beside him and expected him to be sitting there, looking for a funny mistake in the bulletin that he could point out to Alan.

The pastor walked swiftly by on the left and the choir director raised up his arms as the entire congregation stood for an opening hymn. Alan felt tears welling up in his eyes. He bit his tongue and clenched his jaw to keep himself from crying and pulled out the hymnal.

"Hymn 389," she announced, "In the Garden."

He flipped through the pages, reaching it just as everyone sang in unison, "I come to the garden alone."

Alan knew he wasn't going to sing though. He never did. He just opened his mouth and moved his lips as everyone else sang around him.

It was an odd feeling, pretending to sing while those around you actually are. For a second, you can nearly convince yourself that the words are coming from your own mouth.

"*...and He talks with me...*"

A warm tear bubbled up in his left eye. With a quick cough and a discreet wipe of his left sleeve, he cleared it away.

"*...the joy we share as we tarry there, none other has ever known...*"

His face felt hot and flushed, but it angered him, like a red face angers you when you're embarrassed in front of your whole class. With suppressed curiosity, Alan sneaked glances to either side, hoping to find that no one was paying any attention to him.

He nearly gasped when he saw a feeble woman staring right at him and pushing her walker up the center aisle. She was dressed in clothes as faded as the pages of the pew Bibles, but her face was kind and smiling.

When she got to his row, she picked up the walker and turned it, slowly and tediously in fifteen degree increments. He looked around, but there was no other observer, no one in the congregation to come to her aid.

He finished turning the walker for her and retired from her side to return to his seat on the other end of the pew. She was, however, still walking. A minute later she took a seat at his side and folded her hands in her lap.

"*...bids me go; through the voice of woe. His voice to me is calling.*"

The pastor stood, a bald man with a rigid face and a royal blue tie, and flung his outstretched hands up and down in a motion to be seated. He began to read off the announcements of the week. Austin Cowne's bypass surgery had gone well; praise the Lord. Dottie's doctor visit showed she would have twins. God is good. The outside A/C unit was fixed for half of what the first business quoted because the repairman was in need of a little salvation. God is good *all the time.*

The lady from the walker leaned over to Alan and whispered, "Boy, good thing, too. It's not like repairmen need to buy milk and bread for their children."

Alan looked at her, stricken with a counterbalance of situational obliviousness and hysteria. She broke into a soft cackle and smacked the pew Bible that now lay in her lap.

"Oh c'mon. You kids are supposed to say something when the pastor is full of it. That's why we work so hard to get the youth through that door."

Alan responded, also in a whisper. "You think that he cheated the repairman?"

"Cheated's an odd way of puttin' it. Cheated is too black and white. I think he went ramblin' a little too long about giving to God what is God's and guilted the poor fella into it." She took a breath in and glared at a man one aisle over, who seemed to be disdainfully distracted by her whispering. She spoke a bit lower. "Can't say he cheated him, but you sure can't say the church couldn't have afforded it, neither. I put a big fat check in the pot every month."

"Well, if you don't mind me saying so, why do you keep putting the money in if you don't like what he does with it?"

"God or him?" she asked.

"Well, him, right?"

"You tell me."

Alan sat quiet for a moment while the pastor quickly resolved a prayer for the two members of Ladies of Joy who were finishing chemo this week.

"So you just put the money in for what? Why do you do it?"

"Only way I can hound Reverend Jensen. I'm the only reason there's been chocolate milk with the donuts for the past seven years. And guess what?"

"What?"

She snickered. "I'm lactose intolerant."

"Let me ask you something," she whispered.

"Shoot."

"Why do you pretend to sing the hymns?"

Alan looked at her and she stared back, not coldly, but genuinely interested. He thought for a moment.

"I guess I saw my dad doing it. I've never liked the singing much, anyway. That's one thing I've never liked about church. The ones who sing the loudest—it always seems like showmanship."

She grinned. "Now what could you possibly mean by that? Do you mean to tell me Jesus wouldn't show up in diamond studs and $200 heels with a clutch that costs more than most people make in a month?"

Alan smiled back at her.

"Now, let me ask you one more thing," she said. "What's a young man that doesn't like church doing in one without any family to make him be there?"

Alan sat quiet, longer this time, without looking over at her. As he thought about his answer, the pastor drawled on about the wall of Jericho, about "insurmountable" faith.

"I guess," Alan whispered, "I thought I'd find something."

"Did you?"

"Can't tell yet," he said, "but, sometimes it's less about looking in the right place...and more about being able to see at all."

She laughed. "That's a good one. Maybe you should be up there preaching."

***

Alan didn't stay for the sermon.

An hour later he was back at 1227 Eversley Circle. Inside, the place was a mess. There were cardboard boxes everywhere, some taped shut, some stuffed full of clothes and dishes. On the refrigerator, which had also been nearly ransacked aside from a few boxes of Chef Billy, there was a note that read:

Hey, bro. Not sure when you'll be back. Sarah's folks got us an engagement present - a house! LOL (laughing out loud). She wants me to move in ASAP (as speedy as possible). We already took a few loads over today. Taking the rest tomorrow, but not sure when you'll be in or out. Obviously I didn't have much here. Two months of rent are on the counter. We'll have to catch back up if I don't see you again soon, for sure. Thanks for the good times, bro. Best of luck with the grocery store.

Suddenly, the house seemed much emptier than when he had walked in. Even though Micah was hardly there as it was, his absence now somehow seemed to cast a longer shadow. He didn't even have that much in common with him, but the sudden dullness was unbearable.

There was nobody to serve as a testament to not dating. No one not doing much with their life just across the hall. There was nobody in the house but Alan.

He languidly traipsed to his room and threw on a record. There was no singing. He didn't want anyone else talking. The record was classical: Liszt's Consolations. Alan didn't know it, or maybe he did in a way that he couldn't comprehend, but this was the same record his mother would play twenty years ago to lull him to sleep. At number 3, he would be out like a light, snoring softly.

The piano was soft on the record and quiet in his room. A book, to read, that's what he wanted. That's what he hadn't done in so long.

He dug around underneath his bed for sometime and finally uncovered his second copy of *The Hobbit,* which was really his first and the one in better shape, but had gotten read much less than the one in his work locker. Instinctively, he knew where he was going; his favorite part where Gandalf and Bilbo speak to one another just before the last battle.

As he flipped through the pages, he stopped. Mid-flip, likely somewhere on the river, floating away from the wood-elves.

Alan didn't want to read the part at the end. He didn't want to throw himself in the battle or on the eaves of it, even though it was his favorite part. His eaves of battle was real. He was likely in it, he thought, next time he fell asleep.

Instead, he flipped a few chapters prior and read about Beorn, their odd giant host who so kindly offered them so many snacks and treats that filled their belly in the midst of such a difficult adventure. That was where he would like to be. Somewhere filling his stomach, in front of a warm fire, and maybe with a pot of tea. Where all the adventure to be had can wait until tomorrow and none of the adventure already had seemed more important than the plate in front of you. He was, after all, a casual adventurer.

And then Alan did something that he was not quite sure of, even at the time of doing it. But as of late, a harsh compelling something or another had driven him to do things where before he would not have been as decisive. So it was with this.

The phone had hardly rung for one full buzz.

"Hello?"

"Hey, mom."

"Alan! Hi, sweetie! How are you?"

"I'm doing pretty okay, I think. How are you?"

"Well," she sighed heavily, "we're okay, really. You know how it is."

"Yeah."

"So what are you calling for? It's not your car is it? I can call—"

"No, no. My car's fine. Thanks again."

"Oh. Of course. What is it then?"

He felt his chest tense up and the urge to take a deep breath nearly overwhelmed his ability to speak. "I—well...is it too late to RSVP for the birthday party?"

"Oh no!" She responded immediately, "Not at all. I mean, we weren't going to do anything big. I don't think it should be anyone besides you and your sister. If you're okay with that?"

"Sure, that sounds good."

"Okay, great. I'll tell her—she'll be so happy. It really will mean so much to her, Alan. Thank you."

"Yeah."

"I thought that we should go to Pizza Inn. You know, your dad didn't like to flaunt it, but that was his favorite place. If you still eat pizza—"

"Pizza Inn sounds great."

"Good...good. Well, I'll figure the rest out. Maybe I can go pickup a cake or something and we can have that. How is your job going?"

"Oh...yeah. Well, actually, I got moved around a little bit. I'm working night shift now."

"Night shift? Oh, okay. Is that something that you wanted? I know you have a bad habit of not sleeping at night as it is."

"I didn't really have much of a choice in the matter, but it's been okay. My sleep schedule has been okay, too."

"Well good. That's just really good, sweetie. Is the record player working like you thought it would?"

"Yeah, yeah. It really...well, it really plays them good. I—"

His mom sniffled and interrupted. "I'm just so glad you called Alan. I've just...well, I've been having a hard time lately. It's...well, you know. It's the same things over and over. I just want you and your sister to be happy now. That's all I care about."

"Are you okay?"

"Yeah...yes. I'm sorry, I shouldn't have thrown that on you. Really, I'm okay. It just...it really means a lot that you called. I'm really glad you're coming to eat pizza with us."

"Sure. Absolutely, mom. Besides, you know that Pizza Inn was really *my* favorite restaurant. Dad was just siding with me so I could get what I wanted."

She laughed shakily, but threw off her sniffles. "Oh, *sure* he was. Your dad liked anything with cheese and bread on the same plate."

Alan laughed audibly enough that she could hear it.

"Well," she asked, "what are your big plans this evening? Do you have to go into work?"

"No, no big plans. I think I might meet up with some friends tonight. I have a couple of days off."

"Well that's just great. You owe yourself a good time. Just don't get into too much trouble."

There was a pause, as Alan couldn't think of anything else to say, a problem that often plagued him in conversations.

"Well, I'll let you go. I don't want to make these calls stretch out so long you never want to make one again." She chuckled to herself. "Stay safe, sweetie. I love you."

"I love you too, mom."

He hung up the phone and returned to the solace of the abandoned duplex. He had put it off long enough now, he thought. It was time to return to Imp Lode.

He would gather his book, his notes, his tea, and a last-minute snack, and soon he would be off to learn his fate. To return to the world, to his world, at the most dangerous as it had ever been—the most formidable sleep. If only it were that simple.

There was, as he well knew, a choice to be made. He could return to Imp Lode with the intention of arriving at the crack of dawn, at the precise moment when all risk of attack and harm were no more, or he could return without missing a beat. He could wander into the middle of it, right as he had closed his eyes to go to sleep.

Regret; he recognized it, the feeling that he felt right now. Regret that he hadn't asked the old man about his mistake in skipping ahead in time—if there was a good way to do it. Of course, he couldn't foresee the future. Who would have guessed that he would have been world-hopping right in the middle of this?

The more that Alan pondered the idea of skipping ahead in time, the more it soured in his mind. Sure, he had done it on other nights, nearly every other one in fact. But it wasn't to skip something. It wasn't to bypass a part of the story, a part of his story, that he didn't want to face. That didn't seem like a good choice. If he'd learned anything from the old man, it was not to cheat his subconscious. He *couldn't* cheat it, in fact. He knew that. Besides, he was tired of avoiding things.

And so the ritual began.

He munched on a bag of cheese curls this time as he sipped the tea, a splurge he'd allowed himself at the Atlanta bus station before he'd realized how quiet a red-eye bus trip would be. The combination was horrific, but in a slightly exciting way.

The pages of notes flipped by; he reviewed every single one he'd taken since his first time there. Alan couldn't leave this one up to chance. He knew how important it was that the circumstances remain as they had been. It had all been calculated.

As he considered this risk, for a brief skipped beat of the heart, he thought about the chances of something going wrong. What would happen, he fearfully considered, if he were to die in the dream? If he was to meet the same end as Riddle? He knew the answer for a normal dream, sure. But this was Imp Lode.

After only a moment's hesitation, he resolved that it would do no good to dwell on the concern. He would have to sleep eventually, and even if he didn't go through the ritual, who was to say he wouldn't end right back up in Imp Lode. It was inevitable, he knew. *I have to face this.*

Tonight, his pinky toe served as the sacrificial uncomfortable body part, twisted up too tightly in a sock that had shrunken far too much in Alan's futile attempts to properly launder. *Your generation doesn't have the self-respect to do laundry,* he heard Vick's phantastic voice whisper in his fading mind, but it didn't bother him. He found the irritants of the man nearly humorous now, as he fought to keep his eyes from closing.

But then, he was asleep.

XXIII. In the dead of night

Of all the wakings Alan did in Imp Lode, this had to be the oddest. For upon entering the dream, it did not appear that he was awake at all. It took him longer than he'd like to admit to realize that he was merely squeezing his eyes shut and need only open them.

There he was, in the bed. In the bed in the treehouse in Fortis Forest in Oognysse in Imp Lode. That was his address. Beside him, Rime lay still, fast asleep in fact, or at least the appearance of it. Nor did any sound of rummaging or even snoring (for which he was known) come from the wee cellar down below where Kard stowed away. Alan was the only one awake.

He knew the plan was for all of them to appear as though they were out, calmly drifting away into a dreamscape. But his heart was racing. He needed this, these few moments of silence, to calm his nerves. Slowly, as he took deep breaths and let his eyes scan over all the defenses and weapons available to them in the treehouse, he grew less anxious. Along with that came a feeling of pride.

Alan, just like most well-raised children, had first learned of pride as a bad feeling. A feeling, in fact, that one should not be proud of. Pride came from too much confidence in oneself, a confidence that might lend itself to a bloating of ego or lack of humility. But this time, the pride did not feel so bad. The pride that he was worth protecting, that he was putting his life in danger to do something good. He didn't feel guilty about basking in this pride.

Not so much as a scratching or stirring came from within or without the tree since the time that Alan's mind had returned. It was reassuring enough that he could now lay flat on his back instead of on his side facing the window, and he stared up through the trunk of the tree.

He had not taken notice of it when they first arrived, but the *ceiling*, if you wish to call it such, of the treehouse was simply wonderful. Rather than the popcorn and tile varieties he had grown up with, this ceiling was so great because it was not there. The tree had been hollowed, likely quite far, but he could not see past the darkness which began around the three-story mark. As he thought about the reasons why humans enjoy tall ceilings quite as much as they do, he closed his eyes, not to drift to sleep, but to give the appearance of the same.

He thought of his dad and imagined that he was now the guard of this treehouse. That he was making his way around the premises of the tree with a big stick to beat down any imp that dared come down into the pit. A great bopping stick. He grinned.

Alan embellished this image, as a tired mind routed to other means of wandering by closed eyes often does, and allowed it to wander—to his first day in Imp Lode, in the tavern with his first pint of elder ale, how delicious it had been. He thought about the night hiding from the storm, burrowed into the ground with his friends that now watched over him. He thought about Riddle and all of his stories.

His wanderings were soon thrown to a halt, however, as he heard a tapping from up above—as if a woodpecker had just selected the tree for his next gig. Next came a scratching, just as delicate and incessant as the time he'd heard it only just the day before. They had come for him, after all.

His face ran hot and his neck now rushed with the full force of every heartbeat. He kept his eyes closed to keep up the appearance, but he could not do so without squeezing them. There was no longer a single ounce of relaxation left in his body.

The scratching grew louder still and began to reverberate throughout the tree. He realized, with another hot flush, that the imps were on the very tree that he was inside, descending the branches it seemed. Their descent did not take long, for soon he heard right in front of him, just above the door, the grating scraping of bark being torn and clawed by whatever it was that composed the imps.

He was using every fiber of his discipline not to look down at Rime to see if he heard it too, or even to give a knock on the cellar door where Kard hid. Alan couldn't. He knew that he couldn't. But even so, the tempting thought crossed his mind.

Then, there was nothing. No sound or stirring to speak of. There was just enough of a silence that for the briefest moment of time, Alan thought that they might have gone; that he might be okay.

It was hot. Sticky and wet, even. He felt it on the back of his neck. Breath. Breath full of rasp and drool and wickedness. His ears wanted to twist up inside themselves just to get away from it, and he felt chills like a splash of hot ice run down his spine.

The imp's breath on his neck paused. Then it whispered.

It was a growl, like before, but there was something else to it. It was rhythmic, melodious almost. The ugliest meter you could imagine, but there it was. A harmony was there. Something planned, like poetry.

Alan felt a sudden emptiness then that he had never felt before, followed quickly by a fearsome flurry of memories and images. It was as if all the nightmares he'd ever had had suddenly been conjured up for the briefest of slideshows. There was nothing definitive, only the abstraction of ideas, quite like a dream.

Then it stopped. No breath, no whispering. Nothing at all except for the uncomfortable cooling he felt now on his neck from where the residual moisture was wicking the heat away from his body like demonic sweat. But it had left him.

He knew that he must act. It had come to him without a fight. Rime had not seen it, nor had Kard woken upon its entry. He must sound the alarm.

With the slightest twitches of muscle he could muster, he rolled his body so that he was facing his rear. His eyes were still closed, as he thought if the creature were still watching, it might appear as if he were merely readjusting his position while still fast asleep.

Now that he was facing the imp, and he *knew* that he was facing it, he felt for the sword. He felt the cold metal of the pommel and slowly slipped his fingers around the grip.

This was it.

He opened his eyes, and pulled the sword quickly, but rather clumsily, out in front of him, simultaneously waking Rime in the disturbance, who frighteningly muttered some slurred expletive and reached for the crossbow.

The imp, however, was not poised to strike. It was holding the gold cat's eye marble, its face, if you could call it that, completely possessed by the sphere. Curiously, however, in its other hand was Rid's journal.

"Rime—" was all that Alan had the courage to mutter in a hoarse whisper, and just as the name left his mouth, a bolt left the bow whizzing across the room with a whistle.

Next there was a horrible shriek, and the black shape shifted and manipulated its mass, once, twice, each separated by milliseconds. Its shriek ended abruptly with a soft pop, and then it was no more. There was no longer an imp across the room, just the marble falling to the ground with a rolling thud, and the journal slapping flatly next to it, and an awful bumbling groan from below, as a newly awakened Kard struggled to heave open the cellar door.

"Aye, what in the hell was that?!" Kard exclaimed, as he came tottering up from below with a helmet turned nearly backwards on his head.

Rime stood next to him, eyes wide, still apparently speechless.

"It's okay, Kard. It was an imp, but Rime took care of it. It's left us now. Would you run and find Stellis and the others? Lock the door behind you."

As he dashed out the door, heaving it closed with a loud grunt, Rime slowly walked over to the journal and marble.

"I—I'm so sorry, Alandriel. It was as if I had fallen into an enchanted sleep. I had not even dreamed, I swear it. Did it attack you?"

"No...no, I don't think so. Something happened. It was close to me. I could feel it on my neck, but I don't think that it hurt me. It was just such an awful..." Alan shook his head to shake the feeling. "Well, never mind. What matters is you shot it."

"Shot at it, you mean. I do not think I hit it. So strange that it was just the one. Some trap. Two sleeping idiots and you."

Alan approached the scene and reached down to gather up his belongings.

"Well, isn't this odd," he said, "was it holding this book?"

Alan held up Rid's journal for Rime to see. He beheld it with an odd glint of curiosity.

"I would say it is odd, yes, save for I know nothing of the beasts except for what we've learned in the past few days."

"I wonder..." Alan thought aloud. As he turned the journal over in his hands, finding some of the black tarry residue coating the back face of it.

Just then a mighty orange bolt of light shot out from behind the hill outside the window, streaking through the sky like a meteor returning to space.

"Stellis!" Rime shouted. "That is the warning. More must be on their way! Quickly, while there's time. Stow yourself away in the cellar. I will lay in the bed to fool the wicked creatures. You will have to stay low and seated, but there is a nook large enough for a candle so you do not bump your head. Go now!"

"But," Alan began to protest, as Rime shoved a well-burnt cream candle to him, "how am I to know when to come out? I have to help you if they return!"

"My only duty now is to protect you, Alandriel. If they do return and I follow Rid in death, I want you to know that you've become like a brother to me. Now get in there before it is too late!"

He threw open the cellar door and shoved Alan into it. The muddy floor was cold on his legs, but it wasn't entirely uncomfortable. Next to him on the left side was the little nook, just large enough for the candle, with several stray matches he just caught sight of before the door slammed down from above. He heard Rime slide the rug back on top of it with one brisk motion, followed by the shuffling of him getting into the bed, and then there was nothing but silence.

He struck the match on the spine of Rid's journal, which he still held in his hands, and lit the nook candle. It burned furiously at first, a sharp pink light, and then mellowed to a warm yellow that danced about the wee cellar.

Conveniently enough, there was a tiny chimney in the nook just big enough for the smoke to escape through. It was pleasant beneath the treehouse. Chilly, and a fearful aura was in the air, but it still could not smother out the joys that Rid and Rime must have had down here, hidden away from the world with nothing but their stories.

It was then that Alan realized he was still holding Rid's book tightly in his hands, and he felt the sticky black tar peeling off of his palm as he pulled it away.

It was odd that the imp was holding the book, wasn't it?

Still trying to breathe as quiet as possible to hear any sign of a second assault, he silently flipped the book open, right to the spot where he had earlier shoved the leaf that had fallen from the tree in Synn; a beautiful red-gold leaf just beginning to tear apart.

He had to squirm over to the left wall and nearly press the side of his head into the candle to get enough light to see the page. But there it was:

SAGA OF THE IMPES (FROM HILLES) AND THE STOR

He felt his heart in his throat. His tongue went dry, and for a time, he didn't breathe, swallow, or blink. All along, it had been here. This story. Beneath the title, before the written word began, there was a crude drawing. A black, shattered shape of a man and many more just like it swarming up and over a hill in a formation. Then, the words:

THE HILLES OF NYSSEN ONCE AGO WERE DESOLATE,
VOIDE OF BEAST, CREATURE, AND PERSON THE SAME.
BUT SOON SWAM MEN OF THE EAST,
WHO HELD GREED FAR TOO GREAT.

THEY STRIPPED WOODE FROM TREE,
AND TORE FRUIT FROM THE LIVING BUD.
BUT THIS ALONE WOULD NOT QUENCH
THE HEAT OF DRAGON IN THEIR BLOOD.

TWAS NAUGHT TWELVE MOONS ON,
NOR EVEN BENEATH FALL OF NIGHT,
THAT KALIR, SON OF KILN, RAISED PICK
AND BROKE THE SACRED SLEEP OF HILLES.

THE HILLES WERE WRIT WITH MAGIC OLDER THAN HE,
AND THOUGH HE WROUGHT THE GEMS HE DESIRED,
SO TOO, DID A SECOND PRIZE RISE FROM DARK;
A REWARD FOR GREED, FOR GLUTTONY.

THEY SLITHERED AT NIGHT, BLACK AND SWIFT,
THE IMPES BORNE OF THE DARK—

NOW FREE & ADRIFT.

A WHISPER, A HISS, THEIR POISON CAME LIKE THOUGHTS
UNDER SHADE OF NIGHT, THEY DISPENSED THEIR LIES—
FOR THE EAR, JUST A KISS.

ITS ONLY REMEDY,
A DUST OF GLIMMER.
BUT ONE OF SUCH DENSITY AND DEVILRY
THAT IN THE GROUND IT WAS STOWED,
PRECIOUSLY.

HATRED, DISGUST, THESE WERE THEIR VIRUSES SO SPREAD.
AT ITS FORE—A NOTION, AN INKLING,
THAT UGLINESS—THE MONSTER—BESIDE YOU TREAD.

THE WORLD UNRAVELED AT ITS BEQUEST,
FALLING BLOODIED TO BITTERNESS AND FEAR.

NONE SO SLEPT THAT HAD NOT HEARD THEIR TALE,
AND SO IT WAS
THAT ALL HOPE FOR LOVE COULD NOT PREVAIL.

OR SO IT WAS THOUGHT—TORMENTED
BY I, THAT THE CURSE WAS INESCAPABLE,
UNRELENTED.

BUT BENEATHE THE HILLES LIVED ANOTHER,
BRIGHTER, AND INDISPUTABLY GIANTER.

WHOSE BLOOD HAD NEVER FELLED TREE,
NOR FELT WANT FOR SHINE AS ONLY A THING.

WHO BORE THE STRENGTH TO DO IT,

TO BURY THAT WHICH SON OF KILN UNCOVERED.

TO GIVE BACK TO IT WHAT IT DID NOT WISH

FOR MEN TO HOLD,

TO WANT,
TO MAKE THEM GROW OLD.

SO STOR, THE ONE OF STRENGTH
HAD BUT LITTLE CHOICE.
SO HE DID IT—

THE BURIAL, WHICH IT REJOICED.

Alan read the verses again and again, taking it all in just the same as he had the first time, but repeating the task still, for there was nothing else to do with the thrill bubbling through his body. It was, as he saw it, discovery. He read over each word again, his breath held in limbo as he quietly whispered each line in the flickering candlelight. This was more than a story of legend. He knew it.

How long had he been hidden away? He'd lost track of time reading the story. Thoughts raced through his mind in a frantic rush of conclusions. *The imps. They caused the blindness. The gold in his marble prevented it. The whispers.* Had they whispered to him? *Is that what they had tried to do only moments ago?*

And who was Stor, the one that was gianter? He'd fixed it, hadn't he? He buried it, the story said.

Alan was nearly bursting at the seams. It felt as though he knew so much more than before but now had so many new questions that he didn't have the answers to. He brought himself back into his surroundings and listened quietly. It was still as silent as could be in the room above him; the same could be said for outside. Had the imps arrived yet?

He felt for the marble, for one last mystery to test. He pulled it from his pocket and held it over the candle. This time he let it get hot, burning the tips of his fingers. He waited and waited but the gold did not glimmer. It did not move, and it did not swirl. He waited for as long as he could until minutes felt like hours, but no imps came. There was no stirring above.

He couldn't help it anymore. This was urgent information, and he knew it.

He threw open the hatch to the cellar and leapt out, journal in hand. Rime shot out of bed, alarmed at first, but then gathered himself.

"What are you doing?" He asked, a bit angry. "You *have* to stay below. We do not know yet if it is safe!"

"You don't understand! In the book—this book here. Rid's book! There's a story about the imps. But...well, I don't think it's a story at all. I think it's true, or that there's some truth in it. See—" Alan pointedly laid the book and marble down on the table.

"Woah, woah. Slow down. What are you talking about, Alandriel?"

"There's a story, some sort of poem it seems like. It talks about the imps. *They* are the ones causing the blindness. They whisper to men at night...or something like that. They change the way you see other living things. I know that it's true!"

"Okay..." Rime sat on the edge of the bed and stared off into the distance in deep contemplation. "Do you think—well, what do we do—I mean, do you think that's why they killed my brother?"

"What do you mean?"

"He knew. Is that why they killed him?"

"I don't know that he knew yet, Rime. Don't you think he would have told us? What a story to tell. I don't think he knew until—well..."

"Right. Until he was killed by one."

"Right."

Just then the door was thrown open, and Stellis, Kard, and Klio came out of the darkness. As they tumbled through the entryway, behind them came three horrid looking creatures, further off yet, still in the shadows. But they were close enough to make out the terrible details of their faces and gruesome figures, and Alan dashed to the door to close it quickly behind their friends.

Right as it slammed shut, Stellis shouted, though nearly out of breath herself, "Alandriel, what are you doing?! You wish to lock them out in the black of night?"

"*Them*? What do you mean, *them*? They were ferocious looking. You don't mean to tell me that they mean us no harm?"

Stellis paused, still catching her breath, and looked confusedly at Alan. "What are you talking about?" She looked over to Rime. "Is this a joke?"

"Who were they," Rime pointed, "outside the door?"

Rather than answer, Stellis nodded towards it as she swung it open, and the three creatures scurried inside as Alan nearly leapt back out of fear.

The first, and the shortest, was a wee little goblin or devil of sorts. His teeth were gnarled about his wrinkled and scarred face, barely humanoid at that, and his eyes were agitated and narrow. He wore a purple cap with a point at the end, that Alan thought looked awfully familiar, and it swayed to and fro as he rasped odd mumblings in Kard's direction.

Behind him was another, nearly as short, but perhaps even uglier. He didn't look human at all, more like a demented frog or lizard in the face, and was covered in filth and sweat. He stank as bad as he looked.

Trailing behind the two of them was an evil-faced female with sharp facial features and eyes that seemed to glow red in the low light. She was towering over them all and gave off a frightening aura as though she was liable to snatch up any member of their party and disappear off into the night.

"Had you not met them earlier, Alandriel?" Klio asked, twirling a blade in her hand. "I could have sworn that you had."

"No...no I hadn't. You really mean to say they're friendly?"

Rime walked closer to Alan, examining his face closely as if attempting to detect any trace of a lie or fabrication. He nodded to the marble that lay on the table, and just as Rime opened his mouth, Alan realized what had happened.

"As Kard has no doubt alerted you all, an imp came upon us," Rime said.

"Why do you think that I have out this blade, brother of Riddle?" Klio mocked. "It is not unsheathed lightly."

"Yes, yes, I know. But we have learned—or, rather, Alandriel has learned—much since Kard's absence. It seems he has also..." He paused again, searching for one last time in Alandriel's eyes. "...confirmed how the Blindness works."

"What do you mean by this?" Stellis's face softened as she looked back and forth from Alan to the creatures at the door, then to the marble on the table. "You are blind?"

Alan nodded and held up Riddle's book of stories for all to see. "But that's not all! Or that's important, sure, but there's something else. Once the imp had come, and with the help of a fired bolt, gone, Rime asked that I hide in the cellar until things were safe now that the imps had some knowledge that this was a trap. I've carried this book with me since...well...for a while, but had not read much from it until tonight. There's a story in here about someone defeating them."

Alan paused, now realizing the full implication of the situation.

"Elouise?" he asked, looking at the tall woman that had just entered. She humbly bowed her head and smiled softly. "And Lucas...Forty-Two?" He asked, now looking at the other two. The short gnome and the sprite bowed in turn.

"At your service," said Lucas, wielding a tiny sharp hammer.

"So I'm really...I'm blind then. Just like that." He looked at the marble, hovering his fingers over it as he watched the creatures at the door. Alan touched it for a second and their former appearance flashed back, faster than his eyes could comprehend. He lifted his fingers and their present appearance returned.

Alan took a seat upon the bed, rubbing his eyes and blinking intensely as if that would turn him back to the way he had been. After a moment, he looked back to his friends.

"So it was just the marble, then."

Rime sat on the bed next to him. "My friend, you are more than your eyes. You are more than what your eyes are with the marble. I will not have you so soon forget that you saved my life. I would not be sitting here without you. That's something. More than that, you're the only one that's bothered to crack open that old book which may have just told us all we need to know. If we can find a way to stop the imps, then..."

Alan looked at the marble longingly, wanting to return his vision to what it had been. But something deeper inside of him shook the thought away. There was another purpose for it yet. He looked back up, confidently now. "Right. The end of the story. Something comes and stops the imps. In the tale it was called a Stor—something gianter."

Wide eyes spread to every face in the room and several seemed entirely unnerved by the new piece of information.

"No, lad." Kard said, shaking his head. "That cannot be. There is only one Stor near here, and he is a ferocious beast. Perhaps someone else ought to read the story."

The others mumbled and nodded in agreement, though Stellis seemed unsure.

Alan pulled the book open to the story in protest, shoving his index finger onto the bottom of the page.

"No, right here! *But beneathe the Hilles lived another, brighter, and indisputably gianter...who bore the strength to do it, to bury that which son of Kiln uncovered...so Stor, the one of Strength, had but little choice. So he did it."* He looked back up at them. "That's how it ends! Stor does it, he buries it."

Stellis seemed enchanted about something as she reached for the book. "*Son of Kiln?* May I see that, Alandriel?"

She took the book in her hands and whispered softly as she read through the whole of the poem line by line, then the last half a second time, nodding her head in rhythm with each word.

"It is true. This is what the tale says. More than that, it holds more history than fiction. Kalir, son of Kiln, was the first to break rock in the depths of Cavus Selledune. Kalir started the boom that settled Nyssen long ago." Her voice began to trail off as she retreated to the back of the room with the book. "Could it really be so simple?"

Meanwhile, Rime was rummaging around in ratty and moldy notebooks that were strewn about the treehouse, mumbling some variation of, "we've been there," every minute as he finished flipping through another notebook and tossed it aside.

"What exactly is Cavus Selledune?" asked Alandriel.

"The mine," Stellis began, "didn't you see it on your way into town with Kard?"

Alan nodded his head.

"Today that mine is the only way that the gemsmen have of getting deep beneath the rock. In the early days of Nyssen, they used Cavus Selledune, a cavern that lies beneath the mines of today. Every precious stone that left the harbors of Nyssen came from Selledune. The coins stamped in those days still swap hands today. It was a time of great wealth."

"So you think that...well, that the mine broke into the same rock that they did a long time ago? That that's how the imps came back?"

Stellis didn't have time to respond for an outburst of Rime—a great, excited, "I've got it!"

"Got what?" Kard asked, himself foraging around in the cellar for a snack.

"The drawing! I knew that I remembered the old tales of Stor. We must have heard it when we were young..." He paused, looking over the yellowed sheet of parchment in his hand. "Yeah...that must have been it. I remember now. We went out looking for the giant. I was convinced I could catch him. Rid was scared out of his own skin, but he had to know."

"You found the giant?" Stellis asked defiantly, "And how did you do that?"

"Well, so far as I remember, Rid went around asking all the townspeople what and where to find the giant. Everyone thought we were dead as fools, so more than a few didn't mind telling us what they'd heard. I guess we put all the stories together, and that's how we found him."

"Where?" Stellis asked, still unconvinced. "Where did you find him?"

"Well, here," Rime said, offering the drawing. "It's not a great map, but I couldn't have been very old. That's what it looked like. That's the place everyone told us to go to. Deep as could be in the old forest, you'll find a circle of trees growing shorter than all the others. We knew that would stick out like a sore thumb, seeing as Fortis is the oldest thing around here, and you can't see the tops of most the trees."

"Hang on a second," Alan said, approaching Stellis, "can I take a look at that?"

She handed him the map after another minute of studying, still only half-convinced, and Alan felt it right when he took it in his hands. It was something, deep down in his soul, some sort of knowing that he couldn't quite put a finger on. But it was strong.

There, on the page, was a short ring of trees, creating a shady fortress of interlocking branches within them. He knew this place.

"What happened when you got there?" Alan asked.

"Well, that's just it. We ran away as fast as our legs could carry us. As soon as we got there, the ground shook, trembled even, but rhythmically. That's how we knew it was something smart. That's how we knew it was him, the giant."

"Aye, but ye lads never saw him?" Kard asked with a chuckle, returning to the conversation now that he had found some cheese.

"I believe you." Alan said. And he did. He knew that Rime was telling the truth. But more than that, he knew what he had to do.

XXIV. Talking with giants

"Well, it sounds as though you've made up your mind, lad," Kard said as he munched on a piece of sharp white cheese and licked his fingertips clean.

Alan sat across the table staring at the drawing of the ring of trees. "I know that I've got to do it."

Stellis was pacing around the room, while Rime and Klio took a post at each of the windows, both taking special care to perform non-routine maintenance on their weapons. The three volunteers, Elouise, Lucas, and Forty-Two, had all gone back outside to return to their patrols around the perimeter of the basin.

Stellis, frantically flipping through pages and scribbling down new notes as she went, had only paid minor attention to the conversation at hand. At the sound of Alan's recent declaration, she had allowed herself to neglect the book, but only slightly.

"This is not a decision that you should take lightly, Alandriel. I know that you were asked to risk your life in coming here, but I did not intend to put you in this great of harm."

Alan nodded. "I know. I take full responsibility for what I am about to do. I am seeking the giant of my own free will."

"And you really think," Rime proffered, approaching the seated group now with a newly sprung crossbow, "that he's the one that the story speaks of?"

"I thought you were on my side?" Alan asked, surprised.

"Well, yes, I am. But, friend, I do not wish you to undertake a task so daunting just because of silly legends shared between two young brothers. You truly believe it in your own heart?"

Alan nodded.

"I trust 'im," Kard grumbled defiantly. "Alandriel ain't been wrong about a single thing yet. Who's to say his special sight aren't lettin' 'im see the end o'this neither?"

Stellis closed a heavy book and placed her palms on the table. "I just had hoped to find an answer affirmative before such deadly risks were taken."

"No offense," Alan said, holding up the book, "but I think that we do have an affirmative answer. I trust the writings of Riddle, even though he is no longer here to share them aloud."

Rime nodded to Stellis and spoke hesitantly. "I think he's decided this for himself. To be forthcoming, I think we'd be fools to stop him. As Kard said, Alandriel has been our guiding star. I too trust my brother, even more in death."

Stellis sat in contemplation for a moment longer. "Then so be it. I do not have time to orate the debts and gratitude to you which will be owed if your inquiry is successful. We must ready you and get you on your way to this meeting. Imps will return for that sphere and that book if what we know is true. If that story might mean their death."

Rime nodded. "Agreed. I can gather armor for him, though it may take a short time for—"

"I don't think that'll be necessary," Alan interrupted. "I'd like to go without any armor. No armor, no weapons, no threat. I am not meeting an enemy. I am seeking help from a savior. I would also like to leave you with something else."

Rime looked at Alan oddly. Alan pulled his hand towards him and placed the marble in his palm.

"I do not need this. At least not right now. I have hoarded it for far too long. Find as many allies as you can by giving them the sight for a moment. Remind them what they are blind to. We will need as many on our side as we can muster to sneak in a giant."

Rime nodded solemnly and looked at Alan with great reverence. "You are not blinded, Alandriel. Without the marble, too."

Alan met his eyes and, for a moment, they glimmered like his brother's.

"Very well." Stellis got up from the table. "The sun rises as we speak. If you two wish not to attract attention, then Rime, I recommend that you guide him to the dwelling of this being, as best as you can recall... and Alandriel—"

"Yes?"

"If you are going without the marble, then you must remember that this giant will appear just as fierce, just as savage, as it would to any other man. Do not enter his domain lightly."

Alan nodded solemnly, considering the full gravity of what he was about to do, and he and Rime left the sanctity of the treehouse.

***

Fortis was a disorienting, meddling beast of a place to those that it did not favor, but to its keepings, it was a place of solace, difficult to navigate, but known to nudge in the right direction every now and again.

To Alan, this did not matter much at all, for he was not the one doing the pathfinding. Rime walked ahead of him, gauging the incline of this slope and that, checking the direction of the moss, even laying his head flat on the ground at one point to listen. It was nothing new;

this was how Rime had led the party from the first day. But now it felt to Alan as though he were his stalwart guide, a fortress of solitude against the true fears to come.

As they walked, not leisurely but not rushing either, Alan did consider it. He considered that gnawing possibility, that perhaps he could ask Rime to continue with him into the lair of the giant. Alan would consider it for a moment, but there was so much more of his mind telling him to do the opposite. He knew that he had to do this alone for a multitude of reasons, not the least of which was the indisputable fact that they were only on this path because of him. This was a risk he had chosen to take.

The oddest fuzziness, though, was that he could not identify the key motivator. The strongest sense that he must do this alone came from a place within his constitution that he could not easily see. It wasn't as simple as responsibility, or courage, or one of those feelings easily described by a single English word.

Nonetheless, they walked. They walked past more fungi, some even more brilliant (and quite purple) than those that they had seen in the wetter parts of the wood earlier on. They passed more trees, some normal, some great, though nobody appeared to be home in any of these. As they walked though, there was a sense that they were getting further from the heart of the forest. That soon, they would be in a place where very few living things dwelled other than the forest itself.

"Are you nervous?" Rime asked, as he gauged the position of several stars against their route.

"Nervous about the giant?"

"Yes." He dipped his fingers in a muddy puddle and touched it to his tongue. "But also speaking to the giant."

"What do you mean by that?"

Rime focused himself again on the direction they should travel and glanced behind him just for a moment at Alan.

"Well, I've never spoken to a giant."

"Me neither."

"So do you know what language they speak?"

"What do you mean? You don't think they speak...this?"

Rime said nothing for a moment. "You're probably right. He probably speaks this tongue. But do you think that he is quick to anger? That you have to dance around what you say?"

"I hadn't thought of it. Why?"

"Well, I only say it because all the tales I've heard of giants go that way. Easily brought to a boiling rage. Not unlike a gnome, I suppose, but gnomes are much easier to wrestle to the ground."

Just then, Rime stood deathly silent and stared off straight ahead.

"Do you feel it?" he asked, pointing to the ground.

"Feel what?"

"The tremors. We are close, and Stor is awake."

Alan held his breath and touched a hand to a moss-covered stump in front of him. He felt it: just a light vibration, rumbling and patterned like footsteps.

"That's the giant?"

"It is, my friend. We are near." He pointed out in front, a little to the right up over another thicket of fungi, and as they approached, Alan could see the clearing down below.

For a moment, he had déjà vu, which was an awfully strange rattling of the mind to have during a dream. Just as he had imagined it, a small circle of short tree trunks, the color of ivory, and a beautifully interwoven canopy of leaves in their shared space. Or, was it how he *remembered* it?

The ground rumbled again, stronger now. Alan nearly swayed off balance to brace himself against it. Rime looked at him with a pale expression.

"Are you ready, Alandriel?"

"Yeah...yeah." Every pulse rang out in his head like a metronome. "How do I get in, you think?"

"Well...he's a giant, right? If he comes and goes, the way in has got to be pretty large. I've heard giants don't take too kindly to trespassers though, so it might be hidden away."

"Right...okay."

Alan stood in place, looking down the slope and trying to ignore the rumblings that continued to shake his body, one after another.

"Okay, well, you better get out of here, Rime. Might not be safe for much longer. I will meet you after. I still have one more use for that marble."

Rime looked at him pensively and, after a while, grinned. "You have one courageous heart, brother. Be swift." He embraced Alandriel warmly before departing into the heart of the forest.

Alan's stomach sank as he watched Rime walk away. But he knew it was right.

Okay, think. If I were a giant, how would I get into my hole? Alan looked around him and took in the surroundings anew. There was a gentle breeze blowing through the upper rows of branches in the tallest trees, and the soft grasses and flowers around him swayed in time with it. It smelled pleasant, not unlike spruce or fir.

The wind picked up, just a bit, and off to the east of him he heard a faint knocking. *Tap-tap. Tap-tap.* Something sharp, like dry wood or rock. It couldn't be a branch rustling or a creature scurrying.

He walked towards it, and another gust came. *Tap-tap-tap.* It only came with the wind, then it stopped. He went a bit further, then waited. The air was still. Then another flight of wind buzzed through, and along with it, two more taps. He ran to the sound now; it was close.

There in front of him, dirtied and fractured, nearly blending in with the earth beneath it, was a small door. It was square, no more than three feet on either side. It was not unlike the cellar door in the treehouse, but he would have believed that it was a thousand years older. The wood no longer even seemed to be wood, as it was smooth and polished by time itself.

Another breeze came, and the lip of the door lifted just slightly. *Tap. Tap-tap.*

Could it be? It didn't make any sense to him, not really. To get to the lair of a giant, I have to take a trapdoor the size of a small rug?

Just a peek. That won't hurt. Just so I can get a better idea of what's beneath. He sneaked closer and shot quick glances behind himself as though someone were about to push him in. The forest was empty.

He lifted the edge of the trapdoor. It felt warm like the bark of the large trees. He got down onto his knees and leaned over, lifting the door a bit higher so that a ray of sunlight would find its way into the hole.

Just a whisper. That's all he heard. It couldn't be, he knew that. He knew it couldn't have been what he had heard.

It couldn't be his dad.

But he couldn't help but lean in even closer, straining his ear down toward the depths.

Then came another gust of wind, all more ferocious and stronger than the others. Then it did exactly what winds often do. It knocked something over. Here, it knocked Alan Hendershot into the hole of a giant named Stor.

***

Often in instances of make-believe, a very long fall can end without the degree of severity that you would have expected. The fall does not seem to inflict the pain upon the faller that you thought it might.

This was not the case for Alan. As he gathered himself up off of the ground, he could identify every square inch of his body that had impacted the floor. Fortunately, the floor itself was softer. It was something like hay or dried grass, but with nothing but cold, dry dirt beneath.

As he looked around himself, he realized that the room that he stood within was an anomaly of the place. With the bedded floor and dirt walls, it stood out as the only rough part of the abode. Further on, down a little hallway lined more elegantly with stone, it opened up to a larger room, not unlike a kitchen (for giants, that is). Beyond that, another labyrinthine hallway trailed away into a place only lit by dim candles.

The smell floating through the air was absolutely intoxicating, as Alan realized that he had not had a real meal in quite some time. It smelled richly of smoked meat, sharper scents of onion and garlic, all blanketed in a warm, salty tomato cloud. It smelled delicious.

He wandered quietly but courageously through the hallway and into the kitchen, considering whether to announce himself. The ceilings in the kitchen were large, but not as large as he expected. It looked to be fashioned from tree bark and was no more than twice the height of Alan's own kitchen. Around the room sat wooden tables and counters all at least the height of Alan's head, with various utensils and dishes scattered about, all twice the size of the ones that Alan was familiar with.

In the corner, there appeared to be an open oven hewn from some bleak, grey bricks, and a chimney above it crawled all the way up through the ceiling into the dirt above. There was a large pot perched above some dying coals, and steam was billowing out of it carrying the scent Alan had followed.

It was then, as he was drooling over the giant's dinner, that he felt like a trespasser. He had been in the home for several minutes already, uninvited, and had only cared to quest after these fixings rather than announce himself to his involuntary host.

He picked up a large wooden spoon dripping in the drippings of the pot and smacked the side of it. The sound rang out like a deep church bell full of mud, and immediately the rumbling reverberated through the place from the direction of the winding hallway.

The stomps (as being within the confines of the home, he could now place them as footsteps) grew louder, surely coming to snap the neck and cook the meats of whatever thief had broken into his home. Alan huddled himself away in a corner, which turned out to be underneath a rack full of very large and sharp knives, and tried to quell the instinctual shivers as the giant approached.

Boom. Boom. Boooom. The steps were ever closer and a massive dancing shadow crept onto the hallway wall. *Boom. Boom. Boom. Boom.* Then he saw him.

He was, of course, gigantic. Alan's best approximation was eight witchits. His head sat upon a torso the size of a well-gathered hay bale, and his arms hung at his sides like punching bags. His face was truly terrifying. The beard was fiery red, quite literally, as Alan's open-jawed stare traced the flames dancing through the locks. Scars adorned nearly every unbearded inch, and the same spark flickered in his eyes. Pure rage took up residence on his face, and Alan felt every ounce of his blood boiling up to his head, ready to burst.

Then, Alan Hendershot did something very, very right. Very right, indeed. He closed his eyes as tight as he could and pictured Ruteeter, that friendly giant he knew from childhood. A giant gardener, he was, picking the fruits from the roots of the trees that grew around his home in the ground. He wore a smile upon his face, and a beard of red that was so very not on fire. A kind soul.

With his eyes still closed, Alan said (in a somewhat shaky voice), "Hello, friend. I've come to talk with you, if you'll have the company. My name is Alan."

There was silence for a moment, and Alan opened his right eye halfway, just enough to see the giant. In his left hand, he held a stone bowl, and in the other, a spoon full of stew. His back was to Alan, and when he turned, there was no longer any fire on his face or fury in his eyes. There was, however, a grin.

"'Tis good to have company after so many years. So many long years. Would you have a bowl of stew?"

His eyes were sad, like a baby or a dog, or a baby dog, or a puppy. He wore an apron Alan hadn't noticed before, and wiped stew-covered hands on the front as he sat the bowl down.

"Please don't run away." He swayed back and forth, staring at Alan humbly, who was still in quite a state of shock and searching for something to say. The giant scratched the back of his head. "If you just want the stew, I can leave and you can eat it alone. I've been cooking it for several days. It ought to be good."

Alan stepped out from beneath the knife rack and took in a big, ostentatious whiff of scent. "It smells delicious. What kind of stew do you make for several whole days?"

His eyes lit up at Alan's not-running-away, and he opened a little pantry door in the corner that Alan had also not seen before. He rummaged as he spoke excitedly.

"It's an old recipe from my mother. She called it kindletick." He turned his head back, grinning, and returned to the rummaging. "Like a candle wick, I think. If you like it hot, it can be very hot. Spices."

He returned from the pantry with a tiny little chair and laid it down next to Alan. As the giant stepped back, perspective teetered once again, and Alan realized it was a normal, adult-sized piece of furniture.

"Have a seat." He scratched his head again. "I...uh...don't have a table for you, but...oh!"

He dashed off again down the hallway. *Boom. Boom. Boom.* After a sound of tumbling and a bit of grumbling, the *booms* came back down towards Alan. The giant held a plate of some variety of old china in his hand, but once it was stationed on Alan's lap, he realized it to be an appropriate tabletop.

"I'll join you!" he exclaimed, and sat Alan's bowl on the plate before filling his own and taking a seat at the table.

The stew really did smell quite delicious, and though he still felt a bit anxious, he took a spoonful in his mouth to appease the eager eyes of his host.

"Mm—mm! That's a tasty stew."

He grinned and nodded, but didn't take a taste of his own. "My arms and legs. A human in my cubby. As I breathe. Why have you come? Was it just the smell of the stew?"

Before Alan had a chance to speak the giant slapped the table. "Where are my manners? My name is Ruteeter. You can call me Rut, if you please. Or 'R.' I've become quite fond of single letters rather than names. Your name is Alan, you said?"

Alan nodded and took another bite of the stew. It warmed him as he ate. "It is. Your mother made this stew? It has got to be one of the best stews I've ever had."

He smiled and took a big bite of it himself, as though he had just remembered it was sitting in front of him. "Not this particular pot, but it is the way that she made it, yes. So you come from the humans above? The Nyssians?"

Alan shook his head and swallowed. "No. I come from quite far from here, actually. A place called Ashtabula."

"Ash-tuh-bew-luh," the giant sounded out slowly, "I can't say I've ever heard of it. Must be a lovely place though, I'm sure. So why have you wandered into my cubby, A? If you don't mind me calling you so."

"Not at all," Alan said. "I came down here searching for a giant. Or...sorry, I don't mean to call you that if you don't like the name. Someone gianter than myself."

Ruteeter chuckled. "I do not mind it, though I find it such an odd way of speaking. I do not call you a little. Nor do I call any humans smalls."

"Well, what do you prefer? What is your *human*?"

"My word for what I am?"

Alan nodded.

"I suppose...friend."

"Friend?"

"Yes. Friend. It's such a nice word that you all have in this tongue; I think it suits me best."

"But there's nothing you call each other? What did you call your family? Or the others that are...well, your size?"

"Well, often friend. But their names, my mother and father, were Persel and Stor. But we have no word like human in our tongue. Our tongue was spoken before there were any others."

"Stor? You said Stor? That was your father's name?"

Ruteeter shrunk down in his seat just a bit. "It was."

"Is he the one from the old story?" Alan pulled out the book and reached up to lay it in front of the gianter friend, flipped open to the tale.

R pondered the page for a moment and his face grew softly withdrawn as he neared the bottom of it.

"Was that him?" Alan asked.

"That was him," R responded, now avoiding Alan's gaze.

"What's the matter?"

"I cannot do it."

"You can't do what?"

"I know what you wish me to do. To undam the harbor. To flood the mine. To bury it again. I cannot do it."

Alan didn't know quite what to say, for the conversation had not gone anywhere near what he had expected or feared.

"Well, why not?" he asked.

Ruteeter got up from his seat abruptly and left the room, back down the winding hallway. Alan was alone in his kitchen now, with nothing more than a bubbling pot of stew making any bit of noise. He looked around at the charms of the place, the tasseled cloth that hung from above the oven, the woven mat on the floor, the drawings of what must have been R's mother and father above a tiny corner nook of fine dishes. It was no place for a giant, he thought. It was that of a friend.

Boom. Boom. Boom. R reappeared, carrying two large clay vessels in his hands. Both were ornately decorated like fine pottery, one with beautiful blue and gold floral patterns, and the other with a geometric dark green striping.

"This is why," he said, and laid them on the table.

"What are those?"

"Persel and Stor. Stor the one with strength to do it."

"I don't understand," Alan said, but as he looked at the urns, he realized more than he did a moment ago.

"My father loved humans. For much of his life, he was Above. He enjoyed it there; the friendly giant that came to Nyssen to rescue a stranded fishing vessel or hold the weight of a bridge as men refixed the foundation. He was a good friend to men. But he watched them closely. He knew they were growin' sick from that hole they dug in the ground. Deeper and deeper they went. Men shouldn't go that deep in the ground. They'll not find anything that'll bring good to their soul."

R flecked a piece of dirt from one of the clay vessels and rubbed it between two fingers. He took a big breath and nearly blew out the stew fire.

"He didn't want to be around them no more. He dug this cubby for us; I wasn't more than a year old. We stayed below from then on, living on the fruits of the roots he knew how to tend so well. But he loved the men too much. I've found it all, his journals tell a tale sadder than all I've ever read. It gnawed at him, being underground, unable to help. He wanted to fix it for them, for he knew they'd not gain the strength to do it on their own. So he left one night, against my mother's wishes, and did it. He broke down all the barriers to the sea and let it in. The water filled up the mine and that was that. He buried it, as your story says."

His eyes looked away from the dirt and over to the other clay vessel. They were red and watering.

"Only he came home and found that the men had slain her. They'd filled our hole with smoke and she choked on it. She'd hidden me away beneath the floor where they wouldn't find me."

Tears were streaming down Ruteeter's face now as he spoke, and he held his giant spoon tightly in his fist.

"He raised me to love men, even with what they took from him. But the sadness overwhelmed him. He died of it, though by no intentionality of his own. It just took him one night, his broken heart. So, no, Alan. I am sorry, but I will not do it. I cannot do it. I will befriend men all I can to stay in their good graces, but I will not leave my cubby. It is not safe to be a giant in town. I know that they fear me. They would not be kind if I was seen."

"But that's just it!" Alan said, "You can stop the sickness. If you stop it, they'll no longer fear you. It'll all be back to normal. The sickness makes them see you differently—it made me see you differently."

"That's no more than a fairytale, A. A giant is a giant is a giant. I'm no friend to men. I leave that trapdoor open hoping a visitor will come, but every time I see a man they run from me. In town, they're all together. They talk and scheme. They can take me with the strength of many."

"But what if they came here? You leave the door open. What if a hunting party came out here to slay you? You must have some faith in men to allow in visitors."

R looked at Alan but did not say anything. He took another bite of stew and spit it out quickly.

"It's gone cold."

"I have the sickness, and I didn't run from you." Alan said.

Ruteeter said nothing and took his bowl of stew over to the pot. He dumped it all back in and gave it a long stir. He wiped his eyes on a dirty sleeve, and after a minute, he slumped his arms and stopped stirring.

"And that's mighty odd of you, A. You are an odd friend."

"You are the only one, Ruteeter. You are the only one who is strong enough to open up the sea. If you don't do it, all those hidden away in the forest, all those that the men look at the same as you, will be killed."

"That's just a tale. My father thought it would fix it, too. Look how that went."

"But it did! Those that took your mother from you; they must have still been sick. But no one came hunting for you and your father. It must have worked for some time."

"For some time. Then what? They go digging around again and spring back up that same evil? Then I come back to my hole and hide? What kind of life is that?"

Alan didn't say anything for a moment, but looked at R, who still had his back turned and was facing the oven.

"What kind of life is this?" Alan asked. "You're letting fear keep you alone. If you fix it, maybe men will learn. Maybe they will remember. I will write it down! Others will, too. Men will learn what that evil comes from. They must."

Ruteeter continued to move his arm slowly, clockwise around the pot, but not speaking a word. Then, after several minutes, he turned to Alan.

"You will write it down?"

Alan nodded reassuringly. "I will. I will tell everyone I can. They will tell everyone they can. People will learn from the story."

There was another minute of silence, as R poured another pot of stew.

"And you will continue to visit me after I do it?"

Alan nodded. "Of course. We're friends now."

R took another sip of stew, but did not say anything else. But he also did not say no again. Alan pulled out the journal and opened it to the last page.

"Besides, I have a secret weapon for us to use." He pointed to Rid's drawing of the golden cat's eye marble. "This marble is a precious family heirloom. It has been studied by many and used for its unique powers. In fact, a friend is currently using it to gather folks in support of us. But it has one secret power I have told no one else about."

R looked up, very intrigued.

"If you have this marble, you cannot fail at something twice. That means we cannot fail at burying the mine *twice*. Your father tried once, and it wore off, so that means it's guaranteed to succeed this time. Forever."

R looked at the drawing delicately, now holding the book in his massive hands. He looked back to Alan and nodded. "I have never seen anything like this before." He paused, drinking the entirety of his stew. He burped so loudly Alan nearly covered his ears. "I believe you."

XXV. Beneath the sea

It was dark when they set out from the giant's cubby, and the moon was already visible in the sky, barely glancing over the tops of the trees.

They had talked at length—about other stews, bird sightings near the western wood, shoes that fit well, and the sound of a crackling fire. Though the conversation had been about little in particular, it was about quite a lot as far as Alan was concerned, and it had distracted him so deeply that he had forgotten Rime was hidden away in a makeshift encampment under some dense foliage awaiting his return to the surface.

They came upon him now in the pale of the moonlight, and from his position on the giant's back just above Ruteeter's rucksack, Alan could barely see the whites of his eyes and the glint of a sword blade.

"Ho! Rime, my friend," he shouted, "It's okay!"

Ruteeter, who had been searching high up in the trees for signs of bats (the only "tiny creature" that he loved more than birds), had not noticed their aggressor and wheeled himself around in sudden fright.

"Alandriel, are you sure? This great giant has not taken you hostage?" Rime asked in a shaky voice, his sword still drawn. "I must say, he looks friendlier than I imagined."

"I'm sure! He's agreed to do it. We're on our way to the dam right now," Alan shouted down from on high.

"Alandriel? Is that your name, A?" R asked, puzzled.

"A? You two have gotten that casual in a matter of hours?" Rime asked, "Can I come up there so that I can hear better?"

And with that, Ruteeter swept Rime up off his feet and shifted Alan to the right shoulder, giving the newcomer the left.

"It's a real pleasure to meet you," Ruteeter said.

"Likewise," Rime said hesitantly, "are you Stor? The one from the tales?"

"He's not," Alan answered, "this is Ruteeter. Stor was his father."

"He was indeed. What is your name?"

"Rime. Muddle was my father's name. So you're a real-life giant?"

"I suppose I am," R answered, chuckling, "I suppose that I am."

"How did the brief recruitment efforts fair, Rime?" Alan asked.

Rime pulled the marble from his pocket and handed it back to Alan. "Better than we could have expected without this, that is surely true. There is a small group of folks that will meet Stellis and the others in town. They will do their best to distract the Poliserd to sneak the giant in, but we still have the imps to worry about."

Alan nodded. "I have a plan for the imps. But what about you?"

"I'm going with you to the end. I will not leave another brother." In the cool light, Alan could see a slight glimmer in Rime's eyes. He nodded silently.

As the night wore on, the trio chatted more, sharing tales of misfortunes and triumphs in the great old forests of Oognysse, or in Alan's case, the forests of Ashtabula which he lent more ancient and regal names than those he knew in his head. After passing once more through Synn, they had reached the coast, and the smell of salty air and sound of crashing waves reinvigorated them as they traversed down the edge of the land.

Ruteeter walked barefooted, as he always did, and every once in a while, he would kick up a great clump of wet sand with his big toes right onto the back of Alan and Rime. Alan, who did not mind and at present had oddly found himself enjoying the attached company of the giant, was currently discussing the naming of Rime as Ry by his traveling host, who thought that it was close enough to a single letter without causing confusion with his own lettered designation. Ry was holding on dearly to the giant and had no thoughts on the designation.

As they grew closer to the populated area of Nyssen, as R still preferred to call it, Alan hopped off the back of him with Rime close behind. Ruteeter hunched over quite meekly, so that they hid beneath the shadows of the trees as much as they could. For now, inching closer still to the roar of the dam, they were also inching closer to the tall houses of the nosy and fanciful members of the higher-class that could afford to live closer to the coast than others.

"Without much to do," Ruteeter whispered, "they've got plenty of time to mind business that is not their own. They were the first to stir up trouble and put out coin for the 'migration of freks,' as they called it."

"Do you think that they're watching here right now? That they see us?"

"I do not doubt that they watch," Ruteeter answered, "but that they see us—that is not likely. Don't you smell it?"

Alan took in a great whiff of air and scrunched his eyebrows, for all he smelled was the saltiness of the air and a light taste of conifer, pleasant as though it were the scent of Christmas.

"Sorry," he said, "but what am I supposed to be smelling?"

"The trees, silly man! Their allegiance—my father said it can always be smelled in the air by their friends. Surely, they will hide us tonight."

Rime nodded. "Rid used to say the same."

And so the three drudged on, all on foot, now traversing heavy beds of needles from the trees and the wet mud of ocean water that was seeping through. They stayed low in the shadows of their guards, keeping the tall houses out of sight.

"So we just smash it up?" Ruteeter asked suddenly, out of the blue.

"The dam blocking the sea?"

"Yes," the giant answered, "you want me to just smash it up? So that the water from the sea floods over the mine?"

"I suppose that would do it. Then they won't be able to use the mine anymore. Then the imps will lose their desire for their work, or the cause to do it, I reckon. Doesn't that sound right to you?"

"It does. But—and do not judge me as mistrustful, as you are surely cast out from many circles of men just by talking with me—but does it not seem rather simple to you? That we just go in there and smash it up and the job is done?"

Alan hopped over a rock that jutted out from the ground. They were now working their way into a harsher terrain closer to the ravine.

"I think," Alan said, suggestively, "that it ought to seem that way to you."

"What do you mean by that?" the giant asked, himself now taking special care to navigate through some of the sharp outcroppings.

"Well, I'm no master of lore, but I've read many tales and stories of things like this—where some sort of unthinkable thing needs to be done that fixes a lot of other things. Destroying this dam for example—to myself or Ry, we could never do it. The physical strength alone is formidable. But more than that, our hearts likely suffer the same spell of greed that drove men to build the dam in the first place. To put it there to mine those stones from the earth. I have to admit, it seems like a bad idea to me to rid the merchants of such a great source of wealth, but that's just it. Of course it seems that way to me. Of course it seems simple to you, because the soul of your heart that wants things does not want after the same things as men."

Alan turned on the rock he had just climbed and pointed up at Ruteeter. "That is the very reason why you must be the one to do it."

"Hmph," the giant said. He pulled a few rocks to the side to make his path easier.

"Well, A, I must admit to you now—before I had judged that you only sought me for my size and strength, but it seems that preconception was shallow. I feel awfully silly."

Alan smiled up at his friend. "Not to worry. You weren't entirely wrong, either. Strength has got a lot more to do with your heart than your size. I'm just glad I could see it!"

"Just as that is true," the giant said, "I would also impart that sight has a lot more to do with your heart than your eyes. For if you had not come down my door and eaten a bowl of stew with a fearful old giant, I would not be here now—the giant that does not care about smashing up a great wall."

Now they were crawling up a small mound close to the dam. To their west, Alan could see the faint orange glow of torch and oil light in the city—no doubt the restless roving of the Poliserd, the patrol that Stellis and the others would surely be attracting soon. Alan wondered if they had any inkling of what they were about to attempt. He shivered at the thought.

As they scrambled up the mound (which for Ruteeter, was only two swift steps), the situation appeared more grim than it had before. Here they could see the seawall that he and Kard had kept their distance from before. It was fashioned from the craggly black rock that came from deep within the earth, all that had remained of the time before the first flooding. Atop it sat a short rail, not unlike a fence, and nearby there was a small tower.

As Alan tried to focus his vision, gazing as best he could through the sea spray and low clouds, he now saw moving torchlight in the distance walking along the south side of the ravine in their direction. It was a small group, no more than ten men, who all wore the bleached white Poliserd robes. They hadn't seen them, Alan was sure, and he guessed that they probably couldn't, as he and the giant were both only illuminated by the waning light of the moon.

They watched intently, waiting for the Poliserd to be lured away from the mine. Shortly, smoke began rising in the northeast corner of town, and minutes later, Alan saw the spreading flames coming out of one shop.

Suddenly, just in front of the Poliserd, a group of townsfolk, no doubt pretty and very much not ugly to the patrol, began to emerge from shops and homes. They did what they had great power to do, not enact violence or physically intimidate the patrol, but to manifest fear of the frek. Alan could not hear them from this far, but he knew that the sobbing women and children had conjured up excellently horrific stories of a frek uprising taking place in that northeast corner of town. That corner that would take the Poliserd a great distance away from the ravine. Alan smiled and felt the marble in his pocket.

He knew that it was time.

"We cannot have come all this way for nothing, Ruteeter. Although for you, it has only been a short stroll from the forest, for myself it has been a journey across land and sea, and for my friends, nearly the whole world twice over. No, we cannot fail them. Not now. We must split up, for Ry and I have another duty to ensure your job goes off without a hitch. Do not worry. We cannot fail twice."

R looked at him, momentarily drawing his attention away from erupting shouting and screams following the mobilized Poliserd. "I trust you, A."

Alan paused for a moment, considering what he was about to do. He knew that it was the right decision.

"According to our plan, aye? Do you carry it with you still?"

The giant unfurled the rucksack he had carried, and the boulder, about the size of a small child, rolled out onto the ground. It was the same black rock as the dam.

"And you're sure that'll do it?"

The giant touched a crack on the rock. "See that? That's from the first burial. I'm sure it'll do it. Nothing breaks frosk rock better than older frosk rock. Now will you tell me what your plan is?"

Alan seemed distracted, still staring off through the fog that lay heavy on the ground and carefully watching the guard of Poliserd, now nearly disappeared to the far corner of town. He turned to face the giant now, though his attention seemed to be elsewhere.

"Ruteeter, I have not known you for very long, but I feel as if I've known you my entire life. In a way, I have. If we never meet again, I hope that life goes back to normal for you. That perhaps more friends wander through your door."

The giant looked at him intently, but a sadness overwhelmed him. He wiped a sniffle from his nose. "I would not want any to walk through it before you, A. Why would we never meet—"

Alan held up a hand, his attention drawn back to the patrol. "I don't have the time to explain it all now. They're drawing in closer. When they're distracted, go for it. Bury it. Be swift about it."

He made eye contact with Ruteeter one final time, smiling. "And keep a pot of that wick stew warm for me." And with that, he dashed off towards the ravine with Ry following close behind.

They made their way down a precarious path of crumbling stones and slipped rocks; the pair often scooting on their behinds to get down without losing their footing.

"What exactly are we doing, Alandriel?"

"We're burying it, Rime."

"Burying it? I thought that's what the giant is doing?"

Alan smiled to himself as he hopped down another short drop. They were almost to the edge now.

"Oh he is. He's burying the mine. We're burying this."

Alan held up the marble, and it glimmered in the moonlight.

"What do you mean? Why do you want to get rid of it?"

"The imps came out of this great hole, right Rime? So we have to make sure they get put back into it before it's flooded."

Rime looked off into the fog, now seeing that they were approaching a sheer drop-off. He was beginning to realize the plan "Do you have a match or a candle? To make them come?"

Alan paused and looked at the marble. "I thought it was the fire, too. Fire seems so flashy and powerful, of course that would be what activates it. But it's not. It's the ground. The ground that connects us all. Even the imps. They can feel it when it touches the ground. When I bury it, when I throw it into the ravine, they will go down after it."

Rime stood there for a moment, not saying anything. "Y'know, you really are a lot like him. The way you two figure out the stories. I would never have seen it."

The two came over one last sharp ridge in the sidewall of the ravine, and then they were staring into it. Just a black abyss. Alan turned to the side and could feel the sharp mist of the sea falling as light as the air.

"We have to wait until just as it starts to crack. As soon as you feel that rumble in your feet, that's when we throw it. You tell me when, Rime."

Rime looked down at his feet, and then back to Alan. He got down on his knees and dug his hand into the fine, pebbled rock. He closed his eyes and listened.

"It's close," he whispered.

Alan paused, taking in a deep breath and looking up at the stars.

"Now, throw it in!"

Alan reached out his hand and took one last look at the marble. He whispered something to someone that was not with him. Then he let it go.

The marble fell as the salt spray crested over the crack forming at the top of the sea wall, as it started to burst forth all along the wall. Alan and Rime leaned back against the rock, bracing themselves. In a flash, they saw the black skittering shapes of the imps, dive-bombing for the marble like sea birds after a fish.

As the water flooded in, it had a fluid intention to it, gushing and crashing with a monstrous noise. A piercing, shrieking call that could have come from nothing but the imps rang out. Alan could feel it throughout his body, but most of all in his eyes, where the sound itself felt like a piercing blindness.

Alan felt a pain too, though not as intensely. It was like the feeling you get after you've stared at a bright light for a second too long. The overwhelming of the eyes, the burning of the brightness.

A great spray of foam shot up out of the blackness to their right and nearly knocked Rime over. It was steam, the cool water of the sea meeting the hot cracks in the rocks below.

As they hurried to climb back out of the sidewall, he tried to squirm his eyes above the horizon towards the sea. To see R. He knew it was done. He could feel it.

He could hear shouts far off in the city. Rays of sun were just beginning to creep up over the edges of the world.

"It's flooded!" He heard a far-off voice shout. Another man yelled, "Seal it! Seal it off!"

"It's gone," a hoarse cry echoed down the steps of the keep, "it's too late."

Alan smiled.

He slumped to the ground with Rime at his side. He nodded at Alan and also whispered something to someone who was not with him. They sat there for a minute, maybe longer, doing nothing at all. They had buried it.

"Did you do it? Did you finish it?" a voice asked, fast approaching from behind. Alan turned and could see her shape emerging in the light of dawn. It was Elouise, the elf.

She was beautiful.

Alan soon passed out, falling asleep once again.

XXVI. A long-awaited party

The tomato sauce: rich, hearty, and balanced with just the right amount of basil and oregano. The cheese: salty, browned and blistered in all the right places and six inches of stretch before it tore. The crust: crisp and browned on the bottom; warm, bubbly and flaky on the inside. The bite was the same every time, a moment where your tongue and taste buds overwhelmed the rest of your sensory organs and took you to another place altogether. It was Pizza Inn.

It was Tuesday afternoon. They had come for a dinner-lunch hybrid so that Alan could be at work for the early night shift. Because of this, the place was empty. They had the dining room to themselves other than a single employee sluggishly busing tables and listening to a Walkman.

Nikki, Alan's sister, sat directly across from him. She was cheerful and upbeat, taking in every word that was said. Alan's mom sat next to her. She was not a fan of pizza, but had waited for Alan to finish his last piece before she put the candles on the cake.

"So, Alan. A shared cake for you and your dad." She smiled. "Just like he always wanted, even though we know that was just to avoid the attention of having his own birthday cake."

She put the last candle, a twirly green one, into the cake next to the letter Y, before folding her hands and smiling at her son.

"My big guy. Another year older. A hard year, needless to say, but I know we're so happy we've had you to help us through it, Alan."

He finished wiping his mouth with his napkin and looked up at her. He offered a hesitant grin and cleared his throat. "I know I haven't been around a lot for you guys, and I'm sorry. But...well, that's gonna be different now." He looked at his sister. "Nik, I don't know if mom's told you, but I'm moving back in for a couple of months."

Her eyes lit up, and she grinned ear to ear. "Really?! To live with us? Do you want your old room back? I can move my stuff out...probably tonight! We can—"

He laughed softly. "No, no. That's okay. I'm gonna be in the guest room. I'll only be there for a little while I think. I applied to a school in Youngstown. If they let me in...well, I'll have to live there the first year."

He could see the lights dim in her eyes and she picked at a piece of pizza crust. "Well, that's okay. You'll be here for some big holidays, at least. We can do fireworks for the Fourth of July again." She looked over to their mom. "And I bet that you'll need help when you need to move in to your dorm."

"Oh, I'm sure I will! And it's only an hour away. I'm still counting on mom doing my laundry on the weekends." Alan smiled coyly at his mom and they all laughed.

"I know we're both really happy for you, honey. And I know— well..." She looked at the empty seat next to Alan and nodded her head as her eyes watered. "Well, you know."

As they sang happy birthday to him, Alan's eyes watered too. But that's all it was. There was probably something in the pizza that had irritated them, or maybe pet dander floating around in the air. Yeah, that was it. But it was a happy birthday.

He walked into Elmwood's sporting a full belly and made his way straight to the bakery, not for further dessert to stress-test the seams of his stomach, but to have a chat. A chat which, for the past week, he had very much looked forward to.

She was scrubbing down the tops of her cases with a white rag and shutting the display lights off. Just as he got near, Miss Etta looked up and saw him. A sweet smile spread across her tired face, and she put both her hands on her hips in a protesting sort of manner.

"Well, I haven't seen *you* in a while. You get tired of my donuts?"

Alan took a seat at the cafe table he always ate his breakfast at. "You know that I'll be dead long before I grow tired of your baking, Miss Etta."

She smiled and walked around to the front of the cooler. "How is night shift treatin' you? Gotta be nice without Vick on your ass all day."

"Now *that* is something I did get tired of. Lotta late shifts though. That's why I haven't seen any of the day folks in a while. Not since I got back from Georgia."

Her eyes got wide as she took a seat in front of him. "Oh yes! How was it? Hot, I imagine. Surely many other things, but none more than hot."

"It was absolutely hot," Alan said, remembering the old man's garden fondly in his mind, "but beautiful to the same degree."

"And your man—you find him?" She cackled. "Musta gave him quite a fright I imagine. Some stranger showing up from middle o' God's country, Ohio."

"I did. I found him and I got to ask him everything I wanted to."

"And?" she asked slyly.

"Well, we'll just have to wait and see, but I've got faith."

"Faith *is* a virtue. That's what they say, yes it is." She folded up a paper napkin and blew her nose. "But I'm sure there's a whole lot more bloomin' in Georgia than what's bloomin' here. I don't miss the allergies."

Alan nodded and stared off in the distance for a second, watching the slow lull of afternoon customers trickle out before the after-work crowd hit.

"Hey, Miss Etta, I've been meaning to ask you something—after last week."

She nodded.

"Your mom—you said you'd do anything to see her again."

She nodded. "Yes, yes I would."

"What would you say to her?"

She pursed her lips and sat back in a coy smile. "Now God knows I've thought about that many nights. Hmph." She reclined and folded her arms, sitting in silence for a few minutes gazing off into the dark corners of the end-of-day bakery.

"Well, I think first I'd say how much I love her. Never feels like I said it enough. Never does, once someone's gone." She sat quiet again.

"And then what?"

She laughed dryly. "Well, then I'd probably get her to talk about peppermint bark. She loved peppermint bark. She could talk your ear off about fifty-seven different ways to make it and which ones were right and wrong. She was never more alive than when she was boring you to death about it. That's the part of somebody that you can never get back, you know."

She looked at Alan now and nodded. "The piece of them that talks about what they love. You can remember what they thought about something or how they laughed or even the way a hug felt, but you can never get that back. You can never have something that feels the way it does when you know they love something. Even if it's peppermint bark. There's too much of their soul in it for you to really remember."

She looked back at the bakery case and twiddled her fingers.

"You know, I never bake with peppermint here. Seems awful silly sittin' here talkin' about it, but it just doesn't feel right. It's like I don't want anyone else to get part of her from me. I want to keep it all to myself."

She looked back at Alan and managed a tiny smile.

"Well, did that answer your question good enough?"

It did, and Alan said it did, and he thought about her answer for the rest of his shift. The whole time he was stocking the jumbo eggs and checking for breaks, the whole time he was rotating the cottage cheese, and the whole time he was seeing which spray whipped cream cans had already been opened by kids.

On his way out of the store, he was still thinking about it to the point that he was hardly watching the space in front of him as he walked. Raphl was on his way in to "close" up before the store opened for the day and Alan ran right into him.

"Woah, Hendershot. Sorry, there. How'd the shift go?"

Alan shook himself awake and blushed. "Oh, no problems at all. There were a few more cases of the yogurt with the candy pieces than we ordered but I left a message with the distributor. They're in the back cooler."

"The ones with the caramel nougat?"

"Umm yeah, I think so. Golden box."

"That wasn't a mistake. I shoulda let you know. Be a real pal and don't mention it to Vick. Even when I pay for the yogurt, he rides me for keeping *personal goods* in company coolers."

"Uh...yeah, what yogurt?" Alan winked.

Raphl smiled and waved as he headed back for his closet office and then turned to Alan again.

"Hey, Hendershot?"

"Yeah?"

"How are you sleeping?"

"Pretty good, thanks!" He grinned. "Pretty good."

Raphl offered a final pleasant nod before disappearing into Laska. Alan made straight for his car and headed back to the duplex. Tonight was his last night sleeping there. He would sleep well, he hoped.

Tonight, the routine went a little bit differently than it had every other night. He still drank the tea, he still read his notes, he still let part of his body grow numb, but he wasn't going to the same time that he had left. Tonight, he would try a time jump.

It had been over a week since he had last left Imp Lode, passing out from exhaustion precariously perched in a crack of the ravine's wall. It only made sense to him that it would be easiest to skip the same amount of time as he had experienced in the real world. He looked back over Tollers's notes about time-skipping, about how his had gone so horrifically. He decided he wouldn't try to force any circumstances; he would just leave it up to fate. Alan had a good feeling about fate, anyway.

He took one last look over his book of notes. It was turned to the page where he'd written *Ruteeter's lair* at the top, but had left the rest blank. He grinned.

Alan swallowed up the last sip of tea that had grown cold and shimmied into bed. Within a few minutes, he fell asleep—

—when he awoke, he couldn't see a thing. It wasn't like before, where he had forgotten to open his eyes. He could feel his eyes opening and shutting, but his vision remained the same.

Alan was also walking, slowly and in a straight line. He wondered if he was being marched along to some terrible death. Perhaps this was his execution by the Poliserd. The next step would be the gallows at the edge of town.

He reached up to his face and touched his eyes, but didn't feel his eyes, rather, a wet, scratchy fabric. It ran in a band around his head—a blindfold. He smelled, because that was all he had left to do, and the air smelled pleasant—of pine and wet bark, of a cool breeze blowing through the needles in the trees, of *cheese?*

"Is the poor lad sniffin' the air?" Kard asked, jubilantly, "perhaps we should pull Rime's underwear off 'is head now." He roared with laughter, and Alan felt the joy swell in his own heart with the dismissal of fear.

"Oh, give it a rest, Kard," Rime's voice said, "just give us one more minute...there! Take it off of him!"

With a flash of blinding daylight, a brisk hand leapt up and pulled the blindfold from his face. In front of him, Alan saw the middle of the forest, the meadow hidden away where Rime and Rid's treehouse stood. Around him, crowded up in bundles with eyes brimming and voices ringing out sounds of great cheer, there was every being Alan had met in Fortis. Hung from the great branches of several of the lower trees, a great banner was stretched across which had "ALANDRIEL, THE GREATEST SEER OF IMP LODE." written on it in big colorful letters. It was a party, a surprise party just for him.

Alan swayed and rotated on an axis, his mouth hanging open in a lopsided grin, and his eyes scanned over every face and whimsical decoration in sight. The creatures of the wood were nothing if not crafty, he could see. Rime had just finished tying the right rope of the banner to a treehouse limb and was hopping down to come and meet him.

Kard and Stellis made their presence known, his guides from behind, and Alan didn't know what else to do but to give them all a great hug.

"This is...this is all for me?" Alan asked, still in disbelief, "this whole party? I don't understand."

Stellis smiled, perhaps more than Alan had ever seen before, and waved her hand across all the creatures gathered, some of whom were now serving themselves ale and snacks, and others who were watching Alan, hoping to have a chance to greet him. "Yes, Alandriel. After you two were pulled up from the mine and put on bedrest, they got together and planned it all in secret. We were sorry to give you a fright and kidnap you away like that after your long night, but, well," she grinned cheekily, "not *that sorry*."

"Why a party for me? Did—did it..." Alan did not know quite how to word it, but he looked across at Kard's big toothy grin and Rime's cheery face, and they understood that his memory had gone hazy, as Alan Hendershot's memory always seemed to do.

"You did it, Alandriel. The 'frek' market was reinstated the night before you were released, and the word frek has been stricken from any town registry. All who want it have been welcomed back into town," Rime looked out over all the different creatures, the sprites, the elves, the gnomes, even a wee little fairy that was trying to lift a wedge of cheese to no avail, "though I expect many will choose to remain residents of the forest."

"What do you mean? The dam—breaking it, that worked? Wait!" Alan took another long panning gaze at the crowd of the party, "Oh my! I didn't even realize that I see them all as I should! Of course! So you all can see them too?"

"Aye lad," Kard clapped his hands together, "we can. Although there's one gnome I'm still not too keen on." He chuckled.

"And the townspeople? They just got over it like that?"

"Well, not quite," Stellis answered. "There are several holdouts—Poliserd loyalists, if you will. But even they will have to reckon with their own sight soon enough. Even those that still clung to some illegitimate bias, even they couldn't deny that the economy of the town would fall apart now that the mine is destroyed—without the market of these creatures, that is."

"Besides," Rime chimed in, "their registry of wanted faces was ruined! No one looks the same anymore. I've heard some say that the lifting of the curse even made some men uglier...though the only man I've seen since is Kard, and he's as beautiful as ever."

"I'll let that slide, for I am hungry!" Kard declared. "I promised Alan a tall pint of elder ale at the end of this journey, and I will be damned if I can't hold to my word."

Alan grinned and laughed with the others as they migrated towards the long feasting tables of wonderful snacks, but he couldn't help scanning the entirety of the wood once more.

There was somebody missing. He told his friends that he would be right back and slipped away off deep into the trees.

The trapdoor was right where he'd found it the first time, and he braced himself for the landing as he slid back down into the hole. Before he stood up and gathered himself, he already smelled something pleasant coming from the kitchen.

Ruteeter was standing next to the fire flipping thin pieces of sizzly, pork-smelling meat on a flat rock that lay atop the coals. The pop and fizzle of the fat was so loud he hadn't even heard Alan approach.

"Hello, friend!" Alan shouted through cupped hands.

Ruteeter turned around, startled, and nearly dropped his tongs. He was so overjoyed to see his one friend that tears welled up in his great big eyes. He said that he had to sit down, for the emotion had overcome him.

"So you two made it out, aye? I feared you may have been drowned in the ravine! Are you anything more than bruised?"

"I'm solid. Very good." Alan said reassuringly. "I actually don't even remember that much of it. But you did it! Destroying the mine, it cured the blindness! The townsfolk have let all the exiled creatures back into the town."

Ruteeter smiled and nodded before sitting silent for a moment. "I heard. It really is wonderful for them. I bet they're all quite overjoyed. It's good." Though he spoke positively, his face was glum, and Alan could tell that he felt a bit sad.

"Well, yeah, it is! It's really great! In fact, they're having a party right now!"

Ruteeter didn't turn, but went back to flipping the fatty meat. "Well, give them my best. I'm glad the forest is in harmony again."

"Ruteeter," Alan said protestingly.

"Yes?"

"We want you to be at the party."

Ruteeter faced Alan with a bewildered expression on his face. He pointed the tongs at his chest. "Me?"

"You did it. You were the one that broke the wall. The one that had the strength. It wouldn't be a celebration at all if you weren't there."

Ruteeter stared down at the sizzling meat in contemplation. A slight grin crept upon his face and then vanished as he turned back to Alan.

"No, I couldn't. I just started cooking this meat. It would spoil."

"So bring it along!"

The giant looked at Alan inquisitively and then back to the meat. "You're sure?"

"Yes, and if I have to ask you again, there'll be no ale left by the time we get back, and our friendship will have sunken to a low place."

Ruteeter looked at him hesitantly and then broke into a chuckle.

"It is odd that you choose to be such a friend to a giant like me, A, but I am thankful for it." And he finished frying the meat on the rock and packed it all up into a neat leather parcel, and they were off to the party.

Alan had come a long way for this pint of elder ale, and somehow it lived up to the expectation. Of course, Alan thought as he sat beneath the warm glowing sun setting atop the trees, the setting didn't hurt. It didn't hurt that he sat here with Kard on his right, who was taking long swigs of booze out of hollowed out cheese, Rime in front of him, who had nearly eaten the whole plate of Ruteeter's fried meat on his own, grinning the whole way through, and Stellis further down the table with Klio and the others from her order, laughing and basking in the tomfoolery of her companions.

It was a good cup of ale.

As the night crept upon them, Rime suggested that the four of them transform into a walking party to gain a bit of their sobriety back in the cool air beneath the moon. So the adventuring party stumbled along a dusty stone path that wove in and out of the forest, slinking ever closer to the town itself.

None was drunker than Kard, though it also seemed to be true that none held their booze better than Kard, for if you had weighed both the alcohol he took in and the food that he ate that night, it would be a toss up which one was the greater. As they wobbled onward, "towards our homes so that Alan can sleep in a real bed!" Rime had spat into the air, Kard began to whistle a tune once again.

It was the same one from before, the one Alan had heard him harmonize several different times. His whistle was scattered and wavering, not unlike jazz, and after a minute or two of the rest of them trying to match his melody (one they all knew well at this point), he decided it better to sing the words.

IF THE DARK CLOUDS COME ERE THE SAME

THEN BE NO DARKER IN THEIR NAME.

IF THE STORM WERE LONG, EVERMORE,

THEN BE THERE NOT SUN TO YEARN FOR.

THE EMPTY BELLY DOES NOT QUIVER

IF NOT FOR HOPE OF FISH DOWNRIVER.

THE CRYING CHILD STRAYED FROM FATHER,

WITHOUT LOVE FEELS LITTLE BOTHER.

TIS THE DEEP VALLEY 'TWEEN THE HILLTOPS

WHEN PADS OF FEET KNOW THE ROCK OF BOTTOM,

THAT LENDS NO LESS THAN HOPE AS CROPS

AND ONWARD! ASCENT! BETHOUGHT HIM.

Kard reared himself up boisterously, spitting to the sky.

AND SO FORTH WE BOOT!

TO GALE, TO CHILL, TO STENCH OF DEATH,

FOR AT THE TOP, ONLY THERE!

TRULY CAN WE WELCOME BREATH.

He belted out the last verse heavily with full gusto, and by then they realized they were coming upon a few cottages nestled between a vast meadow of lilies on one side and the forest at the rear.

"This is our little...neck of the woods...you could say!" Kard shouted, burping in between words.

The cottage closest to them was built up from stone so perfectly old that it began to look like a natural formation, with moss crawling up every side and the iron windows nearly hidden away in recesses. It looked cozy, Alan thought, as they all now followed his line of sight to the great wooden door, arched at the top with beautiful carvings on its face.

"That's me," Rime said, pointing at the house, "that's the home of our family. Has been since before most of these trees were more than a sapling. It's a bit empty now, I suppose."

"I think it just looks brilliant." Alan said, his eyes still beaming as he took in every detail of the charming exterior in the moonlight.

"Well," he chuckled, "that's good, because I reckon that's where you'll be sleeping tonight."

Kard burped again loudly. "Good, lads, good. Yes, we love the house of the doppelbrothers. Onwards to my humble abode." He pointed a stubby finger further down the little dirt lane.

As they went along, Alan could not help but remark upon how peaceful it felt out in this part of the wood, and he did it often. There was just something about the temperature of the wind, the way it felt blowing on his skin, and the cheer from his friends walking alongside him. But more than that, the knowledge that everything had gone right. Everything really was at peace.

Kard's house looked to be more of a cabin, humble in size and crafted entirely from wood. In the front, there was a nice dressing of flowers and ferns dotting the little path that led to his door. On the right side of the house, not far from it, lay a small shack nearly identical in style, but with open-air windows. A place for butchering, Alan thought. Behind the house, there was a gate.

As Alan noticed it, it was as though all of his actions following that, following the noticing of the gate—and what lay beyond—were instinctual. That there was nothing he could do differently in that moment; it just happened.

"Um, beautiful house, Kard. I really love it." Alan said.

"Why, thank you, lad. It's not much, but it's a place to live, that's for sure."

"Would you mind," Alan said confidently, "if I went into your garden to relieve myself? I've had an awful lot to drink, and we've walked a long ways."

Kard, more cheese fat and alcohol in his blood than perceptiveness, did not consider it strange at all that Alan would rather pee outside behind his house instead of within it. "Go ahead, lad, absolutely. Don't let us bother you! If you can, water the bluebells with it—they're surely withered now I fear!"

Alan nodded and wandered down the path, looking behind him a few times to make sure the party's attention was elsewhere (it was, for Rime had just sworn he'd seen a shooting star and was proposing that they climb into a tree or up on a roof to get a better glimpse in case a second should appear). He made his way to the gate of the garden.

It was just as Alan hoped, perhaps even better in the white light of the moon. There were signs dug into the ground nearly everywhere you turned with plants labeled as they were—Rime's handwriting of course, for Kard could not read or write. There were great rose bushes, sprawling squashes of some variety, and even pepper plants that looked like the ones Dard had given them.

But there, behind a trellis of what was surely beans, a figure moved in the dark. Alan wasn't startled by it. He had no reason to be, after all. Everything in Oognysse was as safe as it had ever been. He didn't call out to the figure, who he could now see had their back turned to him, but he approached, quietly and calmly.

When he was nearly within arm's reach, he smelled it. Coffee and aftershave. The man was gazing up at the stars, but now let on that he was aware of Alan's presence.

His dad turned and faced him.

Alan's eyes immediately flooded with saltwater, and all he could see was a hazy warping of moonlight on the face of his father as he ran to his open embrace. He hugged him for an amount of time that later felt like nothing at all, but at the moment, time had lost its relevance. They were the only two people in the world.

He took a step back now, looking at him. His beard and face were just as dirty as they had been that night he first glimpsed him in The Ferryman. He was in his work clothes, black pants and jacket and a knit cap. He laughed and wiped tears from his own eyes.

"How are you, bud?"

Alan cleared his throat and took in a sharp breath of the cold air, but he hardly had the strength to speak. "I'm good, but I miss you like hell."

His dad sniffled and nodded, then opened his mouth once or twice about to say something, but just stood there grinning. Finally, he said, "I'm sorry—I—well, obviously I never wanted you to have to deal with this."

"It's okay," Alan said in a broken voice, fighting the urge to walk up to him and give him another hug.

His dad walked up beside him and put an arm around his shoulder, bringing him into a half-embrace. The two of them looked up at the sky.

"It's a beautiful night for stars," he said.

"They're the same here," Alan whispered, "as in the real world."

The minutes rushed by, gone in a flash, as Alan stared at the stars and thought of something to say. But those minutes were good, the ones of saying nothing at all.

"You remember the pizza at Pizza Inn?" he asked after a while.

"Yeah," his dad answered, "yeah, no one makes it like they do."

Alan nodded and didn't say anything for a little bit.

"Did you really like it?"

"What do you mean?"

"Well, I've always wondered...did you really like the pizza that much and that's why we always went there for your birthday..." he cleared his throat, "or did you just pick it because I liked it?"

His dad laughed and looked over at Alan. "Do you think you're old enough to know the truth?"

Alan nodded.

"Well, I don't think those two answers are as different as you might think. Sure, I like pizza. Good pizza, even more. The first time me and your mom took you there...well, you were just a little guy, barely talking probably. But oh boy did you talk about that pizza. All the way home, that's all you wanted to talk about. That pizza seemed to change your whole world." He chuckled. "Call it what you want, but it started tasting a whole lot better to me after that, too. You were a good little salesman."

Alan laughed softly to himself and sniffled again, but it felt like he had stopped crying. They went to sit on a bench now in the back of the garden where time seemed to slow down even more, and Alan found himself looking for the right words to say next. There was a part of him that enjoyed the quiet so much he wished he could not say anything and just spend the rest of his life here on this bench, but he knew that wouldn't work.

"Can I ask you something?" Alan said.

His dad grinned. "That's what I'm here for, isn't it?"

"Are you—or, I guess, were you—ever disappointed in me? With where I'm at right now and what I'm doing?"

His dad looked at him, his eyes soft almost as though he were hurt by the question, and then he folded his hands and gazed off in front of him at the moonlight dancing upon the garden.

"The day we brought you home from the hospital was the happiest day of my life. I could just watch you do nothing for hours. Nothing else in the world seemed as special as you." He paused and took a deep breath in. "As you grew up, I was always there to come check underneath your bed or sit up with you for hours explaining that the witch in The Wizard of Oz would never come find you and take you away in the middle of the night." He looked at Alan and laughed. "You were really scared of her, bud. But the older you got, the more I realized that I was the one with more fears. The worst one, or at least the one that really scared me the most, was what you thought of your old man. You were always so good at telling stories, I mean, your imagination just blew my mind. What would you think of your dad the dock worker? Would we still have what we had then when you got older?"

He sat silent again for a minute or two, and Alan could see tears glistening on his eyes in the faint light.

"So, to answer your question," he said in a hoarse voice, "never for one minute have I felt anything but pride in who you are. My kid, the one that never leaves the house without a book in his hands. My kid, the one that'll learn about more people and places than I ever knew existed. My kid, the one that can dream up a world and everything in it while he's laying out underneath a tree in the woods. I never cared what kind of job you ended up getting, what kind of pay or status or something like that. I just wanted you to be happy. I just wanted you to keep dreaming."

Alan felt a warm spot rising up in his throat that he knew was a floodgate of tears, but he found it hard to care. He had never felt much happier than he did right now.

"Well, dad," Alan said, chuckling to throw off the joyful tears from stopping him, "to answer your question, I thought a lot of you. Sure, I read a lot of books, but the best stories, the ones that always seemed most real, those always came from you. Sometimes I'd try to come up with something really wild and crazy just to see the look in your eye and hear you laugh when I told it to you like it was real. To match the master at his craft. The world seemed to be full of so much more magic with you in it. And now—"

He could see the tears rolling down his dad's face, drying up in the beard and the wipe of a brisk hand. They sat in silence once again, but Alan didn't feel like he needed to say anything. He could just enjoy the stars. He knew happiness again.

A bumbling of footsteps came from off in the distance behind them, and a slurred voice hollered, "Alandriel, c'mon with it lad! I didn't say you could shit in my roses now, did I?"

His dad looked over at him and grinned. "I'll let you get back to your friends." He took Alan up in a great warm hug and rubbed the back of his head. He seemed larger than life. Gianter, when he hugged Alan. "But, before you go, remember something," he said faintly, "even if you can't find me or don't see me, I *am* here. I was here long before tonight."

"I love you, dad."

And with that, the heat seemed to dissolve away into the air and surrounded Alan for a moment, like a pleasant, warm pillow. His dad was gone.

Kard came stumbling into the garden whistling the tune of his song and found Alan sitting on the bench alone, looking up at the stars.

"They're really something, aren't they laddy? They've enchanted me too on many a'night." Kard stood there quiet as well and finally said, "would you walk a drunken friend to his bed? I'll have a bastard of a headache in the morn', but please get your I-told-you-sos out of your system now."

Alan laughed and obliged, himself soon retiring to Rime's bed in the doppelbrothers' cottage. Nearly as soon as he lay down, he was asleep.

XXVII. A necessary epilogue

"And that was all a couple of months ago, now, must have been," Alan said, adding up the days in his mind, "but I wanted to come here before my classes started."

The old man had already packed and began smoking his pipe. He was in more casual attire this time, though he still donned a patterned vest which held his tobacco. They were walking out behind the garden now, underneath the great sprawling branches of moss-covered oaks.

"So you found what your mind had hidden away from you, there in the end. It's really something, isn't it? I've often come out here on walks in the dead of night wondering what else mine has buried somewhere deep."

He took a good puff from the pipe and pointed with it at a large, wandering tree they had come upon.

"This tree, here, in fact. It's the only thing shared."

"Shared with what?"

"The only thing shared between the two worlds. Of course, there were always my shipmates, but they were difficult to be with even after I had found them. It seemed that the more time I spent with them there, the more faded my memories of them grew. But this tree has always carried its majesty. It's an evergreen oak. I knew I could never imagine something I'd rather look at, so I brought this one in."

For a minute, Alan took the tree in without speaking, letting his eyes trace over all the twisting branches and the great canopy up above.

Then he asked, "So you think that I shouldn't look for my dad in the dream anymore?"

"Well, I wouldn't be quite so declarative, Alan Hendershot. It would be ill-advised, I think, to not look for something in our dreams. You never know what you might not find then. But I've come to the personal decision not to seek the once-living in the dreams, or at least not their true self. You might be surprised where you'll find them if you're really paying attention."

He took another pull from the pipe and popped his lips together.

"Besides, you had that night with him, with what sounds like a very true version of him. You have all the adventure that led to that. That's quite a lot to come out of being asleep, I would say."

Alan pondered what he said while gazing off into the wood, enjoying the breeze on his skin and the sun on his neck.

"It was something. But in the end, it was only just a dream. That's what's bothered me so much. It feels as though I've been cheated out of life. Like when you're a kid and dream that it's Christmas Eve and wake up to find not a single present or even a Christmas tree."

"Yes," the old man said, smiling, "but in the end, is there a great difference between the dream and a Christmas past? They both have become memories, and we only take with us what we have learned from them. I've always thought the real value of the dream is the story you take from it. Just like a story you can tell of a wonderful gift you opened when you were young, so too you can tell the story of the dream. I'm a sleepy old man, and it didn't bore me, after all. Besides," he grinned, "it's as good an excuse as any to keep returning to your world."

Alan nodded, considering and agreeing with what the old man said as they walked back to the garden. On their way, he asked, "did you ever tell it? Your story from your world, I mean."

The man did not say anything at first, but began whistling a tune that Alan knew felt familiar, though he could not identify it. Then he said, "Perhaps, Alan Hendershot. Perhaps I did."

In the days since, Alan continued to do most of what he had just recently started. He continued to visit his mother and sister, more often than not with a tub full of dirty laundry and news of his tidings away at school. He no longer worked at Elmwood's on Elm, but he patronized the store frequently for a danish or donut when he was on his way out of town.

Alan also continued to dream. Imp Lode changed and evolved as any world inevitably does. He chose to spend much of his time with his companions, his adventuring party, and rarely they would get up to mischief and often would share a pint of elder ale. It was also not uncommon that Alan Hendershot found himself wandering down a trapdoor in the middle of the wood to have a chat and a cup of tea with a great friend. In these talks, he often found what he was not looking for at all.

And finally, he continued school, a recent engagement at the close of this story. Several years into his studies, he enrolled in his final creative fiction class, a class where each student was required to complete a long-form project by the end of term. As classmates entered on the first day, one in particular caught his eye. He knew them from somewhere, but just couldn't recall the time or place.

To his surprise, she chose a seat next to his and pulled out a book to pass the time before the class began.

"Is that a good one," Alan asked, "if you don't mind me asking?"

She looked up at him, a bit startled, and caught his eyes. Alan knew her face now, and it looked as though she had just made the same discovery.

"Um, yeah," she grinned, "it is good. It's a re-read, actually."

She turned the book and closed it, showing him the cover.

"Would you mind if borrowed it when you finish, actually? I know that might be an odd request, but I've been meaning to read that for quite a long time."

She nodded and Alan returned her smile. He decided that this was as good a place as any to finish off one story and begin with the next.

Acknowledgements

I began writing what became *Alan Dreams of Giants* in 2020. Of course, there was a lot going on at the time. The book became an escape for me as Imp Lode is for Alan. I, too, had to be careful not to stray too far into the imaginative and forget to live. Perhaps this is why I kept it a secret from almost everyone. Many who are not thanked were a creative support without knowing it.

Cait, thank you for being the first beta-reader for the story and subjecting yourself to endless quizzing regarding the viability of the plot, proper idiomatic application, and how to make non-fantasy people like my book. As a hater of dream sequences, I truly don't know how you finished it.

Daniel, Anna, Sarah, and Andy, thank you for being release candidate-readers. Nothing convinced me more that I had hit the right note with this story than when my siblings told me they cried at the end. They say you write for yourself, and that's certainly true, but right after that, I think you write for your siblings.

Farewell

I refuse to surrender to my ego and dedicate an entire page to myself. So instead, I have included a brief biography of my beagle, Gimli.

About the Author's Dog

Gimli is probably mostly beagle. We do not know, and we will not be testing him. He has been through enough. He is an excellent, top-of-the-class snuggler. He does not resemble Snoopy, but he does have a small heart-shaped patch of white fur on the back of his neck. In his wilder days, he enjoyed scraping shriveled worms off the sidewalk as a savory snack during a midday walk. Of late, the stresses of adopted parenthood have multiplied his anxiety, and he has become a [less] vocal proponent of canine medication for mental wellbeing. Dogs should be happy, too.